Tell Me Again

This book is a work of fiction. Names, characters, places and incidents are the product of the author's imagination or are used fictitiously. Any resemblance to actual events, locales or persons, living or dead, is coincidental.

For those who embrace the journey

PART I

Chapter 1

2000 –

Hope can be killed quickly. My hope was killed in the five minutes it took my husband, Dr. Ken Faigan, and his mentor, Dr. David Lambert, to explain my situation. I had suffered damage to my spinal cord. Something to do with the thrashing my back had received the instant my car had crashed into a telephone pole a month earlier.

I wasn't really listening. After *spinal cord* I'd heard little else. I was fully aware of the kind of irreversible damage such an injury could cause. Ken was a pediatrician but he also coached a softball team for disabled children, and I'd seen some of his crippled patients. They rolled around a baseball diamond in their tiny wheelchairs like smiling sacks of potatoes. I'd gone to two games and had refused to go to another.

"They learn to live with it," Ken had once said when I'd commented on how the sight of the children made me want to cry. It was after the first game of the season, which my husband's team had lost, and we were sitting in a small deli across from the baseball field having a sandwich. "You have to understand, Meagan," he'd said, "some of those children have never walked. To them this isn't suffering; it's life."

To me it was worse than death.

One day had passed since I'd woken from a month-long coma only to find that I couldn't feel my legs. Twenty-four painstaking hours of concerned faces and worried glances stolen from the sides of eyes. I had been checked, re-checked, and finally, diagnosed. My family hovered around me like flies buzzing around a dead body, their voices an irritating hum I didn't want to have to hear. They frowned, constantly shifted positions, wrung their hands, and paced. They were driving me crazy. Dr. Lambert was explaining my situation with words like *incomplete paraplegia*, and *most likely permanent,* while my mother and father exchanged fearful glances and my siblings stared at me with blank dumb faces. They wondered if I was strong enough to face this. I wondered too.

"Are you saying she'll never walk again?" my father, Patrick Summers, asked, avoiding my eyes and crushing my sobbing mother, Joan, against his chest. It annoyed me that she couldn't even pull herself together for my sake. I turned my face to the wall and felt like we'd gone over my condition a hundred times even though Dr. Lambert had only said it once.

"Well, I suppose nothing is ever truly impossible," he responded. I glared at his wrinkled face. Why was he saying that? Doctors were supposed to give you the hard facts, not their opinions on miracles or the powers of some God who had already forsaken me.

Ken noticed my annoyance with the feeble old doctor and interjected quickly. "It's unlikely," he said, quietly. "Meagan will have control of her bladder and intestinal functions." My face flushed embarrassment. "She'll have full use of everything except her legs. Dr. Lambert has recommended an excellent physical therapist to help strengthen her upper body so she'll be able to do most things for herself once she leaves the hospital."

"*But will she walk?*" my father pressed. He hadn't wanted to accept Ken's answer of unlikely.

Ken met his gaze squarely. "The chance is very small, Patrick. Maybe ten percent of all cases like this recover fully. It happens, but rarely."

"So then it's not impossible," Jenna said. Jenna was my sister-in-law, but she had also been my best friend long before she married my older brother, Josh. For years, Jenna and I had occupied the two apartments on the tenth floor of a building across the street from a popular coffee house we frequented. Jenna and I now both lived in the suburbs with our husbands. She'd recently had a baby with hers, and I'd recently requested a divorce from mine.

"I mean, this is Meagan we're talking about," she continued, using the words *I mean* the same way I always did when I was grasping at something. "If anyone would fall within that ten percent, it would be her."

My sister Danielle patted the back of my hand and I

yanked it away. Danielle was seven years younger than me, but no less stubborn. She was a strong-willed girl who rarely backed down from a challenge. Often, I pictured her as a miniature version of myself. I had always looked out for Danielle and continued to do so, even now. She lived in my old apartment. She was "subletting" it, but she rarely paid the rent because she knew if she didn't, I would. I didn't mind.

Ken shook his head. "It's not a matter of will, Jenna," he said in that same quiet voice. His tone was soft, like he was explaining something to a particularly slow-witted child. "If it were, no one would be paralyzed."

I wanted to cry, and I wanted them to leave because I couldn't cry in front of them. They had been doing a good enough job of that on their own for the last twenty-four hours. Tears of joy when they first heard I'd awakened turned into tears of horror when Ken told them about my condition and now they were tears of grief.

Mourning my dead legs, I thought cynically, *as if they were the ones who'd never walk again. The ones who should have died. The ones whose pregnancy was terminated in the crash.* I hated their selfishness. I knew they were wondering what they'd do with me, whose job it would be to take care of me. Well, they could take their selfish worry elsewhere, because I didn't want it.

"Get out," I whispered. No one moved except Dr. Lambert, who scurried out the door like a nervous rat, relieved to be sent away. "Do you hear me?" I yelled at their stunned faces. "I said get out!" My mother sobbed into her hands and my tone softened. "I just need some time alone."

Ken kissed my forehead and pulled the blankets up to my chin like he was tucking in a small child. "Do you want me to stay, honey?" he asked, his eyes full of mocking pity.

The look brought out the worst in me. This was how people would look at me from now on, like I wasn't real, just another crumpled sack of potatoes. My temper flared and I felt heat fill my face.

"Why would I want you to stay?" I snapped, knowing I was about to start an embarrassing. I didn't care. My husband was going to pay for his concern, I'd see to that. "Do you think I'd lock you into this marriage now?" I demanded, tossing back the offending blankets and sitting up like an angry amputee. "Is that the kind of person you think I am?"

Ken's eyes were soft, his voice frail. "You're paralyzed, honey."

"And you want to spend the rest of your life taking care of me, is that it? Ken the hero," I mocked, "with his poor crippled wife and their cold dead baby. What a happy little family they'll make." His eyes grew wet but I didn't stop. I was no one's little victim, and once anger seized me, I was beyond controlling. "You think less of me than I ever could have imagined. We both know what I said before the accident and I still mean it. The divorce request stands. I refuse to stay married to you simply because you think I need you now and it's your duty as a husband to stand by me. Well, let me tell you something; I don't need you. I don't need anyone. I never have."

My eyes darted around the room angrily and I thought, *better to do the rest of them now too than drag this out*. "That goes for all of you," I raged. "You think I need your pitying eyes? The constant care you'll give me? No. I want each and every one of you the fuck out of my life!"

"Meagan!" my mother scolded, probably more at the use of my language than anything else.

Dad massaged her shoulders. "Let her go, Joan," he said, pushing his glasses back up his nose. They were always slipping. "She's angry. She needs to get it out." His words were so confident my temper flared more violently.

"Fuck you!" I yelled at my father. How dare he presume to understand? He who'd never been sick a day in his life. "You have no idea what I need. You're just a pathetic little man with no balls and a shrew for a wife."

My father took a hurt step back and Danielle snickered behind her hands. Big mistake. I turned my venom on her.

"Oh, you think that's funny, Princess?"

She stopped snickering, fast. "W-What?"

"Why don't you get a fucking job instead of letting me foot all the bills while you skip classes so you can lay around in bed all day watching Jerry Springer and screwing your yuppie boyfriend?"

"Danielle!" Mom shrieked. She was an expert at screaming our names when we shocked her.

"I--I don't," Danny stammered, her eyes wide with

disbelief and fear. "I go to school."

"Yeah, when there's a frat party on campus."

I didn't know how I knew these things, but I could tell from my sister's face that my words were the absolute truth. She looked at me fearfully, like I'd come back from the dead with psychic powers.

"Are you people going to leave?" I demanded. "Or do I have to insult each of you in turn? Cause I've got plenty more. Just try me."

One by one they slunk into the hallway like battered children. Jenna turned and glanced at me, but I shot her a warning look. She probably wanted to turn around and have me *breathe* with her, or pick my aura clean. She was always doing things like that. "Practice tree pose with me, Meagan. Come to my yoga class. Try this tea. Your cells are storing up those negative energies again. I know a Reiki Master... a Feng Shui guy... a woman who does reflexology down at the health center." She'd made it her practice in life to heal me. I didn't think I was sick. I was now, but there wasn't a naturopath in the world who could give me back the use of my legs.

I lay in bed, twisting the sheets around my fingers and hoping I'd hurt them, because I wanted them all as far away from me as possible. I hated them right now. Hated their pitying eyes and their functioning limbs. They had no clue what I was going through. Dr. Lambert may as well have chopped off my legs, for all it would matter. I was going to spend the rest of my life an invalid. A divorced invalid with a dead baby and no legs. How could any of them understand the horror my life would become? None of them had ever seen any real suffering. Unless you counted the three months Jenna had spent in Ethiopia digging water wells with some Greenpeace-type group, but then, that suffering hadn't been hers, had it? She'd seen the skinny limbs and swollen stomachs of the children around her, the black flies buzzing around their scabby heads in the blistering heat, but her body was as strong and healthy as any North American's, and it simply didn't count. Her life, like the others' had been all sunshine and roses, from the wealthy roots she'd abandoned in favor of a more spiritually aware lifestyle, to her happy little marriage and her gurgling baby boy. I didn't begrudge her this happiness, because I knew no one deserved it more; it just bothered me that not even she, my best friend, could understand my torment. Didn't I deserve happiness as well? Why was my life always fraught with challenge? I knew of only one person who could possibly understand, my feared and loathed uncle Seamus. His sweet head was as screwed up as my legs.

I reached for the phone, and then realizing I couldn't make an international call from the hospital, slammed it down in frustration. Seamus lived in Ireland. I bit my lower lip so I wouldn't scream. I was a prisoner. A prisoner who only really wanted one visitor, but couldn't have him. I was trapped. Had anyone even told Seamus what had happened to me? I didn't think so because I knew my uncle would have been on the next flight out of Dublin if he'd known, and I cursed my mother for her loathing of her brother. Everyone thought Seamus was the devil incarnate. They were wrong. The man would walk through fire for me and aside from an incident three years earlier in which he'd attacked a bartender who was sleeping with his wife, he'd never hurt anyone. He was sensitive, that was all; sometimes unreasonably so, and that caused him to do stupid things. We were one and the same.

The muffled voices in the hall grew louder.

"What do we do now?" I heard Jenna ask.

If I were out there, I would have seen my brother wrap a protective arm around his wife's waist. "I think we give her some time. Just be grateful she didn't turn her wrath on us," he joked.

My lips tightened into a thin line. I hadn't turned my wrath on them because I couldn't. They were squeaky clean, my brother and his wife. Not a speck of dirt on either of them, and it annoyed me that such perfection was even possible. Josh with his laid-back manner, Jenna with her love for all things great and small. Sooner or later I would crowbar them out of my life too. They'd just take a little more time than the rest.

The voices continued their worried murmurings and I lay in my bed and stewed. Footsteps approached. The clunk of heavy boots.

"What's going on?" a new voice asked. "What are you all doing out here in the hall?"

My heart broke. It was Amber. The woman I loved. The woman who'd left her girlfriend, Gwynne Patterson, the instant I'd gotten hurt, and hadn't left my side since. She had waited a month while I slept, never really knowing if I'd even want her back when

I woke up.

My heart gave a sickened twist at yet another loss I 'd have to suffer. The world was coming down around me. I'd lost my legs, my baby, Ken, and soon, the poet I was in love with, Amber Reed.

Amber was my soul mate. I'd always known it. I'd loved her from the beginning, but had never been good at showing it. In our brief relationship, we'd spent just as much time arguing about our differences as we had laughing and loving. In the end, I'd decided I just couldn't be what I thought she needed, and quite suddenly and viciously ended our relationship.

Amber didn't take it well. I hadn't taken it well either, but I also hadn't been the one to write a book about it. Amber had done that. Within weeks of our breakup, *When Butterflies Wear Their Armor* hit bookshelves across the country and exposed me to the world as the cunt that I'd been.

We didn't talk for a while after that. We ran into each other briefly at Jenna's wedding, and there had been an incident between us in the bathroom in which we'd gotten a little carried away and kissed. But other than that, I didn't run into Amber again until I had just returned home from running a magazine in London. But by then I was engaged to Ken, and Amber was living with Gwynne.

Now Gwynne was history, and Ken would soon be gone too. My plan had been to reunite with Amber, but I saw now that I just couldn't allow that to happen. Amber had come into my hospital room just days before and she'd placed a ring on my finger, my grandmother's ring, in fact, and she'd asked me to remember what it meant.

I'd never forgotten what it meant. My grandmother's secret lover Rosalie Fitzpatrick, had given her the ring when they were young girls in Ireland. Rosalie and my Gran had been in love, but my Gran decided she wanted to marry my grandfather and live what she saw as a normal life, and Rosalie had given her a silver moonstone ring. The ring was a symbol of their love, and I was one of the few people who knew. My Gran had confided in me when I was very young and, when she passed away, she'd left the ring to me with the thought that I'd know what to do with it. Gran's soul mate had given her the ring, and one day, I was to give it to mine.

I'd given it to Amber. The ring had remained in her possession even long after we'd broken up. Now she'd given it back to me, with the desire that we start our lives together again, and I knew what I had to do.

I had to drive her away again. There was no way I could expect her to honor the promise of the ring, not when she'd given it back to me before knowing I'd be paralyzed for the rest of my life. She intended to pick up where Ken left off, but I knew now I couldn't let her do that. Fate had taken another harrowing turn, and I hated God for what he was forcing me to do.

"You don't want to go in there," I heard Danielle warn. First time anyone had been right about anything since I woke up. "She's having a fit. Kicked us all out. She told Dad he has no balls, called Mom a shrew, and me a Springer-watching princess."

Amber chuckled. "So she's back to her old tricks, then. I knew it wouldn't take long."

"What do you mean?" my mother asked, her voice sounding slightly annoyed that Amber should know something about me that she didn't. If I listened hard enough, I could probably hear her jaw tighten into a grimace.

Amber's boot squeaked on the floor as she shifted. "She's scared, right?"

"Of course."

"This is what she does when she's scared. She insults you, attacks you, because she thinks if she can make you hate her, you'll go away and no one will ever see how afraid she truly is." She thought she was so smart. "You'd be surprised how typical this behavior is for her. Only this time it's not going to work, not on me, anyway."

The easy way Amber spoke of standing by me in front of my mother and Ken shocked me. It seemed she was telling them, in her own gentle way, that they weren't getting rid of her, and she didn't care if they liked it or not. I grinned, then scolded myself for admiring her and reminded myself of what I had to do.

My mother sighed as only she could, a long-winded effect with a slight whistle at the end. "What do you suggest?" she asked.

I couldn't believe what I was hearing. Was my mother actually being nice to Amber? She hadn't had a kind word for her since the day the book came out.

Now she was out in the hallway soliciting Amber's

advice, and I couldn't figure it out. Had my mother finally decided that my personal life was none of her business? I doubted it. That would be too much to ask of any proud matriarch.

"Give me a bit of time alone with her," I heard Amber say.

My brother laughed. "She's shooting blind in there, Amber. I don't think you know what you're setting yourself up for."

"Believe me, I do."

"She'll pulverize you."

"No, she only thinks she will."

Amber, it seemed, never learned her lesson. She was about to walk straight into a verbal attack and she knew it. Why wasn't she smart enough to just walk away? She was going to make me do it. I cringed. She was actually going to make me destroy her with my cruelty.

Ken cleared his throat. "Do what you have to," he said quietly. "It's out of my hands now."

"Oh, Kenny," Mom simpered. She loved my husband, I thought, probably more than I did.

Another squeak on the floor and I heard my broken husband walk away. Amber entered the room and closed the door behind her. She strolled toward me purposefully, like she knew exactly how to handle me, each step a confident clunk against the floor.

"Having a good time?" she asked, tossing her leather jacket on the bed and sitting with her legs crossed under her in a chair. She looked as gorgeous as ever with her platinum hair and bright green eyes.

"Oh, it's a freakin' party," I said snottily. "Go away."

"Nope."

I shot her a look. "Things have changed. I don't want you now. Go find Gwynne."

Amber didn't flinch. "Not this time, Meagan," she said easily. "You can't drive me away."

I was determined to prove her wrong.

"You've forgotten who I am, Amber," I hissed, full of my own importance. "I can do whatever I want."

Amber only shrugged. "Get up and walk then."

My mouth fell open. "W-What?"

"You can do anything. Get up and walk."

I stared at her in disbelief. This was not my loving Amber. This woman was cruel, as cruel as I could be, and I had absolutely no answer for her. She'd managed to do what no one else could --shock me into silence.

"Well?" she demanded, her hard eyes daring me to make a move. When I did nothing, she gave a satisfied smile. "You see, Meagan, you are no longer invincible. What you don't realize is that you never were."

"Fuck you."

She ignored me. "Whether you admit it or not, you need people now."

"I don't need anyone," I barked. "Particularly not you." Tearing the ring off my finger, I whipped it at her feet, and it hit the floor with a tiny metal clink. "Give it to someone who can walk," I said, bitterly. "My life is over."

I turned my face to the wall. Amber grabbed the ring off the floor and sat beside me on the bed. "I'm giving it back to you, Meagan," she said, prying my fist open. "I'm giving it back *knowing* you're paralyzed. That's what concerns you, isn't it? The fact that I gave it back before I knew?" She slid the ring back into place on my finger. "Now I've done it again so you don't have to worry. Paralysis or not, I've made my decision." I kept my head to the wall and Amber cupped my face in her hands, turning me to face her. "But I won't lie to you either, Meagan," she continued in that same easy tone. "Your condition does scare me. I've never seen you so desperate, and truthfully, it terrifies me."

"Well, you don't have to deal with it, do you?" I snapped, yanking my head from her hands.

"Yes, I do," she said. "I have to deal with it because I love you, because you love me-- don't bother trying to deny it --and because as soon as you get out of this hospital, we're going to move in together and live happily ever after."

Her words surprised me, scared me. She wanted something I was incapable of giving her. "Have you lost your mind?" I accused. "This isn't a fairy tale, Amber. When Sleeping Beauty woke up it was not to discover she'd become a goddamn paraplegic. You have no idea what you'd be setting yourself up for. I'm letting you off the hook here. You don't owe me anything, so I suggest you take your chance to run. I've never been any good for you anyway, and I'll only be worse now. My life may be through, but I'll be damned if I drag you down with me. Now take this ring and get the hell out!"

Amber crossed her arms in front of her chest. "Are you done now? Because if you are, I'd like to tell you what's really going to happen here."

Again my mouth fell open. *Who was this woman?* Not my fragile Amber, that was for certain. This woman was in control, with a take-charge attitude that was reminiscent of me when I wanted something. She was completely calculating. "*You're going to tell me--?*"

"What's going to happen, yes."

I was flabbergasted. Amber didn't interrupt people, I did. Suddenly she was me, and I was scared as hell. Was this how I really behaved? She'd even adopted my impatient mannerisms, the pacing, the head scratching, the fingers rapping on the tabletop. I wanted to scream at her to stop it, but suddenly I had no such words in my vocabulary.

"Are you ready for it?" she asked. If she were really me, then she was going to tell me whether I was ready or not. The blond me didn't disappoint.

"Tonight," she began, as if addressing a congregation, "I'm going to take your sister out to dinner, where I will explain to her that she will be moving into my apartment, since my building doesn't have an elevator, and you and I will be moving into your old one. Your mother is going to mind her own business for once," she said, steepling her fingers. "That will be your job. And I'll work out a convenient schedule with your physical therapist. Ken thinks it will probably end up being about four times a week."

Ken thinks?

"Wait a minute," I said, finally finding my voice and cutting her off mid-declaration. "How do you know about my physical therapy? About everything?"

Amber shrugged. "I had a meeting with Ken and Dr. Lambert this morning."

"*You what?*"

"Ten percent chance, Meagan. That's you. You will walk again. I don't care what anyone tells you, or what you tell yourself." Amber, the eternal optimist.

"You knew about my condition even before I did?" I was

incredulous. "How dare you go behind my back and--"

"I dare it because I love you. I also know that Ken will honor your divorce request if you ask him again."

What in God's unholy name was going on?

"You're unbelievable," I muttered. "What makes you think you have the right to plan out my life for me? To tell me to divorce my husband? As if I really would."

Amber peered at me and gave me a sly grin. "You already told him, didn't you? You told Ken you still want a divorce and you're pissed because I knew you'd do it."

"I'm pissed," I asserted, "because you think you suddenly have the right to control me simply because you put a ring on my finger, which means absolutely nothing, and tell me you love me."

"Your grandmother had a meaning for that ring," she said smoothly. Just like me to hit me with the facts, and in such a reasonable manner.

"My grandmother was insane!" I yelled. "She thought she saw fairies for Christ's sake. If the symbolism of that ring is anything it's only the delusional ramblings of a senile old woman who died in the arms of some invisible beansidhe. Do you know what a beansidhe is, Amber? It's a goddamn ghost woman she believed was a fairy. *That's* how crazy my grandmother was, okay? She was off her freaking rocker. More loops in her brain than a slinky." I prayed Gran wasn't up there somewhere listening to me.

Amber was unaffected by my little speech. "Cut it out," she said sternly. "So what if your grandmother was senile? She left you a legacy, one that you've upheld despite your claims of her dementia. She gave you something to believe in and you chose to believe it. Denying it now only proves your fear. And I am not trying to control your life; I am only doing what you won't. You won't ask me to be with you because you think it's selfish and unfair considering your circumstances."

"Well, isn't it?" I demanded.

"No. It's not selfish because I *want* to be with you. I know I have the option to walk away, but I don't want it. I want *you*. When are you going to understand that, Meagan? This isn't anything new. I've always wanted you. And as for unfair, well, who the hell ever said life was fair? Is it fair that you should be paralyzed? No. But it's a reality right now. I can't change your circumstances, Meagan, but I can love you with all my heart and soul. The same way I always have. Why take that away from us? If it's all we can have right now, why destroy it?"

Slowly, she was convincing me. Maybe I didn't have to drive everyone away, and maybe it wasn't so wrong to keep her. I certainly did love her. I'd gotten into an accident a month ago because I was leaving my husband just on the off-chance she'd take me back, so why *did* now have to be so different?

A new ambition crept into my heart. What if Jenna and Amber were right? What if I was in that ten percent? I'd failed at so few things in life, so why was I convincing myself I'd fail at this? Because Ken said the chances were slim? Long shots were my specialty. It seemed strange then that I would choose to believe in his pessimism, when all my life I'd only believed in myself. I would need that confidence now, because it was unreasonable to weaken or let doubt creep into my heart. I'd always been a fighter, and damn Ken for trying to make me accept what the survivor in me could change. I *would* walk again. Maybe I needed Amber to point that out to me, but she was right. I was Meagan Summers, for Christ's sake, and no matter how egomaniacal that sounded, Meagan Summers rarely lost.

I felt a grin crack the corners of my mouth and Amber squeezed me close to her. "See, you're not ready to lie down and die just yet."

"No," I agreed, "not quite yet."

"Good. Does this mean you'll take me back, then?" She asked this as if I had a choice in the matter, or as if she'd done something that required my forgiveness and a welcome back into my heart. Either way, she made it seem like my situation meant nothing and we were only two people making up after a fight.

"It won't be easy, Amber," I warned.

Laughing, she cupped my face in her hands and kissed me. "When has life with you ever been easy, Meagan?" True enough.

Chapter 2

Amber took charge of things with expert precision. The mission: move Danielle into Amber's apartment and Amber into mine. The smiling cohorts: Danielle, her boyfriend Mark, and Josh and Jenna. My parents took Josh and Jenna's son, Sammy, for the day and the group was happy to have all three of them out of the way.

I was leaving the hospital, going home to a past and a future that intertwined like the vines of the fake ivy creeping up the walls in the hospital waiting room. So tacky to have a room painted like that, I thought, especially in a hospital. I was leaving Ken and the fantasy life we'd tried to create behind. I'd never go back to the house we'd shared, and was surprised to find that I didn't even care. There was nothing there for me. I made a mental list. It began and ended with clothes. For six months I'd shared the house with my husband, and not once during that time did I think about taking my belongings out of my old apartment, or pulling the things I'd owned in London out of storage. It was as if I'd known all along that the marriage would be over before the paint dried on the walls. I wanted nothing from Ken, only my freedom. He had purchased the house, paid for the remodeling, and bought all the furniture, and as far as I was concerned, he could keep every last bit of it.

Initially, he'd tried to protest. "Why won't' you take anything?" he'd complained. The real question was why I would want to.

He sat on the edge of my bed in his white lab coat, his stethoscope dangling around his neck. Trying to be the good guy. Always. I couldn't imagine taking his money, or him taking mine, for that matter. I thought it was best if we each just walked away from the marriage with whatever we had before going into it. A clean divorce was what I wanted. No fighting or squabbling over whose aunt had given the crystal stemware, or who really owned the first edition copy of *The Scarlet Letter* in the library. I figured each of us was wealthy enough not to care. I certainly didn't care.

Reluctantly, Ken had agreed and said he would find a lawyer to draw up the papers. There probably could have been an annulment, I supposed, but that would have erased the marriage entirely, and suddenly six months of my life would never have existed. I preferred divorce. If the marriage had been a mistake, then it was *my* mistake, and I was responsible enough to own up to that. I would not delete those months and pretend they'd never happened, because that would have been a lie, as if to say I'd never screwed up to begin with. Annulment, as a concept, is a lie. Surprisingly, for once everyone understood my logic.

Ken and I would remain friends. That was the conclusion we came to as we sat alone in my room for what would be the last time, discussing our divorce as easily as if we were making vacation plans.

"Maybe we won't see each other much in the beginning," he said, "because it will be hard at first. But I'll always be there for you, Meagan. Just call and you know I'll come running."

I wondered where I found such people. Here was my husband, soon to be ex-husband, sitting on the side of my bed and calmly asserting his unending loyalty to me, as if I hadn't screwed with the past year of his life. I thought maybe I brought out some sort of co-dependency in my lovers so that they refused to let me go out of some sad need of their own.

Ken was calm. He was calm because he'd had a month to deal with the fact that I would probably still divorce him when I woke up. Perhaps he'd grieved the end of our marriage before I even opened my eyes. I had yet to grieve. It didn't matter that I was the one who wanted the divorce; Ken was still an important part of my life I had to grieve losing.

I kissed his cheek and playfully flicked the ever-present stethoscope. Ken and his stethoscope. It was like Amber and her dangling bootlace, little slices of reality one could always count on to exist. These were the hallmarks of my loves.

"Thank you, Ken," I whispered. "But I think I'm going to let you get on with your life. I've wasted enough of your time already."

He looked at me sincerely. "Not wasted, Meagan. I've loved the time we've had together. I may not have been the one, but I know you tried to love me the best way you knew how."

I thought I would cry. People like Ken were too understanding. Why couldn't they scream at you? Tell you what a horrible person you were so you'd have reason to be angry instead of guilty? That rarely happened with my people. Mine were the kind who forgave more sins than Jesus. They turned so many cheeks you almost couldn't help but keep slapping them.

"I do love you, Ken." I wished I could take away his pain as easily as I'd taken his heart. "It just hasn't been the kind of love you deserve. You deserve someone who can give herself to you one hundred percent. I hope you find her someday."

And those were my parting words. It was as much comfort as I could offer to a man who had given me his all and only asked for my love in return. He really did deserve more.

Amber and the others arrived shortly after Ken left. It had taken them less than six hours to make the switches, and I marveled at their efficiency. They were like a small army of denim-clad movers. They entered the room all smiles, wearing white painter's caps turned backwards on their heads, going for a cheap laugh. They got it.

"Wait till you see what's outside," Amber gushed as one of the nurses helped me into a wheelchair and Jenna swept the room for any remaining belongings. There were none.

My clothes felt big. The wheelchair was cold and confining. It was a mobile prison and a small shudder of loathing passed through me. I looked at the large wheels that were now my legs, and jammed a fist in my mouth to keep from screaming. Temporary, I told myself. *Soon you'll start physical therapy and you'll be walking again in no time.* I wrestled with myself to believe that while Amber wheeled me down the florescent lit corridor, passing several open doors with curious patients inside, and down to the red and black exit sign around the corner. It was hospital policy to remain in a wheel chair until you reached the exit, so I didn't feel too uncomfortable until we got outside. Then I felt like a sideshow freak.

Jenna kept her hand on my shoulder as we passed through the parking lot and moved toward a waiting white van. The one they'd rented to move, I assumed, until we got closer and I noticed the pretty pink flower painted on the side door with the familiar NB woven through the vines. *Natural Beauty* was written across the face of the van in large, girlish script, like something that would mock you in traffic as you strained to read the backwards letters through your rearview mirror. The magazine I co-owned didn't have any vans, only a few trucks left over from the days when Ted Markham, my partner, was first starting out and delivered the magazine to local merchants himself in an effort to cut down on distribution costs.

"What the hell is that?" I shrieked as Amber pushed me toward the mortifying vehicle. It stood out in the parking lot like a snowdrift in the middle of a black desert.

"Isn't it great?" Jenna gushed. Her face said she knew I didn't think so.

Josh slid the lightweight side door open and reached inside, pressing a button or pulling a latch that made a large metal ramp slide out from the bottom of the van. It reached the pavement with a small clank and the noise was deafening to my ears. Horrifying. Like the sound of a garbage truck waking you from a deep sleep at five a.m. on a Monday, and I recoiled from it like a frightened turtle.

Amber wrapped her arms around me from behind. "Ted bought it for you," she said. "So you can get back and forth to work, and physical therapy of course."

They were all grinning like the monstrosity before me was a good thing.

"Isn't it cool?" Danielle said.

Cool? Were they all insane? It was a death sentence. It was a vehicle for people whose legs were on death row. People who *knew* the governor wasn't going to call.

"It's going back," I said.

"Why?" They asked in unison, harmonizing like the Village People, and I fought to control my temper.

"Ted bought it specifically for you," Amber stated. Again, like this was a good thing.

I pressed my fingers to my temples to block out the voice that called me a cripple. "I'm not riding around in a van meant for disabled people, he's wasting company money." The ramp frightened me with its assertion of my need for it. "We'll get a car. My arms will be strong enough that I can push my way in and out of a car." I looked at Amber meaningfully. "We're taking this back." I didn't want to be bossy, but I was truly terrified.

"But it will be easier," Josh reasoned.

My teeth clenched together. "I don't want *easier*, I want normal. I said it's going back and that's the end of it." I was getting tired of repeating myself.

"But work-- ". They were all ganging up on me.

"I'll go back to work when I can walk. If I never walk again, then I guess I'll never go back. Who fucking cares? I can *afford* to be an invalid, alright?" My sarcasm was cutting.

"What about the publishing company?" Danielle probed.

Before the accident, Ted and I had been in the process of starting a new book publishing company together. We'd even purchased a money-making tabloid called *The Watcher* to help finance the venture.

"What about it? It's dead. Now can we just get out of here? People are staring at me."

There was only one man walking through the parking lot and he'd done nothing more than nod at us as he passed but I knew what he was thinking. *What's up with the angry cripple?* I wanted to disappear.

Josh and Jenna followed in their car as Amber and I brought the van back to the Natural Beauty offices. We barely spoke. Amber went into the building to give Ted the keys and Josh helped me into the passenger seat of their car. Mark and Danielle had gone home. I hung onto Josh's shoulder as he helped me through the door and refused to admit it was an effort to jam my stiff legs under the dash. I used my arms to bend my legs at the knee, acting as if this was the way I'd been getting into cars my whole life. Josh and Jenna exchanged a look, but said nothing. Amber appeared outside with Ted following close behind. She got in the seat behind me and played with my hair while Ted poked his head through the window, kissed my cheek, and tried to convince me to keep the van.

"Come back to work whenever you want," he said. "We'll find something for you to do until we get the publishing company off the ground." He still believed we were expanding our business together. I told him I would call him when I could walk and he shrugged as if he knew I'd change my mind. I knew I wouldn't. I would not go back to my old stomping ground unable to stomp.

Josh and Jenna drove us home. Amber wheeled me into the building, into the elevator, and down the tenth floor hallway, stopping me in front of the familiar old door while she groped in her purse for the key. I wanted to throw myself from the wheelchair and crawl, if I had to, across the threshold and into the place where I had lived for seven years as a successful, functional woman. I did nothing, only stared at Amber's tiny back as she turned the key in the lock. The metal door swung open and she wheeled me inside. The place even smelled the same, fruity. Like an orange rind, or maybe a lemon. Either way it was the citrus smell of clean.

The living room looked like it always had, spotless. Amber must have helped Danielle clean in order to meet my fussy standards before they moved her stuff out, because my sister was a slob and there was simply no way she would have kept the apartment this clean. Amber had probably had to bring cleaning supplies with her, because Danny never had anything more than a bottle of Windex, which she used on everything.

Amber bit her thumbnail and followed as I wheeled my way around the apartment, inspecting everything. I entered the kitchen. Again, spotless. Amber had done a fine job. Bare counter tops except for a microwave and a black cappuccino maker. I imagined Jenna bursting through the door from her apartment across the hall the way she always had when I gave her phone a quick ring to let her know the cappuccino was ready. I felt a small sadness that those days were gone. We had been so young and free. Now Jenna was married to my brother and she had a baby. She was a grown up. She lived across town in a grownup person's house and a stranger lived across the hall. It made me uneasy. It was the same but different, like going home after a sabbatical in the woods only to find that your tribe has picked up their tents and dropped stakes in another part of the world, leaving you only a map in the dirt to follow-- and when had I ever been good with directions?

I wheeled past the bathroom with the linoleum floor with the black and white octagon design I'd always meant to change, the pedestal sink, and claw-footed tub painted dark purple on the bottom and a strange, transparent shower curtain with yellow rubber ducks on it. I laughed. *That* wasn't mine.

Obviously Danielle had thought to add her own decorative touch to this room.

Lastly, I wheeled into the bedroom. Danielle hadn't changed anything about this room. Deep burgundy walls, plush green drapes as soft as velvet but made of some other fabric for which I didn't have a name. This used to be Amber's favorite room. She loved deep colors, romantic atmospheres with soft lighting, and this room had all of those things. A tall bureau rested against one wall and on top of that sat a glass vase filled with white daffodils. I grinned. Amber could remember the minutest details, like that daffodils were my favorite flower.

The four-post bed with cream-colored sheers tied at the posts loomed before us, and I peered at it quizzically. "Hmm, we'll need a new mattress."

"Why?" Amber asked.

"My sister's been having sex on that one."

She laughed. "So? I'm assuming she used sheets."

"Yeah, and we'll be getting rid of those too. And don't look at me like that. I can't help it if it grosses me out. Did you know that after I caught Basil in bed with that stoned nineteen-year-old, I totally re-did this room from top to bottom just to erase the memory?" Basil was a longhaired drummer who'd been my boyfriend right before I'd gotten together with Amber. Eventually, Basil's band had gotten a hit record and he'd moved to LA. "Jenna helped. It was beige and white before but we painted, hung new drapes, and of course, I bought a new mattress." I shrugged. "The thing about having money is that you can afford to be strange."

Laughing, she kissed the top of my head. "Well, I love you, you big nut. Or maybe I should start calling you Gran."

"Yeah, see how far that gets you."

"Okay. So what do you want to do? Switch it with my mattress?"

"A slow and painful death is what you had in mind for me? The only thing worse than the image of Danielle and Mark is the image of you and--God help me for saying this--the most beautiful woman I've ever seen besides you, Gwynne."

"She wasn't that beautiful," Amber said.

I laughed at her. "Oh, come on! Aside from those cold blue eyes the woman is stunning. In fact, the cruelty of her eyes probably only adds to her beauty."

"She has inverted nipples."

"*What?*" Amber's attempt to find a flaw on Gwynne was hilarious.

She nodded her head emphatically. "It's true. On the outside you see that perfect face and the curves, but it's no picture naked I'll tell you that. Massive cellulite on her thighs and ass. Big, hairy mole on her back."

"You're lying."

"I swear to God, I'm not. Gwynne has a horrible body under those clothes. Why do you think she hated you so much?"

"Probably for the same reason I couldn't stand her."

Amber shook her head. "She was jealous of you. Big time. She knew she couldn't compete."

"Whatever you say."

"I'm dead serious. One day, when you were still in London, Gwynne and I were visiting Jenna and Jenna started complaining about how the pregnancy was making her fat. She was nothing but stomach, thin everywhere else, but it was getting to her. I think she must have forgotten who she was talking to because suddenly she said, 'You know whose body I would kill to have? Meagan's. Absolutely incredible. Have you ever seen that woman naked?' Well, my face flushed and Gwynne barked,' "What the hell do you think, Jenna?'" She could lose her temper so easily. You think you're bad, but Gwynne could lose it over the slightest thing, especially any mention of you. I told her too much, I think. Anyway, Jenna apologized like she'd shot the pope, but the damage had already been done. She'd pissed Gwynne off and put such a vivid picture in my head I couldn't help but miss making love to you. I always missed making love to you."

My eyes shot down to my crippled legs and I felt tears sting the backs of them. If my body really had been that incredible, it certainly wasn't now. Now I was a stump. I didn't even know if I *could* make love to Amber because of the shame tied up in my legs, let alone do it well. Gwynne had me beat there. Amber's eyes met mine and I looked away, feeling the tears roll down my cheeks.

"I'm sorry, Meagan," she said, crouching in front of my chair. "I didn't mean to upset you. Please. Don't cry. This is temporary, remember?"

I couldn't look at her. "What if it isn't, Amber?" I whispered. We hadn't discussed that possibility.

"It is."

"You say that because you want to believe it, but what if I never regain the use of my legs? Do you want to be tied down to a stump the rest of your life?"

"You're not a stump," she said angrily. "And wheelchair or not, yes, I want to be with you the rest of my life. I'll tell you that a hundred and fifty times a day if I have to. You're still beautiful, still smart, and still the crazy, neurotic woman I fell in love with. Can you tell me that you don't love me?"

"No."

"Then you're stuck with me, okay?"

"I really hate this," I complained.

"I know, but you're not in it alone." Lovingly, she took me by the arms. "Come sit on the bed with me." She tugged on me gently and helped me to my feet. She wrapped her arm around my waist and eased me onto the bed before crawling beside me and resting her head on her arm. She looked up at me. "Are you really not going back to work, Meagan?"

I shook my head. "Not right away. It's too humiliating right now."

"So what will you do?"

"I don't know. Work on getting better, I guess."

"Okay."

"Amber?"

She rested back against the pillows. "Yes?"

"Where did Gwynne go?"

"I don't know. She moved out the first week of your coma."

"Do you miss her?"

"No."

"Honestly?"

"Honestly," she replied.

"Good, because I really, *really* disliked her."

Amber laughed. "Careful selection of words there. You more than disliked her."

I nodded. "She thought she could keep us apart but

then she'd try forcing us together. I never got that."

"She wanted you to see me with her," Amber said quietly.

"And for you to see me with Ken," I agreed. "The night of our wedding--oh, I could have killed her for that little stunt. Having Ken and me meet her at your apartment. I didn't even want her to decorate our house because I knew she'd pull something but Ken kept telling me I was being paranoid and that she was one of the best interior designers in the city. Then when we were sitting on the couch in your apartment all I could think about was how many times you and I had made love on it."

"Me too," Amber admitted.

"But the worst part was thinking you and Gwynne had probably done it there too."

"We hadn't."

I nodded again. "That's about as far as I want to go with that topic. I don't ever want to know what you and Gwynne did together."

"I'm not exactly thrilled with the idea of you and Ken either," she said. "We should probably just leave them behind us."

"Good idea." Another, more painful, thought occurred to me. "Jenna told you about Zoe, didn't she?" I asked, feeling the vise grip my heart and then release a little. I was going to name my baby Zoe because the name meant "life" but now she'd never have one.

"Yes."

"And she knew that I was coming for you the night of the accident?"

"Yeah." Amber glanced down at the bed. "But I didn't believe her."

"Would you have done it, Amber?" I asked in the softest voice I could muster without crying. "Would you have been her mother?"

Amber grinned. "Is that how you saw it? That I would have been her mother too?"

"I'm sorry, but yes."

"Meagan, why are you sorry? Can you imagine how that makes me feel? That's a wonderful thing to say. You're saying she would have been *our* baby."

"And Ken's," I pointed out. "He was her father, after all."

"But you wanted more from me than to just be in her life. You wanted me to be her *parent*."

My heart ached. "Yes. Do you know what she would have been, Amber? If she took the better qualities of all three of us? Imagine a person with Ken's compassion and interest in healing, with my determination and instinct, with your creativity, kindness and intelligence. She would have been amazing. I don't like to think she would have taken my sense of vengeance, but even if she did, the other qualities would knock it right out."

"She would have been wonderful, Meagan," Amber said, stroking my arm. "And yes, I would have done it."

"I was so afraid you'd say no. Worse, I was afraid you'd laugh at me, or hate me and say you never wanted to see me again."

"And would you have gone back to Ken then?"

"No, my marriage was over no matter what happened between you and me. I refused to raise my child in a lie. I was gonna take off, pregnant stomach and all, but I couldn't do it. It wouldn't have been fair to the baby."

Amber smiled. "Which reminds me, your five thousand dollars is in the nightstand."

I ground my palm against my forehead and groaned. Right before the accident I had packed a bag with my passport, a few pieces of clothing, and five thousand dollars in cash, just in case I decided to disappear. "Everyone knows, don't they?"

"Yes."

I shook my head, embarrassed.

Amber's head flopped against my shoulder and she curled her body to fit mine on the bed.

"I like that," I said, wrapping my arms around her back and kissing her forehead.

"Me too. I've really missed being near you like this."

"So don't let go."

"I won't."

"Never?"

"Never," she said.

We were back with a vengeance.

Bathing, I soon learned, was a difficult chore. It took effort to lift myself in and out of the tub, to wash my hair under the tap without sinking down far enough to drown. But to Amber's dismay, I refused her assistance and went about the task on my own like a normal person.

The first time took an hour and a half. Even the simple things like undressing weren't simple for me. It was a slow, painstaking process. Remove the clothes over the dead legs and place them somewhere (usually on the folded-down toilet seat) where I could reach them again later to throw them in the hamper in the bedroom.

Slipping over the edge of the tub and dropping down into the water felt like a baby's first splash in a pool, frightening. It was amazing to find that my legs had had so many more uses than just walking. They had been my balance. Now that balance was gone and I fumbled through the bathing ritual like someone who'd never done this before.

In the water, my legs almost felt real. I had no real control over them, but depending on my position in the tub, they either floated or sank. If I sat up straight, they rested against the bottom of the tub the same way they would if they functioned. If I lay back, they wanted to float, but couldn't quite reach the top of the water.

Amber knocked on the door occasionally to make sure I was alright. She'd offer to help, I'd say no thank you, and she'd walk away for a little while longer. I couldn't bear her help. I needed it, especially when the time came to get out of the water, but I couldn't bear the thought of her seeing me naked and weak. Naked wasn't the problem. Weak wasn't entirely the problem either. It was the combination of the two that filled me with shame and forced me to go about this toughest of tasks alone.

With a sigh of apprehension, I crawled over the edge of the tub like a soldier crawling out of a bunker and slithered to the floor like a tired, wet snake. Then I elbowed my way across the linoleum tiles and reached for the towel rack, shivering at the coldness that chilled my damp body as it glided across the icy floor. If I never walked again, I would feel this coldness every day for the rest of my life. The thought chilled me even more. We would have to get a removable shower head soon, I realized, to replace the one that seemed to be welded to the wall and was, at this point, useless to me. A removable shower head would help *a lot.*

Drying myself was, thankfully, the simplest task. That, I was able to do in a fairly reasonable amount of time. Dressing again wasn't so simple. I had chosen a brown wool sweater that slipped over my head easily and a pair of faded blue jeans that were somewhat loose because I wanted to be comfortable while still looking human.

The jeans were the problem. It took several attempts before I was finally able to shove my legs through them and drag them over my hips while lying on the floor with my head balanced against the outside wall of the tub. I pressed against it to lift my hips, shoulders flattened against the tub wall, elbows pressed to the floor, neck angled so that the lip of the old tub snuggled in the back of it, forcing those few muscles to hold the bulk of my weight as my heels dug into the floor and my hips lifted by the mere force of the contraction. Finally, the jeans slid over my hips and I released the pressure in my neck, freed my elbows, and allowed my lower body to drop as I tugged on the zipper and fastened the button. Done. I allowed myself a weak smile and breathed a little more easily.

Climbing back into my chair, I pulled my discarded clothes into my lap, brushed my hair and touched on a small amount of makeup. Smudgy brown eyeliner at the lower lashes and a deeper brown mascara to bring out whatever life was still left in my eyes. No eye shadow. A touch of bronze at the cheeks and a dab of mocha gloss on the lips that somehow seemed fuller than they were before the accident.

A glance in the mirror said I looked like me, or as close to me as I was going to get sitting in a wheelchair.

I   did   my   best   not   to   cry.

Chapter 3

My physical therapist was a tall, muscular man of indeterminate age with white-blond hair, blue eyes, and enormous hands. He reminded me of a giant Swede, a masseur in one of those upper-end health spas rich women flocked to for their weekly mud baths and Pilates classes. He wore baggy grey track pants with light grey lines down the legs and pockets on the sides that he shoved his hands into and a white t-shirt that accented his massive shoulders and thick arms. The hair on his arms was also blond, but more golden blond than white. He introduced himself as Derek but my mind said *Sven*.

My mother had dropped me off at the hospital, where my therapy was to take place in the basement rehabilitation room, and left me with the promise of returning in two hours to pick me up. She couldn't bear to watch what "Sven" would have to do to me, and I hadn't wanted her to. This was something I had to face alone. Amber had wanted to come. So had Jenna and Danielle but my mother had helped me convince them to stay behind. We both knew therapy was going to be a struggle and my mother understood why I didn't want anyone to watch that.

Derek spent the first half-hour explaining what we'd be doing together. Then he lifted me onto a massage table and told me to lie back and began moving my left leg back and forth, bending it at the knee. I watched this as if from a detached place in my head. After a few minutes he started the same process on the other leg.

"You see this a lot, right Derek?" I asked, watching him do his job with an air of quiet professionalism. He was the sort of man who had to be encouraged to talk, but when he did, he'd tell you a lot. I'd almost called him Sven.

"Mm-hmm," came the response.

"Tell me something then. Have you ever seen anyone recover from injuries like mine?"

"Frequently."

"Really?" A spark of hope danced within me.

Derek propped me forward and placed three-pound

weights in my hands. "We have to strengthen your upper body," he said, instructing me on which way he wanted me to lift the weights. He raised my arms out to the sides and I pumped the weights up and down, flapping my arms like I was trying to fly.

"Frequently?" I pressed, wanting to hear more about recovery and less about preparing my upper body for a lifetime of work.

"Oh yeah." He looked around the sterile white rehabilitation room like he was about to disclose a great secret. I pressed forward. "These damn doctors are always telling people they'll never walk again but half the time they're wrong. I don't know exactly what happens physiologically, but suddenly these people who were supposed to be paralyzed start feeling sensations. Before you know it, they're on crutches, and then walking. I can't count how many times I've seen it and each time their doctors act like it's a miracle."

I wondered how many of them had seen Dr. Lambert, and decided to cut the old buzzard out of my life. After his first assertion that nothing was impossible, Dr. Lambert had suddenly become the voice of doom, telling me I had to accept what I'd become and try to live a healthy, productive life with my disability. Many people did it, he'd said, and there was no reason why I couldn't go back to work and continue on the way I always had. In less than two weeks he had completely reversed his opinion and I didn't like it. He was about to be history, like Ken and anyone else who tried to tell me I would never go back to my former self.

When my mother came back later that morning she was pleasantly surprised by my positive attitude. In fact, she seemed a different person altogether these days. Not once since I'd decided to move back into my old apartment with Amber did she utter one word of protest. I knew she wasn't happy with the idea but she wasn't fighting me either. She seemed to have reached some sort of acceptance about it, or perhaps tolerance, and to my great relief kept her opinions to herself.

The divorce papers arrived by courier later that day. Ken hadn't wasted any time. After scanning the few pages detailing an amicable divorce in which both parties agreed to terminate the marriage without any requests for alimony or the divvying up of accumulated belongings or monies, I signed them quickly and handed them back to the courier, who gave me a copy before marching out the door on his way to his next delivery. It was an easy divorce. It didn't take long to finalize. Two weeks later, the finished document arrived with a big red seal across the front of it. The marriage was over. I was barely out of the hospital and already divorced.

Amber and I celebrated with a bottle of wine, though it didn't feel like much of a victory; it was more like a disturbing release. I was a free woman, but free to do what? Until I walked again, there was little freedom in anything.

Ted kept calling. Every other day he called to see how therapy was going and to find out when I was coming back to work.

"Come on, Meagan, I need you," he'd plead.

"No. Run it yourself."

Then four weeks after we'd returned the van, Ted called again, this time to tell me to look out the window.

"What for?" I asked. He hung up on me.

Amber rolled me to the window, something I could have done for myself, and there across the street, parked in front of The Purple Cauldron, was the van again. Only this time the *Natural Beauty* logo had been removed and emblazoned across the side door were the words *Markham-Summers Publications.*

"He's not going to give up," Amber said, grinning. "He's like you, doesn't understand the meaning of no."

"Old me, Amber. I understand it now."

"The two of you make excellent business partners. Besides, I'm still in the market for a new publisher."

"Stick with Hector Publications," I warned. "I'm not going into book publishing."

Again the van was sent back and I continued on my usual routine of having my mother drive me to therapy. When I realized it might be too much for her, I called my father and told him to take Amber down to the Mercedes lot and help her pick out a good car.

"Why a Mercedes?" Amber had questioned, her pretty nose wrinkling like she thought the car was pretentious. It probably was.

I shrugged. "Mercedes, BMW, a Jag--I don't care. Get whatever you want. Just make sure it's black and not a Saab. I'm through with those." My mind pictured my crumpled car and I shuddered. "My father will help you pick out a good car. When you find it, come get me and I'll go down to the dealership with you and write a check."

"We'll go half," Amber suggested. It was amazing she wasn't broke, because the woman cared nothing for money. She was the antithesis of me.

I didn't think Amber had much money, so I declined her offer. Why expect her to help pay for a car she wouldn't buy in the first place? Amber's tastes were more sporty than classic. If she were going to buy an expensive car, it would probably be something like a Porsche. Red, to match her vibrant personality. I hated red cars, they seemed sleazy somehow. White was too pure, blue too boring, and any other color too obvious. Black was the only way to go, sleek but elegant. Noticeable but understated.

Amber left with my father, and three hours later we were the owners of a black Jaguar. I wasn't sure I actually liked the car, but it would serve its purpose. There was something old lady-ish about it, I thought, picturing a bespectacled, grey-haired woman at the wheel. It didn't really seem like the car for a twenty-eight-year-old cripple.

Amber hated it when I called myself a cripple. They all did. It made them think I had resigned myself to a life of cynicism, but I hadn't quite yet. I worked with Derek four times a week, and on the other three days I worked on my own, using my arms to push my legs back and forth the way Derek always did, and lifting the five and seven pound weights I had gotten Josh to purchase for me from the sporting goods store across the street from the gym he worked out in. I was careful not to overdo it. I wanted strong arms, not muscular ones. Toned was good. Miss Biceps Universe was not.

During week six of my convalescence, Seamus arrived from Ireland. Amber picked him up at the airport, meeting my uncle for the first time in a crowded terminal by herself. It didn't bother her. Few things did.

"Sorry it took me so long, Meggie Pie," Seamus said, strolling through the door carrying a navy blue duffel bag and a bottle of Irish whiskey. He dropped the duffel bag by the door and scooped me into a hug, half-lifting me out of my chair.

"You're too thin," he admonished. "Nothing Seamus can't fix, though. A few big breakfasts--we'll set you up. Girlie over there could use some meat on her bones too." He nodded at Amber and she laughed. I thought she had a perfect body. "I can't believe no one told me you'd been hurt," Seamus went on, not giving anyone a chance to talk. "No bother, though. I'm here now and I'll be having a long talk with your mother, you can be sure of dat. Why, if you hadn't called..." He waved away his own words. "Anyway, I brought the whiskey cause I thought I'd give you another chance at beating yer old uncle." He turned to Amber. "The last time me niece was in Ireland with her pretty boy husband, she had da nerve to challenge me to a drinking contest. Lost, of course".

I laughed. Seamus was the first person to ignore my wheelchair. His eyes did mist for a second, but he recovered quickly and said it must be jet lag. He knew I wouldn't have wanted his pity, so he didn't give it to me.

Taking the bottle of whiskey from his hand, I tilted it in the light, and the golden liquid swished to the side with a gurgle. "What are you talking about, Seamus?" I said. "I won. I believe the loser was gonna be the next one to visit and you're here, aren't you? Ken warned you that I didn't lose well."

Seamus saw where I was going with this and grinned. "So you cracked up yer car just to get me here, eh?"

I grinned back. "I told you, I do what it takes to win."

The two of us broke out laughing and Amber said, "Would you like some coffee, Seamus?" She was uncomfortable with the conversation and the way Seamus and I were making light of my paralysis. Amber didn't understand that this was how Seamus and I dealt with tragedy. We joked about it, as if to say, *screw it, we've always got each other*.

Seamus shook his head at her. "Not unless you've got some Bailey's to throw in it." It was everything Irish with him.

"Like we wouldn't," I said. "With you coming to town?" I turned to Amber. "He'll take one, honey. Three quarters coffee, a quarter Bailey's."

"You too?" she asked.

"Sure."

Amber poured three cups of coffee and we gathered in the living room to catch up. Seamus looked tired after the long flight, but a shot of whiskey and two cups of coffee later he was back to his old, bright-eyed self. He sat beside Amber on the couch and peered at her with amused eyes.

"What?" She asked, nervously.

Seamus only grinned and I knew what was going on in his dirty little mind. He was picturing Amber naked and thinking what a fine job I'd done getting this one. I wouldn't doubt if he was also remembering everything I'd ever told him about her. I kept no secrets from Seamus. He was like my other self, the physical manifestation of my animus.

"So," he said, turning his smiling eyes on me. "You dumped yer little pantywaist husband den."

"Seamus." He didn't have to be rude.

Amber smirked and Seamus nudged her. "When the wee one brought the boy to Ireland with her, I took one look at him and thought, if she's going to be with a girl, she might as well go back to the girl. Dat would be you."

Amber threw back her head and laughed, and I glared at my uncle.

"Me poor little Meggie Pie didn't know if she was coming or going, marrying that boy in some silly little chapel, *without* her Uncle Seamus, and all da while she was still in love with you. She's like me, does stupid things sometimes. I once married a trampy little stripper and Meggie married the pretty boy pantywaist. Limp Willy, I'll bet."

I'd heard enough. No one bad-mouthed Ken. That was where I drew the line. The man had been an ideal husband, and I was guilt-ridden over what I'd done to him.

"Ken liked you, Seamus," I bitched. "He wanted to invite you to stay with us for a month."

Seamus, as usual, was amused. "Did the marriage even last a month?" he joked. Another smirk from Amber. "Besides, where would I have slept? In your husband's bed while you made time in hers?" He nudged Amber again and she turned her head to hide her amusement, knowing I wouldn't like it.

"It wasn't like that and you know it," I fumed. "I was completely faithful to my husband. Marrying him may have been a mistake, but I never screwed around."

"Dat five minutes of monogamy must have killed you, I think. Were you celibate as well?"

"You're pissing me off."

"Okay, okay." Seamus waved his handkerchief like a snotty white flag. "Don't get bitchy."

"Well, if you can't say anything nice about my ex-husband then keep your freaking Mick mouth shut. I hurt the man enough, and if you think insulting him makes me proud of that, you're wrong."

Amber didn't say a word, but Seamus's eyes stopped being amused. "A word of warning, Meagan," he growled. He never called me Meagan. "The last person who called me a Mick ended up with eight stitches in his face."

"Yeah?" His words didn't frighten me a bit, but I saw Amber inch away and glance at him fearfully. "And who bailed your drunken ass out of jail? Who hired you the best goddamn attorney around? Don't you ever fucking threaten me, or I'll cut you out of my life so fast you'll wish you never said those words." Amber's eyes were pleading with me to be quiet. She didn't realize that this was no big deal, just another, albeit gruesome, part of the strange relationship Seamus and I shared.

He glanced down at his feet, then rose to pull me into another giant hug. "Aw, I'm sorry sweetie," he said, kissing my cheek. "You know I'd never lay a hand on you."

"But you say things like that and everyone thinks you're a maniac."

"Is that why none of them called me?" His face grew angry again. "What did they think I was gonna do? Put you out of yer misery? What about dat Jenna?"

"She wanted to call you," Amber said, quietly. "But she lost your number when they moved and Joan wouldn't give it to her."

"That fucking bitch!" I yelled.

"Hey now," Seamus reprimanded. "Dat's yer mother. I'll deal with her. You mind yer business."

"My coma wasn't my business?"

"Don't get smart. You have so much respect for yer ex-husband but why didn't *he* call me?"

I didn't have a response. Seamus was absolutely right. Why *hadn't* Ken called him?

"Well Meggie?" he taunted.

"I don't know," I snapped. "Are you happy now?

You've given me a reason to be mad at him."

"Better than guilt," Amber commented.

"True."

Seamus's eyes danced happily with a challenge, and I knew what was coming. "Drinking contest, Meggie?"

I shook my head. "I'll have a couple with you but no more. I have therapy in the morning."

"I thought you dropped the shrink a long time ago?"

"Not that kind of therapy. I fucking wish it was for my head."

Seamus's expression softened. "You'll walk, Meggie."

"Yeah." It was a bored acceptance.

"You will. Remember who you are. What did I teach you about fighting back?"

"This isn't an enemy, Seamus. If it is, then the enemy is God and I've done plenty over the years to get Him good and pissed off."

"That's not true, Meagan," Amber said. "You can't look at this from a spiritual point of view, it's physical. You're not being punished, you're just facing a challenge, and you always win those, right?"

"Why don't we talk about something else?" I suggested.

By evening Seamus had managed to get Amber drunk. She wasn't much of a drinker, but he had been refilling her glass of whiskey almost since the minute he cracked open the bottle and Amber was too polite to refuse his constant requests for her to "drink up because it came all the way from Ireland."

I'd stopped drinking at dinner when we'd called in for Italian, but Seamus and Amber were still going at it, and she was starting to look ill.

"I can't," she pleaded, when he moved to refill her glass from a second bottle he had pulled from his luggage.

"Jesus, Seamus, how much whiskey did you bring?" I asked.

"Just a few bottles, Meggie. I'm gonna be here a while, right?"

"Well quit giving it to her. She's gonna puke. She doesn't drink."

"Never?"

"Not really. A couple of glasses of wine here and there, and you've been pouring her that stuff all day."

"I do feel schlick," she murmured. "Schtick...sick. That one. Sick."

I fought the urge to laugh. I had never seen Amber drunk. It was almost midnight, and I thought if I didn't get her to bed soon, she was going to start throwing up and then she'd spend the rest of the night doing so. "Can you walk?" I asked her.

"Can you*?"* She giggled. Then her eyes suddenly snapped open, a look of surprise on her face. "Oh my... I'm slorry. I didn't mean --"

"I know. It's okay. I think we just need to get you to bed. Seamus, can you please carry her into the bedroom?"

Seamus rose from his chair. "Alright, c'mere, Blondie," he said, pulling her from the couch.

She looked up at him. "Blondie?"

"Yeah, dat'll be you."

"Okay."

Seamus carried Amber into the bedroom and placed her on the bed while I grabbed a bucket from under the sink and wheeled in after them. "There are blankets and pillows in the closet Seamus," I said, pointing across the room. "You'll have to grab them because they're too high for me. Sorry we don't have another bedroom."

"Nah, da couch is fine. Do you need help with her?" He nodded at the bed.

"No, I'm okay. Is she asleep?"

"Noooo," Amber moaned.

I rolled toward the bed. "I'll take care of her. You go get some sleep. You must be exhausted after that flight and then all the drinking."

"Yeah," Seamus agreed. "Goodnight, Meggie." He grabbed two blankets and a pillow and strolled out, closing the door behind him.

Amber lay sprawled out on the bed in her jeans and a black t-shirt. I hoisted myself to the side of the bed and began unfastening her jeans.

"Are you coming on to me?" She giggled.

"I'm helping you get more comfortable."

"Too bad."

I took off her jeans and tossed them on the floor, pulled back the blankets and helped her under them before removing my own jeans and sliding in beside her. I didn't have the energy to change into anything else, to cross the room again and dig through the dresser in search of something to put on because I wasn't comfortable with my nakedness anymore. It seemed perverse for someone like me to sleep naked. I didn't like the idea that my body might twist in my sleep but my legs wouldn't and I would be naked like that --looking like half of me wasn't real; human upper half, mannequin legs. It made me shudder with loathing.

"How are you feeling?" I asked, once I was positioned in bed beside her, stroking her hair.

"I'm not sure. I feel sick and then I don't." She pressed up against me. "I'm really sorry, Meagan, I didn't mean it like that."

"It's okay. You weren't thinking."

"You'll walk," she murmured. "Because it's you."

"You need to get some sleep."

"I need you." She pressed closer and I felt a small flutter of fear in my heart. There had been a few times but it was awkward. It wasn't easy. Amber didn't seem to mind the effort, but for me it was horrifying. Heartbreaking that it should be any effort at all. "Did you hear me, Meagan? I said I need you."

"Yes," I said, quietly. "I heard you. But you're really drunk."

"So?" She leaned forward and kissed me. "I want you. Don't you want me?"

There was an ache in the pit of my stomach. "I always want you but---"

"I don't want to hear your 'buts.' Let's make love."

Before I could respond, her head fell back against the pillows and she was asleep. Relief flooded my body. Then anger that I should find myself relieved. And in one terrifying instant I realized I was going to sink. If I didn't regain the use of my legs I was going to sink into a black hole that I might never dig my way out of again. Amber was asleep beside me and I willed myself not to cry.

In the morning I was prepared for Amber's hangover. I

had skipped therapy and Seamus had gone out to pick up the remedies I knew she'd need. By the time he returned, she was staggering out of bed. I sat in the living room, listening to her stumbling around the bedroom, presumably in search of clothes. She must have given up quickly, because she emerged in her jeans from the night before. Puffy-eyed and weak, she slowly crossed the room and dropped onto the couch with a whispered, "hey."

"Good morning." I couldn't help laughing.

"Oh God, Meagan." She pressed her fingers to her temples. "It really isn't funny."

Seamus poked his head out of the kitchen. "How ya feelin,' Blondie?" he yelled.

She cringed. "Please ask him not to yell." It was barely a whisper.

"Don't yell, Seamus. Did you get everything I asked for?"

He carried the bag toward me. "All but the tree bark."

"Tree bark?" Amber looked at me, confused.

I nodded. "One of Jenna's remedies. Willow bark. Supposedly when you chew on it, it acts as a pain reliever. You'll have to deal with Tylenol."

"Thank God," she grumbled. "I said something really offensive to you last night, didn't I?"

"No."

"I did. I'm sure of it. What did I say?"

I sighed. "You asked me if I could walk."

She let out a guilty groan and pressed her face into her hands. "Did I apologize?"

"Twice." Digging into the bag, I pulled out a bottle of Vitamin B, a small carton of orange juice, Tylenol, Evian, and a jar of honey. Amber watched me shake out two vitamins and two Tylenol while Seamus brought me a tablespoon.

"Had many hangovers?" she questioned.

"A few. I drank as a teenager. Not compulsively, but I did party a bit more than my body could handle. Take this stuff and in about an hour you'll feel pretty much back to normal."

She washed down the pills with the Evian and opened the carton of orange juice. "What does it do?"

"The fructose in the orange juice will help burn up any

remaining alcohol in your system. Same thing with the honey." I scooped out a spoonful and handed it to her. She ate it with a wince. "I guess we could have put it on a cracker or something," I said.

"Now you tell me."

"Or I could just let you suffer," I teased. "Anyway, your body's been depleted of Vitamin B. Drinking does that. Taking some should lessen the length of your hangover."

Seamus chuckled. "Me Meggie knows everything."

"Yeah, unfortunately it's the wrong things. Remember Janie, Seamus?" Janie had been my best friend in high school. She'd died in a car accident a few years after graduation and I had never gotten over the loss.

"Aye. Snobby little girl, as I recall."

I laughed. "We ran in a snobby clique. Janie wasn't the only one, just the richest. But she was also the one who really taught me how to deal with a hangover. She'd certainly had enough of them. She had problems at home. Her parents were always fighting and then buying her things to make up for it. It was really sad. I felt so bad for her I'd let her convince me to do almost anything, and we got in a hell of a lot of trouble together."

"That surprises me," Amber said. "You've never seemed like the type who could be manipulated."

Seamus gave a hearty chuckle. "Oh, dat Janie could do it, alright. Poor Meggie, she was always such a sucker for a sob story."

"Me too." Amber nodded. "When I was younger anyway."

"Yeah," Seamus said. "But did you almost get yourself arrested?"

"Not almost, I did. But that wasn't because of a sob story. I was at an abortion rally protesting against the pro-lifers with some friends outside a clinic on Main Street."

"Oh my God," I gasped. "Was it in '93?"

"You were there?"

I nodded emphatically. "With Jenna. She had to go to the bathroom, so we left for a few minutes and by the time we got back everyone was gone. Someone told us our friends had been arrested, so we went down to bail them out. There were only two other girls in there, so we posted their bail too."

"Holy shit!" Amber exclaimed. "Meagan, you bailed me out of jail! Oh my God, it was you. I can't believe it!"

"*You* were one of them?"

She was jumping in her seat. Seamus looked amazed. "I was in the cell with my friend Rachel," she explained. "And a few other girls. The other girls were bitching about how their friends had abandoned them and one of them said 'Meagan wouldn't do that.' *You* were that Meagan! This is unbelievable. Then one of the others said 'Neither would her side-kick. They'll get us out.' I didn't know how Rachel and I were going to get out but then we could hear talking coming from down the hall, voices discussing how many had been arrested. And I heard you! Now that I think about it, I'm sure it was your voice. You said 'Well, if there are only two others, we'll get them out too.'"

"I did say that."

"Rachel and I were stunned. We just looked at each other and the first girl giggled and said, 'I told you she'd get us out, she's even getting *them* out.' Well, we wanted to thank you, of course, but by the time we got out of the cell you'd already left with the other girls. I can't believe this, Meagan. This is too weird."

"Did they file any charges?" Seamus asked.

Amber shook her head. "The charges were dropped and I was so relieved to be let out of jail that I completely forgot to ask who bailed us out. But I always thought about it. What's even weirder is that Rachel used to tease me that I was in love with this mystery woman."

"Seriously?"

Amber pulled one of Seamus's discarded blankets over her legs. "Yeah, she used to say if only I had seen your face I would have been completely in love with you. She didn't see you either, but the way I went on about you--she thought it was hilarious. I just couldn't believe a complete stranger would do something like that. She's gonna shit when I tell her this."

"Tell her she owes me fifty bucks too," I teased. I was still reeling in disbelief. "I can't believe this never came up before. How could we have known each other this long without knowing this?"

"Ah," Seamus said. "The best part is when you never

stop learning about each other. You know what your Gran would call this, Meggie?"

"Fate?"

He grinned. "Dat she would. There are no accidents, she'd say. Life has a purpose." He stretched his arms over his head then reached for his coat. "Okay, I'm gonna go see your Aunt Celia now. Wanna come?"

I felt annoyance appear on my face. Seamus knew I couldn't stand Celia. Celia was a religious nut and the family gossiper to boot. "She's not my aunt, and no."

"She *is* your aunt. She's your mother's sister."

"My mother doesn't have a sister, as far as I'm concerned."

"Meggie." He frowned.

"You know I can't stand Celia or her pasty-faced husband Ralph. They talk about everyone behind their backs, especially you and me. And it's not like she came to see me in the hospital either, so why would I want to go see her?"

"Meggie, Celia just has a big mouth, like your mother."

I shook my head. "No, my mother is not malicious. She may gossip, but she never says anything she wouldn't also say to your face. Celia's a two-faced bitch. She's sneaky and condescending--she even has a fat, bitchy face."

Seamus placed his hands on his hips. "Dat's enough now," he said, sternly. "Celia is your blood."

"Fuck off, Seamus, I know who belongs to my tribe, and Celia doesn't."

"Your *tribe*?" He hated when I said such things, because they didn't make sense to him.

"She really is loyal to her family, Seamus," Amber defended. "She's just never liked her aunt."

"Why, Meggie?"

I rolled my eyes. "You know why. She calls you a big drunk. When Gran was alive she wanted to stick her in a nursing home because she didn't like taking her turn caring for her. Then when Gran died she all but raided the poor woman's house, grabbing whatever she could, and I was ashamed of the way you and my mother let her get away with it."

"You were ashamed?" He scoffed. "You were *ten!*"

"And *you* were a pussy." Amber hid behind her blanket

because she wanted to laugh. She found it funny when I said things that were out of character. "Celia calls Jenna 'that freak of nature who married my nephew,' and she has several names for me. Go on, Seamus. Tell me what dear Aunt Celia calls me."

He looked at his feet. His face looked guilty. "I don't know."

"You do so. She's called me everything from a little tramp to a sinner. A *sinner!* She's got her religion stuffed so far up her ass she even made my mother cry by telling her I was going to hell because of my relationship with Amber. Gramps must have been pretty damn Catholic, because Gran certainly wasn't and that's the only way I can figure out how Celia turned out the way she did. Even Mom can be a bit too religious, but she has enough education, or perhaps just enough common sense, to rein it in. No, you go see Celia, Seamus, and when you do, tell her the little sinner says 'bite me.'"

Seamus threw back his head and laughed. "You have a nasty mouth, Meggie, always did. But you call it like you see it, and I taught you dat, so it always makes me proud. I won't tell Celia to 'bite you,' as you say, but I won't let her shoot her mouth off either, okay?"

"Whatever."

Seamus left and Amber lay on the couch, rubbing her forehead. She looked so pathetic. "Not feeling any better?" I asked sympathetically.

"A bit. What all happened last night?"

"Seamus got you drunk, carried you to bed, and you passed out."

"Who undressed me?"

"Seamus." Her head snapped up and I laughed. "I did. Seamus got you into bed and I took off your jeans after he left."

"Oh." Her eyes searched mine. "But that's not all of it, is it?"

"No. Listen, I'll go make you some tea." I started toward the kitchen but Amber rose from the couch and stopped me.

"What else?" she asked, her hand clamped to the arm of my wheelchair.

My gaze didn't meet hers easily, and with a heavy sigh, I told her. "You said you wanted to make love and then you passed out."

She was thinking, remembering. I could see the memory becoming visible on her face. "You were scared," she realized.

I blinked. "What?"

"You were scared--of *me*. I could feel your body grow tense. Meagan, I think we should talk about this. I don't want you to be afraid of me."

Again my gaze darted away. "It's not you I'm afraid of. Please, just let me make you some tea."

Amber followed me into the kitchen, where I filled a kettle with water and placed it on the stove. I pulled the cream from the fridge, the sugar and tea from the pantry. Amber reached for a mug in one of the high cupboards, but I told her to sit down. "We'll have to move things around a bit," I said. "But I've learned to improvise."

I grabbed the broom from between the fridge and the wall and opened the cupboard door with it. Then I looped the handle through the handle of a mug and pulled it down, and then went for a second mug.

"See," I said, scooping sugar into the mugs. "No big deal."

"I want to talk to you, Meagan."

The water boiled quickly and I poured it over the tea bags in the mugs and added cream. "So talk."

"What are you afraid of? That it's not like it was?"

"Yes," I said. "That's exactly what I'm afraid of. I hate being naked and looking down at my legs that don't function and I hate the idea that you're probably thinking the same thing, that I'm limited."

"I don't think that," she said, savoring a small sip of her tea. "I don't see you as a crippled person. I see you the same way I always did. You're no one's little victim, Meagan."

Familiar words. Only weeks ago I'd said them to myself. "Not yet," I muttered.

"Not ever. Yes, I wish you could walk and I'm praying for the day you will, but I don't think less of you because you can't. I love us together."

"Loved," I whispered.

"No, *love*. I love the way we talk and the way we

laugh, and I love the way we make love–even now. I wish you would let me touch you more, but I understand that you feel self-conscious right now, and you'll get over it. You'll get over it because soon enough you'll realize that it's only me, and we've always been comfortable with each other. You know me, Meagan. You know my body, and even like this you can still elicit a reaction from me like no one else ever could."

"I'm sorry," I said, quietly. "But I don't believe you."

"I'm not lying. I don't lie about sex."

"You've never had sex with a cripple before."

"And you'd never had sex with a woman before me, so what? Life is full of firsts. I don't think it's as critical as you make it out to be. It's not like you used to fuck me with your feet."

"Very funny."

"I'm just trying to make a point. You're still you in every other way and I'm still the person who loves you. Only one thing has changed, but we can deal with that. Together, okay? Meagan, we can handle this." A sly grin spread across her face. "We can be as inventive in the bedroom as you've figured out how to be in the kitchen."

That got me to smirk. "Well, that has never been a problem for us."

"No." She chuckled. "It never has."

"And to think, I once bailed you out of jail only to put you in one of my own."

"I still can't believe that was you. But I'm not imprisoned, honey, I want to be here with you. Deal with that or you're gonna start pissing me off."

My smile matched hers. "Okay, Scary Spice, you can be the boss for a while."

"For a while?"

"Yep, but when I walk again, it's back to being equals."

"We're always equals, Meagan," she said. "Don't ever think we're not."

Seamus stayed for two weeks, during which time he woke up early every morning to make huge breakfasts of pancakes and waffles and bacon and eggs--which I never ate because I had a slight phobia about foods that were runny looking, or in actuality a cooked fetus. Seamus ate the eggs. Amber ate them. But I couldn't even bring myself to look at them. They made me think of my baby. Unborn and dead. They made me want to cry, so badly that one morning I almost shoved Amber's fork away from her mouth and demanded that she stop eating my baby. It was insane. I knew it wasn't the slightest bit rational, but it bothered me.

"You're gonna eat," Seamus said one morning. "You're too damn thin."

I was almost back to my regular weight. My hair had taken on its usual luster and my eyes were bright and alert. Aside from the wheelchair, I'd never looked better.

Seamus slid two squirmy fried eggs onto my plate. I saw a fetus and pushed the plate away.

"She doesn't eat eggs," Amber said, watching me. "She's put herself on a diet that's eighty-five percent vegetarian. Rarely touches a piece of meat." She smiled at me encouragingly.

"That's ridiculous," Seamus said, sounding exactly like my mother. "You need your iron."

"I get that from vegetables and I take supplements. Don't worry, Seamus, I'm getting all my vitamins. I'm very healthy. I'll eat the toast, but I'm not touching those eggs."

"Bacon?" He pleaded.

"No." Jenna had once had a pet pig named Bacon, and I hadn't eaten pork since he died.

"No bacon?" Seamus asked again.

Amber grinned around a mouthful of food. She was going to love saying this, so I let her. She shook her head at Seamus. "Pet pig."

My uncle's eyes widened. "Did you just say *pet pig*?"

"Mm-hmm. A hundred and seventy-five pounds of uncooked ham."

"Very funny," I said. "He was at Jenna's wedding."

"I didn't see it."

"Ringbearer. Went home early and he wasn't an *it*."

Seamus was distraught. "Let me get this straight. No pork. No eggs."

"No tuna," Amber said. "Dolphins get caught in the nets. I keep telling her they have dolphin-friendly tuna now, but she refuses to eat it anyway. Thinks it's a conspiracy." She grinned at me. She was having a lot of fun with this.

"Are you done now?" I asked. "Or maybe you'd like to tell him how I don't eat pearl onions because they make me think of eyeballs." I turned to my uncle. "Amber doesn't eat anything phallic in appearance because she's afraid it will turn her straight."

Roaring with laughter, she threw her napkin at me. "You're so full of shit."

"It could be true."

"For Christ's sake," Seamus cried. "What the hell do you eat?"

I shrugged. "Mostly food without a heartbeat."

"Well da heart stops beating when they kill it, you know."

He pushed the plate back across the table at me. "You're eating the eggs."

"No, I'm not. Do you want me to be sick? That's a baby." They looked at me strangely and I stopped talking. I'd said too much.

"Okay," Seamus said. He knew which road I was on, and he wasn't going to walk down it with me. "No eggs. No pork. No tuna. And no pearl onions. How 'bout I fix you up a nice piece of celery?"

Finally, he got me to crack a smile. From then on it was lightly buttered toast or grapefruit for me in the mornings, and Seamus took it all so well that on his last night in town I decided to make him happy, and ate a steak smothered in mushrooms and onions (not pearl) and about a gallon of HP Sauce. It sat in my stomach like lead.

Amber and Seamus became fast friends during his visit. They whiled away the hours I was in therapy playing poker and dirty Scrabble. She discovered he wasn't the maniac my family made him out to be, and began seeing him in the same light I did.

My mother came twice to see Seamus. The first time they fought over why he wasn't told about my accident, and she'd called him a drunk and stormed out of the apartment. The second time they reached an uneasy alliance. Josh and Jenna came a few times with Sammy, and Danielle, surprisingly, came almost every day. She introduced Seamus to Mark, and after they left he commented on how both his nieces should just become lesbians, because the men they went for were nothing but a bunch of women anyway. I laughed. Mark was even more of a yuppie than Ken had been, and Seamus hadn't missed an opportunity to call him a girlie-boy. When he finally left it was with kisses and promises of future visits.

"Take care of my niece," I heard him tell Amber as he crushed her in hug and a voice overhead announced that his flight was now boarding. "She really loves ya so if she gets nasty just try to remember dat, okay?"

Amber squeezed him back. "Don't worry, Seamus. I've learned how to handle Meagan."

"Hey, I'm not dead, you know," I teased. "I *can* hear the two of you."

Seamus picked up his duffel bag. "Good. Then I don't have to tell you to watch that mouth of yours, because this one's a keeper."

I grinned at Amber. "Dat, I know."

"Smartass." Seamus gave a small wave as he passed through the gate. We had a habit of embarrassing each other in public, seeing who could be the most outrageous. I'd done it last when Ken and I were drinking with Seamus in the pub and I'd loudly asked him if he had successfully impregnated his sheep yet. It was mild compared to some of the things we did to each other and as Seamus disappeared onto the covered ramp leading up to the plane, I thought he'd let me off the hook and breathed a sigh of relief.

Suddenly, he reappeared and in a *very* loud voice called out, "Hey, everyone, there's a crippled dyke over there if you want to 'ave a look."

People turned to stare and, howling with laughter, Seamus once again disappeared onto the covered ramp.

Amber's hands shot to her face. "Oh my God!" she cried, desperately fighting to control her giggles as people continued to look at us. "I can't believe he just did that!"

From far away I heard Seamus's voice call, "You lose, Meggie Pie."

I was never more humiliated in my life.

Chapter 4

Something was wrong with Amber. I knew it from the instant she rose from bed in the morning, quiet and sullen. She tried to shrug it off, smiled weakly, and asked if I'd like some breakfast. No, I didn't want any breakfast. I wanted to know why she'd tossed and turned all night and I wasn't appeased by her response of having had a bad dream she couldn't quite recall.

In the afternoon she disappeared for several hours. By evening she was back at home and still quiet. At ten she feigned tiredness and went to bed with a book. Was it me? Had I unknowingly done something wrong? Glumly, I followed her into the bedroom and got into bed beside her. Again she gave me a weak smile and went back to reading her book. Fifteen times her hand rose to brush away her bangs. She stared at the same page for ten minutes, as if the words just wouldn't sink into her head and she had to read them over and over again.

What had I done? She didn't seem mad at me--more like hurt. Had my paralysis finally gotten to her? I couldn't take the silence any longer.

"I'm trying to respect your privacy, Amber," I said, taking the book from her hands, "but I can't anymore. Something is obviously bothering you and I want to know what it is. Did I do something to hurt you?"

"No," she responded quietly.

"Is it my paralysis? Do you want to leave?"

Her eyes widened with surprise. "Of course not. How could you even think that? Meagan, I love you."

"So what's the problem? You can tell me, Amber. Whatever it is--maybe I can help you."

"It's my brother's birthday today," she whispered.

I was shocked. "You never told me you have a brother."

"Because I don't have one. I had one."

"He died?"

"When I was in college. He was twenty-four and I

haven't spoken his name since." She started to cry and I pulled her to me.

"What happened?" I asked, softly.

My question made her cry harder and she clung to me. "He...He was beaten to death by an anti-gay group after a pride parade."

"He was gay too?"

"No." She shook her head and I felt her tears on my neck. "He was there for me. I'd just come out to my family and Jeff wanted to show that he supported me. He went to the parade with some of my friends and I was supposed to be there but I got tied up with something else."

"You were late?"

"Worse. I--I didn't show up at all! My brother was beaten to death in an alley and it was *my* fault. My parents have never really forgiven me. That's why we're not close. I can't even forgive myself."

"It wasn't your fault, Amber."

"They called him a fag-lover," she sobbed. "My friends tried to stop it but they got beaten up too and Jeff died of a brain hemorrhage three hours later."

"I'm sorry, Amber." I wiped her tears and held her close.

"I wanted to tell you, Meagan, but I could never bring myself to mention his name."

"It's okay. I understand."

"I know. I always knew you would, but it just wouldn't come out of me. I've never talked about Jeff. Even Zeppo doesn't know about him." Zeppo was an up and coming artist and Amber's best friend. "Rachel knew Jeff, but she hasn't mentioned his name in five years. Jeff died and my parents and I pretty much closed off from each other. They live an hour away and we speak maybe three times a year. Oh God Meagan, I killed my own brother!"

"No. You didn't kill him anymore than I killed Janie. Do you believe I killed Janie?" Amber knew the story of Janie Metcalf. She knew that Janie had died in a car accident because she'd been drunk and waiting for my cousin Laura and me to meet her. Laura had kept me tied up dealing with her relationship issues with her boyfriend, and Janie had gotten upset and driven off drunk. I'd never fully gotten over the guilt.

"No."

"Then you didn't kill Jeff either. It's the same thing." But I *had* killed. I had killed my baby with my own accident. Zoe's death was my fault and I thought I might never truly escape the agony of *that*.

"I'm sorry I never told you."

"It's okay. You were at the cemetery today?"

She nodded into my arm. "My mother showed up and I left. She didn't see me."

"If you want to go back tomorrow, I'll go with you."

"No, I don't want to go back but thank you. I feel better just having told you."

"You don't ever have to be afraid to tell me anything, Amber. I'll always be here for you."

"Tell me, Meagan." *Tell me* was a game we'd started after our very first fight. If one person said 'Tell me', the other had to reply 'I love you.' It was silly, but it was part of our history together.

"I love you," I said.

"You're obsessed with me, huh?" She was smiling and I thought she had remarkable powers of recuperation.

"What answer do you want?"

"The true one."

I laughed. "Yeah, I'm obsessed with you."

"Same in reverse."

"Really?"

Something suddenly amused her and she snickered. "Remember that time you called Gwynne a fat Natalie Imbruglia?" Amber's ex and I had gotten into an argument the first time we met and some nasty words were exchanged.

"I just *love* discussing Gwynne when we're in bed," I joked.

"No but it was *so* funny. I never worked so hard at not laughing in my life. From then on every once in awhile I'd find myself thinking it when I looked at her. Then I'd think of all those nasty little nicknames you have for people and I'd just start laughing my ass off. Did you ever have a nickname for me?"

"Sounds like you wanted one, but no."

"I always thought you did," she said. "I thought you'd call me like --"Metal Muff"-- or something."

The laughter burst out of me. "Where do you come up with these things?"

"Because I had that clit piercing."

"Yeah, I liked that," I said, remembering when Amber had first gotten pierced. "That took a kind of nerve I'd never have."

"Do you want me to do it again?"

I shrugged. "Up to you."

"But do you like me with it or without it?" she pressed.

"Both."

"You're not much help."

"Would it help if I told you I find nipple rings disgusting?"

"Not really. I don't like them either. Navel rings?"

"On *your* stomach?" I thought about it and smiled. "Very sexy."

"Yeah?"

"Well you don't have to do it. What's with the piercing fetish anyway?"

"There isn't one. I've only had one piercing other than my ears and I did that for you."

"*For me?* I never asked you to do that."

"But I knew you'd like it, and you did. I saw your face that day at Jenna's wedding when you realized it was gone." We had been broken up for months at the time of the wedding but there we were on the bathroom floor at the reception hall, kissing, touching; forgetting that we shouldn't have been doing that at all.

"I was surprised," I defended. "I was just used to it being there."

"And did you miss it?"

"I missed you."

"You're being evasive."

"No, I'm being honest. If it does something for you, then go for it. If it doesn't matter either way, why bother?"

"I don't think it matters," she said, nodding.

"Chicken," I teased.

"Am not. Fine, I will do it again."

"I'm just kidding. Geez, you're defensive. Metal Muff."

Her head fell back against my shoulder and she laughed."I still can't get used to you saying things like that. You've never been good with female anatomy."

"Hey!"

Amber laughed. "I meant describing body parts."

"Because there aren't any decent words for them. You should know you used just about every euphemism there is in *Butterflies*. What's really funny is picturing my mother at the podium reading those words to her class." A part of Amber's revenge had been to send copies of her book to the university where my mother was an English professor, and to my office.

"Even funnier that it was her own daughter's genitals she was talking about."

"Christ," I groaned. "That's another awful word. I think at this point I almost prefer *cunt*. And you cannot share my amusement because you meant to humiliate me. You should be hanging your head in shame."

"I have," she admitted, softly. "I just, well, I thought we were past that now."

"We are."

She smiled. "Yeah?"

"Yes." My glance fell down to my legs and a new weight turned up in my heart. "We have bigger problems now."

"Right, *we* do. You and me. Don't forget that, okay?"

"I won't," I replied, quietly. But I didn't want her to be a part of my problem. It was my burden and I thought I should carry it alone.

There was a familiar feeling about time being the enemy. I watched it slipping away from me like nothing I did mattered. It was beating me. My legs refused to function, no matter how hard I worked them, and I began drifting into a hell of my own design. Amber fought to keep me afloat. Sometimes she enlisted Jenna's help and together the two women fought to keep me from vanishing into myself as I was wont to do when thing got too rough. They kept me talking; forcing words out of my mouth when I'd lapse into bouts of silence. Kept me dreaming when I closed my mind to the world around me, wishing I could self-destruct. I wanted to sleep. They dragged me out of bed. Whatever I wanted, I was forced to have the opposite.

Slowly, I was becoming a hermit, a frightened turtle that refused to poke its head out of its safe little shell. People stared at me on the street. I couldn't handle it. Their glassy eyes made darting movements. First at the chair--the chair always came first--then at my face, then away.

One night Amber convinced me to go across the street to The Purple Cauldron. We hadn't been in there in well over a year but Amber was writing with a fury and needed audience approval.

"It'll be like old times," she said. "I'll get up on the stage, read my poetry, and pretend I'm not looking at you when I really am."

Reluctantly, I agreed and we crossed over to the familiar old coffeehouse with the purple walls and the dim lights. We chose the same table Jenna and I used to share a lifetime ago when we'd come in to watch Amber on stage arousing her audience.

"You were wearing a black silk shirt," I told her as she prepared her notes for her eight o'clock set. She looked up at me. "Faded blue jeans. Black Doc Martens. Your hair was shorter than it is now, sort of a razored effect with uneven bangs that fell seductively into your left eye. The way they still do. You read from a purple spiral notebook and every once in awhile, your hand rose to brush away your bangs. You recited three poems, the third one so racy it made me blush. Jenna called you over to our table when you were done and I could barely get out the words when you asked me what I thought. Jenna said she thought you got everyone horny and I blushed again. I couldn't stop staring at you and I realized, with genuine shock, that I wanted to kiss you. But like the true chickenshit that I was I darted out of here instead, making up some lame excuse about an early morning meeting I had to get home and prepare for. There really was a meeting in the morning but I'd been prepared for days. Never left anything for the last minute. I battled with myself at home over what I'd been thinking and then Jenna came in an hour later. She asked me what was wrong, because she could always see right through me, and I told her. Then she convinced me to come over to her apartment for some tea."

Amber's eyes misted. She was surprised I remembered every detail of the first night we kissed. "When you and Jenna came in I almost had a heart attack. I didn't know Jenna was bringing you over and you looked horrified when you saw me. Your eyes never left my face when Jenna disappeared into the kitchen to make the raspberry tea you so quietly requested. I said I thought I should leave, that I thought I was making you uncomfortable. You said, 'You are, but probably not in the way you're thinking.' You were so honest. I didn't expect that. It made me curious to know what you'd do if I kissed you." Amber grinned. "So I put my cigarette out, leaned across the coffee table and did it. I was terrified you'd recoil or freak out or something, but you didn't. Instead you surprised me by kissing back, even sticking your tongue in my mouth, and I almost groaned out loud."

I laughed. "It was a reflex. You tasted good."

"Hey Amber," Mitch, the owner of the coffeehouse, complained, "Get your ass on the stage or I'm putting someone else on first."

"Okay, relax."

Mitch shook his head. "Some things never change. Meagan strolls back into the neighborhood," he didn't see my wheelchair behind the table, "and suddenly you can't focus."

I gave Amber's hand a squeeze. "Go," I urged. "You have work to do. Get up there and wow me with your words all over again." Amber grinned.

"Wow everyone," Mitch barked. "But do it now because I don't care if you are a best-selling poet these days, you get the same treatment as everyone else." He was lying. He'd give Amber special treatment and we all knew it.

"You're still a prick," Amber said good-naturedly as she headed for the stage. "That never changes either." She could always make me laugh.

That was the night I decided to stop venturing out, unless it was to therapy. Amber got up on the stage and she was as great as she'd ever been, but halfway through her second poem the whispers began.

"Is she with the woman in the wheelchair?" I heard

someone ask.

"Yeah," another voice offered. "Zeppo says she refuses to leave her even though the woman was an awful bitch before she ended up paralyzed. Dumped Amber like it was nothing. Amber wrote a book about it. Now, apparently, they're back together and Amber wouldn't let her go for anything. She must be pretty special to be able to deal with *that*." I could almost see the woman behind me pointing at my wheelchair. Did she think I was deaf as well as paralyzed?

I didn't know who the two women were or how they should know Amber or me but their words cut through me like a hot knife, and I wanted to get out of there before I lost it. I didn't know which would come first, the temper or the tears, and I didn't want to risk either. I thought of Zeppo. The jerk didn't even live in our neighborhood but somehow he had managed to do enough talking to send a couple of people in to gawk at the poet and the freak. Had he planned it? Or had he merely shot his mouth off about me one too many times in the wrong company? Zeppo and I had always had issues but this was really going too far. These two women weren't here for any poetry reading. They were here because their curious minds had to know what someone like Amber saw in an invalid. She could have anyone. Why settle for a cripple who had a reputation for being a bitch?

The clock ticked away the minutes and Mitch placed a French vanilla cappuccino on the table in front of me as if to say, *I only now noticed you have no legs and I'm very sorry for you.* I glared at the offending cup and pushed it away. Where was a cigarette when you needed one? A stiff drink? A joint even? There was nothing in this room that could dull my senses and I wanted out more than anything. I felt a dozen pairs of eyes on me. They were supposed to be looking at Amber. Up on the stage, Amber was frowning and rambling off her words like they were meaningless. She, too, was watching me. She knew something was going on but she didn't know what.

The room became unbearably loud. The voices heightened. The whoosh of the cappuccino maker behind the counter ran its course like a tired old furnace. I turned my head. There was the *beep beep* of buttons being pressed on a cash register and then the *ding* of the money drawer sliding open. The rustling of cash. The man beside me told a dirty joke to his companion and the woman laughed so hard I thought my eardrums would burst. I felt faint.

"Paralyzed," the first voice said again, as if she were mocking me with the truth.

"That must be horrible. Can you imagine?"

I didn't have to imagine. The noises crept into my head like a virus. If I could walk I would have turned around and slapped the woman. I tried to drink the cappuccino but my hand shook on the cup and it slipped from my fingers, the steaming liquid spreading across the top of the table like a growing bacteria.

Mitch jumped from behind the counter, brandishing a checkered dishtowel. "No problem, Meagan," he said, swiping up the liquid and placing a clean ashtray on the table. Dozens of eyes stared. Dilated pupils. Embarrassed for me. The poor thing can't even hold a cup of coffee.

I looked pleadingly at Amber up on stage.

"Thanks, goodnight," she said quickly into the mic. There was a smattering of applause. They wanted to see what she'd do next.

Amber raced over to the table as inconspicuously as she could and crouched before me. "Are you okay? Do you want to leave?" she asked, tucking my hair behind my ear. I could manage no more than a nod and the eyes followed as Amber wheeled me out the door. I imagined the two women discussing the incident as we left.

I hadn't been anywhere since. Amber was guilt-ridden over the incident, like it had somehow been her fault, and I was distraught. I started staying up until all hours of the night so she would be forced to go to bed without me and I wouldn't have to feel her curl her body to mine in that protective, maternal way she'd adopted.

I wasn't recovering. Frustrated, I stopped doing my workouts at home and became uncooperative in therapy. Derek pushed me and I did as he asked, but gone were the days of me grabbing the weights for myself or asking Derek to help me down to the mat on the floor so I could do backwards push-ups, strengthening my triceps by repeatedly lifting my body off the ground until my arms ached and Derek urged me to stop. Now he had to plead with me to begin.

My family came less and less. It seemed no one could look at me with hope in their eyes anymore, and it was easier to avoid me altogether. I didn't care. I was tired of them looking at me at all. It was such an effort to be nice, to be real, when all I wanted was to fade away. The monotony of my daily life was draining. Nothing changed. Get up. Have breakfast. Go to therapy. Return home. Do nothing.

Amber too had stopped talking about recovery. Often she looked past me, like she was afraid that if she looked directly at me I would ask her what she really thought and she'd be forced to tell me the truth, that she no longer believed I would get well.

Jenna brought Sammy over regularly. She hadn't gone back to the job she'd held before her pregnancy as an aromatherapist/yoga instructor at the healing center across the street, and only continued to write her monthly column for *Natural Beauty*. Had it really been only two years since I'd gotten her the job? It seemed like a century ago. There was no recent past for me. Only the present and a future that stretched out before me like a nightmare that never went away. I tried to occupy my mind. I read with such a volatile passion that I sometimes went through up to six books a week. Zeppo, for some reason, had dropped off some art supplies and I tried my hand at painting. I sucked. I tried sculpting. Even worse. I was no artist. I was nothing more than a businesswoman who no longer had any business to attend to, and my lack of any other talent was frustrating.

Then I did what I thought I'd never do. I felt sorry for myself. Desperately sorry. Meagan Summers had finally lost one. There was nothing to do now but accept that and battle the daily thoughts of suicide. I wondered if I would survive. I decided I didn't care and did what I always did when things got to be too much, repressed them. At least that was one thing I could still do better than anyone.

Chapter 5

Eventually God sent me an angel of mercy.

Adrian Barrett sat on the couch in my living room, crouched over a tiny mirror on the coffee table, working little piles of white crystals into a fine powder with the blade of a small knife he always carried with him. A promising young dancer once, he had given it up to become an art dealer and sometimes drug peddler when the life of auditioning and being rejected by dozens of dance companies finally got to him. He was good, he'd said, but he never had the inner strength or confidence being a professional dancer required.

Adrian was Zeppo's boyfriend. I hadn't liked him much when he first came around because I thought anyone who'd be with Zeppo must be just as artificial. I was wrong. In fact, sometimes it seemed like Adrian found Zeppo as annoying as I did. He cracked jokes behind his back and we became fast friends.

Zeppo's constant presence in my home irritated me, but I kept my distaste to myself. First for Amber, and later because I would need Adrian in my life.

Adrian knew what losing everything meant. He understood. He didn't pity me the way everyone else did. He only got me high.

"We should start mainlining this stuff," he said now, annoyed by the way his smooth, black hand shook as he scratched the blade across the mirror, separating his work into sections. He tugged at the gold hoop in his right ear, and looked at me with questioning brown eyes.

"No," I said. This wasn't the first time Adrian had suggested we get into needles. We'd been getting high together for almost two months and he'd told me several times about his diabetic grandmother and her closet full of unused syringes. "Clean," he was fond of saying. "No chance of disease because there wouldn't be any sharing." He said this as if getting AIDS and dying would really scare someone like me. Truth was, it would probably be a blessing. I kept refusing. Then Adrian would explain that his grandmother would never even know the needles were missing. She might be suspicious about his visit, but as long as he brought her a carton of cigarettes, which she wasn't supposed to have, she'd let it drop. It made me think of my own crazy Gran and I wondered what kind of a person Adrian was. I never could have stolen from my Gran--and there was no way I was sticking needles in my arms, either.

"Why not?" Adrian whined. He hated when I rejected this offer.

I took a sip from the bottle of Jack Daniel's on the table and felt the undiluted liquid scorch the inside of my throat. It was a good sting. Numbing. Like when you have a sore tooth and keep pressing your tongue into the cavity, first because you liked the pain, and later because it becomes a habit.

"I couldn't exactly hide the track marks, Adrian," I said. "Amber would see them. Or worse, my physical therapist would and then I'd be right back in the hospital, only this time in a rehab program."

My mind pictured the padded room my family would insist on because I was insane and I almost screamed at the fear that pressed around my heart. They would lock me away and I'd be alone again. Only this time I'd be conscious, and worst of all, sober. No, I had to be careful, because if I were ever completely sober again, I'd kill myself. I needed the fog. It took away the shame.

"I could score us some heroin," Adrian suggested. He scooped a small pile of the powder onto his long pinkie nail and held it under my left nostril.

I knew the routine. Pressing my finger against my right nostril, I bent my head to the coke and snorted. The substance filled my brain almost instantaneously and I scratched my itchy nose. It always itched after a good snort.

"I don't want any heroin," I said as Adrian took care of the right nostril. He took a snort for himself and rubbed his nose from side to side with his index finger. "Do I *look* like a model? Besides, I don't think I could control the heroin like I can with this."

Adrian laughed at me. "You think you're in control of this?"

"Yes."

"Babe, your nose has seen more candy than Willy Wonka in The Chocolate Factory."

"Who?"

"Never mind."

Adrian took another snort, lit a joint, and settled himself on the floor, his black leather pants making an obscene noise against the hardwood.

"Where's Zeppo today?" I asked. I didn't care.

Adrian rolled his eyes. "Home. Working on his next masterpiece. Probably rolling his dick in paint to get just the right *effect*."

I laughed. Adrian and I were of the same opinion concerning Zeppo's work. Pretentious garbage. He passed me the joint. I inhaled deeply, savoring the rich flavor of the red label hash I had once hated when Basil used to smoke it constantly in this very apartment. Basil. He seemed a million years away now. Back when I was the straight arrow and he, the struggling musician trying to catch a break. But Basil had never touched anything stronger than pot. He'd be stunned to see me now, hard-working Meagan, stoned to the eyeballs.

I was a master at hiding what I'd become. No one knew. Not my family. Not Ted who still called from time to time trying to convince me to join him in his publishing venture. Even Amber didn't know about the secret Adrian and I shared. She knew Adrian had a problem, Zeppo had told her that, but she didn't know about me. She suspected something was amiss, but she thought she knew me too well to really believe I was sinking. Meagan would never touch drugs. I knew that's what she'd convinced herself of. Not corporate Meagan. Straight-living Meagan. Meagan with the ambition as ferocious as a hungry lion. Didn't she know that Meagan was dead? I thought not; she saw the me she wanted to see. Her eyes didn't catch the wet stare of my own. The fidgeting. The constant sniffling. She believed my complaints of a chronic cold because that's what she wanted to believe, and the medicine cabinet in the bathroom grew fuller every day with cold remedies that never got used.

I was drinking too much, that was what she thought. That Adrian was bringing me alcohol and I drank while he snorted. The woman could be as naive as she'd once accused me of being. The real problem was that she could never catch me with my guard down. People who take drugs learn a whole new way to be smart. They learn how to manipulate--a skill I already possessed due to my years of convincing the public they needed Natural Beauty Magazine--and as long as I usually appeared sober Amber couldn't convince herself otherwise.

"Blind love," Adrian had once commented. "People like you and me depend on it." I didn't want to admit he was right.

Adrian and I snorted another line and laughed as my hand shook around the mirror, nearly knocking the whole mess to the floor. So I got the shakes sometimes. Who didn't?

"Shit," Adrian joked. "Do that again and we'll be down on the ground snorting the cracks in the hardwood. Can you imagine Amber and Zeppo walking in on that? Seeing you and me sprawled out on the floor, our noses pressed against the wood like a couple of stoned anteaters? They'd shit."

I pictured a long snout coming out of Adrian's face and roared with laughter. Adrian cranked the stereo and we sat there in stoned oblivion.

Keys jangled in the door and my eyes darted to the drugs spread out on the coffee table like pleasure toys in a sex shop. Our party was about to be crashed by a blond narc.

"Fuck," I said. "Amber's home."

Adrian darted across the room, swept the table clean, and threw the vial of coke in his pocket. There was a tiny bit left on the mirror and he pressed it under our noses. We snorted away the evidence and I wiped the small amount of coke that powdered Adrian's nose like icing sugar on a chocolate cake. The door swung back on its hinges and Amber stepped through, covering her ears with her hands.

"Jesus," she complained, marching over to the stereo and turning it down so we could barely hear it.

"Is it loud?" I deadpanned. Adrian snickered.

Amber crossed the room and bent to kiss me, a frown creasing her face as her eyes spotted the bottle of Jack Daniel's on the table. Two unused glasses.

"You're drinking again?" The bottle was half-full.

"We had a couple," I said easily. "How's Jenna?"

I almost never asked about my brother. I didn't really care.

"Jenna's fine," Amber said, entering the kitchen and grabbing a can of Pepsi from the fridge. She snapped open the can and took a healthy sip. "I had to take her down to turn in her column. You know how archaic she is. No fax. No email. Anyway, Ted says hi and he wants you to call him."

"And Sammy?" I asked, ignoring the information about my business partner and focusing my hazy mind on the picture it drew of my sweet little nephew.

"Sam's great. We're going to take him off their hands this weekend."

"*The whole weekend?*" My nose twitched in annoyance. That meant two whole days of sobriety. No sneaking into the bathroom for a quick fix. Shit!

Adrian poured the whiskey into two glasses with ice and handed me one. He seemed to know the news of Sammy's impending visit would rattle me, but instead of handing me the bottle like he would have if we were alone, he decided on us appearing civilized. Smart move. The cubes clanked together in the glass and I downed half the tan liquid in one gulp.

"I thought you'd be happy," Amber said, frowning again at the easy way I consumed the alcohol and pouring half of her Pepsi into my glass. "You're the one who's always saying we should take him more often."

Yeah, I was always saying it but that didn't mean I actually meant it. I loved Sammy, but being around him meant I had to behave and I didn't exactly relish the idea of two whole days of childish laughter and falling into the role of Sammy's favorite aunt on wheels while I itched for a joint or a snort I couldn't have. He loved when I sped him around the apartment like a maniac (something I would never do high; even I had my limits) and would make me do it again and again until my arms got sore and Amber lifted him off of me, explaining that Auntie Meg was tired. She had taken to treating me like an invalid and I hated it. Hated the way she insisted on doing everything for me, even the things I could do for myself. Sometimes, I thought I hated her.

Adrian lit another joint and handed it to me. Absentmindedly, I took it and Amber's eyes flashed surprise, then anger, as I inhaled the thick smoke, holding it in my lungs for several seconds like I'd been doing this all my life, before releasing it.

"What the hell is this?" she demanded, as I reached around to pass the joint back to Adrian.

Suddenly realizing what I'd done, I tried to shrug it off. "It's just hash." I shot Adrian a look. What the hell was he thinking handing me a joint like that? He should have been paying attention. It never occurred to me that *I* should have been paying attention.

Adrian held the roach out to Amber. "Want a toke?" He always seemed desperate to get others to join in his sickness.

Amber was incorruptible and she crushed him with a look. "Is this what goes on when I'm not around? You come over here and get her all baked?" She said this as if I didn't have a mind of my own. Adrian shrugged and she turned her hard eyes on me. "What else has he got you doing?" Shit. She was going to start watching me now.

"Uh-oh," Adrian said. "Your mom is pissed."

I broke out laughing. Amber was not amused.

"You better watch out, Adrian," I said. "She's likely to call Daddy Zeppo."

Adrian and I roared with laughter. We were two people hurdling our way toward thirty and behaving like children while Amber's head snapped from left to right, glaring at each of us in turn.

"Oh, you two are real funny, aren't you?"

"She is," Adrian said in his best Paul Reiser. "Me, not so much."

I laughed and Amber pushed her fingers through her hair, scratching the top of her head.

"I don't believe you, Meagan," she said turning my chair to face her and locking the wheels. It drove me crazy when she did that. As far as I could tell Amber got more use out of my fucking chair than I did, always directing it wherever she wanted me to be. She crouched in front of me. "Do you remember when we first got together?" she asked.

What a stupid question. "When I had legs, you mean."

Every time the past came up I thought of the present and hated what I'd become. I wished I had died in that coma. What kind of God had sent me back for this?

Amber ignored my sarcasm. She was getting used to it.

"We'd been together about a month," she continued, "and your idiot ex-boyfriend showed up, trying to coerce us into a threesome."

I laughed at the memory.

"Yeah, Basil thought I'd do it too. He thought he was so good in bed." Actually, he had been. One of the reasons I put up with his shit. "*You* thought I'd do it. Thought I'd try forcing you into bed with him."

"That's beside the point," Amber said, annoyed that I would mention her distrust of me. *She* brought it up. "Do you remember what else happened that day?" I opened my mouth to speak but she cut off my words. "Basil put his filthy boots on the coffee table and sparked up a joint. When I took it you got really pissed, thinking I was just like him, and I could see the fear on your face. You didn't say anything but you started cleaning and I *knew* because, by then, I had already discovered that you cleaned when you were pissed. I handed it back to Basil and I haven't touched a joint since that day."

"Good for you," I mocked. How dare she throw my sobriety in my face? "I'd get up and dance you a victory jig, but as I recall, *I have useless fucking legs*!"

Adrian laughed and Amber looked like she would cry, which would be no great shock because the woman could cry at a documentary on the field mouse. But I was the true source of her angst. She couldn't reach me and she knew it. Only Adrian could reach me now and Amber turned on him fiercely.

"Is this the kind of friend you are?" she yelled. "You think her paralysis is funny? Well, let me tell you something, Adrian, you don't know this woman. She may joke about her situation and sit around here getting drunk with you, but do you think she'd give you a second look if she could walk? Do you think she'd let a junkie like you into her home? She wouldn't. Meagan has no tolerance for losers."

"Hey." Adrian shrugged like he didn't have a care in the world. Nothing Amber said could really affect him. "Maybe you're the one who doesn't know her," he said. "Did you ever think of that? You treat her like she's a vegetable, but she's not. She still has a mind and just because she's in a wheelchair doesn't mean she doesn't deserve your respect. *I* respect her. That's why she calls me over here."

I could have laughed. We both knew that was *not* the reason I called him over.

"I-I respect her," Amber stammered. "I'd do anything for her."

"Maybe that's the problem. Why don't you leave her the hell alone and let her do what she wants?"

"So she can end up like you?" she accused. "You don't know anything about it, Adrian, so just stay out of this."

My head was swimming in a pleasant euphoria. I didn't care what they said to each other as long as Amber didn't drive Adrian away because he was the only one I needed now. Adrian and his drugs that could take away the ache and make me happy and carefree even as I sat with my wheels locked in the middle of a war zone. My mind drifted to a thousand things then focused on one thought.

"What does Ted want now?" I asked, cutting off Amber's verbal massacre. My brain did this often--just switched modes when I wasn't looking, and my mouth expressed whatever thought happened to pop up in my head.

Amber spun around to face me. "Ted?" She shook her head like she was trying to grasp my thought process. "What are you talking about?"

I sighed. Couldn't anyone remember one minute from the next? Was I the only one around here with half a brain? Seriously, half a brain.

"You came in and said Ted wanted me to call him. Why?"

She didn't like that I had interrupted her tirade. She was desperate to fight with Adrian because she couldn't bring herself to fight with me. I was too frail, she thought. It would be cruel to yell at someone like me. If only she knew I would have relished it. Would have loved for her to scream at me rather than smother me in the soothing maternal tones she had taken to using. Everyone talked to me like that now, like they were cooing at a particularly colicky baby. Everyone except Adrian.

"You know what Ted wants, Meagan," she said. "He wants a publishing firm and he wants you to be his partner. It used to be your dream too. I don't know why you keep refusing."

I shrugged. "Not interested."

"Well, what are you interested in?" she barked. "Sitting around here getting stoned with *him*?" She pointed at Adrian and I hid my amusement behind a carefully constructed frown. Finally there was an edge to her voice, a second of anger I was glad to hear. My grip tightened on the arms of my chair as I mentally prepared myself for a battle I knew I was about to start.

"Aw, leave her alone," Adrian said.

"Shut up, Adrian," I said through clenched teeth.

"But Meagan---"

His voice sounded hurt, but I shot him a warning look. Amber was about to blow her stack. I could almost see the blood boiling under her skin. She was tempted to get angry with me, fighting herself not to, but I was going to make her and no one was taking that away from me. All I had to do was offer up the bait. Push her buttons a little and I knew I could crack her wall of reserve. It had to be cruel. Cruel enough to really make her lose it on me.

"I don't know. Maybe I'll take up poetry," I mocked. "We can collaborate on a book about my legs or something. I've even got the perfect title. How's this? When Butterflies Crash Their Cars."

Adrian threw back his head and roared with laughter, his open mouth revealing clean white teeth without a single cavity.

"Is that supposed to hurt me?" Amber said.

"Not at all," I said. "Just think about it. It's perfect. We can make it a trilogy. In the first book the butterfly wore armor. Okay, so we expand on that. Second book she smashes up her car, terminating her pregnancy, but who cares about that since she was only three months along anyway right? People have abortions at three months along all the time, right Amber? And who knows, maybe the butterfly even considered it but then thought, *Why the hell should I? I'm a rich insect.* She was cocky, that butterfly. Thought she could do anything. Even raise a baby on her own. Until she killed it that is. Just as dead as if she'd shoved a hanger up herself and scraped out her insides." I scratched my head. "Anyway, where was I going with this? Oh, right. Book three. This where we get to be creative. We can turn her into an insomniac and have her ride around in a little insect wheelchair. What do you think, Amber? Three books doing exactly what you do best, writing about me."

Amber didn't say a word. She looked away and I took a sip from my glass, glaring at her, daring her to fight me. She didn't break. But I knew her weakness. *Okay*, I thought. *Time to pull out the big guns.*

I waited until I again had her attention then raised my arm like a Shakespearian actor on stage and in a loud voice I began.

"Butterfly," I said, quoting from her book. "Winged one of the colorful lie--" I knew every poem by heart. "How your satin hues confuse me--"

"Stop it," she whispered. Mentioning the book was the worst thing I could do to her. It filled her with guilt and pain and I knew it.

"Questions. Fluttering. Flitting by like--"

"*Stop it!*"

"What?" I asked, innocently. "I'm only admiring your words. Imitation is the kindest form of flattery, you know." I had no idea what I was talking about, only that it was working. Amber looked like she was going to cry, or scream. I was hoping it would be the latter because I couldn't handle the tears. "And your subject," I went on. "Fascinating."

Adrian sat in a chair by the bookshelf, his stoned eyes staring out the window.

"Hey, Adrian," I called.

"Yeah, babe."

"Hand me that book over there. Fourth one from the right with the giant butterfly on the cover."

"No problem." Adrian grabbed the book from the shelf and tossed it across the room. It landed in my lap and Amber watched silently as my fingers lovingly stroked the cover, tracing a line around the raised imprint of the iron insect.

"A bestseller," I said appreciatively, turning the book in my hands. I sneered up at her. "Weren't you clever, honey? The way you just turned me into a little bug like that." I was twisting the knife where it hurt most, but still she refused to break. She was good but it wasn't going to matter because I had more time than anyone. I could do this all day--all year. Flipping through the pages, I picked out certain words, reading them out loud and specifically choosing the ones that had injured me most when the book first came out. Words like, *porcelain princess* and *cold-hearted cunt*, all wrapped up in the pretty package of poetry. On and on I read until Amber finally snapped.

"You're not gonna stop, are you?" she yelled. "You won't stop until you're sure you've hurt me. Well job accomplished, alright? Are you satisfied now?"

No, I wasn't. I wanted an explosion, not a spark.

"What's the matter, Amber? Can't take it?" I was being cruel. As cruel as I could be. Pushing her even harder. I turned the page and started to read further when Amber suddenly smacked the book out of my hands. This was more like it. It slammed to the floor with a dull thud.

"When are you going to let it drop?" she yelled. "That was almost two fucking years ago!"

I reached for the book, but Amber snatched it up quickly and waved it in front of my face. "You wanna know what I think of this book?" she screamed. "This is what I think of it!" She began tearing it to shreds. "This is what I fucking think!" She ripped the pages from the spine and they scattered to the floor like leaves. I let her go, knowing she needed this release. It was high time she let her frustrations out.

She stomped on the fallen pages, twisting them under her heavy boots like an angry cartoon character.

"There," she growled, ripping the cover off the front and tossing the whole thing on the floor. She kicked it across the room and the spine crashed against the back of the couch. "Are you happy now? I've destroyed it."

I gave a mocking laugh. "Can you tear it out of my memory, Amber? Can you reach into my fucking head and erase the damage you've done? No. You can tear up every copy ever printed of that book but you can't *ever* take away what you did. You sold me. Like I was nothing more to you than a shot at making a few bucks. You could have just asked me for the money if you were that hard up, you know. You didn't have to sell my soul."

"I sold my rage!" she screamed. "I transformed my pain into words and, yes, I sold it. I'm a poet, Meagan, what the hell else would I do with it?"

"See a fucking shrink!" I screamed back. "Work it out like a normal person."

"Like you?" she scoffed. "Yeah, I can really see how thousands of dollars worth of therapy has helped you."

"Fuck you!"

"Hey, you guys…" Adrian interjected.

"Shut up!" we screamed. Adrian took a step back.

"Go the fuck home, Adrian," Amber barked. "This doesn't concern you."

He looked at me and I nodded. She didn't see him slip the vial between the couch cushions before he left.

Amber stomped around the living room, raging, her thick boots hammering against the hardwood like an angry Nazi's. That amused me.

"Nazi," I said out loud, and found that really funny.

She glared at me. "You're insane, do you know that? Do you know how fucked up you truly are?"

Yes, and I was loving this. Feeling alive again and absolutely loving it. I could scarcely hide the grin on my face and gleefully bounced in my chair like a disabled kid on pixie sticks. Not even a shot of Ritalin could bring me down now. Amber looked at me like she really believed I'd lost my mind. Perhaps I had. It wouldn't have mattered. No job, no life, no reason to be sane. I thought she was stunning in her anger. A furious beauty.

"What the hell are you grinning at?" she demanded, looking up and down her body like I saw something she couldn't. I did. I saw life. It was time to end this.

"I'm grinning at you."

"Why?"

"You're so beautiful."

Her eyes softened. "What?"

"I said I think you're beautiful."

She searched my face for a hint of sarcasm that simply wasn't there. "I'm confused, Meagan. Aren't we fighting?"

"Yes, but that doesn't make you any less stunning. You awe me. In fact, I think you're even prettier this way. Your eyes flash fire instead of patronizing me with pity. Passion instead of worry. For fifteen minutes you've forgotten I'm in this chair and you've treated me like you would anyone else who got under your skin." My grin widened. "Thank you."

She walked toward me. "Are you telling me you set me up? Purposely provoked me into losing my temper with you? You manipulated me."

"Yes." My head bobbed up and down happily. "Pretty good, huh? Fortunately, I haven't forgotten all my skills."

"But why?" She could never quite figure me out, why I did the strange things I did. "And the book." She indicated the tattered crumpled pages on the floor. "I tore it to shreds."

"Yeah, you did do that." I shrugged. "Felt good too, didn't it? Doesn't matter though because I've got about ten more on a shelf in the bedroom closet. Obviously you never clean in there," I joked. "Or you'd know."

She gave a guilty laugh and sat on my lap. I crushed her to me.

"So you really don't care about the book?" She asked, her eyes staring directly into my dilated pupils. How could she not know how stoned I was? *Because she doesn't want to know*, I reminded myself.

"No," I said easily. "Truth is, I love that book."

"*You love it?*"

"Well, not at first, but it grew on me. It's not every day you get a book written about you, even a nasty one. The fact that it slams me all over the place only makes it more flattering."

Amber laughed. "You're so strange." We had always been able to stop fighting as quickly as we started.

"You're just figuring that out? Sorry, but the book was an easy way to get at you. You don't have to forgive me right away but you have to understand, Amber, I need you to be *real* with me. I need your anger sometimes because it forces you to look past my situation and at who I really am, the same person I've always been, only slightly damaged. Your pity makes me insane. It makes me think I'm no good for you and that I should drive you away again."

She shook her head. "You couldn't."

"I could and we both know it. As you've just seen I am not so injured that I've forgotten how to be cruel."

"There's a quality to be proud of," she joked. Wrapping her arms around my neck, she kissed my ear and whispered,

"Do your worst, Meagan. See how far it gets you."

"Hmm. Threatening. I like it."

"We'll see," she singsonged, "when we're eighty years old and you're still stuck with me. We'll see how much you like it then."

I thought of the coke in the couch and shuddered, squeezing her just a little tighter because the moment felt like it could be one of our last. "I'll never be eighty, Amber," I said quietly and thought, *I'll be surprised if I live to see forty.*

It didn't bother me. Much.

Sammy arrived at 10:35 on Saturday morning. I knew it was 10:35 because I checked the clock the second he bounced through the door, holding Amber's hand and humming a song of his own creation. Amber smiled at me. She didn't see the guilty way I turned my head. Sammy said, "Hi ya," and jumped in my lap. I kissed his cheek, mussed his sandy-brown hair (Josh's genes), and placed him on the floor. It was too early for rides. I wasn't in the right frame of mind yet.

I had stayed up half the night watching TV. Trying out sobriety and not liking it much. At three, Amber came out of the bedroom and pleaded with me come to bed. She didn't sleep well when I wasn't beside her. I relented. It took another hour for me to pass out, and when Amber woke at seven I could barely drag myself from the bed. I felt like my head had just hit the pillow and already it was time to get up and start the day. Amber made coffee. It didn't help. She asked me what I wanted to eat and I said I didn't want anything. If I decided I was hungry, I was more than capable of getting something for myself. She asked if I wanted to come with her to pick up Sammy. I said no. I needed to wake up a bit first. Amber left.

I watched the car pull into the street from the garage under our building and breathed a sigh of relief. It was so hard to find a minute alone. Now I had at least an hour, enough time to do what I promised myself I wouldn't. Amber would visit with Jenna for a while, so that left me plenty of time to "wake myself up" and be straight again by the time she returned with Sammy.

I had my supplies, given to me by Adrian. They were

in a constant state of preparation in a small wooden box at the bottom of a dresser drawer Amber never opened. The mirror, the razor blade, and the pipe if I wanted, but rarely did I have to use these things. Adrian usually powdered the product before bringing it to me. It was his little act of kindness. He made it as easy on me as possible.

The promise was a fast-fading memory, and I made a new one as I groped the vial. I could have a snort now, before Amber and Sammy came, and I could snort again, if I wanted to, after Sammy had gone to bed. I wouldn't do it in the hours in between even though Sammy would be safe with Amber and she'd probably do most of the taking care of him. I would stay straight while he was awake in case he wanted a ride in my lap. How tough could that be? I had once gone without a snort for three days when Adrian had gone away for a long weekend with Zeppo and had forgotten to drop off my coke before they left town. That had been when I'd first started, but I didn't see how now should be any different. I was still in control. I could take it or leave it. I just preferred to take it.

Ken had seen me stoned once. He had come to check on me like he sometimes did, still wanting to be my friend, and I had just finished smoking a joint with Adrian. He hadn't known. I could tell he didn't much like the look of Adrian, who couldn't have appeared higher, but I told him Adrian had been drinking and that I hadn't been sleeping well, and he wrote me out a prescription for some sort of barbiturate, which I never got filled but now wondered if I should. I could use something to help me sleep. But then I didn't want to become one of those people who needed one thing to bring them down and another to bring them back up. I didn't want to be a *drug addict*. It never occurred to me that I might already be one.

I snorted two lines, lifted myself in and out of a steaming bath, and felt more prepared for Sammy and his smiles. But no rides. Not yet. Another fifteen minutes and the buzz would be gone, and then I would be all his. In the meantime I left him to Auntie Am.

Auntie Meg and Auntie Am. I wondered how Josh and Jenna would explain that to Sammy, or if any explanation would even be necessary. Maybe it wouldn't. Maybe this was just one of those things kids see and don't think is strange because it's what they've always known. Zoe would have had two mothers. She would have had a father and two mothers and I would have had to explain why. I drove away the thought. It was getting easier to do that.

Amber carried the playpen that would be Sammy's bed into the bedroom and set it up with blankets and pillows and stuffed animals. She came back into the living room and unpacked his Power Rangers knapsack, removing two clean outfits and more toys. The knapsack had to have been Josh's influence because I knew Jenna thought the Power Rangers were too violent. She was an excellent mother. She never raised her voice or her hand to Sammy and he was turning out to be one of the smartest, most polite children I had ever encountered.

I allowed him to misbehave. I was an aunt and that was my job.

By eight that evening Sammy was fast asleep and curled up on the couch beside Amber like a slumbering cherub. Amber carried him into the bedroom and I snuck off to the bathroom.

"He's so cute," she said when she returned. "The thumb goes straight in his mouth and he grins around it. He almost makes me wish we had a kid around here all the time."

I thought of Zoe and frowned.

"Sorry," Amber said.

"Why do you apologize every time you see a kid? You're not the one who killed her, Amber, I did that all by myself. Gwynne would attest to that, I'm sure." I maneuvered myself onto the couch beside her.

"I wish you wouldn't talk like that. It was an accident. You have to learn to let it go." Her eyebrows puckered. "And what does Gwynne have to do with any of it?"

There was a flash of words in my head. Words Gwynne had spoken. "She knows I'm a murderer," I said. "She wanted me to die too."

Amber stared at me, speechless. My brain was somewhat clouded and I said strange things at times like this. I looked at her and thought I would cry at a memory I couldn't quite grasp. Gwynne had said something while I was in the coma. "She said, 'I hope you hear me in there. I hope you know what a murdering selfish bitch you are'. And she called me a corpse. Brain dead. Something about broccoli."

Amber couldn't stop staring. Her eyes were wide and her mouth, open. She was frightened. I was frightening her.

"It's true, isn't it?" I asked. She looked away. "Amber, don't let me think I'm losing my mind. You look like I just told you the scariest thing in the world, so it has to be true. That really happened. She really said those things. That I killed my baby and she wanted me to die."

"Yes," Amber said quietly. "It happened."

She was terrified by my words, and I knew I had to change the subject, because coma talk always scared her.

"You look exhausted," I said. "Come here." She rested her head in my lap and I caressed her back, thinking of how I would someday make Gwynne pay for those comments. I played with her hair and bent forward and kissed her.

"He can really tire you out," she murmured, relaxing into my body. "I'm ready to crash and it's barely nine-thirty."

I wasn't tired. Why would I be? Amber was the one who had chased Sammy around all day as he struggled to get into all of the things he knew he shouldn't. He was like a tiny tornado, spinning around the apartment and touching all the expensive things that would not be in a child-proofed home. We had no child. No point in hiding the good stuff to be pulled out later when the terrible twos had passed. Sammy was only one and a half, but he was ahead of his time.

At eleven o'clock Amber rose to go to bed. "You'll come soon, won't you?" she pleaded.

I sighed. Why did she always need me there?

"Twenty minutes," I said. "I'm just gonna watch a bit of the news." As if I really cared what was happening in the world outside. I was only avoiding the bedroom because I knew the minute my head hit the pillow my mind would start to wander and I'd have to lie there, counting in my head for two hours just to fall asleep. I counted backwards from a hundred. Usually several times and really fast until the numbers lost all meaning and I began to drift. It was a process that took forever and I dreaded having to do it.

At two in the morning I was still counting. Sammy woke up and cried, calling for his mom. I sat on the edge of the bed and whispered soothing words. He would not be appeased.

"Is he alright?" Amber asked sleepily.

"Yeah. I'm gonna take him in the other room and tell him a story." Sammy's leg shot out and kicked her and I squeezed him closer. "Do you want to go in the living room, buddy?"

That got me a nod.

Amber wiped her eyes. "I'll get up." She moved to rise from the bed but I urged her back down.

"Go back to sleep."

"Are you sure?"

"I'm up anyway. I'll take care of him."

Her eyes fell closed again and I maneuvered myself back into the loathsome contraption and placed Sammy in my lap, kissing the top of his head.

"Come on, Sam," I whispered. "I'll tell you a really good story. One my Gran used to tell me about a place called Fairyland and all the little fairy people who live there." I saw Amber grin.

Sammy rested his arms around my neck and used my shoulder for a pillow. He fell asleep in my arms before I even got to "once upon a time". Smiling, I wheeled him back into the bedroom where I placed him on the bed beside Amber because I couldn't reach down far enough to put him in the playpen. I hadn't gotten to tell him about fairyland. I climbed in the other side of the bed, sandwiching him in just in case he should roll away during the night. Amber's arm went around him easily as she slept. Protectively. So like her to be on her guard even when she wasn't conscious.

It was a trait she hadn't had before. Amber had once been the freest person I'd ever known. She had been lively. Sometimes carelessly so. She had been an adventurer and it saddened me how my disability had changed her. Now she was responsible. A bit of a worrier. She didn't seem to have any fun anymore and it was all my fault. I couldn't change what either of us had become.

I thought about these things, and at 4:42a.m. I looked at the clock for the last time.

Chapter 6

On Wednesday Amber left to help Zeppo display some new work at the gallery, and I was feeling lonely. I went to call Adrian but when I reached for the phone I found myself dialing my brother's number instead, and realized it was Jenna I really wanted to see.

I hadn't taken a drug all day and I was feeling a bit edgy. Adrian had called me a drug addict again--said I was no better than him--and I was determined to prove him wrong. For the first time in weeks I turned down his offer to come over and get me high. Then I had almost called him right back to say yes. I stopped myself because I still had a half-gram of coke stuffed away in the dresser if I needed it, and I was teaching him a lesson. I would also need to stop at the ATM outside the hospital on my next trip to therapy, I realized. Cocaine was a cash business and it wasn't cheap. Adrian would front me some blow if I wanted him to, but I preferred to pay my debts on the spot. That part of me *hadn't* changed.

"I made tea," I said when Jenna bounced through the door an hour later, minus Sammy. Dad was on vacation and had taken him for the day.

"I'm glad you called," Jenna said, dropping her hand-woven bag on the table and filling two cups with steaming water. "I was so bored at home. Danny doesn't have any classes today so she's gonna stop by too." She sat at the table and tilted her head at me. "You look good. Not so tired."

"Got a full night's sleep last night," I admitted. "Surprised me so much I almost got scared."

Jenna chuckled. "No Adrian today?"

"Working," I lied. "When's Danny coming?"

"Soon, I think."

Soon ended up being about twenty minutes later. Danny arrived and Amber returned shortly after, smiling when she stepped through the door, happy to see people in our home. People who weren't Adrian.

"What's this?" she asked, leaning in to kiss me. "Are

we doing the girl thing today?"

"You do the girl thing every day," Danielle commented, smirking.

Amber laughed. "You never get tired of your little dyke jokes, do you?"

"Not really. Does it offend you?"

"Nope."

Danny nodded. "Ah, but watch this."

"Don't, Danny," Jenna giggled. She knew what was coming. We *all* knew what was coming. Danny loved to try to get a rise out of me and she knew there were certain words I couldn't stand.

"Meagan, I think Amber's a big old dyke," she baited.

I shrugged. "So?" Did she really think *that* was going to do it?

"You're one too."

"Whatever." I rolled my eyes.

"Whatever?" Amber laughed.

"It's pretty old, Danielle," I said. "Try something new."

"I don't have anything new."

"Then I guess you're stuck, huh?"

"Do you have any beer?"

"Beer," I scoffed. "You're gonna get fat, Danielle. We have everything but beer. And how much are you drinking?"

"How much are *you* drinking?"

I blinked. "What?" The room became quiet. Amber and Jenna exchanged an uncomfortable look.

"Are you drinking, Meagan?" Danny pressed.

"So you've found something new after all."

"Answer the question."

"Mind your own business."

"Oh, but it's okay for you to ask me, isn't it?"

"I'm not the one requesting beer, you are."

"Yeah, because JD is your drink."

I groaned. "And we're starting already. Can you and I have one conversation where we're not bitching at each other? How would you know whether or not I drink? You show up once a month for money and that's it."

"Okay," Jenna soothed, always the peacemaker. ""Let's not start fighting." She turned to Danielle. "Why are you trying to get a rise out of her?"

Danny shrugged. "Because I'd like to see it."

"Why?" Amber asked.

"Because every once in awhile someone needs to check to see if she's still in there. The two of you obviously aren't doing it, so that leaves me."

"Fuck off, Danny," I said. "You just enjoy pissing me off and we both know it. And if you're afraid I'm not in my head, it's only because I might forget to hit the ATM for you. Don't worry Danielle, I won't forget to let you bleed me dry."

"Who the fuck said this was about money?" she barked.

"If you want a fight, go pick it with someone else. I'm not in the mood."

"You're pissing me off."

"What else is new? I've been pissing you off since the day you were born. Did you know your first words were, *Mom, Meagan's pissing me off*?"

Amber laughed and Jenna smirked. Danielle turned on them. "When are the two of you gonna realize she's not funny?"

"When are you gonna get off her back?" Amber countered. "For almost three years I've been watching you give your sister a hard time and she's done nothing but take it. I love you Danny, but you gotta ease off a bit."

"Amber, no offense, but you don't know anything about it."

"I do, Danielle," Amber stressed. "I know your sister's spent the better part of her life doing whatever it takes to make you happy."

"It's okay, Amber," I said. "Just let it go."

Amber threw her arms in the air. "See what I mean? You're jumping all over her but *still* she's protecting you."

"She's not protecting me," Danny scoffed. "She just doesn't want to hear the bitching."

"Well neither do I," Jenna said. "It's *tiresome*. Can we just have a nice afternoon together the way we used to? Don't any of you remember how much fun we used to have together?"

"Things change," I mumbled.

Jenna heard me anyway. "They don't have to. Now this is what's gonna happen: Josh is gonna pick up Sammy from your parent's tonight and the four of us are gonna order Chinese, crack open a bottle of wine, and have a slumber party."

"Jenna, I'm twenty-eight years old."

"So? Amber's twenty-seven, I'm twenty-six, Danny's twenty-one. What's your point? Just because you're the *oldest*," she teased, "doesn't mean you're the wisest."

"It's a Wednesday."

"Gotta get up early for work, do you?"

"You're funny. Aren't you working tomorrow?"

"Not till the afternoon."

"My classes don't start till eleven," Danny chimed in.

Amber shrugged. "You know my schedule."

"There isn't one."

"Precisely."

Jenna tilted her head at me. "Don't you want us around, Meagan?" She asked quietly.

"Nice guilt trip."

She grinned. "I thought it was alright. So are we gonna have a slumber party tonight or not?"

"Okay." I nodded. "Somebody order Danny her twelve pack. Or does wine suit you?"

"Does it suit you?" she countered.

"Doesn't matter." I shrugged and wondered how I was going to get away for a snort later with two extra pairs of eyes in the apartment.

Jenna's plan came to fruition. Josh agreed to "babysit" Sammy for the night and Danielle and Amber went out to pick up some Chinese food and wine. They returned with a six-pack of beer too.

"You couldn't do it, could you?" I asked, grinning at Danielle.

"It's for all of us," she defended.

"A six-pack? You're full of shit. None of us drink beer."

"What about you hitting the Guinness with Seamus?"

"That's in Ireland. And it happens maybe once a year."

"So pretend you're in Dublin. When's Seamus coming back anyway?"

"Who knows? I still have to pay him back for that little stunt at the airport."

"That was hilarious," Amber said, chuckling.

"Wait till you see what I do to him."

"What?"

"Not yet. I have to set it up first but it's gonna be big." I was working out an intricate plan to get my uncle back and it was coming soon. If it all worked out, Seamus was going to be good and humiliated. He thought he'd won the game but he was wrong. I knew someone who could help me pull off something huge.

"Soon?" Amber asked eagerly.

I grinned. "Very soon."

"Let's eat," Jenna suggested. "I'm starving."

In the kitchen we chowed down on Jade Gardens' best dishes and then everyone settled into the living room. The music went on and we cracked open a bottle of wine. Danny snapped open a can of beer and told me to shut up before I even uttered a word. I was edgy. I hadn't touched a drug all day and the wine was doing little to dull the desire. I could feel my jaw tightening even as we sat on the couches swapping stories and laughing.

"Quit grinding your teeth," Jenna suddenly said, turning to face me.

"Am I?" Her words startled me.

She nodded. "It's really annoying too."

"Sorry." I forced my jaw to sit in one position but I knew what I really had to do to stop its motion. Easily, I swung myself into the wheelchair and excused myself from the room. I had been smart enough to hide a vial in the bathroom earlier when I realized everyone would be spending the night and I locked the door behind me, reached behind the sink, and yanked it free. I took it off the back of my hand like I sometimes had to in situations like this, replaced the vial, and emerged from the bathroom a far calmer person. I threw myself back on the couch beside Amber.

"Truth or Dare?" Danny suggested. Amber and Jenna grinned.

"No," I said.

"Why not?"

"You haven't prank called your mom in over two years," Jenna chimed in.

"You hate that," I reminded her.

"But I kind of miss it. Just once," she pleaded.

"You're kidding me, right?"

"Do it, Meagan," Danny bugged me. Amber only leaned into me and smiled.

"And what the hell would I say to her?" I demanded.

"You always come up with something."

"No, Jenna."

"Why?"

Why did she think? "Because I'm not that person anymore. I'm almost twenty-nine. I'm a divorced woman with a dead baby and I'm fucking paralyzed. Are any of these good enough reasons for you?"

Jenna bowed her head. "Sorry."

I felt bad. "Well, don't look all guilty about it. It's not like any of those things are your fault."

I'll do it," Amber said, grinning and lightening the mood.

My head whipped around to look at her. "*You'll* prank call my mother?"

"Or mine--whichever you prefer."

"And what would be the big revelation? That you're actually straight?"

Amber sipped her wine and her eyes flashed mischief. "We'll do your mother. I'll tell her I'm sleeping with Danny now."

I broke out laughing. "That's pretty good."

"Do you want to give her a heart attack?" Danny complained.

"Can you picture her face?" Jenna asked, smirking. "Thinking both her daughters prefer women?"

"You can't do that," Danny reasoned. "She'll hate you."

"You're right." I nodded at Danielle's wisdom. "*You'll* have to do it."

"*Me?* No way."

"You wanted to play, Danielle. And as I recall, the last time we played this game you got away without having to do a damn thing."

Danielle crossed her arms in front of her chest. "I am not doing that."

"Oh yes, you are," I said, tossing her the cordless phone. "You call Mom right now and tell her you've been sleeping with Amber and you feel really guilty about it." My mind bounced to Basil and I looked at Amber. She was the only one who knew my sister had once slept with my ex-boyfriend. My sister didn't even know that I knew. Amber grinned because she knew I thought I'd stuck my foot in my mouth.

"Do it, Danny," Jenna said. "Meagan's right, you wanted to play and now you've been dared."

"Then I double-dare *you*," Danny said.

Jenna arched an eyebrow. "To do what?"

"The same."

"The *same*?"

"Yeah, you're cheating on my brother with Amber."

"Geez, I'm a freaking slut," Amber quipped. I laughed.

"But that doesn't make sense," Jenna stalled. "Everyone is sleeping with Amber? Joan's not gonna believe that."

"That's not the point," I said. "The point is the call."

"Yeah," Danny agreed. "So if I'm doing it, you are too."

Jenna relented. "You first," she said, pouring herself another glass of wine. She was going to need it.

Danny dialed the number with a horrified look on her face and I switched the call to speakerphone. "Umm...Mom?" she said, easing her way in. "I need to talk to you about something." And then carefully she went on to explain that she'd been sleeping with Amber for three weeks and the guilt was killing her.

"You've been what?" our mother shrieked. The rest of us hid our laughter behind throw pillows.

"I'm sorry," Danny whined. "I didn't know I was gay."

"Gay? Danielle, how in God's name could you do that to your sister? Your own sister!"

My head snapped up. Oh, no! This was going all wrong. We hadn't planned ahead and for once in her life my mother was actually defending me. And why? Because I was a cripple! Suddenly everyone became aware of it and the room grew uncomfortable. I looked at Danielle and realized this was exactly what she'd have to suffer if she ever told anyone about

Basil. Danielle looked like she knew it too but she was a sport and didn't put a stop to the game.

"And you are not gay," Mom huffed. "There must just be something about that Amber." The amusement came back and again we muffled our laughter with the pillows.

"I have to go Mom," Danielle said. "I'm meeting with Amber and I'm gonna tell her it's over."

"I am not finished with you Danielle. You go tell that woman you are not seeing her anymore and first thing tomorrow morning I'm going over there to tell your sister. She'll move back in here with us."

"Okay," Danny said glumly. "Goodbye." She clicked off the phone and we broke into hysterics.

"Move back in there with them?" I howled. "I wouldn't move back into that house if I was nothing more than a head and Amber was force-feeding me bacon. You were really good, Danny. I think you should take over my reign."

"Yeah but someday Mom will wise up and get caller ID," Danielle warned. "Now Jenna."

"Don't you think we should wait awhile?" Jenna asked.

I shook my head. "If she thinks Amber's gone off to meet Danielle she might just get a bug up her ass to come tell me now." Everyone agreed and Jenna took the phone. Another call was made. Again we flipped it to speaker.

"Hi Joan," Jenna whispered, sadly. "I suppose you've heard by now, huh?"

"About Amber?" my mother asked, cautiously.

"Boy, Josh sure didn't waste any time telling you."

"*Josh knows?* He knows Danielle's been sleeping with Amber?"

"*Danielle?*" Jenna shrieked. She sounded horrified. "She's been sleeping with her too?"

"What do you mean *too?*"

"Oh Goddess, I'm sorry. I better go."

"Jenna, don't you dare hang up that phone! What do you mean *too?*"

"I...I thought Josh told you about me."

"*You?*"

"I'm sorry," Jenna pleaded. "It's just...well, it's Amber. She just has this power over women."

The pillows weren't enough to muffle the amusement of that one, and the room suddenly broke into raucous laughter. Mom caught on quickly and was not impressed.

"What is the matter with you people?" she barked. "Who's all there?"

"Just the girls," Jenna giggled.

"I can't believe this. Do you have any idea how old you are? And I suppose I'm on the goddamn speaker!"

"Yes," I said, laughing. Amber was howling beside me and Danny was in a fit of giggles on the floor.

"Meagan, I would expect this from you, maybe even Danielle, but *Jenna*--I can't believe you would do this. And Amber, I cannot believe you would allow such things to be said about you."

"It was a joke," I defended.

"Four women in their twenties. One almost thirty---"

"I am not!" I complained.

"And this is how you spend your time. Don't you people have anything better to do than harass me?"

"Come on, Mom," Danny giggled. "It was funny."

"We're sorry, Joan," Amber apologized, still grinning.

"That was the most childish, immature--" She stopped. The humor of it seemed to hit her then and she suddenly burst out laughing. "Two years, Meagan," she said. "I thought you'd finally given up on me."

"I had," I admitted. "It was Danny who revived the game."

"Do you know what I thought? I thought Amber was like some blond seductress who had the power to go around turning the whole world gay."

Amber laughed again. "Sorry, I'm only human."

"But not an unattractive one," my mother said.

"Thank you."

"Are you mad, Mom?" I asked.

She thought about it. "No," she said, slowly. "I just think you're a bunch of children. Goodnight, *kids.*"

"Bye!" We hung up still laughing.

"Jenna you were great," I praised. "The way you played that -- it was perfect. '*Danny's sleeping with her too*?' You sounded so horrified. I can't believe you did it."

"Did you hear how horrified *Mom* sounded?" Danny piped in.

"And we're down to one," I said, raising my wine glass to Amber.

"What should I do?" she asked.

"I'm not sure. We might have to save it for next time."

"Next time?" Danny squealed, excitedly. "So we'll do it again?"

I shrugged. "Why not? It'll keep us young, right?"

"Yeah," Jenna teased. "Especially those of us who are going on thirty."

"I am not. I'm not even twenty-nine."

Danny giggled. "You're not gonna hit the big three-oh gracefully, are you?"

"Doubt it. It must be freaking nice being twenty-one. I don't remember that."

"You wouldn't," Jenna said. "You weren't twenty-one even when you were."

Danny stretched luxuriously. "It is nice," she commented. "What's it like being a hundred and four?"

"Not much different from a hundred and three. The legs go, but you know---" I shrugged.

"Cynicism, Meagan," Jenna warned.

"Lose a limb, Jenna," I threatened. "Then you can fucking talk to me about cynicism." My mind suddenly wrapped around my own words and I flushed with self-loathing. "Oh God, I didn't mean that. I would never wish---"

"Relax," Jenna soothed, waving her hand like my words had meant nothing. "I know you wouldn't wish your situation on anyone."

"Things pop out of my mouth sometimes, but you believe me right? I wouldn't even wish it on *Gwynne*."

"We know, Meagan," Danny said in a bored tone.

"I'm...I'm not evil."

Amber laughed. "Of course you're not. I could really kill your brother for that antichrist remark he made that time."

"You're still on that?" Jenna demanded. "Meagan, what have you ever done that's evil?"

I killed my baby. "Nevermind," I said.

"Tell me."

"Drop it."

"Don't be so stupid," Danny told Jenna. "She killed her baby."

My heart ripped open and Amber shot to her feet. "She did not kill that baby, Danielle!"

"*I* know that. Everyone knows it but her!"

I stared at the floor fighting back tears and suddenly wishing they would leave so I could go smoke a joint or something and send away the pain. Amber glanced at me, worriedly. "She said drop it but you couldn't leave it alone," she barked at Danielle.

"Why don't we drop it now?" Jenna suggested.

But Danny could never let anything go. "Is she gonna move on from this or what? For Christ's sake, Meagan, you miscarried. It happens."

"Be quiet," I whispered.

"Danny, please stop," Jenna pleaded, nervously.

"Stop what? Forcing her to see the truth? People fucking miscarry!"

"Fuck you!" I yelled. "Does it look like I'm gonna have another baby, Danielle?"

"The pregnancy was an accident to begin with."

"Danielle!" Jenna was disgusted by her words.

"An *accident*," Danny stressed, unaffected by the warning in Jenna's tone. "Three months along and then another accident to remove it. Didn't you once have an abortion, Meagan?"

The room fell into silence and everyone turned to look at me. I had never had an abortion.

"In high school? Didn't you have a fucking abortion?"

"No. What the hell are you talking about?"

"You were pregnant senior year," Danielle accused.

My mouth fell open. "What the fuck are you talking about? I was not."

"Yes, you were," she barked. "I remember because Mom was crying. Her *Catholic* daughter was going to have an abortion."

"That's not true!" I shrieked. Amber and Jenna were staring at me like they weren't sure they believed me and it roused my anger. "Everyone in this fucking room is pro-choice but this one says I had an abortion and look at the way you're all looking at me! Get Mom on the phone right now! I was not pregnant. I skipped a freaking period."

"That's not what Mom thought."

"Because I freaked out, alright? You have to know every goddamn detail of my life? Fine. I fucking freaked! I was afraid I could be pregnant and I was stupid enough to go to Mom with my worries. But I wasn't pregnant. My period came a week later and I spent the rest of that year with Mom checking my room everyday to make sure I was taking my fucking pills. She alternated between telling me I shouldn't be having sex and hiding condoms in my dresser drawers."

Danny didn't believe me. "Then why was she crying about you having an abortion?"

My head was starting to ache. "Why do you fucking think? I was seventeen, Danielle. I didn't see another option."

"So you would have done it!"

"Yes, I would have fucking done it!"

"And that's my point."

"What kind of point is that? You're comparing the fears of a seventeen-year-old high school student to what happened *ten years* later?"

"Yes, because you didn't plan either pregnancy."

I ground my palm against my forehead. "There wasn't a pregnancy," I said, through clenched teeth. "Goddamn it!" I hit speed dial on the phone and Amber said "Honey, it's almost midnight."

"I don't care."

My mother sounded tired when she answered the phone. "What is it now?" she complained.

"Would you please tell your bigmouth daughter what happened my senior year?"

"I don't know. What happened?"

"Did I *ever* have an abortion?"

"To my knowledge, no."

"You're not helping me," I barked. "*Was* I pregnant that time I came to you and told you I skipped a period?"

"No, it came a week later. What's this all about?"

"Just Danny shooting her mouth off. Sorry I woke you. Go back to bed." I clicked off the phone and glared at my sister.

"Happy now? Or do you need documented proof from my fucking gynecologist?"

"You owe your sister an apology," Jenna said.

Danny nodded. "I'm sorry."

"No. Fuck your apologies, Danielle. It never ends with you."

"I was trying to help you!"

"That's helping me? Accusing me of killing two babies?"

"I was saying you didn't kill any. *If* you had been pregnant and had an abortion it would not have been a formed child yet. The other was a miscarriage. And I thought if you'd had an abortion once---"

"That I'd just keep doing it? At twenty-seven-years-old, Danielle? With a husband and a fucking fortune in the bank?"

"You were leaving Ken," she pointed out.

"And she was coming to me, Danny," Amber said softly. "We would have raised the baby together."

Danny scoffed. "And screw Ken, right?"

"You really don't get it, do you, Danny? Ken would have been her father. Yes, she would have lived with u,s but she still would have had her father. Do you think people don't get divorced? Ken would have been a great father and I had no intention of taking that away from him." She opened her mouth to say something else but I stopped her. "Don't," I warned.

"Don't what?"

"I know what you're going to say. Passport. Money. But you also know I *didn't* go anywhere. Now we've discussed this and it's done. There will be no more mention of Zoe. I swear to God, I will shut out anyone who even breathes her name."

"That's real healthy, Meagan."

"Healthy or not, it's my way."

"Or the highway," Danny grumbled under her breath.

My eyes narrowed to slits. "Who told you that?"

Josh."

Jenna looked guiltily at her feet.

"What are you people *doing to me?*" I groaned. I was so close to tears I wanted to bury my head. "I have a brother who calls me names and tells people I'm Satan, a sister who loves to harass me, a mother who never tires of berating me, and Amber---" I looked at her and felt the old sting of the butterfly. "Fuck. If this is what you people call love, then do me a favor and hate me, because your goddamn love is gonna destroy me." I pulled away to maneuver myself back into the wheelchair but Amber latched onto my arm. "Just let me go."

"I can't."

And then she was crying. And then Danielle was crying. And then Jenna decided to join in. "You're all gonna sit here and cry?" I demanded, but my heart was weakening and again I staved off my own tears of frustration. "Just...Christ, don't cry. I still love you. Maybe I just need to go away for awhile."

"*Go away?*" Amber cried. "Where?"

"I don't know," I said, quietly. "Presumably somewhere with a ramp."

Danny looked up at my face and I winked at her. She burst into nervous laughter. Jenna's head snapped up. "What?"

"She's not mad," Danny said, grinning.

"No, I'm not mad."

Amber continued to cling to me. "Tell me you won't go away. I don't want to wake up one day to find you gone."

"I won't go away. Lighten up. Have another drink or something. Come on Danny, I'll have a beer with you."

"Okay." Danny jumped to her feet and ran into the kitchen to grab a couple of cans.

"Get me a glass though," I called after her. "I hate that metallic taste." Amber smirked and I knew what she was thinking. "It's not the same," I whispered.

She laughed. "You always know what I'm thinking."

"Usually."

It had been an exhausting evening but it wasn't over yet. Danny passed out after I drank a beer with her. Jenna soon followed. Then Amber. I finished off the last of the wine, covered Danny and Jenna with a blanket, and gently shook Amber awake. Sleepily, she rubbed her eyes and staggered to her feet.

"You are coming, aren't you?" she asked.

Nodding, I followed her into the bedroom, closed the door, and maneuvered myself into bed beside her. Instantly, her hand moved up the front of my tank top and I felt a small freezing pain press around my heart. She wanted to make up for tonight, for all that had happened, and she didn't wait for a response. Her fingers trailed a soft line across my breasts and it made my insides hurt. Made my head pound with pain. It wasn't easy anymore.

"I--I have a headache," I whispered.

She laughed. "That's so lame, Meagan."

"No, I really do. Just let me take something, okay?"

I reached across the nightstand and pulled two painkillers from a bottle Amber thought my doctor had prescribed and washed them down with a sip of Evian. Painkillers and water. I didn't like the way they sat on the table beside the bed, making me feel like I was eighty-eight instead of twenty-eight.

"Do you think that's such a good idea considering you've been drinking?"

I put away the water. "A little late to worry about that now."

She sighed. "I'll leave you alone." She rolled away from me and I thought she might be quietly crying again. She believed I was rejecting her. Didn't know that I always wanted her and the want was as bad as the ache of not being whole.

"Amber?"

"Yes?" The word was very quiet and it broke my heart.

"I never asked you to leave me alone."

"You don't feel well."

"I didn't say that either. I said I had a headache and I took something for it. It will pass. I...I want you."

She turned and smiled. "You do?"

"Yes."

"You don't say that anymore, Meagan."

"I know," I responded, softly. "I'm sorry."

Her eyes pleaded with mine. "Say it again."

"I want you," I repeated, pressing forward to kiss her. "I always want you."

"Will you ask me?"

She seemed so desperate to hear me say the words that I hurt even more. What was I doing to us? I was allowing my paralysis to come between us, and yet, I couldn't stop it. Sex made it all too real. It reminded me of my limitations and I spent so much time avoiding it, she was feeling undesirable.

"I...I want you to make love to me." The words half-caught in my throat. "I love you and I... want you to make love to me."

She grinned. "I would love to make love to you."

"I don't know if I locked the door."

"They're sleeping."

"Can you check it anyway?"

"Okay." Amber rose from the bed and went to lock the door. "I don't think they'd just barge in here," she said, returning to the bed. "But whatever makes you more comfortable." She hopped on the bed and gave it a little bounce.

"You're so beautiful," I praised.

"So are---"

I shook my head. "Don't."

"Meagan, you *are*." Her hand rose to touch my face. "I think you're breathtaking."

"Could we please change the subject?"

"No. I think you should know how attractive you are."

"You're making me uncomfortable."

"Too bad."

"What?"

"You heard me, I said too bad. It's long enough now. I've allowed you to be uncomfortable around me and I shouldn't have. I want it to stop. You say I'm your soul mate but it seems to me you wouldn't be uncomfortable around such a person. I think you're beautiful, regardless of what *you* think."

"I think I'd rather sleep now."

"No."

"What are you gonna do? Force yourself on me?"

"Maybe I should."

I groaned. "And the next round begins. Am I supposed to fight you now too?"

"No." She looked at my face and her expression softened. Voice lowered. "Show me your body, Meagan. It's so beautiful and you used to be so comfortable with it. Let me see you undress and reach for me the way you used to. Do you remember the way we used to tear each other's clothes off?"

"I remember," I said quietly.

"You wanted me so much then."

Her words were stabbing me. "That hasn't changed."

"Then show me. Undress me and then undress yourself."

Slowly, I nodded. Amber was wearing a button-down shirt, like a man's pajama top, and carefully I began unfastening the buttons. She was on her knees in front of me and her eyes never left mine as I opened the shirt and tenderly slipped it off her shoulders. There was nothing left to remove.

"Now you," she whispered.

That was the hard part. Tears wanted to singe my eyes as I went about the task of revealing myself to her. I pulled my shirt over my head and reached for the covers but she stopped me.

"Please don't. On top of the covers, okay, Meagan?"

And then the tears did come. I tried to look away but Amber cupped my face in her hands. "It's okay baby," she soothed. "Look at how beautiful you are. Look at your body."

"You're hurting me," I said quietly, feeling filled with shame.

"I don't want to hurt you. I want you to see what I see."

"And you're making me cry. And my head hurts again. And it's.....you're *hurting* me."

"I'm sorry, Meagan. I didn't mean to hurt you. Please, don't cry. Does your head really hurt?" She reached for the bottle of pills, shook one out, and grabbed the water. "Just one, okay? You can't have too many of these. The doctor said they can be addictive."

She was handing me Demerol but the bottle said Tylenol 3's.

I washed down the pill. "Thank you."

"I didn't mean to hurt you."

"I know."

She moved back to her side of the bed. "I think I've done enough damage for one night."

"You're not gonna make love to me?" I whispered.

"You still want to?"

"Yes."

Her face looked relieved and she moved to pull the covers up around us. "N-No," I stammered, easing them away and feeling the terror fill my heart. "No covers."

"Are you sure?"

I managed a weak laugh. "No, I'm not sure at all."

She smiled. "I love you, Meagan. If at any time you want to---"

"No. In fact, throw them off the bed so I don't get tempted. I just want to be with you."

"Are you afraid?"

I was terrified. "As long as you don't whip out a giant spotlight I think I'll be okay."

The smile came again and she pushed the blankets to the foot of the bed but didn't shove them off. "We'll leave them there just in case," she said, turning back to me. "Remember who you're with, okay? Does it feel like the first time we made love?"

"No, I didn't care about covers then. It's more like the first time ever being naked in front of someone."

"That's not so bad."

"You're right. I suppose it's more like being naked in front of a lot of people when you weigh six-hundred pounds, have really bad skin, and webbed feet."

Amber chuckled. "The difference is you're none of those things, I'm one person, we love each other, and I've seen you naked more times than I can count. Granted, it's been an undercover operation lately but I still see you, still know how beautiful you are. It's not a risk Meagan, it's just us."

"Are you going to talk all night?"

"Do you want me to?"

"You make me think of Basil asking for a hummer then talking all the way through it."

"Oh God, shut up. Right now you have to tell me about giving Basil hummers?"

"So find a way to shut my mouth."

Again, she laughed. "Come here," she said, yanking me to her. "I'm sure I can find several uses for your mouth."

In the morning I was greeted with another headache. Making love to Amber without the covers had been one of the most trying experiences of my life. I'd felt twisted as we moved about the bed. Incomplete. The mannequin legs mocked me and I wanted to scream at them to bend of their own will, to do anything but lay there looking dead.

Amber was careful not to let me get upset. If my expression started to reveal how disheartened I felt, she would stop whatever was going on and pull me into her arms for a time. Then it would begin again and I would be back to my mixture of humiliation and pleasure. It was nice, but it was awful. It was us, but in the end it was more painful than anything else.

The memories ground the pain into my forehead and I bolted up with a jerk. The top half of me bent forward and I pressed my face against my knees as the lightening smashed behind my eyebrows. Blindly, I reached for the pills while the agony ripped through my head and Amber snapped awake.

"Another one?" she asked worriedly.

I couldn't respond and only nodded into my knees as my hand continued to grope for the pills.

"I'll get them, honey," she said, reaching around me and finding the bottle.

"Four," I muttered.

She snapped open the lid. "No, that's too many. Try two first." She handed me the pills and reached for the water.

"No water." I shook my head. "They work faster when I chew them."

"Are you sure?"

She rubbed my back and I pulled away from my knees to take the pills. "It'll pass," I whispered. It was passing already and I wondered if I shouldn't have dealt with the pain awhile before reaching for the pills.

"Do you want to stay in bed awhile longer?" she asked.

"No, I'll get up."

"You don't have to," she reminded.

"I know. I never have to." Why would it even matter? At least in my dreams I had legs that worked.

Chapter 7

"Guess whose birthday it is today?" It was two days after the slumber party and again I hadn't gone to bed. I'd watched TV, had a few snorts, made a few overseas calls, and before I knew it, it was morning.

"Didn't you come to bed at all?" Amber complained, rubbing her tired eyes.

"No. And since you're not going to guess I'll tell you. It is Seamus's birthday today and he's about to get the surprise of his life."

"Oh no. What did you do?"

I grinned. "Just a little prank involving his favorite pub and a lovely little transsexual I met in London named Jackie."

Amber was amused. "*You* have a friend who's a transsexual? You who thinks Zeppo is a freak?"

"Let's just say my eyes were opened to a whole new world in London. Jackie came to my rescue one night after I did something extremely stupid. It's a bit of a long story."

Amber's curiosity was piqued. She sat on the couch and flicked off the TV. "Tell it."

"Okay. But you have to promise not to get freaked out."

She thought that was funny, like straight little Meagan could never freak her out. She was laughing. "I'm usually pretty un-shock-able, Meagan," she said.

"Don't be so sure."

"I am. You're you and I'm me. I doubt anything you say could even make me raise an eyebrow." She was so condescending.

"I had sex with a vampire," I shot.

That wiped the smirk off her face. Her mouth fell open and she motioned for me to continue.

"I'd been in London about two weeks," I began. "Ken and I hadn't gotten serious yet so it wasn't like I was cheating on him. We were sleeping together but we weren't exclusive, even though he wanted to be. I was still resisting." Amber nodded.

She didn't want to hear about Ken any more than I would have wanted to hear about Gwynne. "Anyway, Becca was one of the assistant editors in the translations department and one night she invited me to a party. She was heavy into the whole underground scene, which I didn't know at the time, and only told me to wear something sexy. People say that. I didn't think to ask why and chose a short black dress, sort of like a slip dress, with super-thin spaghetti straps and a low back. I think I still have it in storage.

"Like the one you wore on our first date?" she asked.

I smiled, "Yeah, I guess it was like that. Anyway, about twenty minutes after we get to the party Becca disappears and I'm left to gawk at my strange surroundings. The party was held in this place that looked like a cross between a brownstone and a dance club. It wasn't really either. There were two large neon bars that seemed to give off the only light in the place and they sat in what appeared to be a giant living room filled with tables and loveseats. There were a few fashion people there. I recognized a few models that I wouldn't have a name for if you asked me, a few photographers, and one designer. But mostly the party was filled with people heavily into Goth. There were half-naked lovers leading each other around on dog chains--that sort of thing"

Amber smiled, but I knew she wouldn't be smiling for long.

"Jackie was part of the entertainment. At eleven-thirty a light came on over a small stage in the corner of the room and Jackie came out doing a slow striptease to some strange music. I stood at the bar, drinking a martini because that seemed to be all they had, and nearly choked on it when she removed her clothes to reveal large silicone breasts and a very large penis. I stared in disbelief. Of course I had never seen anything like it. I was me, right? What did I know about transsexuals and underground parties with S&M themes? The crowd didn't even flinch. They were used to this sort of thing. So, I'm standing there, trying to hide my shock and appear as cool as everyone else when I notice the most incredible looking guy watching me. He was a black guy with light colored skin and a smooth face. Short goatee, long hair. He wore a velvet top hat, a white ruffled-looking shirt with strings hanging down in front, and a long black jacket that made me think of a mortician in the sixteenth century or something. When he stood I noticed that his pants had those old fashioned slits at the ankles and his shoes were very black and shiny. He carried a black cane, which he didn't need, with a golden skull on the handle. He was very Goth. Anne Rice couldn't have written the guy any better. He approached me and I couldn't take my eyes off of his. They were yellow. Cat-like. With his tan colored skin and those yellow eyes and the goatee, he looked like a human tiger. He grinned at me, sort of an animalistic sneer, and I saw that his eye teeth were filed into fangs. Can you picture this guy Amber?"

"Vividly."

I nodded. "He walked right up to me, said his name was Angus--which I though seemed appropriate--and kissed me. I was startled at first but I allowed it. Even kissed back. I stared into his yellow eyes and had the feeling he was devouring me. One of his fangs bit into my lower lip and a small drop of blood appeared. He licked it away. I couldn't tell you why but I found that arousing."

Amber folded her legs under her. "Christ, Meagan. This is getting a little sick."

"It gets sicker. Do you want me to stop?"

"Like hell you're gonna stop."

I laughed. "All right, but you're not gonna like it. Angus took my hand, kissed the inside of my palm, and I watched this as if it was happening to someone else. I don't know if there was something in the martinis or what, but when he moved to lead me away from the party, I followed him. He led me up a winding staircase and down a long hallway to a large bedroom where we had sex. I'm not gonna get into explicit details but there was a bit of an underlying violence involved. Handcuffs, biting, scratching, candle wax – that sort of thing. Then it got a bit weirder."

Amber threw up her arms. "How much freaking weirder could it get?"

"Others," I said. "The door swung open and Angus rose to greet the two women who entered. One of them was very tall. She had long black hair, red eyes, red lips, and frightening fangs. She was wearing a black leather cat suit with thigh high boots and silver spikes on the bottoms of them that must have been four inches long. Angus was tall but she towered over him by at least three inches. I had the feeling that I was in the presence of giants. The other woman crawled in beside her like an animal. This one had short purple hair and, again, the red eyes. I guess they all wore contacts. This one was Asian and she was naked except for the dog collar around her neck and the chain that led up to the other woman's hand. She was boyishly thin. Narrow. I started dressing.

"Angus kissed the tall woman. 'Who's this?' he asked.

The tall woman bent down and stroked the other woman's purple head. 'This is Jasmine,' she said. 'She's going to be our kitty cat tonight.'

Jasmine didn't say anything. She wasn't allowed to speak. The tall woman walked toward me and I backed up against the wall. Something about her terrified me and I realized immediately that Angus wasn't the master around here, she was. That frightened me even more because she was really scary to look at.

"And what role will you be playing tonight?' she asked, stroking my face. Her nails grazed my cheek and I stared into her eyes thinking this must be what it feels like to stare into the face of evil. If evil was a beautiful raven-haired woman who thought she was a vampire with scary fangs and an amused sneer.

I pushed away from the wall. 'The role of a woman leaving,' I said. Seemed appropriate.

She licked her lips and looked me over. 'Are you sure?' she asked. 'You and I could have a lot of fun.'

I felt violently ill. I gathered my purse and shoes from the floor and as I passed the Asian cat she swiped her hand at me like a claw and hissed. I jumped, resisting the urge to kick her in the ribs, and the tall woman laughed at me. Angus only shook his head like it distressed him that he had taught me nothing in all those hours, because it had gone on for hours I realized, and I darted out the door, clutching my purse to my chest and nearly stumbling down the spiral staircase at the end of the hall.

When I got downstairs I found that the party had ended. Becca was nowhere around and only a few people remained, finishing off their martinis and snorting the last of the coke that sat in a large crystal bowl on a coffee table. I realized I would need to call a taxi and searched for a phone. A pretty brown haired woman siddled up beside me and said, 'You don't seem like the type who would leave with the vampires but I guess we all have our oddities. I'm Jackie.'

I looked at her, remembered her penis, and shook her hand.

'You're never going to get a taxi this time of morning,' she said. 'Why don't you let me drive you home? You look like you could use a friend about now.'

What else could I do? Becca had abandoned me, or perhaps thought I'd abandoned her, and I certainly wasn't going back upstairs to have a foursome with the vampires. Jackie seemed the safest bet. She was sober and she was nice. She drove me back to my flat above the NB offices and I invited her in for coffee. We talked until the sun came up and she told me how she hadn't gotten the full sex change yet because she made piles of cash doing the shows. It didn't bother her. When she left she gave me her card; but I've talked to her many times in between."

My throat was getting pretty dry at this point. It was a long story to have to tell in detail.

"After that night I could barely look Becca in the eye again. Becca and I never talked about what happened at the party but I suspected that was because she had her own shame to deal with. Jackie told me that Becca had spent the night in a basement bondage room, chained to a stone wall and being spanked by guys in hoods. Apparently Becca was heavy into S&M and degradation fantasies and she couldn't get off unless someone was beating her and calling her names. Surprising, because the woman looked like a twenty-five year old librarian. It was part of the reason I hired her. She looked smart."

I shrugged. "That's it. That's the whole story."

Amber didn't say anything for long moments. Then she pressed her fingers to her temples, shook her head, and said, "I can't believe you just sat here and calmly told me some vampire guy walked up to you at a party, bit you, sucked away the blood and you willingly followed him to a bedroom where you let him handcuff you to bed, burn you with candle wax, scratch you like an animal and then fuck you!"

"The wax didn't burn. And sure, when you lump it all together like that it sounds pretty bad."

"*It sounds pretty bad?*" she shrieked. "Do you have an idea how dangerous---"

I rolled my eyes. "I know how dangerous, Amber. We used condoms but even still I've been tested for every disease there is a dozen times. I'm clean. I never would have slept with Ken *or* you if I weren't. Don't you think I've thought about all that? Like a thousand times? I've been tested for AIDS so many times my damn doctor told me to stop coming back. Now aside from Seamus, who knows about Angus but not Jackie or the two women because there was no point in telling him that, you're the only other person who knows and I expect you to keep it to yourself. And quit looking at me like that. If you're about to get up on your soapbox then let me first remind you that you too have been tied to a bed. Blindfolded, even."

"*With you!*" Her voice went up five octaves. "There's a bit of a difference, Meagan. There's a level of trust that exists in an intimate relationship. What you did is not the same thing. It doesn't even compare."

I threw up my hands, imitating her earlier gesture. "Fine. Then how does it compare to you having a threesome with your history professor and his wife when you were in college? How old were they, Amber? Sixty? *That's* gross, okay. Compared to your little geriatric adventure having sex with a hot-looking vampire is no big deal. At least he wasn't shuffling off to Denny's for his senior discount."

She made a face and rubbed her hands like my words had chilled her. "Okay. You make a point. Not a very good one but you're right, everyone does something stupid once in awhile. The problem Meagan is that you seem to specialize in it. You stick out relationships with people who aren't any good for you, marry someone you don't really love, run away from your problems, and apparently have a vampire fetish."

I laughed. "I don't have a vampire fetish. I have an Amber fetish and I don't run from you anymore, or wheel from you as the case may be, and you're very good for me. Now what do you have to say?"

She smirked. "I love you."

"Nice save. For the record I love you too. You don't have fangs or anything, but you'll do."

"Ha ha. Why is it I never know what to make of you? Whenever I think I couldn't' know you any better you throw another loop at me. I think you enjoy being mysterious."

"You know everything about my past now," I said. "Promise. Not that it's any of your business but since we both believe true intimacy necessitates full disclosure I'll allow it." I gave a shy grin. "How's that for a couple of two dollar words thrown together to make me sound smart?"

"Please," she said. "You're one of the smartest people I know and you've never even been to college."

"Sure I have. Took a kickboxing course at Preston after we broke up. Then I switched to a gym."

"You know kickboxing?" Amber was amused.

"Yep. If I could walk I could kick your ass".

Amber laughed. "So what does this Jackie have to do with Seamus?"

"This is good," I said, grinning. "Lucky for me, Jackie is already in Ireland on business, a fortunate coincidence I guess, though Jenna would probably say the planets were aligned in my favor." Amber laughed. "Tonight, Jackie's gonna go into the pub where Seamus is having his party, do her thing, and then she'll hop the next flight out."

"And her thing is?"

"Dressed in full Marilyn gear she's gonna sing "Happy Birthday Mr. President" to my uncle. He'll eat it right up, never knowing that the woman he will undoubtedly be flirting with has a penis. Jackie's planning a trip to L.A. soon so she asked me if I could wire her the money in American funds. A thousand bucks."

Amber's eyes widened. "That's a pretty expensive prank, wouldn't you say?"

"She's actually giving me a deal. It's worth it though. And that's where you come in. I'll need you to run down to the ATM, grab the money, and take it over to Western Union. Will you do that?"

She was on the edge of her seat now, glad to be part of the program. "Sure."

"I also promised her another five hundred dollars if she

can get Seamus to drink a shot from between her breasts while doing a bump and grind."

Amber roared with laughter. Then her face grew serious. "But what if Seamus catches on?" she asked. "Won't that be dangerous for your friend?"

I shrugged. "First of all Seamus won't catch on because he'll be too focused on her chest to look anywhere else. Jackie is more woman than Sharon Stone. Plus, I've already prepared for that unlikely eventuality. I talked to Mike, the bartender at the pub, and he's going to make sure everyone in the place knows the real deal. That oughta humiliate Seamus. If he figures it out the other guys will prevent him from getting out of control."

Amber was appreciative. "Same old Meagan, every angle covered."

"Jackie does her thing, sneaks out of the country like a jewel thief, and Seamus learns that if he's going to embarrass me in public he better be ready for retaliation. What do you think?"

She couldn't stop laughing. "I think Seamus will never screw with you again after this one. The poor guy couldn't afford such an elaborate scheme. I'm not sure you can."

I waved away her words. "Money is meaningless when it comes to revenge. The scary part is, one day Seamus will give it right back to me. My uncle doesn't go down without a fight."

"Wonder who that sounds like."

"That's why this game has been going on for about nine years. All I've done is raise the stakes."

The phone rang early the next morning.

"Hi ya, Meggie Pie," the voice slurred.

"Seamus, do you know what time it is here?" Amber turned in her sleep.

"Five?" he asked.

I looked at the clock on the nightstand. "Five-fifteen, Seamus. It's five-fifteen in the goddamn morning."

"Sorry, Meggie, but I had to call and thank you for sending me an angel last night."

That perked me up. I nudged Amber and she rolled over, tossing an arm across my stomach. "It's Seamus," I mouthed. She grinned.

"What do you mean an angel, Seamus?" I said into the

phone. It was late morning in Ireland and Seamus was still drunk.

"Aye. With lips as soft as flower petals."

"*You kissed her?*" I sat bolt upright and Amber turned her head into her pillow to muffle her laughter.

"I wonder what that's gonna cost you," she whispered.

I giggled. "Hang on, Seamus. I'm gonna put you on the speaker so Amber can say hi." I punched the button and hung up the receiver. "Okay."

"Hey, Seamus," Amber called. "Have a good time last night?"

"Aye, Blondie. You should have been there."

"I wish I was."

"Seamus. This is very important-- did Jackie get on the flight?"

"Drove her to the airport meself, Meggie. Dat's where I kissed her. Would have done more, I think, if she didn't have to go."

I howled with laughter. "Then you would have been in for a surprise."

"What do you mean?"

"Jackie is a man, Seamus."

"You're wrong. I felt her tits."

"Well did you feel her dick too? She's a transsexual."

"Aw. You're lying."

"She's not," Amber giggled.

"Come on, Seamus. Did you really think you were going to get away with your little stunt at the airport the last time you were here? You know me better than that. Jackie is a transsexual I met in London and I paid her to give you a show. I never thought you'd kiss her, but thanks, you've only made my victory that much sweeter."

I could almost see my uncle gag. "I think I'm going to be sick, Meggie."

I laughed. "You do that. And when you've got your head in the toilet remember who did this to you. You can't top this one, Seamus. I win."

I hung up the phone and Amber and I roared with laughter.

"Remind me never to embarrass you," she said, coiling

her body to mine. "It's frightening what you're capable of."

Chapter 8

Being at my parent's house wasn't a pleasure trip. I was there because they were having a dinner party and my mother had forced Amber to drag me along. Amber did it because she wanted my mother to accept her.

From my place in the corner of my parents' formal living room I watched Amber flit about the house like a servant, helping my mother serve, refilling wine glasses, clearing away the dinner dishes, cleaning the kitchen. Doing all these things while my mother occasionally checked in on her and busied herself entertaining her guests. I didn't like what I was seeing. I had a tendency to overreact to things sometimes but this didn't feel like one of those times. Amber was doing everything but shine my mother's shoes and my mother didn't seem the least bit appreciative. I grumbled about it to Jenna, bitched to Danielle, drank my champagne and glared at my mother every time she passed with her party smile firmly affixed to her face. When I saw Amber move to empty yet another dirty ashtray, I'd finally had enough and asked Danielle to bring the two women to me.

"Tell them I want to see them in the guest room," I said.

Danielle hurried off to grab them, she loved a good altercation, and I wheeled my way through the party like a friendly amputee, muttering excuse me's and pardon me's in a sweet voice that belied my inner fury. I reached the guest room, wheeled inside, and turned myself around so that I was facing the door. I wanted to look them directly in the eyes when they walked in. My fingers rapped an impatient beat on the arm of my chair as I waited. The two women entered.

"What's this all about, Meagan?" my mother asked in that waspish way of hers. She was annoyed at having been called away from the party. Strained face. Furrowed brows. "I can't be long. We have guests out there, you know."

"Not *we*, Mother," I stressed. "You. *You* have guests."

"Fine." She placed her hands on her hips and let out an exasperated sigh. "*I* have guests. Is there a point to all of this?"

Amber closed the door and my jaw tightened. "*Yes, there's a point.* I've been watching what's been going on and I don't like it. I don't like the way the two of you are behaving."

"What do you mean?" Amber asked, leaning against the dresser beside me. She would have touched me somehow if my mother wasn't staring at us.

I looked up at her. "My mother is running you ragged and you're letting her."

Amber tried to defend her perpetrator. "She's not---" she began but I cut her off.

"Yes, she is."

My mother folded her arms across her chest and glared at me. It was her intimidation move. I glared right back. Her little look may have been able to keep others in the family in line, but for me it was just a face that roused my anger. She thought she could stare me down without saying a word. She never learned that only infuriated me more.

"You want a slave," I growled up at her, "hire one. I'm not gonna let you treat Amber like the hired help around here."

"I was doing no such thing."

She was playing games with me but I knew how to strike terror into her heart.

"You were," I said, "and unless you want me to roll out into that party like a lunatic and loudly proclaim to everyone that I'm a big old crippled dyke you better put a stop to this right now."

She tried to remain calm. Amber looked amused.

"Meagan," my mother said, "you are misunderstanding this whole thing. I haven't told Amber to do anything, she's been offering her help."

"Yeah, because she wants so goddamn desperately for you to accept her. You're taking advantage of that and I won't allow it. Let her lift one more finger and I'll scream dyke so loud your ears will ring. Do we understand each other?"

My mother looked at me fearfully, then at Amber who stared at her shoes. No boots tonight. This was formal affair and Amber shone brilliantly in a green Versace dress that matched her emerald eyes perfectly. She was stunning to look at. I felt like a dressed up stump. It was humiliating to try to look pretty when you were sitting in a wheelchair.

"Thank you for all your help, Amber," my mother said. "But my daughter has obviously lost her mind and if you help me anymore, there's no telling what she'll do."

Amber was embarrassed. "I want to help," she said quietly.

"And I appreciate it but you really have done plenty tonight. Danielle can do a few things and Jenna's been helping so I think it's best if we just leave it at that." She turned her patronizing stare on me. "And *you*. Get a grip on that temper of yours before you return to the party."

Another glare. She saw that it didn't affect me and stalked from the room, closing the door behind her. Her high heels clicked away.

Amber walked to the door and turned the lock. The hem of her dress bounced on her knees as she walked back towards me. She kicked off her heels and sat on the edge of the bed.

"Do you want to tell me what that was all about?" Her head indicated the door my mother had just exited through.

I shrugged. "Exactly what I said. I didn't like the way she was treating you so I called her on it."

"Honey, she wasn't treating me any way. You really did misunderstand. She needed help so I was helping her. That's it. You probably didn't have to threaten her with the dyke thing--as if you would have done it anyway."

"You think I wouldn't?"

Amber laughed. "I'm surprised you were able to say the word at all. There's no way you'd shout it out to a party full of people."

My eyes flashed with the challenge. "That sounds like a dare to me." I wheeled to the door and Amber jumped in front of me, grinning.

"No," she said quickly, stopping me in my tracks. She knew if I thought it was a dare I'd definitely do it. "I believe you, okay? It's not a dare. Do you want to give your mother a heart attack? If you need a challenge then say it to me."

I was amused. "That's supposed to be a challenge?"

"At one time it would have been the greatest challenge of your life. If it's so easy now, say it."

She was baiting me. I opened my mouth but nothing

came out. Amber smirked.

"Well?" she prodded.

"Okay…give me a second." I closed my eyes, wrapped my mine around the word like a vise and gritted my teeth. I was about to give her my lie. Someone had once told me I'd have to, I was sure of it.

Taking a breath, I gripped the arms of my chair and plunged. "I....am a lesbian," I finished it quickly. Winced. Then gave her a triumphant grin.

Laughing, she applauded me. "Very good. Not the slightest bit challenging, huh?" she teased.

"It wouldn't be if it wasn't so damn important to you. But you've waited long enough, I suppose. Tell me, what's changed now that I've finally said it?"

"Absolutely nothing."

"Exactly. You waited two years to hear a word that means nothing. It's just a label, Amber. That's all it's ever been."

"Are we back to that speech?"

"No."

"Good. Shall we go back to the party then?"

I groaned. "How much longer till it's over?"

"We'll leave in an hour. The Dean from your mother's school is here and she wants me to meet him. I think she's on her seminar trip again. Do you think I should do it if she asks?"

"Entirely up to you. A word of warning though; when he approaches don't take any deep breaths. The man has chronic halitosis. I mean, make you gag in his face kind of breath. The first time I met him, I actually did. I was fifteen but I doubt that made it any less insulting."

Amber smirked and I followed her out to the party where I had two more glasses of champagne and saw her give me a sideways glance when Dean Hutchence shook her hand. I grinned. They started talking and the Dean was leaning into her. Amber turned her head, pivoting it on an angle so she could hear his words without having to smell his lethal breath. Jenna passed them. Amber said something to her and she nodded and walked away. She came back with something in her hands, which she handed to Amber. The Dean said something to Jenna and she coughed. Shook her head apologetically. I watched her mouth form the words, "I have a cold" and hid my amusement behind my champagne glass. Jenna had never had a cold in her life.

The champagne was light. After the Jack Daniel's I'd been consuming lately it tasted like water and I craved something stronger. One of my mother's colleagues was saying something to me and I nodded as if I'd heard her then excused myself from the conversation. My mother's parties were so boring. I needed a pick me up.

Grabbing my purse from the hall closet, I rolled into the bathroom where I locked the door, removed the vial from the zippered compartment in my wallet, and anxiously twisted the cap. Half a snort off the back of my hand. Went up wrong. I coughed and sniffed again to fix it. Then I reapplied my makeup, brushed my hair, spritzed on some of my mother's Chanel, and popped a painkiller. Just one. Chewed a breath mint and went back outside.

"You were in there quite a while," Jenna said as I passed through the kitchen. She had a suspicious air about her. She was leaning against the sink with her legs crossed in front of her, staring down into her champagne flute. She set the glass on the counter.

"So?" I demanded.

"What were you doing in there?"

"What do you do in a bathroom, Jenna?"

"I don't pop pills."

My eyes narrowed. What was she doing? Peeping through the keyhole? "Excuse me?"

She picked up her champagne flute again then set it back down like she realized she didn't want it, and sighed.

"Amber asked me to grab her date book out of her purse a few minutes before you went into the bathroom," she said. So that was what she'd handed her. "I grabbed the wrong purse. Now why don't you tell me why *you* have a baggy full of pills in yours." It was more of a statement than a request.

"Who did you tell?" I demanded. She raised an eyebrow. Shouldn't have said *that*. I was only glad she hadn't discovered the coke. She would have had to have searched my wallet for that.

"No one, *yet*," she said. "I thought I'd give you the chance to explain first."

I shrugged. "What's to explain? Ever since the accident I get headaches. You know that. My doctor prescribed some pills for me and that's what you found."

"That's funny," she said, "because usually when my doctor prescribes pills they come in a bottle."

"You don't go to a doctor, Jenna. You go to a naturopath. And just what the hell are you accusing me of?" I hoped I sounded rightfully indignant.

"Why aren't they in a bottle?"

"Why do they have to be? They're easier to get at this way. I keep the bottle at home and I keep some in my purse in case I get a headache when I'm out somewhere. Satisfied?"

Amber strolled into the kitchen and dropped her date book on the counter. "You just about ready to leave?" she asked.

I shot Jenna a look. "Yes. I'm not sure I like the company in here."

Amber gave a curious glance. "What's going on?"

"You wanna tell her, Jenna, or should I?" Jenna looked away and I turned to Amber like a person who'd been victimized. "My supposed best friend here just accused me of being some sort of drug addict."

"What? Jenna that's insane."

"She has pills, Amber," Jenna said quietly.

"I know that. Her doctor prescribes them for her headaches."

"See?" I cried victoriously. "What did I just finish telling you? My *doctor* prescribed them. Now if you're through with your little inquisition I think we'll be leaving."

My doctor *had* prescribed pills but not the ones Jenna found. The prescribed ones really were at home in a bottle. Useless garbage. I could take five of them and not feel a thing. Adrian's were better. More potent. Demerol. A few of those and you were swimming in a pleasant euphoria. He'd also given me some Percocet and Percodan but they weren't as good. Needed too many to get the same effect.

Jenna didn't seem convinced but she apologized and Amber and I left shortly after.

"What's her freaking problem?" I grumbled in the car on the way home. It was dark and the streets of suburbia were almost empty. Only a few cars passed every couple of minutes.

Twisting in my seat, I stared out the window at the trees and houses we passed, not far from the house Ken and I had shared a lifetime ago.

"I don't know," Amber said, as we neared downtown.

It was a short trip but it was like driving into a completely different world. There was life on the streets here. People. Other cars. Nothing isolating about that.

Amber steered the car onto Chestnut and a small flutter of nausea crept into my throat as we passed the corner of the crash that made me this way. I swallowed it back. She didn't notice.

"How could she accuse me of something like that?" I was going on about it and I was more indignant than I deserved to be.

Amber shook her head. "She's been overreacting to things lately. Same way she was when Josh cheated on her that time."

"*When he what?*" My head snapped in her direction.

Amber's face flushed. Her eyes widened fearfully and I was reminded of a deer caught in the glare of headlights. "Oh God. Meagan, you can't tell anyone I let that slip out," she pleaded.

I didn't like her choice of words. It only proved she kept things from me.

"When did he cheat on her?" I demanded. I felt a new feeling of disgust for my brother crawl into my gut.

We stopped at a red light and she turned to look at me.

"It was when you were in the hospital," she said. "Jenna figured he was stressed out over your condition and being a new father and she chose to forgive him. They had a few counseling sessions and worked it out. Everything's back to normal now and they're doing fine."

"That little bastard. How could he do that to her?"

"I don't know."

We passed through the light and seconds later met up with another red one. There was a homeless man on the corner. Old. Tired-looking. Squeezing his filthy coat around his body in an effort to stay warm. He looked in at me and I fumbled in my purse, pulled out a fifty, and pressed the button for the window. It slid down with a squeak and Amber looked at me, alarmed. I motioned for the man to approach and stuck the money out the window.

"Take it," I said. "Get yourself a room somewhere and a hot meal." The words sounded generic. Like something someone would say in a boring old black and white movie. Someone who was strolling down the street after just seeing the ghost of Christmas Future and knew they needed to change. Handing a homeless person money was a way to appease the Gods of Fate.

There were bars up and down this street. Many of them had rooms above that were rented out on a nightly basis. It wouldn't be The Plaza but the man could have a warm bed, a decent meal, and still have enough money left to do the same thing tomorrow nigh --if he didn't blow it all on alcohol first.

He took the money, thanked me, and we drove away.

"That was very generous of you," Amber said. "Dangerous, but generous."

I shrugged. It wouldn't do to let her know I was proud of myself. Then she'd expect me to hand money to every bum we saw. The only reason I gave this one money was because when he looked in at me with those dead bloodshot eyes I got the feeling it could be me; penniless and alone., clutching my coat around my waist and begging strangers for drug money, but from a wheelchair. Maybe if I took care of him, destiny would overlook me. I was banking my karma. I wasn't protecting him from the cold streets; I was protecting me.

"She didn't tell me, Amber," I said, sadly. "*You* didn't tell me."

"I couldn't. Jenna confided in me because there was no one else. She couldn't tell you even if she wanted. Then when you came out of the coma she begged me not to tell you because she was afraid you'd hate your brother. And she wasn't wrong, was she?"

I stared out the window.

"Meagan, you can't say anything to him. I know you care about Jenna but they've worked it out. If you start calling your brother a cheating bastard, or whatever else you might come up with, you're only going to start problems."

"Well, I can't just let this go."

"Yes, you can. It's not even any of your business to

begin with. Don't be like your mother."

"What did you just say to me?" I growled.

Amber sighed. "You know what I mean. You've even said it yourself, everyone makes mistakes, so allow Josh his. Don't turn your back on him simply because he followed the Summers tradition and did something stupid."

"You're really pushing me," I snapped. "Maybe we should just drop this before you say something that really pisses me off. I'm already mad at you for not telling me. So much for full disclosure, huh?" Suddenly I didn't feel so bad about the drugs.

"This wasn't *my* secret, Meagan. I don't keep anything from you. I'm sorry if it hurts you that Jenna did but she was only protecting your relationship with your brother. Even Jenna knows your first loyalty is to her."

"It's to you," I said quietly.

She smiled at me. "I mean your first loyalty when it comes to family. Everyone knows if you had to choose between Jenna and them it would be her. Had anyone else accused you of what she did tonight you would have lost it." We pulled into the underground garage and she looked at me meaningfully. "Sometimes I think Jenna's the one you're in love with."

"Don't be ridiculous."

"Why is that ridiculous? You practically idolize her. You don't even deny that you'd drop your own family for her in a heartbeat. Let's face it, you worship the woman."

Was she jealous of Jenna? I shot her a look.

"But I came back from the dead for *you*. I don't remember much about that coma, Amber, but one thing is abundantly clear to me-- I refused to die because I wanted to be with you. What greater test of my love do you need?"

"None." She cut the engine and turned to face me. "Have you ever thought about hypnosis, Meagan?"

"Why?"

"You just know things sometimes. Like when you woke up and knew Danielle had been skipping school."

"I didn't really know that. It was a guess."

"A guess that was exactly right. She'd been doing exactly what you said, watching TV and screwing Mark. She told Jenna they barely left the bed for two weeks. Then there's the strange things you say, like knowing about Gwynne coming into your hospital room and saying those awful things to you. Or how you've convinced yourself that your baby would have been a girl and would have grown up to become a neurosurgeon. A *neurosurgeon*, Meagan. That's not a word you just pick out of the air.

"One morning you woke up and said the name Beth. The girl in the room across the hall from yours was named Beth, did you know that? You were half-asleep still. I think it was when Sammy was over. You looked at me and said, "Beth wanted me to go up with her," and that freaked the hell out of me because a week before you came out of the coma that girl died."

I shuddered. "Stop it. You're scaring me. I don't want to talk about being dead. I don't want to talk about Zoe anymore than you want to talk about Jeff. I won't go under hypnosis because I don't want to remember. The truth is, I'm doing everything I can to forget."

Again I thought of the drugs. They helped me forget. In the bathroom at my parents' house I'd noticed I was getting low and made a mental note to call Adrian. Tonight, after Amber and Zeppo had gone to bed. It was the perfect time for our transaction. The world slept while Adrian and I crept, that's the way it worked. I was more like Angus the vampire than I ever could have dreamed. I too had become nocturnal.

"So what do you want?" Adrian said, taking off his coat and reaching into his pockets. His supplier was a large man named Seth and I'd seen them on the street together a few times making their deals as if no one else could see what they were doing.

"I saw Seth yesterday," Adrian continued, " I've got some weed, some blow, some heroin--which I know you won't touch--and another friend gave me some Quaaludes and acid."

I glanced at the bedroom door. "Will you be quiet? Amber's sleeping in there and my fucking sister-in-law almost caught me tonight."

Sister-in-law. That's what Jenna had turned into. She'd broken the bond of our friendship when she chose to protect my brother instead of confiding in me. It pissed me off. If she'd been married to anyone else she would have told me about it, would have wanted my support. I felt betrayed.

"Give me the weed and the coke," I said. "No acid. I don't touch that hallucinogenic shit." I glanced at the pills. "What do Quaaludes do?"

"Make you mellow like Jello, babe."

That was something I could use. "Okay, give me a handful of those too." I reached for my purse. "How much?"

Adrian calculated. "One-fifty for the blow, fifteen for the weed, ten for the 'ludes. What's that work out to?" He scratched his head. "One-seventy-five."

I threw a fistful of cash at him.

"Careful with the 'ludes," he said. "Don't take more than a couple or you'll be so relaxed you'll barely be able to talk, and there's no way you'll get that past the blond narc."

He handed me the pills, the weed, and a plastic baggy with two little rocks in it.

"C'mon, Adrian," I complained. "Why are you going to giving it to me like this? Where's the vial?"

He shrugged. "I didn't have time to cut it."

I handed back the bag and removed an empty vial from my box. "Cut it now and put it in here."

Adrian went to work on the coke.

I shoved the stuff in my little wooden box, along with the pills, and Adrian and I snorted a line. Out of my supply, of course, Adrian's was for selling. Zeppo was having a show tomorrow night and Adrian made his best money at the gallery, peddling his coke to all the yuppie snobs who wouldn't dare get their shit off the street. I wondered where they thought Adrian got it.

"Okay," Adrian said, pulling on his jacket, "I gotta go before some idiot who doesn't have the sense to page me calls and wakes Zeppo. By the way, thanks for the hard on."

"What?" I couldn't help laughing.

Adrian grinned. "The pager was on vibrate when you called. *That* woke me up."

I laughed again. "Get out of here, you freak. I'll call you in a couple of days."

"Sure thing, babe." He kissed my cheek and left.

The next morning Jenna showed up with Sammy and three takeout cups of raspberry tea she'd purchased on the way over. She handed me one and I set it on the table without looking at her. Amber frowned. Jenna looked at me and I turned my head. Wheeled into the living room where Sammy was already preoccupying himself with his toys.

"Come on, Sam," I said. "You wanna go for a quick ride?"

Jenna watched me speed Sammy around the apartment and when she glanced at Amber, Amber gave a nervous shrug. She was afraid I'd tell Jenna what I knew. Three laps with Sam and I was done. I dropped him in front of his toys again and wheeled into the bedroom, where I slammed the door behind me. Seconds later Jenna appeared.

"I'm sorry, okay?" She sat on the edge of the bed and began rubbing her bare feet. I knew they were killing her because Jenna never wore heels and she'd been in them for hours last night. "I didn't mean to accuse you of anything. You're just so different lately. You don't sleep. You're losing weight again. You see problems where there are none." She shrugged. "It made sense at the time. I just don't want to see you get hurt."

I thought of the way my brother had hurt her. The way she'd protected him from me. The way we used to be. I had no choice now but to accept her lie.

Sighing, I wheeled to the bed, placed her feet in my lap, and started rubbing them for her.

"I forgive you, Jenna," I said. For more than she would know.

Amber strolled in, an amused sneer on her face. "Bowing at the feet of your Goddess, huh?"

I shot her a look.

"What does that mean?" Jenna asked.

"Oh nothing," I said. "Just that Amber seems to think I'm secretly in love with you."

Jenna fell back on the bed, howling with laughter. "Amber!"

"You have such a big mouth," Amber said to me. "And I was joking."

"Were not. A part of you really believes that or you

wouldn't have said it at all." I grabbed Jenna's wrist, pulling her forward. "Jenna, tell Amber what you told me the night before your wedding."

"About when you first moved into the building?"

I nodded.

Jenna looked up at Amber and shrugged. "I had a crush on her." Amber's mouth fell open and Jenna laughed. "That's the same reaction I got from her; a dropped jaw."

"Tell her what kind of crush, Jenna. Explain it to her."

"A nonsexual one," Jenna said. "I wasn't attracted to her physically, more like psychically. I was drawn to her spirit. There are different types of soul mates in this world. Some connect on a level of friendship. I met Meagan and I knew at once that was us. We clicked. We were complete opposites and that's what made us fit together. Meagan was ambitious and down to earth. I was spiritual and somewhat flighty."

She groped for a metaphor and came up with magnets. "Think of it that way, Amber. If you try to put the positive ends of two magnets together you can struggle forever but you'll never make them connect. Flip one magnet to its negative end and suddenly they fit like yin and yang. You can barely pry them apart. Sometimes like attracts like, true, but other times it's more important for opposite polarities to meet. Meagan was--is--mine. You're hers. The difference is she also loves you in a physical way. That makes you one up on me. She doesn't love me in that way. I'm sure the thought never even occurred to her. It never occurred to me."

"You're not gay," Amber said, easily.

"Neither is Meagan."

I shook my head. "Don't go down that road, Jenna," I said, giving her back her feet.

"Why not?" she asked, crossing her legs under her. "I should think it would be even greater proof of your love that you found her gender unimportant when you really have no interest in women."

"I told her I'm gay last night."

"Gay!" Jenna found that hilarious. "You're barely bisexual."

Amber peeked out the door, saw that Sammy was still playing with his toys and leaning against the wall, surprised me by saying, "She was telling me what she thought I needed to hear. She was only doing it for my benefit."

"And did you need to hear it?" Jenna asked.

"I always thought I did. But if she doesn't want to label herself I'm fine with that now. I used to think it was just denial on her part; that she couldn't own up to who she was. Now I realize maybe I was trying to force her into owning up to who she *wasn't*. I'm sorry, Meagan," she said. "I was insecure and I didn't understand. It's hard for me to see things from a metaphysical perspective. Sexuality is a very earth plane kind of thing for me."

Jenna and I shared an amused glance.

"Did she just say *earth plane*?"

I nodded. "Yeah, I'm pretty sure she did. I think those words were as biting for her as 'lesbian' is for me."

Amber laughed. "Hey, I'm learning."

"It takes time," I offered. "I've known Jenna forever and sometimes she can still shock even me with her strangeness."

"Thanks," Jenna said, "and while we're on the topic of strange, remind me to pick up some pearl onions for you later."

Amber howled with laughter and I shook my head at her. "Geez, do you have to tell everyone about that?"

"I can't help it. It's funny. The fact that you've never even been served a pearl onion only makes it funnier."

"London, Amber," I said. "They put them on my plate in a restaurant in London. So there." I stuck my tongue out at her.

We were back to kidding around like we had in the days before the accident, the days before Josh, and I didn't feel one urge to have a snort. That would come later, when the world settled in once more and I was the only person alive. Left to my own devices, I had to kill the time somehow. It was just a boredom thing, really.

Chapter 9

"I like you," I heard the olive-skinned woman tell Amber. She was about my height, or the five-foot-seven I would stand at if I could stand at all, and she had long brown hair, parted down the middle, and deep dark eyes and red lips. Her name was Nicole, and she was one of two women Adrian and Zeppo had brought with them when they'd arrived an hour earlier to visit. The other woman was a redhead named Holly.

Adrian, Holly, and I sat at the kitchen table chatting and sharing a bottle of wine. Zeppo fiddled with the stereo in the living room and Amber had taken Nicole to the bookshelf along the far wall to show her a book they'd been discussing. I saw the surprise register on Amber's face as she backed up against the wall.

"Excuse me?"

Nicole leaned into her. "I said, I like you."

Amber's eyes darted to the kitchen and I looked away. Pretended I couldn't hear them. I thought Zeppo was smirking and suddenly felt very insecure. I sipped my wine and glanced at Holly who didn't seem to notice what was going on.

"So, how long have you and Nicole been together?" I asked.

She giggled. "Oh, I'm not with Nikki. I'm straight."

"Oh." I glanced back at the living room. Amber was still pressed against the wall and Nicole was still leaning into her. She whispered something I couldn't hear and Amber shook her head. Nicole reached for her purse, pulled something out and placed it in Amber's hand. I knew it was her phone number and felt a lump of fear form in my throat.

"How you doin'?" Adrian whispered. He always knew when I was stressed.

That morning I had quite accidentally come upon Amber's journal. I had been bored and thought reading some of her poetry would cheer me up, but when I pulled one of the spiral notebooks out from where she kept them in a cabinet under the bookshelf, poetry was not what I'd found. Instead I found myself reading Amber's most private thoughts. There were only a few entries, and none of them were dated, but I could tell by the content that they had been written within the past few weeks. I'd wanted to put the book away but couldn't bring myself to do it. And I read.

I feel her slipping away from me; slipping away altogether. I watch the spirit drain from her body and I feel I can't help her. She doesn't see in herself what I see when I look at her. She looks in the mirror and I know she doesn't see beauty anymore. Even in a wheelchair she's lovely, but she doesn't know it. Her confidence is gone with the use of her legs and I don't know how to give it back to her. I tell her I love her and she looks at me like the words hurt her, like she doesn't see how I could possibly love her now, and she shuts me out. Shuts everyone out.

No one is allowed to touch her--only Adrian. From him she accepts all the things she refuses to take from me. She takes his affection. She takes his friendship and she gives him her laughter. Adrian is the only one she is drawn to now. Jenna comes over and Meagan avoids her gaze. Seamus calls and she gives him a brief hello, inquires about his health, then hangs up. She plays with Sammy but her heart isn't in it. Danielle stops by and she is polite but distant. Only Adrian sees the inner Meagan now and I am twisted up with jealousy.

I see her stare down at her legs like they are the ugliest things she's ever seen. They're still remarkable. I don't know how because I always thought people who were paralyzed must have awfully skinny, weak-looking legs, but not Meagan's. I look at them and think they look as great as they always did and it surprises me that they don't function. I half expect her to leap from the wheelchair and tell me she's been faking it the whole time. "Grab a bag, Amber," I imagine her saying. "We're going to Ireland."

Because that would be just like her. "Let's go surprise Seamus." That's the Meagan I know. The one who could pack a bag in a second flat and hop a flight to wherever she felt like going.

I don't think I know this Meagan. She is sad and distant and the spark has gone from her eyes. I'm afraid to touch her sometimes. Rarely does she come to bed and then, often only after she thinks I'm already asleep. Lying in bed with me scares her, I think. She's afraid I'll reach for her and end up disappointed. I know that's the reason, but I just want to feel her beside me and it has little to do with sex. I just want Meagan.

I don't know how to tell her that. Sex was always such a large part of our relationship, it always came so easily between us, and I know she fears the way it is now. She'd rather avoid me altogether than to curl up to me and be reminded of how desperately things have changed. It's so hard. I can't force her to be who she once was and I feel so lonely sometimes. I just want her back. Why doesn't she come back??

I had closed the book in my lap and cried. I was hurting her again. All I ever seemed to do was find some way to hurt her. There had been a shuffling sound in the bedroom, Amber getting out of bed, and I had quickly wiped my eyes and quietly replaced the book in the cabinet. I didn't mention what I had read.

"Hey." Adrian poked me.

I jumped. "*What?*"

"I asked if you want more wine."

I looked at Amber, who was still huddled away by the bookshelf with Nicole. They were whispering to each other. Amber slipped something in the front pocket of her jeans and my heart broke open.

"Yes, please."

Adrian reached for the bottle and poured three glasses of wine. Across the room, I watched Amber sip her drink. Our eyes caught for a second and she looked away. I turned back to our guests around the table. Amber was making a date to cheat on me. I thought I would cry.

"Does anyone have anything stronger?" Holly asked. Holly was Adrian's friend and she had a nasty little secret of her own. She tapped her finger to the side of her nose and Adrian grinned.

"What are you asking me for?" he whispered.

"Don't be a jerk-off. Do you have any or not?"

He shook his head. "Sold the last of it to Meagan."

I nudged him. "Shut up! She's ten feet away." It probably shouldn't have mattered. Amber was off in the corner betraying me. So what if I snorted some coke?

"Right," Adrian said. "The blond narc." Amber had finally gotten her nickname after all.

Holly glanced at the living room. "She seems occupied enough."

Yes, she certainly was occupied, and her face was completely impassive. I tried to discern what I could from her expression but it was as blank as one of Zeppo's untouched canvases and I thought that scared me more than if I saw interest. At least with interest I would know what I was up against. This way, I had no idea. I knew only that Amber was lonely and she was nestled at the far end of the living room with a woman who was attracted to her. Not a bad looking woman either.

I glanced at the bedroom. Wanted to get high. "Okay, Adrian," I said. "You stay here. Holly and I are gonna go in the bedroom for a minute. If Amber pries herself away from Nicole just tell her I'm showing Holly Zeppo's new painting."

Zeppo had given Amber one of his latest works and she had hung it on the bedroom wall above the bed. I didn't care. I had little use for my surroundings anymore.

"Why can't I come?" Adrian whined.

"Because someone has to stand guard and you're already stoned. I saw you sneak off earlier."

I backed away from the table and nodded at Holly, who stood and followed me into the bedroom. We left the door open a crack so we wouldn't look suspicious, and in case Adrian screwed up. As it turned out, our precautions were unnecessary because when we reemerged five minutes later everyone was still exactly where we'd left them. Adrian at the kitchen table, Zeppo at the stereo, and Amber and Nicole by the bookshelf.

"She hasn't budged," Adrian whispered.

I reached for my wine. "Thanks. That's exactly what I wanted to hear."

Holly glanced at Amber and Nicole. "Why don't you do something?" she asked me.

I looked at her. "Isn't Nicole your friend?"

"No, she's Zeppo's. Personally, I can't stand her."

"Meagan, *do* something," Adrian pleaded. "Don't let this go on right in front of your face."

"What should I do? Wheel over there like an angry stump and demand they stop talking?"

"Yes."

"No. I have to let Amber make her own decision."

"And if she decides to sleep with Nicole?"

My heart twisted. "Then I'll know I'm not enough."

"Wow," Holly said. "You're a lot more accepting than I'd be. There's no way I'd let my partner sit away in a corner with some horny bitch."

I cringed. "I need another snort."

Holly's eyebrows shot up. "We just got back."

"I know, but this wine doesn't cut it. You guys up for some tequila shots?" This was my life now, getting high or drunk with whatever guests were on for the ride.

"Should we call the others?" Adrian asked.

I glanced at Amber. "Call Zeppo. The other two can do whatever they want."

"Come on, babe. Fight for her."

"No."

"Okay." Adrian shrugged and waved Zeppo into the kitchen.

Holly helped me slice lemon wedges and we placed them in a large glass bowl, grabbed six shot glasses, cracked open a bottle of tequila, and brought it all to the table along with a saltshaker. Zeppo grabbed a seat beside Adrian and the four of us started doing shots. Amber and Nicole entered the kitchen and sat next to each other, across from Holly and me. I met Amber's eyes and she guiltily looked away.

"So, what do you do?" Nicole asked me politely. Holly had told me Nicole was a secretary. I forgot what Holly did.

I licked the salt off the back of my hand and downed another shot. "I drink."

"I meant as an occupation."

"So did I."

Adrian and Holly laughed. Zeppo just looked blank.

"Meagan was the Overseas President for *Natural*

Beauty magazine," Amber said, twirling her shot glass through her fingers. She couldn't look at me, and I watched the shot glass make half-turns on the table.

Nicole nodded. "I've heard of it. What happened?"

I shrugged. "Car accident. Paralysis. End of story. What do you do?" The fact that I co-owned the magazine was always kept silent. I didn't like people knowing my business and Amber always backed me up on that.

"I'm an administrative assistant," Nicole said.

"Isn't that just a fancy way of saying secretary?"

She laughed good-naturedly and the reaction caught me off guard. "Yeah, I suppose it is. You don't go in for pretenses, do you?"

"Depends." I glanced at Amber. "Some situations necessitate a bit of phoniness."

"What would necessitate it?"

I didn't miss a beat. "Sparing someone else's feelings. If you knew you were about to do something that would hurt someone else, my guess is the kindest way would be to pretend it wasn't happening." Amber remained silent. Taking the advice, I thought.

"You believe a person should close their eyes to what's going on around them?"

"Give me an example."

Nicole lit a cigarette. "Cheating spouses, let's say."
Good example.

I looked at Amber again and again she looked away. Adrian rapped his fingers on the table. "Anyone who would cheat is just garbage anyway," he said.

I shook my head. "Not necessarily."

Adrian threw up his arms. He was trying to make a point for my sake and I wouldn't let him. "That's such bullshit, Meagan. You once told me your brother cheated on his wife and you thought he was the lowest, slimiest thing to crawl up from the sewers."

"That's because I know his wife. She's pretty and she's kind and she'd do anything for anyone. Some of us aren't so good. Some of us shut people out and we probably get exactly what we deserve."

"That's not true, Meagan," Amber said, quietly.

"People who shut others out are only doing so because they're hurt enough already and they're trying to lock it away."

"Possibly," I said. "But that doesn't mean their actions don't have consequences. Everyone pays for their crimes at some point. If karma doesn't take care of them, human nature will." I was having a private conversation with Amber and I sensed she knew it.

"So, you're saying it's okay to cheat on someone like that?" Nicole questioned, obviously hoping I'd say yes so that Amber would be guilt-free when she slept with her.

"It's never okay to cheat," Holly said. I didn't know the red-haired woman but she seemed to want to protect me. I looked at her and she shrugged. Nicole's question lingered in the air.

"I understand the rationalizing that goes on," I said. "That's all I'm saying. When a person cheats it usually has little to do with the person they're actually cheating with and is more about what they feel is lacking in their existing relationship. Personally, I'd just walk away, but that's me." I looked down at my legs. "Sorry, I'd *wheel* away. I never quite get used to that."

Nicole smiled sweetly and Adrian laughed. I didn't notice Holly or Zeppo but Amber looked pained.

"What about you, Zep?" Adrian asked, downing another shot and then lighting a joint. He passed it to Zeppo. "Where do you stand on the cheating issue?"

Zeppo inhaled the smoke and held it in his lungs for a moment. "I think Meagan's right," he said, releasing a gust of grey air. "I think people cheat when their partners aren't fulfilling their needs."

Holly took the joint from Zeppo, sucked in a toke, and handed it to me. I handed it to Nicole without taking a drag myself. Nicole offered the joint to Amber but she waved it away. She was staring down at her shot glass like a lost child. One who had run away from home and was now regretting the decision. She looked at me sadly, then turned to Nicole. "I think I'd appreciate it if you left now," she said. Relief flooded my body.

Nicole blushed. "Excuse me?"

Amber stood up and pulled something out of her pocket. I knew what it was. Nicole looked nervous.

"She gave me her number, Meagan," Amber said. "I'm sorry. I would never cheat on you." She dropped the paper in front of me and I glanced down at it. "Please leave," she said again to Nicole. "It was wrong of you to come into our home and give me that number and it was wrong of me not to rip it up the second you did."

Adrian and Holly grinned. "You heard her," Adrian said. "Get your skank ass out of Meagan's home."

"Adrian!" Zeppo turned on him.

"Fuck you, Zep. You bring that woman in here and you probably knew full well what she'd do."

"I'll take you home," Zeppo said to Nicole. They reached for their jackets and Zeppo turned back to Adrian. "When are you coming home?"

"When I feel like it."

"Fine." Zeppo and Nicole stalked out the door.

Amber walked around the table and bent down beside me. "It was just flattering, Meagan. Please forgive me."

"You didn't do anything."

"No, physically I didn't but it shouldn't have even gone as far as it did. I don't know why I took the number. I could never cheat on you. You mean everything to me."

"It's okay," I said quietly.

Amber rested her forehead on my legs. "Oh, please don't do that," she pleaded. "Don't just accept this as if it never happened."

I managed a weak laugh. "No, I'm well aware of what happened but you're asking me for my forgiveness and I'm giving it to you."

"If it's any consolation, Amber," Adrian said, "she never doubted you for a second." Holly nodded her agreement.

"What do you mean?"

He shrugged. "She's been watching this go on all night and we've been telling her to go do something about it but she wouldn't. She was determined to let you make the decision on your own."

Amber turned back to me. "You knew the whole time?"

"I heard her tell you she liked you. I saw her slip you her number and I saw you put it in your pocket."

Amber groped my hands. "I'm so sorry, Meagan. Nothing would have come of it, I swear."

"It's okay," I said again. "You were honest with me. That's all that matters."

"Meagan, you're gonna make me cry."

"Well, don't," Adrian said. "Because expecting her to comfort you after this is really asking too much."

"It's alright, Adrian," I said. "She doesn't need reprimanding."

Holly looked at me in surprise. "Who *are* you?"

Amber smiled. "She's the woman I'm in love with."

I don't know why I took the number, Amber's journal read. I couldn't stop myself from going back to it. *I could never cheat on Meagan. I've never wanted anyone but her. Zeppo brought that woman here and I think Adrian was right, I think Zeppo did it on purpose. Maybe even told Nicole how lonely I've been feeling and encouraged the whole thing. I don't think it was his intention to hurt Meagan, he's just the type of person who would believe I deserved to have someone on the side. He doesn't understand how much I love her.*

It was just nice having someone to talk to. Meagan and I talk, but we don't talk anymore. Our conversations are completely superficial, like we're both afraid if it goes too deep our words could end up hurting each other. Nicole was talking to me. That's why I took the number, I think, because a part of me just wanted to talk. I told her I love Meagan and she said, "I'm sure you do, but love isn't always easy, is it?" and I thought I would cry. I looked across at Meagan and she was gone and I felt like I'd made her disappear. Then she came back and smiled at me and I thought I'd never felt more ashamed in my life. I was wrong. The real shame would come later when we were sitting around the table and the topic turned to cheating.

She came back to me then. For ten minutes she came back and she spoke in that way that only Meagan can-- backwards logic. She sat there and rationalized the situation, making herself the villainess and me, the person who only deserved to be loved. She was trying to understand why I might do such a thing. I could rip out her heart and she would only try to understand why. That *shamed me. The fact that she would allow me to hurt her if she thought it would give me something more that what she thinks she can offer.*

I don't know how she does that. She'd rather let the pain rip her from the inside out than to share it with me and she'd rather let me cause her even more pain than to deny me anything. A part of her hates Josh for what he did to Jenna but she would allow me to do the same thing to her. She wants so much for me to be happy that it makes me sad.

She said all those things, defending me in my wrongness, protecting me even from Adrian, and when Holly asked "who are you?"... I knew. She was Meagan. And then she was gone again. But she had come back for a minute. She had let me see inside just to remind me of how fully capable she was of loving me, how she'd still do anything for me, and then as easily as she had reappeared, she disappeared. I could see the change happening on her face and I wanted to shake her and cry, "Don't go, Meagan. Please baby, stay with me", and all those things you say when you're watching someone die. But I didn't say those things. Instead I watched the real Meagan go back into hiding. I watched her eyes shift to something dull and defeated, saw the vacancy behind them, and I knew she was already gone.

Again I closed the book in my lap. It was close to 2a.m. and I sat by myself in the dark living room and cried. I burned a stick of incense and smoked a joint laced with the tiniest bit of cocaine. Holly had given it to me the night before when the awful thing almost happened and it was a fat, potent mixture of weed, hash oil and coke. It clouded my head quickly, and dried the tear ducts so that I couldn't cry now even if I wanted to. The effect was a small kindness I was grateful to be given. I didn't want to cry when I did what I knew I had to do. I wanted to speak easily and give her the truth as I saw it.

With the book still in my lap, I rolled into the bedroom, slid it under my pillow, and maneuvered myself into bed beside her. She rolled toward me and I held her, remembering what we'd once been to each other and what we could never be again. I wouldn't be cruel. That wasn't the way this time. I would tell her what I needed to say, and when she was gone, I would finally heed the call of the voice in my head and depart this world in the most dignified manner I could muster. I wasn't cut out to be a cripple. End of story. I didn't want a wake, or a funeral, or Jenna trying to contact my spirit with the help of one of her weirdo friends, I just wanted to go. They could do what they wanted with my body, bury it, donate it to science, make ashes of it; I didn't care. I would no longer be in it.

"Amber?" I gave her a small, gentle shake.

Her eyes fluttered and she pressed closer. "What is it? Are you alright?"

"I'm okay," I whispered. "I just need to talk to you about something."

"Now?"

"I'm sorry, but yes."

Sleepily, she nodded into my neck. "Go ahead."

I stroked her cheek. "I think you should move out."

"No, thanks."

"Don't be flippant."

"Don't tell me to leave."

I reached across the bed and turned on the lamp. "Listen to me."

"I thought you said you'd forgiven me for last night."

"This isn't about last night. It's about what we've become and it's not fair for you to have to live this way."

"What way?"

"You know what way. I think you should leave."

"Do you love me, Meagan?"

"Yes."

"See, if you wanted me to leave, that was the wrong answer. If you honestly didn't love me anymore, I'd go. But not like this. Not because you have some sort of guilt tied up in your legs."

"Why are you making this more difficult?"

"Because I don't ever want to be without you again."

I sighed. "I'll come for you. If I ever walk again, I promise, I'll come find you wherever you are." It was a lie. I knew I'd be dead.

She snuggled up to me. "Well, you won't have to look too hard because I'll be right here. I'm not leaving you, Meagan.

Get a court order."

I snickered. Then I felt tears stinging the backs of my eyes and realized, sadly, that the joint hadn't been strong enough to keep them away for long. "Why are you doing this?"

She looked up at me. "Because when we were apart I spent every day wishing you still loved me, still wanted me. Even when I was with Gwynne all I ever really wanted was for you to one day come to me and tell me you still loved me." She shrugged. "And I'm happy with you."

That was *her* lie. I pulled the notebook out from under my pillow and handed it to her. "Those aren't the words of someone who's happy. I'm sorry I invaded your privacy. I thought it was your poetry and when I realized it wasn't, I couldn't put it down."

"Meagan, those are just thoughts."

"Yes."

"No, you don't understand. Did you read it? *All* of it?"

"Yes."

"Then how could you not see how many times it says I love you? Or that I've only wanted you? Don't pick and choose what you want to see. If you're going to take it in, then take it *all* in."

"I have. But you don't know me, Amber. Not anymore."

"Then let me know you. Show me who you are now."

I gave a bitter laugh. Shook my head. "I don't even know who I am now. You're right, I'm slipping away. I'm sorry but I think maybe I left us both a long time ago."

She sat up and there were tears in her eyes. "No, Meagan, don't say that. You can fight it. Nothing takes you down, remember? You're the strongest person I know, don't let this beat you. Please. Fight it, Meagan. Come back to me."

"I can't," I whispered. "I'm not the strong one, Amber, you are. I crumble. I run away. You don't know what all I do to block out the pain."

"Then let me fight for you."

"That's not even possible. You can't give me back the use of my legs or, at this point, my mind even. Maybe you could give me back my soul but I'd prefer if you kept that because it's safer with you now. Just let me go, Amber. Save yourself and let me go."

"No. If you go down, I go down. It's your choice, Meagan. You can drag me to the bottom with you or you can fight and save us both."

"Don't force me to make that decision."

She shrugged. "It's up to you, Meagan. Do we live together or die together?"

I looked at her meaningfully. "I know where I'm going, Amber, but you can't come with me."

Suddenly she sprang from the bed, came around the other side, folded her arms in front of her chest, and glared down at me. "Where is it?" she growled.

"Where's what?"

"You're on drugs. Lots of them, I think. Now you tell me where they are."

"I'm not---"

"Don't fuck with me. You think I don't see the difference in you? You read the notebook. You *know* I see it."

I looked away. "Just let it go."

"You just sat here and calmly told me you're going to kill yourself! Well, you're not. Do you understand me? And you're not seeing Adrian anymore either--since I'm sure he's the one who's been giving you the drugs--and you're not going to fucking die!"

I glared up at her. "You won't tell me who I will or will not see."

"I just did. You're through with him."

"I'm not on drugs." The words sounded hollow, even to me.

"Nosebleeds. Teeth-grinding." She checked off the symptoms on her fingers. "That dumb, vacant look in your eyes. Jenna had your number. Oh, she had it, alright. You're as fucking wired as Adrian is and we both know it. Now you're going to tell me where the drugs are or I'll turn this whole apartment upside down until I find them."

I shrugged. "Go ahead."

"You're not gonna tell me?"

"There's nothing to tell."

"Fine. Then I'll start with your dresser."

Panic whipped through me. My whole stash was in that

dresser and if she found it I wouldn't be able to kill myself. I didn't own a gun, I couldn't stand up to hang myself, and I was afraid of knives, so slashing my wrists was out of the question too. I needed those drugs. I needed them so I could take away the pain once and for all.

Amber started at the top, yanking one dresser drawer out after another. Clothes flew about the room. She dug through them, searching. The third drawer crashed to the floor. Then the fourth. There was only one left and the terror gripped my heart.

"Oh, just stop," I said in a bored tone that belied my inner panic. Amber ignored me and yanked out the last drawer and tipped it over. The wooden box fell out on top of a pile of clothes.

"What's this?" she said angrily. She snapped open the lid and rummaged around inside. "Weed, hash, coke, *three* bottles of pills. Jesus Christ, you're a one-woman pharmacy."

"Put that back," I demanded.

"I don't think so." She darted for the bathroom and another cold rush of panic whipped through me. I knew what she meant to do. The same thing narcs always did when they found drugs.

"Amber, don't," I called after her. There was the sound of the toilet flushing. "Shit!" I threw myself from the bed and toppled to the floor. I had one other vial in my purse and I had to cross the room and get to it before she came back. The toilet flushed again. I dragged my way across the floor. Another flush. Rage in my head.

"You fucking bitch!" I screamed, digging around in the bottom of my bag. "You're paying for every last bit of that!" My head ached and I felt the familiar pulsing of a migraine behind my left eye, like something was trying to poke the eyeball out from the inside.

Amber returned to the bedroom just as my fingers closed around the vial. She looked down at me on the floor and I jammed my fist between my stomach and the hardwood.

"*There's more?*" she screamed. She dropped down beside me and reached under my stomach. I struggled against her but she was stronger than me now and her fingers met up with mine and began prying them apart.

"Give it to me."

"Fuck you."

The vial slipped from my grasp and I slammed my body on top of it. Amber found it and yanked it out. She struggled to her feet and held it under the light streaming in from the hallway. She tilted the bottle and watched the tiny crystals slide to the right behind the orange glass.

"Oh God, Meagan," she cried. "What have you been doing to yourself?"

"Just give it back," I pleaded. I felt myself growing desperate and trying to rationalize an irrational action. "People do coke all the time. Look at all the people down at Zeppo's gallery. I control it, alright? Give it back." I wrapped myself around her ankles and kissed the tops of her feet like I worshipped her. A statue of a goddess. What she thought I'd do to Jenna. I thought I might be scratching the floor with my nails and she stared down at me, as if realizing for the first time she really didn't know who I was.

"Please, Amber. Please, just give it to me."

She burst into tears and fell to her knees in front of me, the vial clutched tightly in her fist. "Why, Meagan? Why would you do this to yourself?"

She knew why. The pressure built in my head and filled my entire body.

"I just want it to go away," I sobbed. I fell forward into her arms and buried my face in her neck. "Please, Amber, just let me make it go away."

Her face pressed into my hair, arms tightened around my back. "I can't," she whispered.

"You can," I wailed. "Just give me the vial and it will go away. For a little while, it will go away."

She brushed back my hair and pressed her lips to my temple. "Baby, you're paralyzed. Drugs can't make that go away."

She called me baby and I thought I'd rip the hair right out of the back of her head. At some point she had taken to calling me baby and the word infuriated me. It made me feel as if she did not mean it as a term of endearment at all, but rather, was reminded of an actual baby when she looked at me in my deteriorated state. I had never told her how much it bothered me. I couldn't choke out the words.

She rocked me in her arms and I cried into her neck. "Say you'll get clean, Meagan," she pleaded. "Fight with me. I'll help you. *Please.*"

"I--I don't want to."

"You do!" she cried. "I know you, you'll never stop fighting."

"Amber, I can't. It's too late. Just go away."

"I'm not leaving you." Her tone was strong but she was crying. "Now say you're going to fight this. Tell me, Meagan. Tell me how nothing beats Meagan Summers. You refused to die once before, refuse it again. Come back to me, please." She was sobbing now. Rocking me. "Please, just let me help you. Let me be your friend instead of Adrian. Let me be the one you turn to. I want to be the one who holds you again." I felt her tears on my cheek. "Please, Meagan. I never ask you for anything but I'm begging you now. If you won't do it for yourself, then do it for me. I need you. You don't think so, but I do."

"Amber---"

"Please, say it. I can't bear to watch you slipping away anymore."

"Okay," I whispered. I didn't see how I had much choice in the matter now anyway. She'd flushed my drugs, and if I thought I was getting more I was shit out of luck because she knew who my supplier was and she was never going to let Adrian near me again.

She cupped my face in her hands, surprised that I would give in so easily. "Okay? You mean it?"

I nodded. Let out a slow breath of air. "Maybe I have one last fight left in me."

"You do, baby." She crushed me to her. "I know you do."

I wasn't sure how long we stayed on the floor like that but eventually Amber reached for the phone and had me call Adrian. She stood beside me and watched me punch in the numbers. Listened to me speak in hushed tones. I told Adrian I was sorry but I couldn't see him anymore.

"Come on, babe," he said. "We're friends."

"I know but I'm going to die, Adrian. If I don't help myself, I'm gonna die."

"You're not that bad. I tease you about the junkie stuff."

"I'm sorry. You know I love you but I have to get control of my mind again. I feel so sick. I have to get well."

"And you think that's gonna be easy?"

"No, I think I'm gonna suffer like I've never suffered before but I have to try." I looked up at Amber. "I'm tired of dying, or wanting to die. I'm sorry Adrian, but I can't be your friend right now. Maybe when I'm well."

Amber shook her head at me. As far as she was concerned I would never see Adrian again. She'd end her friendship with Zeppo if she had to.

"Goodbye, Adrian."

I hung up the phone and pressed my palm to my forehead. I was starting over, *again*. I wasn't sure I could do it.

Chapter 10

The symptoms came on fast and furious. Amber had wanted me to check myself into a rehab clinic but I'd refused, maintaining that I would handle this problem the way I did all others, on my own. I was ashamed. I didn't want anyone to know how sick I'd become, or how close to the edge I'd pressed, and disappearing into a rehab program would only exasperate my mother's belief that I could not be left alone in my paralyzed state. I wasn't alone. I had Amber. I thought I would die.

Cocaine withdrawal was agony like I'd never known. The sweating, the vomiting, the constant nausea. But none of those things could compare to the tremors that made me shake on the bed and beg for a snort while Amber held me and cried. It wasn't just the coke my body was missing. It was the pills, the pot, the hash, and in the end maybe even the alcohol. I was drifting on a sea of illness and Amber was my anchor. The only bright spot at the bottom of the water and I had to swim toward it to get healthy again. For the second time in our lives she was calling me back from the dead.

She didn't tell my family, only Jenna, who took the news surprisingly well considering how I'd made her feel when she'd first suspected. Ken showed up to check on me one day and Amber sent him away, telling him I was at physical therapy while I remained in the bedroom straining to hear their conversation. She betrayed me to no one and that only made me more determined to heal.

By the third day I felt insane. The tremors were slamming through my body and I bounced against the headboard begging Amber to call Adrian. I sobbed.

"Please, Amber. It hurts!"

She pulled me into her arms. "I know, baby. Just hang on. We just have to get you past the rough stuff."

"I...can't...do it!" My teeth ground together and I thought they would crush against each other and crumble in my mouth.

She stroked my hair. "Tell me who you are."

A groan escaped the wellspring of pain within me. "I don't know."

"Tell me what Seamus calls you."

"Nasty-mouthed...little bitch."

She chuckled. "He calls you Meggie. That's who you are. Go back to her."

"I need Adrian."

"Adrian doesn't exist anymore."

I felt my heart drop. "Is he dead?"

"No. Zeppo finally got the good sense to kick him out. He's gone."

A sudden guilt turned up in my heart, weighted with the agony. "Where will he go?"

"We don't care."

She squeezed me closer as another violent spasm whipped through me and I felt like she was pulling the sickness out of me and taking it into her own, much stronger, form. My upper body stiffened. My back ground against her chest as a knife sliced into my forehead. I thought I would go blind with the pain and my eyes squeezed closed in response.

"It...fucking...hurts."

Tenderly, she brushed back my bangs. "Maybe a rehab program---"

Panic. "No! No hospitals. I can't go back there. They'll lock me up. Please Amber, don't let them do that to me. They'll think I'm crazy and they'll.....lock me away!"

"Shh. Okay, baby. No one's locking you away."

Another jolt. Fire in my stomach. Hungry spiders crawling around my veins in search of their poison.

"Can you please not call me that?"

"Baby?" She asked.

"It hurts me. It makes me feel weak." The devil was at the door and he was waving a syringe. "F-Fuck you!" I yelled. "I don't do needles!" He disappeared.

"That's right, Meagan," Amber said, rubbing my arms. "Push him away and tell me who you are."

He wasn't real. We both knew he wasn't real but I knew what Amber was doing, she was trying to call me home. Forcing me to remember myself. "Tell me what Jenna sees when she looks at you."

"Yang." My mind clutched onto the word.

"What?"

"Yang to her yin. Her counterpart."

"That's right. What does Sammy see?"

I glanced at the doorway. No devil. Felt the sweat on my face. My body lurched forward. She pulled me back. "Tell me what Sammy sees." She was reminding me of what I was to others. Trying to tell me my life was important.

"His Aunt."

"And what do I see, Meagan?"

I started to cry. "A drug addict. A cripple. A pathetic disease."

"No, I see the woman I love. She's smart and she's beautiful, and most of all, she's strong."

I felt icicles creeping over my body and she wrapped the comforter tightly around us. Held a glass of water to my mouth and I sipped it slowly, pulled away and shook my head when I realized it made me want to throw up.

"One last question, Meagan. Tell me who Zoe would have seen."

My head ached. She wasn't supposed to mention Zoe. "She's dead," I whispered.

"Yes."

"She was...supposed to be with us."

"Yes. And what would she have seen when she looked at you?"

"I can't." It hurt. It hurt so badly.

"Tell me, Meagan. Force out the word because you've been holding on to it too long and it's been destroying you."

"I could have had an abortion," I rationalized.

"But you didn't. You wanted her and you lost her. Grieve for that loss, Meagan. Let it go with the drugs. Say the word. What would you have been?" She was pushing it out of me.

"*Her mother*," I sobbed. The tears poured out of my eyes like someone had turned a tap on behind them. "I was supposed to be her mother!" I rocked back and forth. "I was supposed to....*take care of her*. And I killed her!"

"You didn't kill her." Amber rocked with me. Cried with me. "You didn't kill her. You've been killing yourself and

I'm so sorry I didn't see it sooner. Maybe I didn't want to see."

I wiped my eyes. Fought for control. "You're apologizing for my stupidity?"

"Yes. It's gonna be okay though. Jenna's gonna come in the morning with a bunch of remedies her herbalist recommended and she'll show me how to administer them. Tonight is the last of the big suffering, okay? We can make it till morning, right?"

I buried my face in her arm and sobbed. "I'm so sorry. It wasn't supposed to be this way. We were supposed to be happy."

"And we will be again. I told you, Meagan, we're in this together."

"Why? All I do is hurt you. I don't know how you can even stand to look at me."

"I love to look at you." She managed a tired chuckle. "Mind you, you're not so attractive at the moment."

I laughed in spite of myself. "Tell me anyway."

"I love you." She kissed my head. "You're my twin soul and I love you."

I shivered. "I don't know what that means."

"Neither do I but it's the only way I can describe what you are to me. You're that part that goes missing when you're gone. I'm only whole when I'm with you."

I pulled the comforter tighter so that it was squeezing us in, blocking out the cold that kept wanting to slide over me even as I sweated. "Alchemy," I said. "It's alchemical, us. Maybe it's viral."

"As in a virus?"

I nodded as my body continued to ache. "A long time ago---" My body lurched again. She pulled me down again. "I used to tell my therapist about the way you would creep into me. I used to tell her I wanted you out. Now I'm numb from the drugs and I wish I could feel you in me like that again."

"I'm in you, Meagan," she soothed. "Just open your heart and feel me because I'm there. I haven't gone anywhere."

I smiled, weakly. "You're as crazy as I am."

"Yes, because we're one."

I breathed in her skin and knew I would have died without her. I wondered how many times loving her would save my life and once again praised whatever God had sent her to me.

"I've got you, Meagan. I won't let you go."

Where in the world had she come from?

The next morning Jenna arrived with over a dozen remedies. Teas, tinctures, oils to drop in the bath. Some, like passionflower and goldenseal, were mixed into small bottles her herbalist had prepared to promote sleep and ease the headaches. Peppermint and sage were for the dizziness. Anise, ginseng and ginger for the nausea. Scented candles perfumed with oils to promote relaxation and small sachets made of cheesecloth and filled with herbs and flowers to place in the tub with me, again to promote relaxation and sleep.

Then there were Jenna's own "special" remedies. Things like healing gemstones. She gave me a bloodstone to help overcome my depression and to enhance my body's natural vitality. She told me to satisfy whatever cravings I might have because that would be the bloodstone telling me what my body required. It occurred to me that what it probably required was cocaine. I kept the thought to myself and watched as Jenna placed a moss agate on the window sill. She said tonight would be a waning moon, which was conducive to "banishing" something. I was to imagine my problems decreasing, and between the combination of the stone and the power of the moon, they would do so and my anxieties would lessen. She gave me an empty velvet bag. "Have Amber put the stone in here in the morning," she said, "and don't use it again until you need it." I wanted to laugh. I pictured what Amber's face might look like when I told her to put away my healing stones and I wanted to laugh.

She brought me daffodils to cheer me up. Slipped a Goddess pentacle under my pillow so that I would have Her protection. She cleansed my aura and told me a chant to recite in my head because she knew I was too shy to chant out loud in front of Amber.

Lastly, she resorted to superstition. She hung a small piece of stained glass in the window to protect from evil. Jenna didn't believe in evil. What she considered evil was my longing for the drugs. Drugs came from the outside. The stained glass would keep them out.

"I know it sounds silly, Meagan. Just humor me, alright?"

She placed wind chimes on the fire escape for the same reason and left a small offering of bread and wine outside for the entities that would come to protect me.

I laughed. "Entities, my ass. You mean fairies."

Jenna giggled. "Shh, Amber will think we're crazy."

"She thinks we're crazy anyway. Did you see her face when you were cleansing my aura?"

She nodded. "Hers could use some cleansing too. Do you feel better?"

"You know, I think I do."

"Good. I have a talisman for you too." She pulled a small silver pendant out of her woven bag and slid it onto a chain. Placed the chain around my neck and showed me the pendant. It was an image of a Goddess. "This is Macha," she said. "She inspires the fighter within us, revels in battle. She is one of the three aspects of the war Goddess Badb. I haven't heard anything about her being a very kind Goddess, but kindness isn't what you need right now anyway. You want a warrior in your corner and Macha is certainly that."

"Thank you, Jenna." I stared down at the pendant. "Isn't there a Goddess of poets called Brighid?"

Jenna smiled. "You know more than you think you do. You want a symbol of that Goddess for Amber, don't you?" I nodded and she pulled something else out of her bag. "I couldn't find a pendant but I did find this statue."

I stared at it in disbelief. "Jenna, how could you have known I'd say that?"

She shrugged. "Call it a guess. Anyway, I picked up this little statue of Brighid in an occult shop. Same place I got your pendant. Do you want to give it to her now?"

"She's in the living room crying, isn't she?"

"Yes."

"Because of me. Because I hurt her."

Jenna sat on the bed beside me. "Because she loves you."

"How do I keep screwing it up, Jenna?"

"Easy. You're Meagan."

I laughed. "Thanks. Thanks a lot. Can you help me into

that chair? I wanna go out there and see her."

"I don't know, Meagan. You're still pretty weak."

I smiled at her. "What will I do if you don't help me, Jenna?"

She sighed. "You'll throw yourself from the bed and drag your way into the living room."

"Exactly."

Wrapping her arm around my waist, she pulled me to the edge of the bed. "Okay, come on maniac." She lifted me to my feet, helped me into the wheelchair, and wheeled me into the living room where Amber sat, staring out the window with tears in her eyes and a steaming mug of chamomile tea warming her hands. She wiped her eyes when she saw me. Forced a cheery note into her voice.

"Hey. What are you doing out of bed?"

Jenna tousled my hair playfully and did a vanishing act into the kitchen. Amber watched her leave. My arms felt terribly weak but I forced them to roll the wheels on my chair and angle me closer to Amber.

"I'm sorry I've hurt you with all of this. I never wanted to hurt you. I only wanted to love you but apparently I can't even do that right. Don't feel guilty if you want to leave, Amber. I would certainly understand. I'm a mess. But I have Jenna--and my family if I want them--you don't have to feel obligated to stay. I didn't lock Ken into my nightmare and I won't do it to you either. Maybe someday I'll be normal again. Until then, I understand if you can't handle to be around me."

She started to cry and, weakly, I pulled her into my lap and held her. "It's okay. I promise it will be okay. You can start a new life. You're everything anyone would want in another person and I know you'll do fine. You can move past this and forget the nightmare I've allowed you to be a part of for far too long. I was selfish. I wanted you and I wouldn't allow myself to consider what being with me might do to you. Every time the thought came up I pushed it away and I'm sorry for that. I'm sorry I let my desire for you cloud my judgment."

"I don't want to leave you," she whispered. "I just want us back."

"I'll probably never walk again."

"I don't care. It's not your legs I'm in love with."

"I thought I had great legs?" I teased.

She gave a little laugh. "See, that's why I can't leave you. Every part of your body is aching and screaming right now---"

"Except my legs."

Another laugh. "Right, except your legs. But the point is, you're in so much pain and *still* you're trying to make me laugh. How could I leave someone who makes it her sole purpose in life to get me to smile? Even in the worst of circumstances? Just keep your heart and your mind with me, Meagan. That's all I want."

"You're masochistic, do you know that?" I squeezed her closer. "Okay, we're in this together. No more shutting you out or moping around about my legs. If you're willing to accept what I've become, I guess I should too."

"Give her your present," Jenna said from behind us.

I shook my head into Amber's neck. "She's always sneaking up on people."

Amber laughed.

"I don't sneak up," Jenna said.

"And she has supersonic hearing."

"That I do have." She crossed the room. "It's in the pocket of your chair."

"Do you move things around telekinetically too?"

"No. I used my hand. Give it to her."

Reaching into the pocket, I pulled out the small statue and handed it to Amber. "Jenna's psychic powers keep growing stronger. She found this in a store and somehow knew I'd want it for you. It's Brighid, Goddess of poets and creativity. Very beloved in Ireland. She has a shrine in Kildare."

Amber stared at the statue. "It's for inspiration?"

"Yes."

"Thank you. I love it."

"Thank Jenna, she's the one who found it."

"Only because you told me to."

"And there she goes saying strange things again," I joked.

"That's cause I've been taking your drugs."

I laughed but Amber said "Jenna", like she couldn't believe Jenna would mention taking drugs to a person suffering withdrawal.

"Joke about it, Amber," Jenna said. "When you take away the seriousness, few things are as funny as little Miss Clean-Living Corporate over here being a drug addict. Didn't you once tell me she freaked out when you smoked a joint with Basil?"

"Basil." I laughed "I wonder whatever happened to him. And I didn't freak, I cleaned."

"Which means you were freaking out," Jenna said. "Cleaning this room and freaking out."

I started laughing, then the effort suddenly turned my stomach and I patted Amber's leg. "You have to get up, honey, I think I'm gonna be sick."

Jenna grabbed the handles on the back of my chair and speedily wheeled me toward the bathroom. By the time we got there, the feeling had passed.

"Forget it."

"Forget it?"

"It's gone now."

"Headache?"

"Yes."

"Okay, you're going back to bed and I'll make you some tea."

"Will Amber be okay?"

Jenna smiled. "She'll be fine. I'll get her to lay on the couch for awhile. She hasn't slept in three days."

"Oh." My heart ached.

"It's okay, Meagan. No one ever died from lack of sleep. I'll spend the afternoon."

"What about Sammy?"

"Your parents have him."

"Jenna, you didn't---"

"No. They don't know anything."

"Thank you."

Jenna helped me into bed where I quickly passed out after having only two sips of whatever horribly sweet-tasting tea she'd given me. When I awoke it was to the feel of something wet being brushed against my forehead. I peered up through half-closed eyes. "What are you doing now? Anointing me with an anti-hex oil?"

She giggled. "You were sweating in your sleep. I'm wiping it away with a damp cloth."

"Amber?"

"Sleeping."

"Okay." My eyes fell closed again.

Amber and I spent the afternoon sleeping while Jenna scurried back and forth, checking on each of us in turn. By evening I was feeling slightly better. Less shaky. I turned in the bed to find a cup of soup on the nightstand. Still hot. As if Jenna had known exactly when I'd awaken. I reached for the soup, felt the liquid burn my tongue and coughed at the sting. Jenna's head poked in the room.

"You alright?"

I nodded. "Amber?"

Jenna shook her head. "Will you stop worrying about Amber? I told you she's fine." She came into the bedroom smirking. "Don't tell her, but I cleansed her aura while she was sleeping."

"I heard that," Amber's voice said from behind Jenna's head.

Jenna's hands covered her mouth and she giggled. "Well, how do you feel?"

Amber shrugged. "The sleep did me good." She wouldn't give Jenna the satisfaction and I smiled. The only unconventional thing about Amber was that she was gay. No new age mumbo-jumbo for her. She scoffed at things like reflexology and feng shui. The closest she came to alternative anything was that she was willing to believe in the healing properties of herbs and that was only because their benefits had been proven. She wanted hardcore facts before she believed in anything other than what she'd always known.

Except for the ring. In that case she'd allowed herself to believe. She'd believed in the symbolism because I wanted her to believe in it and because it meant so much to me. She looked out the window and came to sit on the bed beside me.

"Why is there a half-eaten loaf of bread on the fire escape?" she questioned.

"Half-eaten?" The words surprised me.

Jenna smirked. "Birds, Meagan."

I nodded. "Right."

Amber looked at me quizzically. "What did you think?"

I shrugged. "Birds."

She grinned. "You're lying."

I pushed my fingers through my hair. "Fine. Fairies, okay? I thought fairies."

Amber fell back against the bed howling with laughter. Jenna smirked again and grabbed her bag from the window sill.

"I have to take off now but I'll come back in the morning. Amber, if she gets those tremors again give her that tea I showed you how to make, light the purple incense, and maybe massage her upper body, particularly her temples and the back of her neck. That should relax her again."

"Got it," Amber said.

"Jenna, thank you," I said. "You know, for everything."

"No problem," she replied, and bounced out the door.

From then on the symptoms eased. The vomiting stopped and the nausea dissipated. I needed less sleep. The tremors still came but they arrived in short spurts and left more quickly. The imaginary devil did not return. The sweating came to an end and I was beginning to feel more and more like my old self. Amber was pleased with my progress. I was recovering quickly and she was happy to see me "coming back to her". I thought I was happy to be back.

Then one night it happened. I had been clean for three weeks, a lifetime in addict-speak, and virtually symptom-free. Amber was asleep beside me and I stared at the ceiling, once again praising whatever deity had sent her to me. I felt an itch at the bottom of my foot. The toes wiggled in response and my breath drew up short. I stared at my foot. I wasn't seeing what I thought I was seeing because I'd accepted my future as a paraplegic and this was impossible.

The itch came again. The toes wiggled again as if to mock me for my stupidity, and I could swear that *this time* I felt them move. Fear gripped my heart. The foot pivoted forward and I burst into tears. Shook Amber awake.

"I'm hallucinating," I sobbed. "I don't know why it's happening now but I'm losing my mind."

"Meagan, what's wrong?"

I couldn't stop sobbing. "It's mocking me. My...my

foot. I keep seeing it *move!*"

Amber glanced down at the bed, looked back at my face, then her head whipped down again, as if she only just realized what she'd actually seen. A gasp escaped her lips.

"Meagan, you are moving it! You're moving your foot!"

"No, I'm hallucinating."

She crawled to the bottom of the bed and lifted my leg. "Well, I'm not hallucinating and that foot is moving."

Hope sparked in my heart. "Are--Are you sure?"

"See for yourself." Grabbing my arms, she helped me sit forward and together we watched in stunned silence as the foot pivoted back and forth at the ankle.

"Can you feel it?" she asked, excitedly.

"I...yes, I can! Oh my God, *I'm* moving it Amber, it's not happening involuntarily. I'm really moving it!"

Amber jumped up and down on her knees and I focused my attention on the other foot. Concentrated. And then that one started to move. I was shocked.

"How am I doing this? I don't understand. Why couldn't I do it before?"

Amber shook her head. "Maybe it was all the drugs. Maybe you've had the feeling back in your feet for awhile but you never noticed because the drugs were making you numb."

That seemed unlikely, but I grasped onto it nonetheless, wanting any reason to hate the drug I had loved. "That must be it," I said, and continued twisting my feet round and round like Linda Blair's head.

Amber threw herself on top of me and attacked my face with kisses. I kissed back. Fervently. Passionately. Like in the days before the accident.

"You're gonna walk again, Meagan!" she cried. "You're really gonna walk!"

"Had you given up hope?" I asked.

"No," she said quickly. Too quickly.

I laughed. "You're such a liar."

"Well, you gave up hope too," she said, giving me one of her playful shoves.

Remarkable how one quick twist of fate can change your whole perspective on life. Suddenly Amber didn't see me as fragile anymore; she wasn't afraid the slightest touch could break me. She was looking at me and her eyes said *Meagan,* not *baby.*

I kissed her cheek and pushed myself to the side of the bed, letting my legs dangle off the mattress and taking a preparatory breath.

"What are you doing?" Amber asked, alarmed. She jumped off the bed and stood before me. Soon I would be able to do that too.

"I'm gonna stand up," I said, bouncing excitedly.

Her arms shot out to shield me. "No---" Her protest fell short when she saw my arched eyebrows and her head cocked in thought. "Are you sure?"

"Yes."

"Okay, but let me help you."

I waved away her hands. "No, I'm gonna do it myself."

"No Meagan, you'll--"

"What? Hurt myself? Small price to pay to be able to walk."

Grinning, she stepped to my left and I knew she was readying herself in case I should fall. "Alright," she said, agreeably. "Go for it."

My hands pressed against the mattress and I pushed myself to my feet. I stood. For the first time in months, I stood. Felt the cold hardwood beneath my feet. The tiny grooves in the wooden planks. Then I quickly lost the balance I never quite had and my body toppled to the right, where Amber couldn't catch me. I fell to the floor and she dropped down beside me.

"Are you okay?" She helped me sit up.

My head shook in disbelief. "I think I hurt my leg."

Amber panicked. Her hands groped my thigh and I was stunned to find I could *feel* it. "Oh God, I knew I shouldn't have let you stand up. Where? Where does it hurt? Shit! It was too soon. I'm sorry, Meagan, I'm so sorry."

She was taking the blame for something she didn't realize was a good thing. A short flash of pain stabbed me in the calf like a charley horse and I gasped. "Oh my God, I really did hurt my leg!"

Now she was seriously panicked. "I'll call Ken--or should I call an ambulance?" She moved to dart away from me but I latched onto her ankle, laughing like a maniac.

"Amber, wait" I squealed. "Listen to what I'm saying. *I hurt my leg.* Just think about what that means for a minute before you race off to call the paramedics."

She stopped. Stared down at me and I watched the realization dawn on her face. "It means you can feel it!" She screamed. She dropped down beside me again and crushed me to her. We were both laughing hysterically, crying simultaneously.

"Now you're catching on," I said. "I'm gonna be walking again in no time."

"And let me guess, you're gonna start practicing right now."

"Nope."

Her eyes widened. "No?"

I gave a wicked grin. "There's something I've missed even more than walking."

She grinned back. "Making love to me?"

"Do you really need to ask?" I teased.

"Yes, after all this time I feel I do."

I laughed. "You'll never have to ask me again, Amber, I promise you that. In fact, you'll be begging me to leave you alone."

I pushed myself to my side then up to my knees, the lower half of my legs folding under me remarkably easily, and I sat back on my ankles like anyone else in the world. Amber gasped at the sight of me.

"Meagan, you're on your knees!"

"Good. That position will be helpful."

She fell back against the floor roaring with laughter. "Did anyone ever tell you that you adjust to sudden change incredibly well? This is a miracle!"

"Yes."

"And you're more concerned with having sex."

I shrugged. "I'm being realistic. Even miracles take time. I'm overjoyed, believe me. I'm stunned. Maybe I'm in shock but I am rational enough to know that I won't be walking tonight. To me, that leaves only one other way to celebrate. It would be an insult to Deities everywhere if we didn't."

She couldn't stop laughing at me. "Why are you so

strange?"

"Because that's the person you're in love with. I'm back, Amber. Everything is coming back and I won't ever leave you like that again."

"You're gonna walk."

"I'm gonna walk."

"Meagan, you're gonna walk!"

The more she screamed it, the more real it became.

PART II

The intercom beside me buzzed in that annoying, distracting way. It buzzed twice. Two short stabs like a bee running out of steam. One that would fight before it hit the ground, dead. I could relate.

I set the author contracts I'd been reviewing on the corner of my desk and placed a pewter paperweight Jenna had given me on top. There wasn't any wind in the office but I used it anyway. I switched off the computer, picked up a letter opener and waited for the bubbly British voice.

"Sorry to disturb you, Meagan," Cynthia crackled through the intercom, "but you have a Jacob Ebstein on line one."

I pressed the red button with the end of the letter opener.

"Thank you, Cynthia," I said. Cynthia had been imported from *Natural Beauty's* London offices. "Any faxes come in from Cicely Bower while I've got you?"

I was expecting a synopsis from the first-time author Amber had convinced me to meet. "You'll like Cicely," she'd said, as if liking someone was conducive to publishing their work. We'd had a meeting and I was intrigued by her proposal and told her to fax me a synopsis to start. So far, no word.

"Nothing yet," Cynthia said.

I scratched my head. Didn't like people who were late. It showed a lack of professionalism. The fax was supposed to come yesterday and if it didn't come today that wasn't going to be good for Cicely. I didn't like people wasting my time. Especially some no-name author when I had bigger clients to deal with. Cicely would spare herself a lot of grief if she just sent the damn fax.

I pressed the button again. "Okay, Cynthia. Who did you say was on line one?"

The box crackled. Expensive piece of junk.

"Jacob Ebstein."

I reached for the receiver. Jacob Ebstein. The name

sounded vaguely familiar but I couldn't put a face to it. Another author Ted and I had stolen away from Hector Publications? Tied up in the files somewhere? Possibly. Hector was a sinking ship and Ted and I had gotten some of their biggest names. Amber had come first. Others followed. We did nothing unethical, only offered more money when their contracts with Hector expired and they came to us in search of a better deal. Amber had put the word out. Markham-Summers was a fresh new company offering larger advances, greater royalties, and we were open to new ideas. We didn't try to alter our writers' products to suit our booklist but we did demand the best. First-time authors were welcome but their books had to be able to catch our notice within the first few manuscript chapters. If needed we'd assign them an editor to work with or one of our regular freelancers most of whom had collaborated on several books and had even ghostwritten a few for a couple of local celebrities.

Markham-Summers wasn't about money. We made it, of course, but the greater idea was to publish good books. Sometimes odd books that would never see the light of day without unconventional support. In our first few months of operation we'd already gotten a reputation as the underdog's ticket into the world of publication, and in two cases, instant celebrity.

Magazine contacts became our greatest supporters. People we had encountered during our years turning *Natural Beauty* into a global rage rallied around us and the word was out: Markham-Summers was taking off like a rocket. It was good to be back in the game.

I pressed the button for line one.

"Meagan Summers," I said. Crisp. Business-like. It was the tone you needed to control a conversation from the second you opened your mouth.

"Meagan." A child's small, excited voice greeted my ears, surprising me.

"How may I help you?" I asked, curious to know why I was getting a call from a child and why he said my first name like we were old friends.

"I knew you'd come back," the voice squealed, happily. "I knew it."

"Excuse me?" This was a most peculiar call.

"Meagan, it's *Jacob*. Remember?"

I searched my memory but came up empty. "I'm sorry," I said. "You must be looking for someone else."

He giggled. "No, it's you. I saw your picture in the paper last week. You were coming out of a museum or something and the caption said: 'Among the guests included were Meagan Summers of Markham-Summers Publications', and a bunch of other names I didn't know."

I knew the picture he was talking about. Amber had clipped it from the *Times* society page, giggling about how well known I was becoming, and placed it in a photo album. I wasn't that well-known. Just a big fish in a medium sized pond. Outside of the publishing world few people knew me at all. I preferred it that way.

The picture had been taken outside a gallery where Zeppo's work was being displayed. Amber was in it. Zeppo was in it. So were Ted and the gallery owner. Everyone's name had been included but Amber focused on mine like it was the most important thing in the world. She took pride in everything I did; even when I did nothing but stand outside a gallery with her waiting for the valet to bring around our car. Leased Mercedes. Company write-off. To Amber's great relief I sold the Jaguar the minute I could walk. I never knew she'd hated it as much as I did.

"I still don't understand why you're calling me, Jacob," I said. There was something familiar about saying his name.

"I was burned in a fire a while back," he said.

"I'm sorry."

"Well, I'm okay now."

"Good." Something came to me. A quick flash. "Did I meet you at the hospital, Jacob?" I asked.

"Yes! You remember!"

"Not really."

"Think," he pressed. "Remember Mrs. Marten? Quin? Winston the snob?" He kept throwing names at me. "Linda? Victor? You have to remember us. You have to remember me! You were like my mom out there."

A cold fear gripped my heart and my nose twitched in response. Fingers shook around the letter opener. I thought I knew what he was implying and it terrified me. I'd been having nightmares lately, and they had something to do with when I was comatose.

"Out where?" I asked suspiciously.

"You know," came the response, "when we were ghosts."

My throat closed and a pressure slipped into my head. "Look, if this is some sort of sick prank---". Something Seamus had set up, perhaps? To get me back for Jackie?

"It's not," the boy said. "I swear. You said I made you think of Zoe."

The phone slipped from my ear and crashed against the top of the desk. I hadn't thought about Zoe in months. Now there was this strange, crazy kid bringing her up like he knew her. Like he knew me!

Cynthia popped her head in the door. "Everything alright, Meagan?" Soothing British tone.

A twitch pulsed behind my eyebrow. "Y-Yes. I just dropped the phone."

There was a taste of blood in my mouth. I'd bitten through the inside of my lower lip. Cynthia closed the door and I stared at the receiver that seemed to vibrate with the small voice inside that called my name. Slowly, I placed it back in its cradle and pressed my palm to my eyebrow to stop the nervous tic. I was going to be sick.

The intercom buzzed again.

"Jacob Ebstein again on line one," Cynthia said. "He said you got disconnected."

I snatched up the receiver in my shaking hand. "Listen kid, I don't know what you're trying to pull here-- "

"I'm not!"

"But you better stop calling this office right now. Do you hear me?" I slammed the phone.

Three minutes passed. Long enough for Jacob to mull over my words. The intercom buzzed again.

"*What*?" I snapped.

"Jacob Eb--- "

A thousand blades of panic sliced through my body. "For Christ's sake, Cynthia, tell that kid to fuck off!"

"I'll...umm...I'll get rid of him," Cynthia said,

nervously. I'd never yelled at her before and she sounded afraid.

Damn it! I pushed my chair away from the desk, stalked across the carpet, and swung open the door. Cynthia jumped in her seat. She glanced at me fearfully.

"I told him if he called again we'd contact his parents."

"Good."

The phone line lit up again and Cynthia's eyes shot to it nervously. It rang twice then stopped. My insides shook. If there was ever a time for a snort it was now. I swallowed back the urge. Bit my lip again.

"I'm sorry, Cynthia," I said noting the fearful way she continued to stare at me. Her eyes were locked on my face. I thought I looked pale. "I didn't mean to yell at you."

"It's okay," she relaxed.

"Listen, I'm gonna try to get some work done now so I'd appreciate if you didn't patch any more calls through, okay?"

She looked guilty. "Okay. Oh, and that fax came if you want it and Amber called earlier to ask if you could pick up some milk on the way home."

"Milk? It doesn't get any more domestic than that, does it?"

Cynthia chuckled and handed me the fax. I felt the beginnings of a headache. One I couldn't remedy with pills because I was a drug addict. Even aspirin was out of the question now. I had to settle for herbal remedies because the thought of taking anything else scared me. In high school I'd known a guy who was addicted to Advil! That showed me that anything was possible, so I switched to Jenna's naturopath.

I turned to go back in my office as the pain crept into my forehead and I pressed my palm against it.

"Cynthia, do we have any more of that lavender oil in the kitchenette?"

"Another headache?" she asked, sympathetically.

I groaned and dropped onto the striped couch across from her desk.

"I'll grab it," she said, and sprinted from the room.

Our offices were on the third floor of the building and the kitchenette, which we only used for making coffee or tea, was directly across the hall. Ted's office was kitty-corner to mine, equal in size, and next to the conference room. We both had doors that opened to Cynthia's reception area. The top floor belonged to the three of us. All other offices were on the first and second levels, several of them empty because we employed a small staff in the trendy brick building we'd purchased for next to nothing and had had restored and decorated to meet our downtown standards. We'd gone for funky over corporate. Young. Vivid colors and framed magazine covers on the walls, couches and coffee tables, instead of swivel chairs and glass tops. Minimal furnishings. Sort of a warehouse effect on the first two levels. Light hardwood floors throughout; giant slanted windows that overlooked the city below, and a sign on the front of the building that said, Markham-Summers Publications in thick silver letters. We'd moved downtown uptown, dropped an artist's building in the middle of all the multi-windowed skyscrapers and corporate monstrosities. It was part of our appeal. People came to us because we appeared down to earth while at the same time capable of getting the job done.

Cynthia returned with the bottle of oil and a bowl of sugar cubes. She twisted the cap and gave me the bottle. I rubbed the oil into my temples. Took a sugar cube. Placed three drops of oil on it and popped it in my mouth. It dissolved slowly.

"Thank you, Cynthia," I said.

"No problem."

I went in the bathroom to brush my teeth. Had to brush your teeth a lot when you were taking your medicine on lumps of sugar. Then I went back in my office, locked the door, sat behind my desk and stared out the window.

Victor. Quin. The names pressed a definite fear around my heart. Terrified me. Turned me to ice and I felt as if someone were pressing my back against a glacier that was freezing me from the outside in. I shivered. The office was suddenly freezing, but the thermostat said sixty-eight.

"Are you cold, Cynthia?" I asked, pressing the button for the intercom. I figured the thermostat was broken. That happened in old buildings.

"Actually, I find it quite stuffy in here, Meagan," she said. Was that because she was a Brit who liked things chilly? "I could come in and turn up the heat if you like."

"No." It was definitely me. "Maybe I'm just coming

down with something."

By three o'clock I hadn't gotten a bit of work done and I could take the cold no longer. I felt like I'd been hit by a snowstorm and only wanted to get home and soak in a long hot bath.

"Leaving for the day?" Cynthia asked, when I stepped into the reception area and passed her desk.

I grabbed my coat and purse from the closet. "Yeah. Listen, if Ted doesn't need you anymore today why don't you knock off early too? Enjoy a long weekend."

"Thank you. Ted left so I think maybe I will."

I smiled sweetly. "Sorry again, Cynthia. I'll see you on Monday."

It was Amber who had helped me learn how to walk again. After those first clumsy steps, it was just a matter of weeks. Derek helped me strengthen my legs and when I returned from therapy in the afternoons I'd practice walking. I fell a lot at first. Got a lot of bruises and scratches. Each time Amber panicked, afraid I would damage my spine again when she wasn't around and she'd come home to find me paralyzed on the floor. The doctors said my spine was fine. There was no reason I couldn't stumble as much as anyone else. It was a miracle. A medical wonder. Derek and I laughed when I told him.

I kept my recovery to myself. The only people who knew I was getting well were the only people who mattered-- Amber and Jenna. They were the ones who'd seen me through the paralysis, the drug addiction, and they were the only ones I wanted involved in my recovery. I owed them my life, especially Amber.

"Promise you won't try to walk," she'd plead, every time she had to leave the apartment even for a minute.

I always promised and it was always a lie. I crossed my fingers behind my back so it didn't count. Sorry babe, but nothing is keeping me down.

One day she came home to find me with a scraped

elbow and a band-aid on my forehead.

"You promised," she cried, lifting my arm to inspect the damage. "What happened?"

I shrugged and gave her a sheepish grin. "Had a disagreement with the coffee table," I said. "Don't worry though, I taught her a lesson." It was tipped over on the Oriental rug where I had thrown it in frustration. She laughed.

I locked my wheels and pushed myself to my feet. "Okay, help me walk now."

"I think you've probably walked enough today," she said.

"Fine, but if you don't help me I'll just do it myself and I don't mind telling you that coat rack's been eyeballing me for days. He wants a piece of me. I can tell."

Another laugh. "Okay, but one lap around the apartment and that's it."

"Yes, boss."

She placed my arm around her shoulders, and wrapped her other arm around my waist.

"One lap," she said again. I made her do three.

When my legs were strong enough and I was walking on my own, I had shown my family. They were shocked. Stunned. Amazed. I wasn't supposed to recover. Fate had given me a miracle and I was a little afraid of the price I'd have to pay for that.

Next I went to see Ken, my jerk of an ex-husband. I drove straight to his office, dumped the Jag in the parking lot across the street, and marched up the steps to his building like an angry soldier in a pair of jeans and the Doc Martens Amber had bought me because she said I'd need some "shit-kicking" boots now. She was right. There were a few things I needed to say to Ken, and it wasn't going to be pleasant.

I stormed into the reception area startling Kelly, his secretarial nurse.

"Mrs. Summers," she exclaimed, her shocked eyes roving over my legs.

"*Ms.* Summers, Kelly. Is Ken in his office?" I stalked toward the door.

"Yes, but you can't just---"

I flung it open. Ken was behind his desk, talking on the

phone with his back to the door. I slammed it shut on Kelly and he spun in his chair, his breath coming up short when he saw me. The phone slipped from his hand and fell to the carpet with a muffled thud. He didn't say a word, only stared.

"Hi ya, Kenny," I said bitterly. I couldn't believe I had once loved this yuppy prick. I moved across the room, dropped myself in the chair in front of him, and plunked my boots on the top of his desk. No wonder Amber wore these things. They were a power trip. I folded my arms and he stared at my legs, speechless.

"What do you think?" I said, pointing a shiny boot at him. "Not bad for a paraplegic, huh? You little *fucker*."

He hung up the phone and I sprang to my feet and slammed my hands down on the desk in front of him.

"You said I'd never walk again," I growled. "You and that senile old jerk off Lambert took away my hope and I wanted to die."

"Meagan." He stood to meet my gaze with his handsome worried face. Some things never changed.

"I wanted to die, Ken!" I repeated. "Because I couldn't see a future for myself with your words of doom hanging over my head. I even became a drug addict."

"A drug addict?" He was stunned.

"Oh yeah. Coke, weed, Demerol--you name it. I was on it all. Hooked myself up real good because I allowed you *supposed* doctors to take away my hope."

He moved to take my hand but I yanked it away.

"I'm sorry, Meagan," he said sincerely. "It wasn't going to happen for you. It was impossible."

I tapped the side of his desk with my boot, making my point without words.

"Improbable," he said, quickly. "It was improbable."

"How many children, Ken?" I accused. "How many parents have you devastated with your diagnosis of irreversible paralysis?"

"Meagan that's not fair."

"No? Is it fair to that poor little kid wheeling around a baseball diamond, wishing he could run but knowing in his heart he never will because Dr. Ken said so? Is it fair of you to take away that child's hope? You are not God, Ken. I'm walking proof of that!"

I stormed from his office and slammed the door behind me. Then I paid a visit to Dr. Lambert and gave him the same speech, but omitted the drugs and added that he was a senile old prick who needed to retire. I felt better after that. And then I called Ted.

"Still want a publishing company?" I asked.

"You bet," he said.

"Let's do it."

Everything snowballed from there. New business. New car. New legs. New life. Meagan Summers was back on top.

Traffic ground to a halt. Everyone had the same idea I did. Get home early. Start the weekend. I turned up the radio and listened to the horns honking all around me. Did they really think that helped? Moved traffic along any quicker? My teeth ground together. The headache had passed but I was still shaken. The heat in the car was blistering. I turned it down. Felt cold and turned it back up. Switched radio stations. Drummed my fingers on the dash. Popped in a CD. Waited.

The man in the car beside me was picking his nose. I shot him a disgusted look. His hand dropped to his lap. On the other side was a woman yelling at her kids in the backseat. I couldn't hear her but I could tell she was yelling by the way her arms flailed about. One of the kids stuck a gooey sucker in her hair and she turned around and slapped him. I looked away. A catering truck was behind me. I struggled to read the words. *Lester Foods*. Didn't sound appetizing. In front of me was a twenty-year-old Camaro that spit black smoke out its tailpipe like the driver had never heard of a thing called the ozone layer. The car was in neutral, about to stall. A rev of the engine caused another black puff of smoke.

There was a 7/11 on the next corner, but I wasn't stopping for milk. There was no way I was getting off this street. If I did, there wasn't a driver around who would let me back on it. I watched each car that reached the corner block the entrance to the store and thought about what a bunch of assholes people were. There was a car at the edge of the lot, waiting. He'd been waiting for ten minutes and no one would let him out. Traffic edged forward and I stopped before my bumper hit the edge of the driveway and waved him in. He waved back, smiling. The catering truck behind me honked and I gave him the finger in my rearview mirror. He honked again. Flipped the bird back at me. Traffic crept forward again but I didn't move. Grinned at the man in my mirror and he laid on his horn. Swung his truck around me and shot me the finger again. I waved him goodbye. Inched forward.

Traffic began to clear at the next stoplight. It spread. Separated down different side streets and the Camaro in front of me darted forward with a roar, an impatient driver at the wheel, much like I had once been.

My foot pressed hard on the accelerator, then instantly released it as a small fistful of fear gripped me. I couldn't drive fast anymore. Every time I tried to speed my throat closed like a clam and my heart pounded. Yellow lights threw me into a panic and I was prone to screeching to a stop whenever I saw one. I had become a phobic driver, but not even fear could keep me from getting behind the wheel of my leased Mercedes. It was a great car. Classic, but sporty. Something Amber and I could both enjoy, though I planned on surprising her with a car of her own soon. She might not accept such a lavish gift but I'd force her to.

I turned onto Riverview, an odd name for a street that did not have a view of the river, and pulled into the garage under our building. I parked the car in the reserved spot and rode the elevator to the tenth floor.

"You're home early," Amber said happily when I stepped through the door and dropped my purse and jacket on the couch, ignoring the coat rack. I smiled back at her. Rarely did I come home early. It pleased her.

"No milk," I said, glancing into the kitchen at a young boy sitting at the table eating an ice cream cone.

"We have company," Amber said, following my eyes. We headed for the kitchen and she indicated the boy. "Jacob…"

"Ebstein!" I gasped.

The boy smiled up at me like I was a long lost relative and I felt like my head might explode under the enormous pressure that suddenly crushed it. Something in me snapped and I marched toward the boy and almost grabbed him.

"What the fuck are you doing here?" I demanded.

His face washed white with fear and Amber whirled around to face me.

"Meagan!" she scolded. "Don't talk to a child like that." Her eyes were wide with disbelief that I would even dare.

"This child," I hissed, pointing an accusing finger, "has been calling my office all day. Harassing me about people I've never met and saying we're old friends."

Amber turned her soft eyes on the boy. "Is that true, Jacob?"

I kicked the side of the counter. "No! I'm making it up!"

"It's true," Jacob said, quietly. His ice cream was melting down his hand. At least the kid wasn't a liar.

I turned to Amber and grabbed her arm. Thought of when Gwynne had once done the same thing and let go.

"How could you let this kid in here?" I demanded. "You don't even know him." I was amazed at her stupidity, terrified and shocked she would do such a thing.

"*You* know him," she said. "He said you did."

"Oh, well as long as he said so!" I threw up my arms.

The ice cream dripped on to the table and I snatched the cone from the boy's fist and tossed it in the garbage.

"Meagan!" Amber cried. She thought I was insane.

I paced the kitchen floor. "How did you find out where I live?" I demanded of the horrified boy. He wasn't any more scared right now than I was.

"On--On my computer," he stammered.

"And you just showed up here? Don't you know how dangerous that is? I could be a child murderer."

Jacob laughed. Shook his brown head. "You'd never hurt me, Meagan, you love me."

I almost lunged at him. He was forcing memories into my head, things I'd rather forget. Things that scared me. "Are you crazy, little boy? I don't love you. I don't even know you! And for Christ's sake, stop calling me Meagan!"

Tears sprang to his eyes and Amber grabbed my arm and pulled me aside.

"What the hell is the matter with you?" she said through clenched teeth. "He's a little boy!"

I shook off her arm and paced the kitchen like a maniac. I squeezed the bridge of my nose to release the pressure in my forehead and winced at the self-inflicted pain.

"Get him out of here, Amber," I warned.

One little boy in my kitchen and my personality underwent a severe change. I didn't like surprises. There were always too many of them and this was the worst one yet.

Suddenly Jacob shot to his feet and the chair he was sitting in flew backwards and crashed to the floor.

"Y--You're mean," he stammered with all the courage a small boy could muster. "You changed. I liked the dead Meagan better."

My mind spun. *Dead Meagan.* Darkness creeping in. I steadied myself on the counter and drove it away.

"What's your phone number?" I demanded. "I'm calling your parents."

"I don't have *parents*," he shot back. "I only have a mother, and good, I hope she does come and get me, because I hate you! You're nothing like you were in the Realm."

"Realm?"

The word drew an instant coldness around my heart. I staggered backwards and Amber's arm shot out to shield me from a fall I wasn't about to take. She was mesmerized by the boy. Staring at him while trying to hold on to me at the same time.

"That Meagan was kind," he cried. "She took me for walks and held me when I was sad and she always came to check on me even when my mom was there just to make sure I was okay. You're nothing like her. You suck and I hate you! Do you hear me? I hate you!"

His words shocked me. Shocked Amber. She was a woman caught in the middle of a dilemma she didn't quite know how to handle. Tears sprang to Jacob's eyes again and she moved to comfort him. I grabbed her wrist and shook my head at her. This was my mess, not hers, and I thought my heart would break as an unbearable guilt turned up inside it. He meant no harm. He wasn't trying to scare me. He was misguided. He thought he meant something to me and I had cruelly told him he meant nothing.

He buried his face in his hands and I crouched on the floor in front of him.

"I'm sorry, Jacob," I said. He dropped his hands to his sides and stared at me with sad, wet eyes. "Please forgive me. If we meant something to each other somewhere I honestly don't remember it. You scared me. I didn't mean to hurt your feelings but you showed up here and that terrified me. I was in a coma for a while, Jacob, and when I came out of it, even worse things happened. So I've worked very hard at trying to forget. Can you understand that?"

Amber watched silently. She pressed her hands to her cheeks and shook her head like she couldn't believe what she was seeing. Jacob threw himself in my arms, and the action startled me. I held him and there was something familiar about doing so. He smelled like chocolate ice cream.

"You really don't remember?" he cried into my neck and Amber's eyes locked onto mine. "I thought you could be like my other mom again. I thought we could be friends." I wiped away the tears on his cheeks.

"Don't cry, Jacob," I said softly. "I don't remember our old friendship but maybe we could start a new one. Would that be okay with you?" He nodded. "But Jacob, you have to promise me something. If we do become friends you have to promise you'll never mention Zoe again." Amber's eyes widened on that one and I shook my head at her, meaning that I would explain later. "Can you promise me that, Jacob? Because I don't talk about Zoe anymore. She's a part of my life that's over now and I have to let her go."

Jacob nodded again and Amber placed her hand on my shoulder. "I think we should call his mother now." She stroked the back of Jacob's head. "What's your number sweetie?"

Jacob rattled off a phone number and Amber dialed. He continued to cling to my neck. Amber spoke in hushed tones on the phone while I urged Jacob back into a chair and went about fixing him another ice cream cone.

Amber hung up. "His mother's on her way."

We'd gone to Ireland. Once Markham-Summers was a definite go and the building was under renovation Amber and I packed a few bags and hopped a flight to the Emerald Isle to shock Seamus. I hadn't told him I could walk. I enjoyed shocking people. I hadn't even told him we were coming.

Amber slept on the plane. I didn't. Flying always made me anxious. It meant you were on an adventure and I had no patience for sitting in a cramped seat for hours, waiting for it to begin. We flew first class but what did that matter? Sitting was sitting and I had sat for six months. Now I was going to run. I was going to go out into the flower field behind Seamus's cottage and I was going to run for miles, until my lungs ached with the loss of breath and my legs were begging me to stop. Then I was going to turn around and run all the way back. You couldn't get me to sit still anymore. I had to *move*, if only to constantly prove to myself that my legs were real.

Amber awakened when the plane touched down. She had a sixth sense about landings. Always woke up when we were just about to reach earth. We'd been on three airplanes together in the time I'd known her and on each trip she did the same thing. Slept for hours and woke on landing. She wasn't the person to fly with if you needed conversation. Only woke up for two reasons: to eat her complimentary meal or to de-board the plane. Never a trip to the bathroom. Never saw an in-flight movie.

I was the opposite. I flitted about the plane until some attendant came along and urged me to return to my seat. I walked around for no reason; brought our trash up to the front of the plane myself instead of waiting for the flight attendant to collect it; kept my seat in the upright position the whole flight and bounced to the beat of the music in my ears. Anyone who got on a plane without their own collection of music was insane.

We rented a car at one of the long counters in the middle of the airport. It had been a long time since I'd driven on the wrong side of the road but I picked it up again after a few turns that put us right in the center of oncoming traffic.

Amber gripped the door handle fearfully and looked out the window like her life was flashing by out there.

"Do you want to drive?" I asked, long after I'd gotten the hang of it.

"Not on your life," she said.

"Then relax. I have no intention of crippling myself twice." Amber relaxed.

It was early evening in Dublin and I realized I was starving. Couldn't eat that awful airplane food. So we stopped at a little restaurant in the Temple Bar district and feasted on vegetarian lasagna and green leaf salad. The food was bland but the company good. Friendly people in Ireland. I thought I might move here myself someday when I was old and tired. The thought made me smile. I might live to be old after all.

"Are we going to Seamus's now?" Amber asked when we paid the check and got back in the car. I cranked the key and she grabbed the door handle, saw my amused expression and let go.

"No, Seamus won't be home yet," I said. "We'll have to surprise him at the pub."

I liked that idea. Strolling into the pub like I owned the place and shocking the shit out of my uncle who would be so drunk he'd think he was hallucinating.

He was sitting at the bar when we entered, his back to the door and talking to Mike. I grinned. Mike looked up at me from behind the bar and his eyes widened but I shook my head, placed my finger to my lips, and crept up on my uncle.

"I think I see a leprechaun Mick," I said, planting a kiss on his ear.

He jumped then whirled around to face me. "Meggie!" His bloodshot eyes popped down to my legs.

"Hey, Seamus."

"Jesus Christ, lass. You can walk! You're in Ireland and you can walk!" He scooped me up in his arms and crushed me to him, nearly cracking my ribs. "I don't believe it, Meggie. I can't believe you're here and you're walking!"

I started laughing. He was going to cry. "Brought you another surprise too," I said, nodding at Amber.

"You brought Blondie with ya," Seamus cried, releasing me and scooping up Amber. She hugged him back, laughing.

"So what do you think, Seamus?" she asked. "Did she shock you or what? She's been planning this moment since she took her first step. You're the first person she thought of. Couldn't wait to get here. Drove the flight attendants nuts."

Seamus roared with laughter. "That's my Meggie Pie. I told you it would happen, Meggie. Nothing can keep my niece down for long. Let's grab a table. We've got some big celebrating to do." He turned to Mike as we sat. "Three pints, Mikey."

I shook my head. "Make it two, Mike. I'll have a mineral water or something if you have it."

"Mineral water!" Seamus found that hilarious and slammed his fist on the table. "That'll be the day me niece comes to Ireland and doesn't have a pint or two with her uncle."

Mike placed two pints in front of Seamus and Amber and handed me a bottle of water. "Good to see you again, Meg." Only in Ireland could people get away with calling me Meggie or Meg.

"Get this girl a pint," Seamus said.

I shook my head. "I can't, Seamus. I don't drink anymore."

"Why?"

Amber looked at me and nodded encouragingly. Seamus caught something odd about the look.

"What's going on here, girls?" he asked.

I took a deep breath and looked him in the eyes. Amber squeezed my hand and Seamus stared at me.

"I have a substance abuse problem, Seamus," I said. I looked around the bar and lowered my voice to a whisper because this was highly embarrassing. "I'm a drug addict." His face flashed surprise. "Or I was," I added quickly. "Until Amber helped me get clean."

He scratched his head, trying to figure out if this was another practical joke. Glanced at Amber for verification and she gave him a small nod.

"She's been clean for a few months," Amber said. "But it can still be a struggle sometimes. Maybe we should get out of this pub." She glanced around worriedly.

I waved away her words. "I'm fine. Alcohol was never the biggest problem anyway. It was the other stuff that was too good to me."

"What other stuff?" Seamus asked, concerned.

"Mostly coke. A few other things. Some pills."

He looked at me meaningfully. "But you're off everything now?"

"Yes."

He turned to Amber. "And you helped her?" She shrugged. He rubbed his eyes. "Was she gonna die, Blondie?"

"I don't know," Amber said. "I don't think so but she was definitely on the edge." She was easing the blow for Seamus. We both knew I was going to die. "She was really strung out and I didn't even notice until it was almost too late." A hint of guilt in her voice. Then fear. "It was scary, Seamus. She was scratching at the floor begging me for a snort and I'd never been so scared in my life. Not even when she was in the coma because at least then I knew who she was. But this was a completely different person I was looking at. It wasn't Meagan. It was a drug addict. A quivering, shaking drug addict and she was kissing my feet and begging me for the vial I'd taken away from her."

I listened to Amber's words as if she really were talking about someone else. I should have been embarrassed but I wasn't. Only sorry. Amber had never told me how frightening the experience had been for her but she told Seamus now because she needed to get it out at long last and he was as good an ear as any.

"Why didn't you call me?" Seamus asked her.

Amber set her pint on the table and met his hurt gaze. "I couldn't call you, Seamus. She was so ashamed. She didn't want anyone to know what she'd allowed herself to become and I promised her I wouldn't tell anyone until it was over."

Amber looked like she could cry at any minute and I rubbed her leg under the table. I didn't know how progressive Ireland had become, so I was limited in how I could comfort her.

"You scared me, Meagan," she said, turning her wet green eyes on me. "You shook in bed and you begged me to call Adrian almost every day and I had to fight the part of me that wanted to just ease your torment. For three days your eyes looked so panicked and you rocked back and forth on the bed like a person in a mental hospital. You kept rocking and your eyes looked like they would pop right out of your head and I thought I would go crazy. I didn't know if I could get you through it. I had to be strong enough for the both of us and I didn't know if I could *do it*!"

Seamus did what I couldn't. He rose from the table,

pulled Amber into his arms, and she sobbed into his neck. "It's okay, Blondie," he soothed. "You shouldn't have had to face that alone but it's over now, right?" He looked at me over his shoulder. "I think we should get the wee one home, Meggie. Let her get it out in private."

I nodded and Seamus threw a few bills on the table. He waved to Mike and walked Amber out with his arm around her waist. She went in his car with him and I followed in the rental. I got the feeling she couldn't handle being around me just then and needed the protection I had always sought from my uncle.

I watched the back of their heads as we drove away from the city and toward Seamus's home in the country. I knew Amber was crying. I could tell by the way her head was bowed down and how her hand rose every few seconds like she was wiping away the tears I should have been there to wipe away. Seamus rested his arm across the back of her seat and her head fell against his bicep. I felt a twinge of jealousy that startled me. He rubbed the back of her neck with his thick fingers and I wondered if she liked it. My uncle was the masculine version of me, except his hair was black and mine was brownish-red. His eyes were dark and mysterious, mine were hazel and flat. He was strong. Muscled. Women flocked to him. He had even bragged how he'd once turned one straight. How could Amber not be attracted to him? My knuckles tightened on the wheel. Whitened. Then I realized what I was thinking and couldn't believe my mind would even venture to such a place, that I could have so little trust in either of them. The only thing that was going on in that car was Seamus comforting Amber. Nothing more.

We turned onto the long stone driveway leading up to the house, parked, and Seamus led Amber toward the door. She glanced back at me as I removed our bags from the trunk and slammed the lid harder than I'd intended. I shrugged and waved her inside. I grabbed the bags from where I'd dropped them on the driveway and was surprised to see the front door close behind them.

What the hell was this? I fought to control my temper, struggled with the bags and kicked the door. Seamus swung it open.

"Sorry, Meggie," he said, taking the bags from me and

placing them on the floor inside. "The door closes by itself sometimes."

I grunted. Stepped inside. Wished we had decided to stay at a hotel. Seamus went off to make tea and I started a fire in the stone fireplace in the living room. Amber and I sat in front of it. We didn't talk. Seamus returned with three steaming mugs, handed one to Amber and one to me. They talked. I felt like I didn't exist. I moved to the window and looked outside at the flower field I would hit in the morning.

Seamus and Amber sat on the couch together like an old married couple and I turned my head, fighting those awful thoughts that once again encumbered me. The cup was warm in my hands. I took a sip, felt a familiar sting on my tongue, and alarmed, spit the liquid across the room, whirling around to glare at my startled uncle.

"Are you fucking crazy, Seamus?" I yelled. "You put *whiskey* in my *tea*?"

Amber gasped and Seamus jumped to his feet.

"I'm sorry, Meggie," he said. "That was supposed to be Amber's, to soothe her nerves."

Amber squeezed her knees to her chest. "You didn't *swallow* any?

"No. But it's not poison, Amber."

"For you it is," she said, with more than a little anger in her voice. Was she afraid one sip of whiskey could send me running back to the coke?

I glared at her. "You want to have this out, don't you?" I said. "Fine, then let's get it over with. I'm a recovering drug addict. That angers you. Then do something about it for Christ's sake. Say something to me. Tell me how it bothers you. I can take it, you know. I'm not gonna crumble."

Seamus looked uncomfortable. "I'm gonna leave you two alone," he said. "There's clean sheets on the bed upstairs and I'll bring up your bags. G'night, girls." He left the room.

"Well?" I said.

"What do you want me to say, Meagan?" she asked. "Should I tell you how I'm afraid that if one little thing goes wrong in your life you'll run back to the drugs? Or maybe I should tell you how angry I am with you for lying to me for three and half months. For letting me believe you were this poor pathetic paraplegic when really you were nothing more than a manipulative drug addict. Do you know how used that makes me feel? I defended you to Jenna when she suspected, and if you think that day in the kitchen was the first time she thought it you're wrong. She'd been telling me for weeks to keep an eye on you but I wouldn't believe that about you. You always said you couldn't lie to me so that's what I chose to believe."

"I'm sorry, Amber, but a drug addict can lie to anyone. Believe me, it was hard, but I had to. And I'm not making excuses for myself, what I did was wrong. I hurt you and I'm sorry for that. Just tell me how to fix it and I will. I'll do whatever you want. Do you want me to beg your forgiveness?"

I dropped to my knees and crawled toward her.

"Get up," she said.

"No. Not until you forgive me."

She sighed. "I do forgive you, Meagan, but that doesn't make it hurt any less."

I sat beside her. "Okay, so how do I take away the pain?"

"You don't. This isn't one of those things that Meagan Summers can just take charge of and twist into something workable. This isn't business. It has to run its course, though I think coming here was a good idea. I think maybe it could heal us both."

I smiled at her. "That's Ireland. Land of magic."

"Dat it is," a voice said from behind us. "And my two girls are going to have a very pleasant stay."

In the morning I watched the sun come up through the bedroom window and cast its glow on Amber's sleeping form. It was time to hit the field, though I didn't feel like running anymore, maybe a long walk.

Kissing Amber's bare shoulder, I pulled the colorful quilt up to her neck, and slid from the bed. There was a dresser with a mirror on the other side of the room and I crossed over to it. I brushed my hair then carried my clothes into the bathroom where I splashed cold water on my face, brushed my teeth, and changed into a long brown wrap-around skirt and a pretty white camisole with a thin border of lace around the low neckline. It was going to be a warm day. I could tell by the way the sun rose high above the field, already beginning to warm the small bathroom as it streamed in through the open window. No screen. Seamus hated screened windows and I liked that I could poke my head out of any window in this house like Rapunzel in her tower.

I slipped the camisole over my bare breasts, brushed my hair again, and quietly made my way outside. Seamus had gone to work. I had listened to the car pull away from the house, the gravel of the driveway crunching under its tires, and had breathed a sigh of relief that he'd be gone until late afternoon. I wanted this place to myself for awhile. I wanted to share the quiet cottage and the acres of unplowed field, the rolling hills, the flowers and the ancient stone well out back with Amber. I wanted us to be alone with the magic.

The back door was unlocked. Seamus never locked his doors. What was the point, he'd say. He was miles away from anyone and this *was* Ireland, after all. His father had never locked his doors and Seamus was his father's son.

Stepping outside, I surveyed my surroundings and thought I would have to bring Jenna here some day. She'd love it. Then I walked out into the field of flowers and across the patch of Heaven. I plucked them as I went, smelled them. Twirled them in my fingers and tucked one behind my ear, then instantly pulled it out. I wasn't the Earth Maiden, Jenna was.

The stone well loomed before me and I made my way over to it. I looked down the dark hole that seemed endless and gave the fragile old bucket hanging from the wooden beam a small shove. It swung back and forth. I drew it to me and placed the flowers I'd been collecting inside it. I lowered the bucket into the well as if these flowers were an offering of my gratitude to whatever had given me my miracle. I imagined tiny fairies dancing inside the well and accepting my gift. I smiled down the hole and shifted into a small twirly dance of my own around the well. I was happy. For the first time in ages, I was happy. And I danced to the music of the fiddles and tin whistles that played their Celtic serenade in my head. I thought I could dance forever and only stopped briefly to once again admire the well.

Amber approached in the near distance, smiling. Even from afar I could see her smiling at how odd I was and I gave her a large happy wave. The quilt from the bed was wrapped around her body and I saw her shiver slightly at a coldness I did not feel.

"I always said you were strange," she teased, nearing the well. She glanced down into the hole with an amused grin on her pretty face. "Is that where the fairies live?"

I shrugged. "Maybe. Or maybe they live in the forest, or in the ponds. Maybe they're not even visible. Maybe they're standing with us right now. All I know is that if millions of people can believe in saints and angels, I can believe in fairies."

"Good point. Aren't you cold? You're practically naked."

"Naked? I couldn't be wearing a longer skirt." Another shrug. "I'm comfortable. What about you?"

She flashed open the quilt and I laughed. "You see, you're the one who's always naked."

"Not always."

"Did you see that tree near the opening of the field? Someone carved their initials into it long ago and it's still there. You can tell it's really old too. The tree is dead but that carving looks like it was always there, like it was part of the tree's design." My head cocked to the left. "You're very pretty like that," I mused, abandoning my tree talk.

"Like what?"

"Out here, in the sun, surrounded by flowers and wrapped in a quilt. You're always beautiful but there's something particularly striking about you right now."

"I felt the same when I watched you do your little dance from the window."

I laughed. "You saw that, huh? How long were you watching?"

"Long enough to know you had music playing in your head. You couldn't live without music, could you?"

"Definitely not. I couldn't live without you either."

"Keep it up and I'm likely to believe that."

"There's nothing I would rather you believed."

A small gust of wind blew from the right and I shivered. Amber opened her quilt to me. "Come here."

"Okay, but I'm warning you, if I get in there with you there's no telling what I might do."

"Is that a promise?"

I stepped into her quilt. "Do you want it to be?"

"Yes."

"Even though you're cold?"

"I won't be for long. Besides, we still have some lost time to make up for."

"No arguments here," I agreed.

She sat on the edge of the well and I took her hand to my face and kissed the inside of her wrist. "That wasn't the place I was hoping you'd start," she said. "But alright."

I laughed. Kissed her throat, her mouth, and slowly slid apart her legs. "You're getting warmer," she whispered against my ear. My hands moved up her legs, mouth lowered to her left breast, licking, sucking, taking her in the way I knew she liked. "Much warmer," she breathed.

My fingers moved upward, stroking her gently. "Am I gonna get a running commentary?"

She groaned. Leaned back and then steadied herself on the small stone wall. "I'm gonna fall in this well."

I dropped to my knees and bent my head to her. Teased her with my tongue. "Will it be worth it?"

She grabbed the wooden beam supporting the top half of the structure and gasped. "Oh God, yes."

I put my mouth on her again, softly because I was still teasing her, allowing her passions to build. Playing with her. Her free hand pressed against the back of my head, pulling me in closer. I pulled away. "Don't get impatient. You're always so impatient." My mouth met hers again and my fingers went back to their stroking. She kissed me passionately, breathing hard against my lips. I moved downward.

"Do it, Meagan," she pleaded.

"Do what?" I deadpanned. I continued to stroke her and she writhed against me.

"Put your mouth on me." Her hand slid under my camisole and then down the front of my skirt. "Please Meagan, do it now."

I bent to her again. Pressed into her warmth and explored her with my tongue. Her breath came in short, quick gasps as she neared the first plateau. It didn't take much. I continued on. Adding pressure then taking it away, feeling the tensions build in her body until she was just about there and calling my name. And then she was over the edge, quivering, pulling me up to her and tearing the camisole up over my head. It fell to the ground beside us. Expertly, she untied the knot at the side of my skirt and the fabric slipped to the earth. I wore nothing underneath. Her mouth met mine. We moved away from the well and she pulled me down on the ground. The flowers were high around us. Secluding us. Folding us in.

I reached to touch her hair. It was longer now, shoulder-length, straight but full. Beautiful hair. Soft. Inviting. My fingers slid into it as she trailed a warm line of kisses across my stomach. Bent to me. Reciprocated the favor until I was the one writhing and calling her name. And then we were tangled in the quilt. Lying in the field and whispering to each other how it had never been like this with anyone else.

"I think you're right, Meagan," she said, as I turned to dress. "I think it is alchemical. There's just something about us together."

"Right. It's not you and it's not me, it's us." I tied my skirt at the waist and helped her to her feet. "You don't believe in fate but that's what this is."

"I think in this case I do believe it. Maybe we chose each other long ago and we're just not conscious of it."

I grinned. "You mean when we were spirit, Amber?"

Slowly, she nodded. "Maybe. There's certainly no logical explanation for it."

"For great sex?"

She squeezed the quilt around her as we walked back toward the house. "Not just the sex… everything. The way we were drawn to each other and the crazy things we'd do just to make it work." She stopped walking and turned to face me. "And the way I love you, Meagan. I would face things with you I would never be willing to face with anyone else. I'd walk through hell if I knew you were waiting there."

"You have. You've met my demons and someday I'll have to meet yours."

"So I'm saying it's *possible* that's there's more to this than regular earth-plane love."

I chuckled. "You kill me when you say things like that. It's so...not you."

She laughed back. "I'm learning to inhabit your world."

"We share the same world. We just view it in different

ways. It's all relative anyway. I like your view though, it's very *real*. A good blend in a person, I think, would be a cross between your views and Jenna's. Logical but spiritual."

She nudged me and shook her head good-naturedly.

"What?" I asked.

"You're describing *you*."

"I am?"

"So you think you're the perfect person, huh?"

"Definitely not."

She wrapped her arms around my neck and kissed me. "You are to me."

Chapter 12

Martha Ebstein was a short, dark-haired woman with hazel eyes and a plump round figure. She arrived twenty minutes after Amber's call, shocked that her only son had taken the number five bus across town to meet with a stranger he claimed was a friend. She was a nice woman. A single mother who worked as a waitress in one of those fancy restaurants uptown and went to school in the evenings to get her high school diploma. She was thirty-five, but looked at least ten years older. Jacob's father had died in a work-related accident, she'd said, when Jacob was five and she'd been raising him on her own ever since. Struggling, but doing her best.

"I'm sorry he did this," she said, after seeing that her son was fine, plopped in front of the TV.

Amber poured her a cup of coffee, frowned at me when she asked for milk, and offered her a scone. I looked at the pastry, wondering why we even had such things in the house because neither of us ate them. We had cookies and ice cream and bags of chips that never got touched until company came because Amber was as fussy about what she ate as I was.

Martha bit into a scone. "He saw your picture in the paper last week," she said. "He started running around the house screaming about how he knew you from the hospital. Jacob was burned pretty badly in a fire a while back and he was in the hospital for some time. Unconscious."

Amber sat down beside me and Martha's eyes misted.

"I thought I was going to lose him," she said. "When he woke up it was like a miracle."

I nodded--I knew about miracles--and motioned for her to continue.

"But something was different about him when he woke up. He *knew* things. That's the only way I can describe it. He knew things he had no way of knowing and it's been happening ever since. He says they're like flashes in front of his eyes. Things pop into his head and he's been keeping a journal so he can keep track of it all. It's very important to him. When he said he knew you I believed him but I never thought he'd try to contact you. He hasn't tried to contact the others."

"Others?" Amber asked.

Martha nodded, put down her scone, and swiped her hands across her thick thighs, removing the crumbs. "Yes," she said. "Jacob says many names. Janine and Meagan are the most important though. He has those two names written in his book with big stars drawn around them. Under Meagan it says *friend*, and under Janine it says, *guide*. I asked him what that meant once but he said he couldn't explain it. That Janine was like a travel guide or something. He hasn't quite put that part together yet."

She looked up at me. "So you see, when he came across your picture in the paper, that part clicked for him. He recognized your face. This is strange for my son, because he doesn't talk like this, but he said it was the face of kindness."

Amber and I shared an amused look.

"Is that funny?" Martha asked, confused.

I poured myself a cup of coffee. "Sort of," I said. "I'm not exactly known for my kindness. My reputation is quite the opposite, truthfully, though I'm not deserving of it. I was the subject of a book once that cast me in a pretty negative light." I shrugged. "People believed it. The book is now out of print and, thankfully, the reputation's subsiding."

"Who wrote the book?" Martha asked.

Another amused look.

Amber played with the back of my hair. "I did," she said.

"Oh." Martha scratched her arm and began to look nervous. Like she just figured out what we were and it scared her. "So you two are...together? Not that it matters. It doesn't matter. Forget I brought it up."

"Tell me what Jacob says about me," I said, changing the subject and releasing the woman from her discomfort. She looked relieved and picked up her scone again.

"Are you sure you wanna talk about this?"

"I don't think I have much choice anymore," I said. "I have nightmares sometimes. They seem meaningless but I know they aren't. They have something to do with when I was unconscious. Jacob called me and I felt like he had tapped into my nightmares. I got scared. Yelled at him pretty fiercely, I'm afraid. I apologized, of course, but I think you should know that I overreacted and I did swear at him. So if he starts using the f-word, you'll probably have to blame me for that."

Martha laughed. "In our neighborhood the f-word is said more often than hello. I don't see how you're to blame for *that*. But Jacob doesn't talk like that anyway. He's more likely to scare you with his talk of the afterlife than with any curse words. He calls the afterlife the Realm and he says it's quite nice, actually. He says a girl named Beth was his friend but she decided to stay in the Realm and sent him to you because she told him you were coming back. That you didn't know it yet but you were."

Amber and I shared another look at the mention of Beth. I was frightened by what Martha was saying but I urged her to continue. It was suddenly very important that I learned what I could.

"Jacob says you were married to a doctor Beth had a crush on."

Flash of familiarity. Words I'd heard somewhere. *You know who else is really hot? Your husband.* And then something else. Something funny.

I grinned. "Invisible dildos."

The words popped out of my mouth and two sets of shocked eyes met mine. Amber fought the urge to laugh. My hands shot out to cover my mouth and I felt my cheeks stain red.

"I'm so sorry." A picture of a young girl sitting with me outside the hospital appeared in my mind and I squinted at it. "He's right about Beth," I said as the image came into focus. "She *was* there and she did have a crush on my husband. I was married when I was in the coma and this girl--this Beth--I can see us talking on the front steps, and she asked me what I thought was so great about the physical world; sex was one of my answers. She agreed to that one, didn't care much about love, and said she wondered if there was some sort of astral equivalent for it." I glanced at the living room and lowered my voice. "She joked about there being invisible dildos and then she stepped through Amber and I got mad."

Amber was alarmed. "What do you mean she stepped

through me?"

The two women stared at me like I was some strange, new exhibit at the zoo and the image was becoming clearer in my mind. It was strange but suddenly I could see Beth. Vividly. She was grinning at me like she knew something I didn't but I wasn't afraid of her. A feeling of pitying her. Liking her. I squinted again. Called the image to the forefront of my mind. Amber on the steps. Tying her shoe. Wanted to touch her but Beth did instead.

"She was tasting your energy," I said, suddenly.

"You're freaking me out," Amber said. Martha remained silent.

"There was a tulip head at my feet," I went on, "Pink. Beth stepped through you twice, liked your energy and I told her to stop. She said you couldn't feel her anyway and I told her I didn't care. That what she was doing was like stealing and that I didn't even pass through you. I wanted to but I didn't want to violate you."

"But what does it mean to pass through?" Amber asked.

I shook my head. "I think it was like a way of knowing what people were feeling or thinking. You stepped through them and you were aware of what it felt like to *be* them. I wanted to crawl into you, Amber. I'm sorry but I know I did. I wouldn't allow myself to do it because you weren't really mine and it *would* have been like stealing. It would have been like rape. That's what I thought when Beth passed through you, that she was somehow raping you of your essence and I would have attacked her had either of us been real, I think."

Martha nodded her agreement. "Jacob says he used to pass through me to make sure I was okay." She frowned and looked over at Jacob who was playing with the TV remote. "Is he okay with that?" she asked, as Jacob zipped through channel after channel.

"He's fine," I said. "Does Jacob know why I came back?" I knew why.

Martha shook her head. "I don't think he knows why *he* came back. He probably came here hoping you'd know but you don't, do you? This is even newer to you than it is to him."

I nodded. "Martha, would you mind if Jacob and I did

become friends? Maybe we can help each other. Obviously, we've been through a lot of the same things."

She shrugged. "I'm okay with that. But I don't want him taking any more buses to get here."

"No, of course not."

"Okay, then. I'll leave you our number and you can just get in touch with us when you want. After the shock of all this wears off, I'm sure."

She reached for her jacket while Amber jotted down our phone number on a piece of paper and handed it to her. She rattled off the one Jacob had given her earlier, asked if that was correct, and smiled when she learned her memory didn't fail her. It never did.

"So what do you think?" Amber asked when Jacob and Martha were gone.

"I think I need to go buy some milk."

"No."

"Why?"

"Because that's avoidance--the first step to shutting down."

"Suddenly you're Carl Jung? It's milk."

We cleared away the empty cups and tidied the kitchen. "Talk to me, Meagan," Amber said, when I placed the stopper at the bottom of the sink and turned on the hot water. I squirted a drop of Palmolive inside and watched the suds spring to life.

"We should get a dishwasher," I said. "Would you like to talk about that?" She frowned at me and I sighed. "Alright, I'm freaked out. That kid shows up here and he knows about me, knows about Zoe---"

She sat on the counter top. "Tell me about that. What did he say about her?"

I turned off the taps and wiped my hands on a towel. "He said I told him he made me think of Zoe, back when we were ghosts. Do you know how absolutely terrifying it is to hear something like that? When we were *ghosts?* I lost it. He kept calling and Cynthia kept patching him through and then I lost it on Cynthia. And then of course the migraine, right? That fucking knife ground into my forehead and I sat in the reception area freezing, with my head pounding, until Cynthia, saint that she is, found me the lavender oil."

"Did you apologize?"

"Of course. But she was probably thinking 'I didn't come over from London for this shit,' you know? I gave her the rest of the day off and came home. I don't think I yelled at her too badly. I think I just barked at her to tell Jacob to fuck off."

Amber shrugged. "That doesn't sound too bad. She was probably a little surprised by your language but I'm sure she recovered. What are you going to do about Jacob?"

"Talk to him, I guess."

"Become his friend again?"

"Possibly. He's kind of cute, isn't he? When those tears burst out of his big, brown eyes I felt like I'd killed a puppy."

She laughed. "I think you almost did."

"And you thought I'd lost my mind."

"I thought you'd lost something. The cool wall of reserve certainly wasn't there today."

"No, I couldn't detach myself from this one. Jacob didn't tap into any part of me that felt real. He went straight for my unconscious mind and I haven't developed a barrier for that part yet. Haven't had to. I think it's okay though. A few hours ago I was terrified, now I'm just strangely calm."

"I noticed. You really refused to pass through me, Meagan?"

"Yes, that I'm sure of."

"I wouldn't have cared."

"But I didn't know that. I would never take from you what you wouldn't freely give. Beth called you 'the chick'. She said 'Aww you're going back to the chick and we both know it'. She knew I was coming home even before I did."

"How do you know that? You didn't know it yesterday."

"I'm not sure really but I'm certain it's true. When Martha said Beth had a crush on Ken it opened something and suddenly I was remembering a scene I'd never known had taken place. Jacob is connected to me somehow, I think. He's a little boy who knows the names of the people in my nightmares--how is that possible?"

"You're asking me?"

"Why not? Maybe you can find some logical

explanation for it because I certainly can't. Maybe I'm way off base but what if he was sent here for a reason?"

She hopped off the counter and smiled. "Now you sound like Jenna."

"The problem there is that I've rarely known Jenna to be wrong."

It was dark in the auditorium. Dark like in those first black moments in a movie theatre before the screen lights up and you've just set your big paper drink down on the sticky floor beside your feet. You won't touch it again because as the coming attractions begin to roll you realize you've just set it down on top of someone's chewed gum. Pink. The gum is always pink. No spearmint Dentyne for the cinema crowd. Strawberry Bubble Yum. Won't stick to your lips but it can do a fine job on the bottom of your shoe.

This wasn't a movie theatre, though. It was a university auditorium with faded gold seats bolted to the slanted floor and big yellow doors in the back that whooshed open every few minutes, casting a bright stream of hallway light inside as another student rushed in to take the seat her friends were saving for her down in front. Then the doors would whoosh closed again and the room would be dark. Clank of steel as the doors closed against each other and fit into place.

There was a short introduction by Professor Child welcoming today's guest speaker. Then Three hundred pairs of hands clapping. Jenna smiled beside me. My mother sat on the other side nodding at Professor Child and eagerly wringing her hands. There was tension among the students. A feeling of wanting Professor Child to get off the stage so they could just get on with this already. It made me think of high school. I was half-expecting someone to nudge me and say, "Let's sneak outside for a smoke." In high school I would have. I would have been the first one out the door and heading for the parking lot with my lighter already in my hand and a cigarette waiting between my fingers. I'd skipped every assembly I was ever supposed to attend. Went to the beach with Janie instead. Janie in her metallic blue jeep and the buff bodies on the sand. Janie was dead now. I was an adult. Times changed quickly.

Jenna pinched my arm. I looked at her and she nodded at the stage where Amber was finally taking the podium. There was more applause from the students. She could have been one of them. Twenty-eight years old and she could have been listening to this lecture instead of giving it.

They were impressed with her look. Doc Martens. Tommy Hilfiger jeans. Black DKNY turtleneck. Trendy blond hair. My mother thought she should have dressed more professionally, but I told her to look around. Amber knew her crowd. Whatever the occasion she always blended right in and made herself one of the group. This crowd was easiest to blend into because Amber really dressed this way. This *young*. In high school we would have said she was cool. I wasn't sure what kids would have called her today, maybe still cool. The students related to Amber in a way they never would have to Jenna or me. Jenna was too earthy, me, not quite trendy enough. I was a cross between the two of them, a hybrid. Designer clothes with a new age awareness. The only thing that separated me from them was ambition. Amber had little and Jenna had none. They were content. I was rarely satisfied.

Amber talked for forty-five minutes and the students were riveted to their seats. She talked about poetry and the books she'd written. About how she was now trying her hand at a novel. She encouraged them. Made them believe anything was possible if they were willing to expose themselves on paper and accept whatever consequences that exposure might bring about. She talked about how hard it was for a poet to get published for the first time. How you had to start with magazines and literary journals and how even after you got a book published it remained a struggle.

"You have to be able to deal with rejection," she said, "because it happens a lot. You have to struggle to believe in yourself when no one else will, and even after you've gotten a book published you have to continue to struggle because now you're faced with the challenge of topping yourself and you have to keep topping yourself or you can linger in obscurity forever."

That wouldn't be a problem for Amber now. She was a Markham-Summers client and we didn't give up so easily. She was Ted's client. Amber and I had decided early on that it was best if we kept our home lives and professional lives separate. My company published her work, I didn't. If there was a disagreement it would be between Ted and Amber. I would be forced to stay out of it. So far, the situation was good.

In the last fifteen minutes she answered questions. She was good at this. She belonged at a podium. Her voice never wavered and she never took more than a moment's deliberation before responding, she simply told the truth. I watched her with pride, always amazed at what a remarkable person she was. I couldn't believe I had ever left her at all. Married someone else, even. Just to keep myself away from this incredible person who awed everyone who came in contact with her.

"Who's your publisher now?" someone asked.

Amber smiled at me in the crowd. "Markham-Summers."

"Are they any good?"

"Very. They're fair and ambitious."

Jenna grinned and patted my hand. My mother smiled. A boy stood up. Football jacket. Short brown hair. Nudged forward by his buddies. He slapped away their hands. Said he was doing it.

"Are you seeing anyone?" he asked Amber, grinning.

There was laughter from the group.

"Sit down, Marcus," Professor Child said.

Marcus sat. The boy beside him stood.

"Are you?" this one pressed.

This time Amber laughed with the group. "Yes," she said into the microphone.

"Ever consider dating someone who's pre-law?"

Professor Child moved to the microphone. "Let's try to keep the focus on literature," she said. "Now are there any questions that don't have to do with Ms. Reed's love life?"

"No," someone called out.

The auditorium filled with laughter again. A girl stood up. She had a Bic pen with a chewed cap in her hand and a notebook. A serious student, this one. She was actually here to learn something.

"I have your second book at home," she said, "*When Butterflies Wear Their Armor*."

Amber nodded and I shifted uncomfortably in my seat.

"What I noticed about *Butterflies*," she went on, "is that it contradicts your earlier and later works. Is there an explanation for that?"

The girl sat. Amber glanced at me. My mother glanced at me. Jenna glanced at me. I cleared my throat and slumped down a little further in my seat.

"Each book," Amber said, leaning into the mic, "is in some form or another based on personal experience. *Butterflies* was written from the gut instead of the heart. I try to avoid that now."

"But it was a bestseller," the girl said. "Are you saying you'll never write another bestseller?"

Amber shook her head and reached for her glass of water. "That's for the critics and the public to decide," she said. "What I'm saying is that *Butterflies* came from a dark place and I have no intention of going back there. The experience taught me that although a writer must expose herself, she must be careful not to expose others in a way that is not truly befitting of them. *Butterflies* was *my* truth at the time. It was my perspective on a particular situation and the other person involved did not have a voice. It was one-sided, and if there's anything I learned from the experience, it is that there is always more than one side to the truth. To quote a friend, "truth is relative and authentically changeable from one person to the next."

Amber was quoting me. I smiled up at her.

"My truth is capable of being your lie," she went on. "So when you asked me if I will ever write another bestseller what you're really asking is if I will ever write from such a one-sided perspective again and the answer to that is no. Will my books continue to be successful? I hope so. I have an excellent publishing firm backing me up and I trust them implicitly. I see no reason why letting go of my anger should have a negative effect on my career. If that's truly the case then so be it," she shrugged, "I'll just move on to other things."

"So you don't take your craft seriously." The girl was pushing Amber but Amber didn't flinch.

"Writing is a part of who I am," she said. "I would never give it up entirely; I would just change its direction. When I was talking about consequences earlier I meant it. Butterflies left several consequences in its wake. The aftermath was not worth the book's success. It nearly destroyed my relationship with its subject and that person has had to overcome many obstacles because of it. Imagine if such things were written about you."

"I gotta get my hands on this book," someone said to more laughter.

"Are there any other questions?" Amber asked.

"Just one," Marcus called. "Will you go out with me tonight?"

Outside, the corridor was packed with people. They formed small intellectual groups and milled about the big yellow doors like the lecture hadn't ended twenty minutes ago. A group of girls to the left discussed Amber's clothes. They were impressed someone so old could look so young. Jenna and I laughed. Another group discussed the content of her lecture, and yet another, the matter of her sexuality. She hadn't used pronouns when discussing the subject of her second book, they'd noticed. She had avoided the use of "he" or "she" by filling in the blanks with words like "this person", and her evasion wasn't lost on these more observant students. The girl with the chewed pen cap was among this group and she confirmed their suspicion by describing the book. Anyone who had read *Butterflies* could have confirmed it.

I kept my hands in my jacket pockets and leaned against the wall, waiting. Listening to the way they dissected Amber as only college students could. I'd never gone to college but as far as I could tell it wasn't much different from high school. Same kind of talk but with a few big words tossed in to show they were maturing. In the end it came down to the same three things it always came down to for the young: fashion, sex, and physical beauty. Amber was a hit. She was still inside talking to Professor Child and I wondered what was taking her so long.

She'd been surprised to see me in the audience. I saw it on her face when she stepped up to the podium and peered into the crowd. Her eyes met mine and she gave a shy grin. I was supposed to be at work. I'd taken the afternoon off, something I rarely did, because this was important. This was the culmination of Amber's years as a struggling poet, the apex of her career thus far, and I would have to be pretty low on love's evolutionary scale to miss it. What had started as a short lecture for one of my mother's English lit classes had turned into a speech for every literature and journalism student in the school. Once Dean Hutchence and Professor Child got involved the lecture became an event. My mother was pleased. She was the one who had found the poet, after all. High marks for her. She would be even more pleased now that the lecture had gone well.

The corridor began to clear. People tired of waiting. The poet had probably gone out the side door to the parking lot. Only a few scattered students remained. Two small groups deciding where to go for coffee, and Jenna and me. The girl with the pen cap looked at me. I smiled. She turned away, embarrassed that she had been caught staring. I didn't care. I was learning to move past such things. She knew who I was. She looked at Jenna and she looked at me and something in her sensed I was the one. A few years ago that would have made me uncomfortable enough to leave. Today it just made me curious to know how she could tell.

I felt the small box in my jacket pocket and smiled. The jeweler had called that morning to tell me it was ready; the duplication complete. A ring to match my own. Silver band. Celtic knotwork; oval moonstone. The stone of dreams and healing. I had gone looking for it myself. The jeweler didn't carry such things, only precious gems like diamonds and rubies and sapphires. They were lovely but they wouldn't serve my purpose. Jenna took me to an occult shop downtown and I sifted through a glass bowl of stones in search of the perfect one. I held several stones to my ring, looking for a match, and after awhile I found it. Then I took the stone to the jeweler, showed him my ring and told him what I wanted. He'd wanted to keep the ring so he could make an exact replica but I told him he would have to settle for a picture because the ring left my hand under no circumstances. It was superstitious but tradition. The man understood. Saw this sort of thing all the time, he'd said, while snapping a picture of the ring on my hand. He could get everything he needed from the shot. One week later he called to say it was ready and it couldn't have happened on a better day. I planned on giving Amber the ring as soon as possible.

The big yellow doors swung open and Amber stepped into the corridor.

"Hey," she said happily, walking toward us. "What are you doing here? You're supposed to be at the office."

I shrugged and pushed myself off the wall. "Couldn't miss your big speech," I said.

"You were great," Jenna said.

"Thanks. I was really nervous at first but then I saw you guys in the audience and it got easier. I'm glad you came."

"Ms. Reed?" The girl with the chewed pen cap interrupted us. She tapped Amber on the shoulder and Amber turned to face her. Amber didn't like being called Ms. Reed but she didn't say anything.

"I just wanted to apologize for all the questions inside," said the girl.

Amber gave a sweet smile. "No problem. One of the journalism students, right?"

The girl gave a shy smile. It looked fake. She nodded. "Vicki Clump," she said, like her name was supposed to mean something. "Reporter for the school paper. I was wondering if I could get an interview to go along with my story." Something about the girl made me uneasy. I thought she looked like the cat that swallowed the canary. Amber looked at Jenna and me. "I'm sorry," she said. "I can't right now but if you call Markham-Summers I'm sure they'll set something up for us. Ask for Ted. Tell him I told you to call."

"Thank you." The girl scribbled something in her notebook and walked away, giving us a sideways glance. She wasn't happy. She wanted her interview now. The way I saw it she was lucky Amber agreed to one at all.

I wanted to yell after her to change her ridiculous name. How many snickers would a byline like Vicki Clump receive? People would be reaching for their newspapers and picturing a fat girl with bad clothes, clicking away on her computer in a messy newsroom with a box of doughnuts beside her. Clump was not the sort of name that suggested you were reading the work of an ace reporter. Clump was the name of an overweight waitress in a greasy diner.

"So what are you up to now?" I asked Amber. I never assumed anything. Just because I had shown up didn't mean she had to change any plans she might have made.

She grinned. "I was thinking of going out for coffee

with Marcus. Think I should?"

I shrugged. "Go nuts."

"Oh, you're real good for a girl's ego. Can't you ever show the slightest amount of jealousy?"

"Nope. Jealousy is a wasted emotion that doesn't belong in a trusting relationship. I would expect that if you wanted to have sex with a little boy you'd tell me first so I could have your bags packed." I was joking around with her.

She laughed at me. "You are so jealous. It just kills you to admit to an emotion like that."

"Possibly, but if a twenty-year-old boy is what you want, go for it. I wouldn't stop you. Truthfully though, I would think your tastes run more toward someone like Seamus. If you were going to be with a man it would probably be someone like him. Strong. Sexy. He could protect you from someone like me, until you found out he's exactly like me."

I'd said too much. Jenna looked at me and Amber gave me that amused grin of hers.

"You're jealous of Seamus," she said. The pieces clicked in her head and she found it very amusing. "You're jealous of your own uncle. When we were in Ireland, it started then, didn't it? That first night. Seamus was comforting me and you thought I was attracted to him because he's like an older, masculine version of you."

I said nothing and just looked at the wall, wondering how she was capable of sizing me up so easily.

Amber laughed. "Talk about ego. You believe that even if I left you I'd go for someone exactly like you."

"Tell me you wouldn't," I said. Supreme confidence. I was nothing like I'd been when I was paralyzed. Now I was back to me.

Jenna joined in Amber's laughter. "Geez Meagan, the Goddess certainly blessed you with a big head, didn't she?"

They were teasing me. Having fun with the peculiar way my mind worked.

"Alright," I said. "If the two of you are done, I'll admit that, yes, the thought did occur to me. So what? It's not that unreasonable to think you're attracted to my excessive kind of personality. Look at how long you waited to get your hands on it. You waited through an exile in London, a marriage, paralysis, drug addiction. Tell me you're not a glutton for punishment and like it or not, mine can be a punishing personality. It's not intentional but it happens. Same thing with Seamus. Same thing with *Gwynne*, if you want to get right down to it. You're a bitch magnet. You draw to you the very people who are capable of breaking your fragile heart if they don't battle with themselves daily not to do it. That being said, I love you, and I don't think I've hurt you in a very long time."

Amber was speechless. Jenna nodded her agreement.

"It's true," she said. "Minus the b-word everything Meagan just said is the absolute truth. I don't know why she insists on seeing herself that way when she's not, but she does have an excessive personality and you *are* attracted to that. Gwynne was ten times worse than Meagan, surely you see that, and I can only suspect that Seamus is even worse than the two of them. Not that I'm saying you're attracted to Seamus."

"I'm not."

"I can just see her line of reasoning. She didn't like it when you were with Gwynne. And not just for the obvious reasons. She didn't like it because she was able to see that Gwynne's personality was even more excessive than her own. More hot-tempered."

"Exactly," Amber said. "They're complete opposites." She turned to me. "When you get mad the wall of ice goes up. Your voice turns to glass and you become distant and cold. When Gwynne got mad it was an explosion of rage. It's like fire and ice. Opposites. Personally, I prefer the ice. But you're changing too. Ever since you started walking again you're calmer. Inside. You still have that nervous energy but now it's just an external thing, like you've found some sort of peace. Maybe I'm a part of that, maybe not, but I guess I'd like to think that I am."

She was the biggest part of it. That's why I had the ring in my pocket, because it was the only way I knew to show her how important she was to me. I wasn't good with words or self-expression but I could whip up a cauldron of symbolism like nobody's business. Thank my Gran for that. She taught me that action was often more important than words. I didn't always follow that advice in my life but when it came to Amber I was willing to try. Gran would have wanted me to. She wouldn't have cared if Amber were a woman or a man. It would have been more important to her that I had found the kind of love she always talked about. The kind you would risk your life for and the kind that only comes along once in a lifetime. It was her greatest wish for me.

Jacob was another impetus for growth in my life. He had come out of nowhere, startling me with his sudden presence, but once he'd arrived, a friendship developed from what seemed the ashes of some long past destruction. We talked and the nightmares lessened. The headaches eased like a pressure that had been building in my head since the day I came out of the coma had, at long last, found its own release. We slashed through each other's memories and the more we shared the more we remembered. It was like awakening to a new spiritual consciousness. Life in the Summerlands. We remembered how beautiful it was and I came to the conclusion that I had, indeed, come back for Amber. I wanted to show her I could be a better person, only I had gotten sidetracked along the way and it had gotten worse before it could get better.

Jacob told me he remembered passing through Ken. Beth had told him Ken was my husband and he wanted to know what my husband thought of my sleep. He didn't get the answer to that. What he got was a vibration of intense anger that scared him. Ken was angry with me and Jacob decided he didn't like him very much.

"Why would he be mad at you?" he asked me one day. "All you were doing was sleeping."

I evaded the question. Didn't tell him Ken had several reasons to be mad at me at the time because, as much as he seemed older, Jacob was still a child.

We saw each other often. Sometimes I'd pick him up after work and take him to a movie so Martha could have some time to do her homework and relax, and Amber could have a few more hours alone working on her novel. I never asked her what she was writing about. She was private when it came to her work and wouldn't show anyone until she was sure it was her best. What I did do was rent the apartment across the hall after Judy moved downstairs so Amber could have a quiet place to write. She didn't like working in any of the spare offices down at Markham-Summers and I grew weary of watching her try to concentrate at the kitchen table while I wanted to watch TV or read and felt like I was distracting her either way.

The apartment became available and I saw an opportunity. Amber was shocked when she returned home one day to find the kitchen table cleared of her debris and her laptop missing. I took her across the hall and thought she was going to faint when she saw the furnished living room, funky, the way she liked it, the new cappuccino maker in the kitchen, and one of the bedrooms turned into a functioning office, complete with its own phone line, a fax machine, and a photo copier that *Natural Beauty* was getting rid of in favor of a newer model. The whole thing had cost me very little. The furniture was Jenna's old stuff, pulled out of storage, the fax machine another *Natural Beauty* throw-away, and the phone line, a fifty-dollar connection fee. The apartment had changed occupants several times since Jenna had moved out, distressing the building's owner, and I was able to finagle a very good deal out of him on a one year lease. I put it in Amber's name so it would be a business write-off, for her. As it turned out, Amber would not let me pay for it at all. Once she saw what I had done, she agreed it was a good idea but asserted that she would pay for it herself. There was no reason for me to pay for her to have a quiet place to write, she'd said. It made her uncomfortable when I did such things. When I bought her a car she accused me of trying to buy her and took it back. Then she apologized, saying she understood it was only my way of expressing love but that it had to stop.

"Be there for me as a person," she'd said, "not as my financial institution."

It was a new concept for me but I tried. Jacob helped with that, too. He reminded me that there was no money in the Realm and I had liked it enough there to consider staying. He was very wise for a child. Sometimes so wise it was hard to remember that he was just a child. He was like a little burst of light and I enjoyed spending time with him.

Amber liked him too. So did Josh and Jenna and Sammy, who looked up to the older boy like he was God. We became like some strange little surrogate family who went to the zoo or the park at least one Saturday a month and Martha couldn't have been happier for her son. She was working hard on bettering herself so she could better their lives and she appreciated the time Jacob got to spend with others, especially since her sister had moved her family away and it was just the two of them now. And us. We were an unconventional group. It didn't get any more twenty-first century than us.

After the lecture Jenna, Amber and I went out for supper then on to The Purple Cauldron, where I had prepared for Zeppo and his new boyfriend Nathan to meet us. No one had heard from Adrian in months and I wondered, in passing, what he was up to. He had been my friend once. Perhaps the wrong kind of friend, but a friend nonetheless, and a part of me missed him.

Nathan was alright. He was older than Zeppo. Thirty-seven and a bank manager in one of the chrome and glass buildings uptown. They'd met at one of Zeppo's shows and had hit it off instantly. Zeppo, at long last, had finally had his fill of twenty-four year old pretty boys who wanted nothing more out of life than to get laid or high, and he settled into a comfortable relationship with the quiet banker. They were good for each other, I supposed. Zeppo drew Nathan out of his shell a bit and Nathan toned down Zeppo's juvenile antics. We were all growing up in our ways. It was scary, but true.

Amber was surprised to find the two men sitting at our regular table when we walked in.

"What are doing here?" she squealed. Zeppo rarely ventured into our neighborhood unless it was to stop by the apartment.

"Meagan invited us," he said. "She wanted to celebrate your speech today."

Amber turned and squeezed me in a hug and I pretended to flinch. I knew what I was about to do so I was just having some fun with her first. Jenna knew too and she gave me a sneaky grin as Amber released me and turned her face to hide the fact that she was pissed off by my reaction to her embrace. Some things never change, she was thinking. After all this time I still flinched when she touched me in public. She was about to find out differently.

She took the chair beside Zeppo and I sat across from Nathan and said hello. Jenna sat beside Amber, unconsciously joining in my little game.

"We're just here for a bit," I told Amber. "I have to do something then we can go on to a club or back to our place if you want."

"What do you have to do?" she asked suspiciously.

"You'll see," I singsonged.

What I had to do was what I'd been terrified of since the day I met her.

I waited for the coffeehouse to fill with the Thursday night crowd. It had been the same crowd for the past few years. They used to come to watch Amber, back when she was the resident poet, and I, the person in the audience they knew she was making uncomfortable. Later they came to watch a different kind of show. That of the poet being affectionate to the woman in the audience and the woman in the audience looking even more uncomfortable. Tonight they would get their final show. The end result of all those hours spent watching my relationship with Amber ebb and flow. Tonight they would see that I was fearless. So would Zeppo, who still had his occasional doubts about me, and so would Amber, who would never expect what was coming.

Eight o'clock. Full house and Mitch approached the mic.

"Before we begin with the poets tonight," he said, "a friend asked if she could borrow the mic for a few minutes. She's not a public speaker, so bear with her, alright?"

Mitch left the stage and Amber's eyes widened when I stood up. She never would have suspected he was talking about me. I hated being a public spectacle. She knew that.

Nervously, I approached the mic and tilted it forward. "Thanks Mitch," I said. My voice echoed through the room and I jumped.

"Christ, that's loud, isn't it?"

Laughter from the crowd. Amber grinned up at me. She knew how to do this; she'd been doing it for years. I was a stage virgin. I removed the mic from the stand and pulled up a stool, sitting on it and hooking the heels of my boots around the bottom rung the way I had seen Amber do it a hundred times before.

"I won't take up much of your time," I said. Jenna was grinning up at me. Her hands were pressed together like she couldn't wait. "A lot of you have been coming in here as long as I have and you've seen me in various stages of erratic behavior." More laughter. "You used to come in to watch Amber but little else escaped your curious notice. Do you know what I'm talking about?

"Oh yeah," someone called.

I nodded and brushed back my bangs. "Good. So that's why I'm up here now, to admit what you've always known anyway. I'm embarrassing the hell out of myself because I want to prove to someone how important she is to me and I'll go to any length to do it."

Amber's eyes misted and she stared up at me like nothing in her life had ever been as important as this moment. I looked at her and smiled.

"You'll call me corny for this later," I said, directly to her. She shook her head and I laughed. "Oh, you will. You won't be able to resist but I don't care. I'm only up here for one purpose, to tell you I love you and I don't care who knows it. I've never known anyone like you and you awe me. I suppose you already know that but you probably don't know how utterly grateful I am for your presence in my life. You've stood by me through so much. Twice, you saved my life. First when you called me out of the coma, and later, when the paralysis had almost beaten me and I was ready to give up. Most importantly, ever since the day I met you, you've been slowly teaching me how to be brave."

She was staring up at me through teary eyes and I gave a little chuckle. "Don't cry, okay? Just come up here for a second because I want to give you something, and then I can stop interrupting the show--or maybe I'm giving my own little show."

A few snickers in the audience as Amber made her way to the stage and climbed the steps to stand beside me. I reached into the pocket of my jacket and felt the cool metal circle, then pulled it out and showed it to her.

"You had a duplicate made?" she whispered. She was smiling. Knew this was very important.

I nodded. "But before I give it to you I have to tell you what it means. You know about my ring and the bond it represents. This ring has basically the same meaning except it comes with a bigger promise because now it's part of a matching set. Do you see where I'm going with this?"

I was afraid of where I was going with this. I was about to say something I never thought I'd say in my life because it was too bizarre. She stared at me, waiting. I sucked in a breath of air and plunged.

"With this ring I'm actually marrying you, Amber. I know it's not legal, and it certainly isn't binding, but if you accept it, then you're accepting my vow to always love you and you're making one in return." I looked at her meaningfully, terrified my next words were going to embarrass us both. "So will you accept it and be my uh...wife?"

Amber threw her arms around my neck and kissed me so passionately the jaded coffee crowd cheered. "Yes," she said. "You know the answer's yes."

I gave her the ring and someone in the audience yelled, "It's about time!"

"Isn't it?" Amber said.

Smiling, I placed the mic back on the stand and gave a little thank you wave to Mitch as Amber and I left the stage.

"I can't believe you did it," Jenna squealed. "You got up in front of all these people and created your own strange little wedding ceremony."

I shook my fingers through my hair. "God, now I know what it feels like to be a man. That was absolutely terrifying."

Zeppo reached across the table and gave my hand a quick squeeze. "It took guts to do what you did and I can't doubt anymore that you really do love her."

"I always did, Zep."

"Can't you let me give you a compliment without turning it into something?"

"Sorry but I'm waiting for the follow-up insult."

He reached for his coffee. "Not tonight."

I turned to Amber. "Were you as embarrassed as I was?"

"Not the slightest bit," she said, shaking her head. "I know what it took for you to do that, Meagan. You don't like people looking at you, let alone seeing you for who you really are. You exposed yourself to all these people for me and I think I'm gonna cry."

"You're always crying," Zeppo said.

"Maybe she learned it from you," Nathan teased. Zeppo scowled at him and I got the feeling this relationship was not going to last long.

"So, what do you want to do now?" I asked Amber. "Go to a club?" I didn't mind if other people drank around me. Amber shook her head. "Do you want to stay here?" She shook her head again and looked at me, waiting for me to catch on. I didn't.

"Meagan," Zeppo said, when it became obvious I wasn't about to catch on. "For someone so smart you sure are stupid." I looked at him blankly. "She wants to go home and fuck you, bonehead."

"Zeppo!" Nathan reprimanded. Jenna and I laughed and Amber smirked. We weren't offended by his language. This was how we talked--right out with it.

"What?" Zeppo demanded. "I almost want to fuck her myself right now."

I laughed. "Does *everyone* want to fuck me right now?" I teased.

The whole table nodded and we roared with laughter.

And no one noticed Vicki Clump in the back of the room eagerly taking notes.

Chapter 13

The story broke in the university gazette the following week. "Lecture Poet Weds Publisher in Bizarre Two Minute Ceremony." Byline: Vicki Clump. It was tabloid journalism at its worst. Two thousand copies printed and circulated among staff and students alike. A scandal, my mother thought. Her reputation destroyed. How would she ever face her colleagues again? The biggest problem was that the story was true. Her daughter had actually gotten up in front of a coffeehouse full of people and symbolically married another woman.

I didn't see the problem. While I wasn't pleased with the article, symbolic *was* the key word. I wasn't *actually* married, only by love--which was more important anyway, but less conflicting for society in general.

Amber was nervous. For the first time since her brother's death she was concerned about the consequences of her sexuality. My mother was going insane. Amber thought I would go insane too, perhaps even break up with her to spare everyone the added embarrassment that was sure to come. I didn't do either of those things. I told Amber to relax, told my mother to be quiet and accept what had been done, and did the only other thing I could do. I called Vicki Clump in for a meeting.

She arrived promptly at eleven am the next day. Cynthia showed her into my office with a sideways glare, and she sat in the chair in front of my desk nervously fiddling with the strap on her purse. I leaned across the desktop and peered at her.

"I'm glad you could come, Miss Clump," I said. "I honestly didn't think you would."

Her eyes darted around the room like a timid animal sensing a trap, paused briefly on my face, then looked away.

"I'll just get on with this," I said. "I've read your article and I can't say I'm pleased. You wanted your interview and Amber put you off so like the true rat that you are, you found another way to get your story." She flinched. "You're an ambitious little thing, aren't you? So ambitious that you followed us from the school and tailed us all night." I'd had plenty of time to figure it out. "Probably sat outside the restaurant for an hour waiting. Then you followed us to the coffeehouse where your efforts paid off and you got an even bigger story than you could have dreamed. You taped every last word of what went on in there. Then you ran home, played the tape, and got down to business on your computer. I'm guessing you used one of those little micro-cassette recorders and there's a tape spinning in your pocket right now. Hand it over."

I'd startled her, proving my hunch was right, and she was as devious as I suspected. She stared at me, deliberated for a moment, then pulled a tape recorder from her pocket and slid it across the desk. I took it, ejected the tape, placed it on the desk in front of me, and gave her a hard look. Who did she think she was screwing with?

"Now the other one," I said.

"Excuse me?"

"Miss Clump, we've already established that you made another tape last week. Your kind always does and I know it's sitting in your other pocket. Maybe you thought you'd use it as some sort of blackmail if things didn't go your way in here. I don't know what your motives might be but you have it and I want it."

Vicki blinked twice. I had her number and she knew it. Her hand fumbled in her left pocket and she handed over the other tape. There wasn't a duplicate. She hadn't considered making one. That's why it took her so long to decide. She feared she was losing her leverage.

I stared at her. She wasn't an attractive girl. She wasn't ugly. Just average. Mousy brown hair, flat brown eyes, plain features. Everything about her screamed a mediocrity she hated having. She'd had an average childhood and average parents. When she grew up she had average boyfriends and average friends. Plain Jane. And no one made a better tabloid reporter than a plain Jane with a heart full of envy. They'd do anything to get their story. Dig through garbage dumpsters, stalk celebrities, harass politicians. Vicki was a plain Jane and she was hungry. I was about to feed her.

I crossed my legs on top of my desk and peered at her

over the silver pen I twisted in my hands, letting her sweat a little.

"Have you ever heard of *The Watcher,* Miss Clump?"

She shrugged. "Sure. It's a tabloid."

I nodded. "One of ours. It's not the publication we're most proud of but it makes us a lot of money and that gives us the opportunity to concentrate our efforts on other projects. Often high-risk projects. My partner and I won't take the chance of being sued so everything printed in *The Watcher* is 100% true. Our editor-in-chief makes sure that not one story gets printed without proof backing it up. Witnesses, a paper trail-- whatever. As long as we can prove it, we're safe. Like you, right?"

I paused, giving my words a chance to soak in, staring at her as if I was just seeing who she really was.

"You are a sneaky, deceitful little bitch, Vicki." Her jaw dropped. Hadn't expected *that.* "I knew it from the moment you stood up in that auditorium with your chewed pen cap. There are only two reasons why people gnaw on things. Either they're bored or they're anxious. You weren't bored. You were a woman anxious to get your story and you went about it in the most underhanded way possible. That is what's required of a tabloid journalist."

Vicki perched forward on her chair. "I don't understand," she said. "Are you offering me a job or insulting me?"

"Both," I said. "I don't like you, Miss Clump. I'll be perfectly honest about that. You're unscrupulous and hard. But those are the exact qualities that can make you an asset to me. Fortunately, I am capable of disliking you and employing you at the same time. So here's the deal. If you want it, there is a position open for a new reporter down at *The Watcher*. The starting pay isn't great but people seem to move up quickly over there. Are you interested?"

Her eyes lit up. "Yes, of course."

I nodded. "Good. Then you'll have to go down and talk to Henry Faulkner, the editor-in-chief. I've already spoken with him and he's expecting your call."

I stood. Vicki stood. She stuck out her hand. I ignored it.

"Thank you," she said. "I don't know how to thank you."

I dropped my pen on the desk.

"Two more things, Vicki," I said. "First thing, you might want to consider changing your name. Use a pseudonym or something. Clump doesn't cut it. Second thing," I stared her down and lowered my voice to a menacing hiss, "Don't ever fuck with me again. This time it got you a job. Next time you'll be the sorriest you've ever been. Understood?"

She gave a guilty nod and scurried out the door, eager to get across town to *The Watcher* building. I settled back in my chair and grinned.

I was a big believer in the old saying: Keep your friends close, your enemies closer. Vicki Clump would never cross me again.

"*You did what?*" my mother screeched.

"I gave her a job."

It was family dinner night at my parent's house and everyone was there; Josh, Jenna and Sammy, Danielle and Mark, and Amber and me. Jenna grinned around a forkful of mashed potatoes, Josh laughed, Dad shook his head and Danielle and Mark giggled. Amber had been surprised when I'd first given her the news as well but she knew business was business and she was amused by the way I was able to separate my personal feelings from my work.

"How could you give her a job after what she did?" my mother demanded.

I shrugged and reached for my glass of water. Everyone else was drinking wine.

"That's precisely why I gave her the job. Think about what the girl did. She tailed us for four and a half hours and for absolutely no other reason than to see what she could come up with. She wasn't tipped off on what was going to happen because no one knew. Maybe she had a hunch. Maybe she's freaking psychic, I don't know. I don't care. But the girl was prepared for whatever might happen. She taped what went on in the Cauldron. I took it from her. She even had the audacity to come into my office with a running tape recorder in her pocket.

Do you know what that says about her?"

"Yes, that she's a deceitful little girl who can't be trusted."

I folded my hands on top of my head and smirked."Exactly. Vicki Clump has a killer instinct. Perfect psychological makeup to be a tabloid reporter. She's a garter snake who thinks she's a python. Put the other stuff aside and you have to kind of admire that. Now she's in the pit with the anacondas and they'll either teach her well or eat her alive. It's my guess she won't get eaten. She's too hungry herself."

"She dropped out of school," my mother said. "Do you know that?"

I shrugged. What did I care?

"I suppose she would have to if she wanted the job. It doesn't bother me. The girl is vicious. People like that rarely fail."

Danny howled with laughter. "You kill me, Meagan. You won't be Amber's publisher, won't give me a job, but you'll hire some girl who tried to destroy you both and did a fine job of embarrassing your own mother along the way."

"It's business, Danny," I said. "I do what's good for business. Vicki Clump will be an asset to *The Watcher* and that makes her an asset to Markham-Summers. I've hired her and that's the end of it."

My father nodded his agreement. "She did the smart thing," he said, drawing on his years of running a sometimes-overzealous accounting staff. He was used to having to watch people like a hawk because if he didn't, a few of them might try to please their clients by playing with the numbers a little, risking an audit for a higher refund.

"Meagan knows what she's doing," he said. "So I suggest we all get off her back and let her run *her* business the way she thinks it needs to be run. She's done well enough thus far."

I patted his hand. "Thanks, Dad. I can always count on you to be on my side."

That got me a glower from Mom. She hated to be disagreed with, especially by my father. She decided to change course and try to find another way of getting under my skin. She was pissed about the article and she wasn't going to let me get away with it. As if I had written it.

"So tell me about this supposed wedding," she said, spitting the word *supposed* at me. She was getting under my skin, fast. "The article said you gave Amber some sort of ring and made a vow. Explain this to me."

I felt my temper flare under the weight of her patronizing eyes.

"You know what?" I said. "I don't have to explain a goddamn thing to you. I'm twenty-nine years old and I'll do whatever the hell pleases me."

My mother could always reduce me to acting like a rebellious adolescent.

Amber's hand moved under the table and gave my thigh a squeeze. The kind of squeeze that said, "Okay, calm down", and I pressed the fleshy space between my eyes that always crinkled when my temper flared. The table remained silent; respectfully waiting for me to calm down.

"Okay," I said, after a few long moments. "You want to understand and maybe you're entitled to that."

"*Maybe?*" my mother demanded.

My temper gave another quick flare. "Don't push it, all right? The article Vicki wrote was one hundred percent accurate. It happened exactly like she said, or wrote, whatever. The point is, I had a duplicate made of Gran's moonstone and gave it to Amber in front of all those people and vowed that I would always love her. I don't know if that makes what happened a wedding, but it was certainly a publicly made commitment. I don't plan on hiding anything, mother. I don't care who knows I love her and you'll just have to accept that. I'm sorry if you got embarrassed but it's over now and you can't be outed twice. At least I don't think you can. And since we're on the topic of pulling things out of hiding I think there's something else I should tell you too. All of you."

Josh looked away. The son of a bitch already knew. I glanced at Jenna and she gave an apologetic shrug. The others stared and Amber squeezed my hand under the table.

"Are you sure?" she whispered.

I squeezed back. I was sure.

"Now, before you all freak out let me assure you that this part of my life is now over and it has been for a long time."

"What did you do this time?" Danielle joked. "Become a drug addict?"

I met her gaze squarely. "Yes."

"*What?*" It was a collective cry.

"That's why you won't have a glass of wine with dinner anymore," Danielle said. "I knew something was up."

I nodded. "It was when I was paralyzed. Amber and Jenna saw me through it. It was a crazy time for all three of us and I owe them my life. Like I said, it's over now and my life is back on track so any worrying at this point would be silly. Just thank Amber I'm alive."

This sort of speech embarrassed her. She stared down at her plate.

"Did you save my daughter's life?" my mother asked. Echoes of Seamus asking essentially the same thing. Ours was a dramatic family. But there was a new respect for Amber creeping into my mother's voice.

"I helped her off drugs," Amber said. "So did Jenna." She didn't like being credited for saving anyone's life. It made her uncomfortable. There is a superstition that says if you save a person's life you become responsible for it. Maybe that was what she was afraid of, being held accountable. I didn't think so. Amber didn't place much stock in superstition, she just didn't want to be praised for something she thought any decent human being would do.

"Who else knows?" my father asked.

"Seamus," I said.

"Of course," my mother said.

"Vicki Clump?" Dad joked.

I laughed. Leave it to him to lighten things up.

"Definitely not," I said. "It's old news. I just thought you should know."

My mother saw Amber in a different light after that. She became more than friendly. Slowly, she was learning to be as affectionate with Amber as she had been with Ken. I told her about Jeff, and as I suspected, it broke her heart. She opened herself even more to Amber and the uneasiness between them passed. Amber stopped bending over backwards and my mother grew to respect her for it. It was a good time for all of us.

I still had the dreams. I didn't look at them as

nightmares anymore because I was starting to accept that they had significance. They meant to tell me something. *What* they meant to tell me I didn't know but I suspected it was something important and asked Jenna to hook me up with a hypnotherapist. She knew all sorts of people like that.

But the experience yielded little help. Instead of finding out what I'd encountered while in the coma I regressed to past life in which I discovered I had been a witch who was hanged and quartered in medieval England after three days of torture during which I refused to confess my crime. Amber and Jenna were also there. Amber had been my husband and Jenna had been my sister, which explained a lot about their influence on my current life. I wasn't sure I believed any of it even though it had come from my memory, but it was interesting to learn. Amber thought it was funny. Jenna thought it was true, and she planned on regressing herself, just to "verify" things. Only Jenna would seek out verification in the unconscious. The eerie thing was she found it. Even returned with greater details, like how I had swung from the gallows because I refused to reveal the whereabouts of my sister whom I had sent away in order to protect her from the hysteria I was caught up in. She figured we were even. I'd saved her life centuries ago and she had been spending this one trying to save mine, even when I didn't need saving.

Jenna wanted Amber to go, but Amber refused. While she didn't fully believe in such things, they scared her. She didn't want to know who she had been centuries ago, her only concern was with who she was now, and that she knew. Aside from Jenna, Amber was the only other person I knew who was completely aware of herself. That she had once been a six foot tall Englishman with stark black hair and penetrating blue eyes only made her laugh. It made *me* wonder why she was always gifted with incredible eyes.

So the experience was amusing but unhelpful. All I really discovered about being in the coma was what I had already known, that I had made the decision to come back.

The dreams spoke to me of a challenge. One night I dreamed I was in an enchanted forest surrounded by foliage and animals and I connected the place to the word, Summerlands. Jacob knew it well. In the dream a man came to me. He was tall and celestial looking and he said his name was Victor.

"I know you, don't I?" I said.

He smiled brightly. "You know me. You may not remember me but you know me. I've come to tell you that you are approaching a challenge. Do you remember we once spoke of this? You didn't want to know what the challenge was then."

I smiled back. "That much I do remember," I said. "But I've faced my challenges. I gave Amber my lie, which she did not accept. I beat the paralysis and I beat the drug addiction."

Victor shook his head. "Those were only obstacles, Meagan. The real challenge has yet to come. I've come here now to tell you and I find you would still prefer to be kept in the dark. Perhaps I will come back again when you are ready."

He started to disappear.

"No," I said. "Don't go. Tell me."

But Victor continued to fade and I woke up yelling, "Tell me what the challenge is!"

Amber got nervous. Fate, it seemed, was not done with us yet and she was learning to think in those terms. Learning to believe in what she never would have imagined possible. She didn't like this forced reality any more than I did but something kept pushing us to face things beyond our human reasoning. Things like the spiritual world Jenna revered and which I continued to drift in and out of. I didn't want to be chosen for any challenge. I just wanted to get on with my life. That, it seemed, wasn't about to happen.

In the second week of October my siblings and I threw a party to celebrate our parents' thirty-fifth wedding anniversary. We rented a hall and invited one hundred and sixty guests. Even Seamus flew in from Ireland for the occasion. He sat at the head table with my parents, my siblings, Amber and me, while Celia, my mother's sister, and her husband Ralph were relegated to a table a few feet away. There simply wasn't room for them at the head table. Too bad.

Celia scowled at me all through dinner, which consisted of three choices of entree--roast lamb (Dad's favorite), prime rib, and vegetarian lasagna for the few of us who didn't care to eat meat. Dessert consisted of a small wedge of marble cheesecake placed on the side of a lovely chocolate flower filled with a scoop of vanilla ice cream and drizzled with creme de menthe. I stared at the green liquid dripping down the ice cream and into the chocolate cup.

"Aren't you going to eat that?" Amber asked, scooping some caviar from one of the bowls that sat on every table. She spread it on a wafer of some sort and popped it in her mouth. I shuddered. Glad I didn't have to eat it.

"There's creme de menthe on the ice cream. I think I better not."

"I'm sure it's fine, Meagan," my mother said.

"Still, I'd rather not."

Celia watched me push away my plate and gave me another condescending scowl. My mother had, at some point, confessed my problem to her and she couldn't resist giving me the eyes that said she thought I was a lowlife. She thought my dress was too revealing. She'd made mention of it when we'd first walked in. It was not revealing at all. I'd chosen a silver sheath with a knee-length hemline for precisely that reason. It was sexy, shimmery, but understated at the same time. I wore silver jewelry, the ring that never left my hand, a few silver bangles on my arm, and silver hoop earrings. I thought maybe it was too much silver but Jenna said I looked like a moon goddess, all shimmery and cosmic. She was decked out in a long white dress that gave her the appearance of a curvaceous yet virginal earth bride.

Danielle had decided on the longest, tightest dress I'd ever seen, and I was surprised at what a remarkable body she had. She was prone to wearing baggy sweatshirts and loose-fitting jeans, but now, in her skin-tight cotton-spandex body vise she looked like a long stretch of red curves.

Amber wore a black dress that cut inward at the waist but hung loosely enough to give her a sexy, comfortable look. I smiled at her. The woman *was* sex. She wore a thin diamond necklace that sparkled against her lightly golden skin, silver nail polish "so that we matched" and of course, the ring. Zeppo had once commented that Amber was sexual and I was sensual. Looking at us now, I thought he was probably right. Amber wore musky perfumes. I wore light, floral scents. Her hair was blond and straight, but choppy enough to give it a sexy edge.

Mine was highlighted and tousled, like I'd just rolled out of bed and had rather enjoyed the experience. Her eyes were deep and lusty, mine were aware but warm. We were complete opposites in every way and yet we went together perfectly.

Dinner came to an end and the band struck up a song that got people on their feet. My parents went up to dance. Josh grabbed a lonely looking cousin, thirteen-year-old Bethany, and led her to the dance floor while she giggled behind her hands and looked up adoringly at her handsome relative. Jenna, Amber, Danielle and I stayed at the table catching up with Seamus. Ralph asked Celia to dance and, reluctantly, she took his hand and followed him to the dance floor, giving our group a disgusted glance as she passed.

"That woman is really pushing me," I bitched.

Jenna sipped her wine. "Well, she hasn't said anything yet so maybe she won't."

We chatted awhile longer and the first dance came to an end. The band jumped into a more upbeat song and some of the older couples went back to their tables, Celia and Ralph included. Celia asked Ralph to go get her a drink and the minute he left for the bar she ambled over to our group. Waddled was more like it, I thought.

"What do you want, Celia?" Seamus complained, taking one look at her bitchy face.

She sneered at him. "Want, Seamus? Look at this table. A drunk, a freak, a drug addict and a lesbian--make that *two* lesbians. You're all corrupt. Seamus, you corrupted Meagan when she was just a little girl and now she corrupts everyone she comes in contact with. Well I have one good niece left and I plan on keeping it that way. Come away from there, Danielle, these people are no good."

"These *people* are my family," Danielle corrected, glaring up at Celia.

Celia's eyes softened on her face. "You have to know where to draw the line, sweetie. You can love your family, but you can't always be around them--not this part of the clan anyway. Do you want your sister to corrupt you? She's sinning Danielle, they all are. And they'll take you straight to hell with them."

"Shut up, Celia," Seamus growled.

"I will not."

I pinched the bridge of my nose in frustration. "*Who* do I corrupt?"

"Your brother, for starters. Weren't you the one who introduced him to that freak of nature?" Her head indicated Jenna. "They have a child, and she carries on with crystals and tarot cards and all the things the church warns us about. She might be the worst one yet because her evils are intentional."

Jenna remained silent and I glared at my aunt. "I suggest you get away from this table, Celia, or I will have you forcibly removed from this party."

"You have no authority to do that," she scoffed.

"Who the fuck do you think is paying for it?" I barked. "The very people you're standing here insulting. One more word about Jenna or anyone else and I'll make sure your fat ass gets thrown out of here."

"Don't you swear at me little lady, with that filthy mouth of yours. No wonder your husband left you." She pulled a small black Bible from her purse and dropped it in front of me. "Read that."

I tossed it aside. "I have. Your problem, Celia, is that your legs are locked together at the knees. Maybe if you let old Uncle Ralph give it to you now and then you wouldn't be so bitchy all the time. And for the record, my husband did not leave me, I left him." I nodded in Amber's direction and smirked. "Cause I get off on eating her pussy."

Celia gasped. "You vulgar little---"

Her words were drowned out by the laughter that erupted from Seamus and Danielle. Jenna flushed and Amber turned her head but she couldn't control the giggle that turned up in her throat. It burst out of her and she buried her face behind my back.

"You are just trash, Meagan Summers."

"And you're a frigid old cow."

Ralph appeared at Celia's side, frowning. "What's going on over here?" He wasn't a bad guy, really. He was just kept on a very short leash.

"Get her away from this table, Ralph," Seamus warned. "Or I will."

Ralph dragged Celia away while she continued to

shake her head in disbelief and Amber fought for control, wiping her eyes and still giggling every few seconds.

"I can't believe you said that," Jenna hissed. "She's gonna spread it all over this party."

"*I* can't believe she said it," Amber howled. "She can do it but she can't say it."

Celia was back at her table now, explaining the events to her husband and watching us. I thought I'd really give her something to look at and picked up the Bible. "Give me your lighter, Seamus."

"Are you crazy, girl?" he screeched. "You're not settin' fire to a Bible. I'm sorry Meggie, but even I have my limits."

"For Christ's sake, Meagan," Danny complained. "Do you have to go right to the edge with everything? It's a Bible!"

"So?"

Amber shook her head. "Don't, Meagan. I know you want to make a point but it's your parents' anniversary."

"You're right." I handed her the Bible. "You always are."

Amber passed the bible on to Jenna who set it at the far corner of the table, clearly out if my reach. Amber knew how to reason with me. She knew I wouldn't care about the book but I would care about ruining my parent's party. She knew me better than anyone, even Jenna.

Relieved, Seamus wiped his brow. "You scared me, Meggie. You wouldn't really burn a Bible, would ya?"

"She would," Amber said. "When Meagan wants to make a point she'll do it by any means necessary."

"You're no different," I said. "What about that day I told you to shut up and you refused to talk to me for three hours?"

"Three hours isn't long," Danny said.

"It is when you're trapped in an elevator."

"You did that to her in an *elevator*?"

Amber giggled. "Well, she kept telling me to shut up. I was freaked out because we were stuck between floors and she just kept saying 'Shut up, Amber. Will you freaking please just shut up?' So I shut up. Within fifteen minutes she was begging me to talk. Then she'd get angry and say "Fine, don't talk", and she'd be pacing the elevator while I sat on the floor laughing in my head."

"Yeah," I said. "Then she pulls out a book and won't even let me read it over her shoulder."

"Amber, you're cruel," Jenna giggled.

"I was making a point."

I chuckled. "Tell them when your point came to an end."

Amber sipped her wine and couldn't help grinning. "She said she was going to leave me there. She got it into her head that she was getting out and somehow managed to get herself up on the railing and popped open the escape hatch at the top of the elevator. With one foot on the railing and one on the wall she starts pulling herself up through the opening like Batgirl or something. I figured it must have been all those months of being paralyzed that helped her, you know, because she learned how to maneuver her body and pull herself around with her arms.

"So she wiggles through and now she's on top of the elevator and, I presume, quite proud of herself and she says 'I swear to God you better say something right now or I'll leave you here and when I get out, I won't send for help.' Well, I knew she would so still I don't say anything. 'Fine,' she says. 'Goodbye'.

"But suddenly the elevator gives a quick jolt and starts moving up. We were stuck between the ninth and tenth floor and the tenth is the top. Meagan can see what it looks like up there but I can't and all I can think is, *Oh my God, she's gonna get crushed!* So I'm gonna talk now, right? I start yelling 'Meagan get out of there, it's going up!' I was terrified.

'I can't,' she says, sounding very afraid. 'My bootlace is stuck on something.'

Now I'm really in a panic. 'Take it off!' I'm screaming. 'Hurry! Take it off!'

'No,' she calls back. 'They're expensive.'

They're expensive? I couldn't believe my ears. She was going to die because her boots were expensive! I'm practically sobbing at this point, so I start screaming louder. 'Are you fucking crazy? Take off the boots!' And the elevator keeps going up.

Suddenly, she drops through the hole in the ceiling and

lands on her feet laughing, bootlaces completely tied. 'Well you're talking now, aren't you?' she says. She hadn't been stuck at all. She'd been playing with me because she could see there was about four feet of space left between the last stop and the top of the elevator shaft. She knew she wasn't gonna get crushed.

Then I really lost it. I couldn't believe she would let me think she was about to die and all because I wouldn't talk to her. I'm screaming at her now, and you know what she says? She says, 'I'm curious, Amber, why didn't you press the 'stop' button?' As if I was trying to kill her! But I hadn't thought about the button because she had me in such a panic I couldn't think straight." Amber laughed. "It's funny now but I could have killed her then."

"Celia's right, Meagan," Danny said. "You truly are insane. How could you do that?"

"You know, I'm getting really tired of people calling me insane."

Seamus waved away Danny's words. "She just can't resist a good practical joke, Danny. Takes after her old uncle."

I fiddled with the bangles on my wrist and grinned. "Still, nothing beats the Jackie encounter."

Seamus chuckled. "Oh, you'll get yours. Seamus never forgets."

"I'm waiting."

"When you least expect it, Meggie."

We were laughing and having a great time when Josh returned to the table and pulled Jenna into his arms. "Come on, wife. Dance with me."

Jenna followed him off and Seamus grabbed Amber. "Us too, Blondie. Let's go for a whirl."

I smiled at them and nodded my approval, glad to see there were some people in the family who really loved Amber. Everyone had warmed to her but Seamus was especially affectionate. I still thought a slight part of him might be attracted to her but I didn't make anything of it. Everyone was attracted to Amber; that was just something I had to deal with on a regular basis. What surprised me was that she never looked like she noticed.

My parents came back to the table and I went off to

dance with my father, who was handsome in a double-breasted suit and a blue silk tie, while my mother spoke with some guests and Danielle scoped the room for eligible men. I spotted one in the corner. A cute brown haired man, who couldn't have been older than twenty-five, with big green eyes and a shy smile. He made me think of my first impression of Ken and I pointed at him over my father's shoulder. Danielle glanced at the corner, smiled, and rose from the table. *Was* I corrupting her? Within seconds she was across the room flirting with him. I watched from my safe distance and the man appeared to be shyly flirting back. They came onto the dance floor. Celia approached my mother and I stiffened. Watched them talk. Dad glanced over and pulled me a little bit closer.

"Don't worry about it," he whispered. "Even your mother's had just about enough of her sister."

I smiled and watched Celia walk away, frowning. "Doesn't Seamus look handsome tonight?" He too was wearing a suit. Only his was grey and shiny. Sharkskin, I thought, though I really didn't know what that was. It just sounded right. And I continued to admire the way the fabric accented my uncle's muscular build.

"He looks good," Dad said. "I also noticed he hasn't had much to drink."

"No, he's cutting down." I was proud of my uncle. "Easing up in his old age, I guess."

The song ended and my father and I went back to the table, followed by Seamus and Amber, then Josh and Jenna. Danielle stayed on the dance floor with her new find and Mom whispered that she'd like to speak with Seamus, Amber and me out in the hallway. We followed her across the room with all the somberness of guilty children about to be punished.

"I know what went on with Celia," she said, closing the banquet room doors behind us. "You made some rather off-color remarks, Meagan?"

"It wasn't her fault, Joan," Seamus said, quickly. "Celia was calling us names and saying we're all going to hell and Meggie was just defendin' herself. And Jenna too. She said some nasty things about Jenna too. Don't blame Meggie."

"I'm not," my mother responded.

I leaned into her like my ears had deceived me. "You're

not?"

"No. In fact, I think Celia deserved to be put in her place. Perhaps you could have done it more tactfully, but I'm not upset with you."

"*You're not?*"

"Meagan, please stop saying that. I called you out here because I want each of you to know how proud I am of the way you look out for one another. I can't say I've always understood it, but I am proud of it. I think I've managed to give each of you a hard time over the years and I'm very sorry for that."

"*You are?*"

"Meagan, can you please just let me finish?"

"Sorry."

"Celia had no right to say anything. If she doesn't accept the three of you, or Jenna, then she doesn't accept me."

"The three of us?" Amber asked, quietly.

My mother patted her hand. "Yes, you too. Meagan loves you so I love you. I think you're actually a good influence on her. You seem to be able to do what no one else can, make her reachable. Meagan has always been the sort who thought she had to take on the world alone. With you, she's vulnerable, and that's a good thing for her. It takes a lot to make her happy but you seem to be able to do it fairly effortlessly. I'm glad you're in her life."

"Me too," Seamus said. "But she's always had me, Joan. And she always will."

Mom gave her brother a genuine smile. "I'm sure she will, Seamus. Along with Jenna. The two of you understood her even when I couldn't. She can be a very peculiar woman."

"Dat, I know."

She crushed him in a hug. "I love you, Seamus."

"You been hittin' the sauce, Joanie? He teased.

"No, I just think it's important that I tell you. We've had our differences but I have always loved you. I love each and every one of you," she continued, giving meaningful looks to each of us in turn, "and we're going to walk back into that room as a family. There are no black sheep here." She reached for the door handle then suddenly turned around to face Amber and me. "Take her hand, Meagan."

My eyes widened in surprise. "Are you sure?"

"We're a family," she said again, wrapping her arm around Seamus' waist. "Take her hand and whoever doesn't like it will have to deal with me."

Seamus pulled her closer. "Dat's the spitfire I remember. You have your mother's blood Meggie, and dat's something to be very proud of."

I felt my eyes mist as I took Amber's hand. "Yes, it is." And together the four of us walked back into the banquet room.

At one in the morning the food was brought out again, only this time it was a buffet table filled with waffles, pancakes, eggs, bacon, sausage, and French toast--an early breakfast for the remaining guests who straggled about the banquet room, popping the last of the balloons and closing down the bar. Celia and Ralph had left shortly after we'd returned from the hallway and Danielle had proceeded to get drunk with her new friend. I wasn't sure I liked what I was seeing and approached her several times to tell her to slow down. Josh told me to leave her alone.

Breakfast came to an end and my parents saw the last of the guests out, stayed for one last glass of champagne, and thanked us for a lovely party before leaving. It *had* been a lovely party, and we were down to the same group who'd sat at the head table earlier being insulted by Celia. Josh and Jenna were cuddled up at the far end of the table and Seamus, Amber and I sat across from them. Danny had disappeared. I thought maybe she'd gone home with our parents because I hadn't seen her since they'd left.

"Maybe we should get going too," Amber said, rubbing her eyes. "Are you staying with us, Seamus?"

"If you'll have me."

"Don't be silly, of course we'll have you."

Everyone reached for their coats and I headed for the bathroom, still wondering about Danielle. I swung open the ladies room door and my wondering came to an abrupt end. There she stood, hunched over the vanity, her dress pressed up around her waist while the man who'd reminded me of Ken furiously pumped into her from behind. She was moaning, thrashing her head about and the man was saying "that's right, baby, I'm fucking you. I'm fucking you good."

Her breath came in short gasps and I screamed, "What the fuck are you doing?" Oh, I knew what she was doing.

The man climaxed at that exact moment. He let out a low, guttural groan and I saw his penis slip out of my sister and spit its liquid across the top of her bare buttocks. Danny yanked down her dress, smearing the mess into her skin, and the man quickly zipped his pants.

"Don't scream," she slurred. "He's really nice."

"*Nice?*" I screamed. "He's fucking a drunk woman in a bathroom! Seamus!"

"Oh God, not Seamus!" Danny was horrified. The man fumbled with his sports jacket and I grabbed Danielle by the ear, pulling her out of the bathroom and into the banquet room where everyone stood stock still as Danielle fought against me crying, "Let go of me! You have no right. Let go!"

But Seamus wasn't the problem. Josh, spotting the man coming out of the bathroom behind us, put the pieces together quickly and charged at him. "You fucking little shit!" He threw the man against the wall and wrapped his hands around his throat while Danielle sobbed, "Stop it! You'll kill him!" and struggled against me.

Seamus pulled Josh off the man while I threw Danielle into a chair, and the man ran for his life. He darted out the banquet room doors and disappeared. Jenna and Amber said nothing, only stared in disbelief.

"Why can't anyone in this family ever mind their own business?" Danny wailed.

"*Mind their own business?*" Josh was irate. Jenna moved to comfort him but he stalked away from her and marched up to Danielle. "What the hell is the matter with you?"

She ignored him and turned her venom on me. "And just who the fuck do you think you are dragging me around by my *ear?*"

"You were having unprotected sex with a complete stranger in a bathroom!"

"Well, I guess I fit into your precious little group now, don't I?" she snapped. "The freak, the drunk, the drug addict, the dyke, and now the little whore! Aren't *we* the model for dysfunction? Are you happy now? I'm just as sick as the rest of you."

"None of us is sick, Danny," I said.

"Celia was right," she moaned.

"That's why you did this? Because of what Celia said?"

She glared up at me. "No, I did this because I like to *fuck!*"

"Jesus Christ." Josh threw up his hands.

"What, you don't like to fuck, Josh? You don't like sticking it to Jenna? And we all know what Meagan likes, don't we?"

"That's enough," Josh barked. "You're the one who's in trouble here."

"I am not. I'm an adult and I'll fuck whoever I want *whenever* I want. Are you proud of me now, Meagan?"

"Why are you making this about me?"

She knocked a bouquet of flowers off the table. "Because it's always about you, isn't it?"

"What are you talking about?"

"Who can compete with perfect Meagan?"

"Perfect? Danny you're drunk. You're not making any sense."

Just like my big sister, right? Oh we're blood, you and me."

"Yes, we are."

"Don't you fucking agree with me!" Her voice was loud and filled with an anger at me that I didn't understand. "It always works out for you, doesn't it Meagan? Do you always have to win? Do you always have to have everything? Just once I'd like to see you fall on your ass."

"I have," I said, thinking of the paralysis and the drug addiction that had nearly destroyed me.

"Oh, that's right, you were paralyzed. It didn't last though, did it? Your suffering never does."

"Is that what you want?" I yelled. "To see me suffer? Do you hate me that much, Danielle?"

"I don't hate you, I hate your luck. I hate how you just walk around falling into things and then making them yours. You wanna know the real reason I dumped Mark? It was your fault!"

"*My fault?*"

Amber stood beside me and Danielle glared at us. "That's right, I had to dump my boyfriend because the two of you are a couple of dykes."

"I don't understand," Amber said, calmly.

"No? You don't understand that it's every man's fantasy to watch two women going at it? Two women who look like you? Every time he saw the two of you together he'd want to have sex. How do you think that made me feel, Meagan? How was I supposed to live with the fact that my boyfriend was screwing me while picturing my sister and her--whatever she is. Your wife? Your bitch?"

"Watch your mouth."

"Please," Danny scoffed. "She *is* your bitch. Ken was your bitch. What exactly do you do to these people? Tell me, because I'm dying to know your secret. What's so goddamn special about you?"

"Danielle, stop this," Jenna said. "Meagan has nothing to do with what went on tonight."

Danny shot her a look. "Does she need your protection, Jenna? From me? Or maybe she needs Seamus to protect her...or Amber. Well, who the fuck protects me?"

"I do," I said, quietly.

"You do? You wouldn't even give me a job!"

"Because I want you to finish your education."

"And it's back to what you want, isn't it?"

"I want it for *you*. I want you to be better than I am. Danny, you're so smart and you're so damn cute, there's no limit to what you can accomplish. Why take my road? Do it the easy way. Finish school and do something you love, not something you ended up with because your sister gave you a job. And I'm sorry if Mark was an asshole but that's not our fault. You can't blame Amber and me because Mark had some adolescent fantasies."

"Well, it wasn't just him," she barked. "That man you caught me with tonight had the same twisted thing going on in his head. You and Amber walked in here holding hands and of course he *knew*. He couldn't take his eyes off you and he kept asking me questions like if you live together and have I ever seen you kiss. He was trying to get off on the picture he was drawing in his head and it turned my stomach."

"So you had sex with him?" Josh demanded. "What kind of sense does that make?"

Seamus and Jenna grabbed a couple of chairs because

it looked like we were going to be here for awhile. The waiters clearing the tables disappeared. Amber leaned against the table I was half-sitting on and pressed against me ever so gently. It was a non-verbal expression of camaraderie, her way of telling me it was going to be okay.

"What's the difference?" Danielle blasted. "I'm used to it anyway. We were in there screwing and you wanna know when he came?"

"Danny, don't," I pleaded.

"He came when he spotted *her!* Because again, it's always about her! I can't even fuck without her being in it somehow."

"You shouldn't have been fucking him at all!" I yelled feeling disgusted at Danielle's words.

"*You* pointed him out," she stressed.

"For someone to talk to Danielle, I didn't mean for you to find an empty bathroom and have sex with him!"

"Well, maybe you've corrupted me after all."

"I don't corrupt people. If you're gonna start talking like Celia, I don't even want to be around you."

"What's next, Meagan? Are you going to teach me how to be a dyke too? Lord knows, I'll pick up more men that way. All I have to do is turn dyke like my drug addict big sister."

"Stop calling me that!" I wasn't sure if it was *dyke* or *drug addict* that bothered me but my patience was thinning.

"It's okay, baby," Amber breathed into my hair. "She's drunk."

"I know." I lowered my voice. "And don't call me *baby*." But I squeezed her hand to let her know I wasn't angry with her.

"I think we should go," Seamus said. He hated public scenes as much as I did.

"We can continue this discussion when you're sober, Danielle," I said, turning away from her and reaching for my purse.

She shot to her feet and jumped in front of me. "No Meagan, you don't control this scene, *I do*. This fight has been a long time coming and you're not walking out on it."

"Fine." I threw my purse back on the table. "You're working up to something here so just get to it."

She shook her head. "You couldn't even handle what I want to tell you."

"Try me." She was going to tell me she'd once had sex with Basil. I'd known since the day after it happened but I'd never confronted her. She'd been young at the time, insecure. I'd never mentioned to her that Basil had confessed the whole thing but I sensed that right now my sister was so desperate to hurt me, she was going to tell me.

She gave me a menacing sneer. "I fucked Basil once when you were away on business."

"You did what?" Josh shrieked. Jaws dropped around the table. I didn't know why because our family was filled with secrets that always got disclosed in such a way. I thought everyone should be used to it by now.

"I know, Danielle," I said, quietly. "But you were seventeen and I forgave you for that a long time ago."

She wasn't pleased. She'd wanted to blow my mind but it hadn't worked. "I said I fucked Basil!"

"And I said, I know. I've known since the day after it happened. Basil broke down and told me everything. You were his first indiscretion so maybe that will please you. You seduced your older sister's boyfriend when you were nothing more than a kid. You win, alright? I don't care. But what you fail to realize is that it was never a competition to begin with. You're my sister and I won't fight you, not over any man. Especially not over one like him."

The sneer never left her face. She was determined to hurt me. "He was good, Meagan. Basil was one mind-blowing lay."

"I know," I said. "It was one of his better attributes. I wouldn't say mind-blowing, but you can draw your own conclusions from the experience."

Josh whirled around on me. "What is the matter with you? Your seventeen year old sister sleeps with your boyfriend and you don't *tell anyone?*"

"It wasn't anyone's business. It was between Danielle, Basil and me."

"She was seventeen!"

"Why are you jumping on me?" I demanded, "I did what I thought was right. And it wasn't like he took her virginity. They both knew what they were doing and don't you dare try to blame this on me. Basil and Danny had sex-- I don't really give a shit. Yes, I was hurt at the time but it was six years ago. I got over it."

The way I minimized the situation only fueled Danny's rage. She tossed a chair to the floor and shrieked, "Why don't you break? There's something fundamentally wrong with you. I don't think you're even capable of tears. You're so goddamn cold it's like you're dead inside."

"Cold?" I yelled. "When have I ever been cold to you? I knew what you did with Basil and not once did I ever throw it in your face. Instead, I've taken care of you. I paid your rent for a year. I could have let the apartment go when I went to London but I didn't because I knew you wanted it. I signed a new lease, *for you.* I paid your bills. I called you every week to make sure you had groceries and spending money and when you didn't, I sent it to you. Who co-signed the loan on your new car? Who let you charge three thousand dollars on her Visa and never once asked for the money back, or even what you'd spent it on? Don't you dare say I don't protect you and you have one hell of a nerve calling me cold!"

The room was eerily quiet, all except for Danielle who wasn't going down without a fight. "Money, Meagan," she hissed. "That's what you're good for, because you're too stupid to know some people aren't worth your dollars."

"She's not stupid, Danielle," Amber said.

Danny placed her hands on her hips and I watched the anger make a mask of her face. "Well, thank God you have your bitch around to shield you from the truth."

My teeth ground together. "You will not call her my bitch. Apologize, right now."

"No."

I stepped up to her. "Danielle, if you don't apologize to her I'm through with you."

Amber pulled me away. "It doesn't matter."

"Did she know about Basil, Meagan?" Danny demanded. "Did you tell your bitch about that?"

"That's it, Danny. The next time you need money, or your gas is being shut off because you didn't pay the bill, or you're out of food, call someone else."

"Meagan, you don't mean that," Amber whispered.

"No, I do mean it. It's time Danny learned to stand on her own two feet anyway." I pointed an accusing finger. "You want the real world, honey? Well, now you've got it. You're on your own."

"Because I called her a bitch?"

"Because it's time you learned to take care of yourself. I've babied you, that's the problem. I'm as much to blame for your immaturity as you are. And yes, Amber did know about what went on between you and Basil because I tell her everything."

Danielle looked ashamed and I could tell by her face that it wasn't the scare of being cut off financially that was causing the emotion. It was the shame of what she'd done, both with Basil and with the man in the bathroom. She was sobering up, fast, and I could see that she wasn't proud of the things she'd been saying. Defeated, she slumped into a chair and groaned. "That's great, Meagan," she said. "She's probably wondering when I'm gonna come on to her."

Amber chuckled. She could find a ray of humor in anything. "No, Danny. I know you wouldn't come on to me. You made a mistake a long time ago. I was surprised when Meagan first told me but I've never thought any less of you because of it. If I wanted to, she wouldn't let me. She loves you very much and she's never held what happened against you. As for tonight," Amber crouched down next to Danielle's chair, turning her knees so that the hem of her dress did not creep up inappropriately. "May I talk to you about what happened tonight?"

Danny shrugged. "Why not? It's all out in the open anyway."

Amber nodded. I couldn't see how she found it in her to be kind to Danielle after the way Danielle had insulted her. "I'm sorry for what happened, Danielle. You never told us about Mark so we couldn't have known what was going on. Our relationship wasn't designed to hurt you. If your sister thought she was hurting you, she couldn't live with herself. She's not cold, Danny, and she's very capable of tears. I know because I've seen them. I've watched your sister hit bottom and I've watched her climb her way back to the top. She doesn't corrupt people, nor does she make them her 'bitches'. I would do anything for her, yes, but not because she controls me--because she loves me. And because I know that she too would do anything for me. For any of us.

Mark and this man from tonight -- they're not good enough for you; not if that's the way they think. I do know about the two women fantasy, but a good man, the kind you deserve, would be completely indifferent to the relationship your sister and I share. He would be in love with you, so he would see only you. You're very pretty, Danielle. You're sweet, you're smart and, usually, you're very kind. You don't want the type of man who would ignore those qualities anyway. The world is full of good men. Maybe you haven't found the right one yet but you're young, and he is out there. And when you find him, you can be sure that when he's making love to you he won't be thinking of anyone but you. At the very least, he won't be thinking of us."

Amber's words had a calming effect on everyone. Josh finally sat down and Jenna leaned into him affectionately while Seamus sipped a glass of wine and nodded at Amber's wisdom.

I pulled a chair up to Danielle. "Do you know why Amber and I were holding hands when we walked back in here tonight? Because Mom told us to. It was actually a pretty special night for us because Mom pulled us aside to tell us she loved us and that she wasn't ashamed of our relationship. It was important to us, Danny. It was important to Mom and she wanted me to take Amber's hand so everyone could see there is nothing wrong with what we are to each other. She reached a new level of acceptance tonight. She opened herself to Seamus and she opened herself to us."

"But Celia---"

"Celia's wrong," Amber said. "I won't speak ill of your aunt, but she's wrong. We're different, that's all. Jenna is different. Seamus is different. You and Josh are more what people would define as normal, I suppose, but I know you don't really believe the rest of us are evil. Look at us, Danielle. Really look and think about what you see."

Danielle burst into tears. "I'm sorry, Amber."

"It's okay," Amber soothed, hugging her. "Don't cry."

"I like you, I really do. I like all of you. *Love* all of you, but I just don't fit in."

"You do fit in," I said. "Everyone fits in, Danielle. It's just a matter of accepting each other, faults and all. None of us is perfect. The important thing is that we realize that and stand by each other nonetheless."

Danielle pulled away from Amber and reached for me. "I didn't mean it with Basil. I was just jealous and I don't think you corrupt me. You just made me mad."

I squeezed her to me and smiled. "Well, if there's anything I know about, it's saying things you don't really mean when you're mad. And I'm sorry too. I'm sorry for not realizing how out of place you felt. Just talk to me, Danny. If you're upset about something, tell me. I promise I'll listen." I raised her chin and wiped her eyes. "I did mean what I said about you standing on your own two feet though. I'll still help you but you have to learn how to manage your finances and I know you can do that-- you work for an accounting firm." She laughed quietly, and rested her head on my shoulder.

Jenna smiled. "Why don't we all go home?" It was the first thing she'd said in forty-five minutes, and I couldn't help laughing. "What?" she asked.

"I was just thinking how sitting here all silent like that must have been killing you."

"It was." she giggled. "But I knew you guys could work it out." She rose from her chair. "Let's go. It's three a.m."

"Yeah," Josh agreed, stretching. "I'm beat." He didn't apologize for his behavior but he was willing to let the situation drop.

"I don't want to go home alone, Meagan," Danny whispered. "Can I stay with you guys?"

What could I do but grin? "Yeah, come on, slut."

That got her to giggle. "You can't ever resist it, can you? You always have to be a smartass."

"Yep." I messed her hair. "Accept my oddities and I'll accept yours."

"Deal."

Chapter 14

The bank was a busy place. End of the month kind of busy. Friday kind of busy. I was there taking care of Markham-Summers business and opening a new checking account for the payroll. Ted and I shared responsibility for the banking and it was my turn. I thought it always seemed like my turn but it didn't bother me much. I liked playing with money, even money I would have to give away. It kept me present in the physical. It kept me feeling grounded to the earth and made me feel safe and in control.

I handled my business, pushed open the big glass doors, and stepped out of the air-conditioned building and into the hot summer air. First National Bank sat in the middle of an uptown heat wave. We didn't notice the heat so much downtown because we had the river nearby and the refreshing air that wafted up from it. Uptown was like any urban setting, suffocating when the temperatures crept into the nineties. People got frustrated and impatient. The heat made even the slightest offense like accidentally bumping into someone an unbearable experience as they were likely to yell at you and tell you to watch where the hell you were going.

I bumped into no one. Didn't feel like an altercation with a corporate crybaby in an Armani suit. Uptown was full of them. Downtown it was jeans and t-shirts, but uptown it was men and women decked out in their most appropriate Armani and Donna Karen, clutching their designer handbags and pushing their Gucci sunglasses back up their surgically altered noses. I didn't like dealing with these people, much less admit I was one of them. I preferred to lie to myself and tell myself I wasn't. Another one my quirks Amber found amusing.

There was a man outside the bank, pacing. He wore black leather pants--insane in this heat--and did not fit in with the uptown crowd. He was fidgeting, like he was deciding if he should go in and rob the place. He had his back to me but I could tell his hands were shoved in his front pockets by the way his elbows poked out to the sides. Dry elbows. Skin flaking off the dark flesh. He turned and I gasped. Adrian! Adrian Barrett. Ex-drug dealer and friend. I had just been thinking of him weeks before and now here he was, standing in front of me like a wish I'd unwittingly sent up. My challenge?

He looked at me. His hazy eyes focusing in on my face like it invoked a memory he couldn't quite grasp. I watched it hit him and he grinned.

"Meagan," he mumbled, like the word was a busy circus act doing a show in his mouth. It sort of fell out, like a stumbling trapeze artist. Adrian stumbled toward me, each step an effort and I took a step back. He wasn't the Adrian I had known, the fit young dancer. He was a junkie. And I suddenly saw myself through Amber's eyes. Saw what she must have seen that first horrible night when she'd discovered what I was. Only I hadn't smelled like I hadn't bathed in weeks and my clothes hadn't been last year's tired rags. But the face. The scared face with the manic eyes. That had been mine. And it *was* terrifying to look at.

"Hello, Adrian," I said.

"Long time, babe. Wanna split a rock? I'm tapped but you can front me the money, right? For an old friend?"

I was surprised he was still on the expensive stuff. Usually, when a cokehead bottoms out he has to turn to something like crack because it's a quarter of the price, and from what I'd heard, it was a pretty good high. I didn't know about that. My nose had only seen the good stuff, though I didn't think you snorted crack anyway. Seemed to me you smoked it.

Adrian was staring at me. So stoned he didn't even notice I could walk. His eyes remained hopelessly locked on my face. He was wearing a short-sleeved shirt, and I could see the bruised track marks up and down his arms. He'd hit bottom. He'd been poking himself to death. I shuddered. It could have been me.

"I don't do that anymore, Adrian," I said. "But I'll buy you lunch if you're interested." He looked horribly thin. Probably hadn't eaten in weeks.

"Naw," he said. "Not much of an appetite anymore. Got fifty bucks?"

"No."

"Come on, Meagan. You do so."

"Let me buy you lunch, Adrian," I said again. The people passing by were giving me strange looks. Wondering what someone like me was doing talking to an obvious junkie. I ignored them. "We could use the time to catch up," I said, giving Adrian's arm an affectionate squeeze. Or, I could use the time to convince him to seek help. He looked like he was at the point where he could go either way, die or get better. Maybe with the help of a friend he'd opt for the latter.

Adrian didn't seem interested in lunch but he agreed. Probably because he thought he could get some money out of me with a sob story told over a sandwich. He'd forgotten I knew the game. Knew all the tricks. We looked at each other, each of us laboring under our own agendas, but my money was on me. He'd take a bit of persuading but he'd go; I was certain of it. He just needed to know someone cared enough to ask.

Slowly, he nodded his head and we stepped into the street and crossed over to the deli on the opposite side. I took his hand like he was my boyfriend, showing him that I wasn't afraid to touch him, and he looked down at our entwined hands and grinned. It was a long time since anyone had dared to touch him. People were afraid of junkies. Sometimes even other junkies. Maybe I should have been afraid too but I wasn't. The worst he could do was run off with my purse but he wouldn't even do that because it felt too good to suddenly have someone caring about him and his face said he wanted the drugs but he was tired of them. I knew the look. I'd seen it in the mirror. It was the look of lucidity trying to slug it out with addiction. Addiction would win if I walked away from Adrian right now. Lucidity had a chance if I stayed.

I made my decision as easily as if I were deciding what I wanted on my pizza.

It was after ten that evening before I got home. I'd spent all day and all evening convincing Adrian to get help. It took work. A lot of work. But by eight-thirty, he was signed into a rehab program and already feeling the shakes coming on. I hastened to leave him. By nine-thirty I had to go and promised him I'd be back.

Amber was furious when I got home. She paced the

living room floor in a pair of cut-off shorts and a baby tee that exposed her flat, tanned stomach.

"Where the hell have you been?" she demanded, her eyes an angry green stare. She was so intense when she was angry, like a fiery fairy with a golden tan. I struggled not to smile because I knew it would only make her angrier. Rarely were we angry at the same time.

"We were supposed to have dinner with Ted and Cicely hours ago," she fumed, "and you totally blew everyone off. This was *your* dinner, and I had to call and cancel when you didn't show up at home. Just who the hell do you think you are strolling through the door whenever you freaking feel like it? No calls. Nothing. Your cell phone has been turned off all day and Cynthia said you left the office at eleven forty-five and never came back."

"I was with an old friend," I said.

"For ten hours? Who?"

I was going to get the suspicious look and I wasn't going to like it.

"Adrian."

"Adrian?"

Amber stalked across the room and inspected my eyes like a mother trying to determine if her kid was drunk. I opened them wider to give her a better look.

"I'm not on anything, Amber," I said. "And I resent that you would even have to check. I was signing Adrian into a rehab clinic."

She stared at me. "How did this come about?"

I led her to the couch and we sat down.

"I ran into Adrian outside the bank today," I said. "Amber, the guy was so fucked up he didn't even notice I could walk. He wanted money. Asked me if I wanted to split a rock with him. I told him no and offered to buy him lunch. We went across the street to the deli and people just stared at us like they were wondering what business we could possibly have together. Adrian sort of smelled and I could tell he was offending some of them with his odor so we took our sandwiches to the park and sat on a bench where I spent the next several hours trying to convince him he needed help. He finally relented and I drove him to a private clinic across town and stayed while he signed himself in. That's why the phone was off. I didn't want any distractions that might scare him off. Anyway, then I spoke with the doctors. Adrian's been on so much shit they'll have to give him methadone therapy so he doesn't die from the heroin withdrawal. That's what he's been on, heroin."

"Why a private clinic?" Amber asked. She was taking it well but she didn't like that I was involved. "Why didn't you just drop him off at the hospital rehab?"

"Those hospital programs suck. They never have the funding they need to deal with all the junkies they get. Half the time they're understaffed. Adrian needs major help and a private clinic is the best place he can get it."

She folded her arms across her chest. "And I suppose you're paying for this too." As far as she was concerned Adrian could just die. She blamed him for my drug addiction and the horrors she'd had to face because of it.

"Yes," I said. "I'm paying for it." Then I dropped the bomb. "I'm also gonna be his sponsor."

That threw her for a loop. She shot to her feet and started pacing again. "Meagan, you cannot be his sponsor. You never got help for your own problem. You don't know that you're psychologically prepared for this. It's not easy. And while you're trying to get Adrian off drugs he might start convincing you to get back on them."

I made her sit again.

"That won't happen," I said. "His doctors know my history and they think I'm probably the best person for the job because of it. Adrian and I used to get high together. I found my way out. They think that will be a good example for him."

"But you never got help yourself," she said again. "In some way the addiction is still there for you."

I sighed. "Yes, Amber. And it always will be. You don't stop being a drug addict just because you've stopped taking drugs. Recovery is a life-long commitment. I may never touch a drug again, but I'll always be a drug addict. It's not pleasant but it's reality. As for seeking help, I didn't need it. I had you. But Adrian doesn't have someone to hold him down on a bed when the tremors come on so badly his body convulses and aches for the drugs with a pain like he's never known. He's in far worse shape than I was and he doesn't have one person in the world who cares whether he lives or dies. I care, Amber. I don't want to scare you, but I can't turn my back on him either. He's alone in this and he needs a friend. Can you try to understand why that matters to me? I never would have gotten through my ordeal without your love and Adrian might not get through his without mine. He needs to know someone cares."

She took a slow breath and rested her head against my shoulder. "I understand," she said. "I don't want you to do this but I understand why you think you have to. You're just this strange wonderful person who does things that make no sense to me but I guess I know you well enough to know that someone who becomes your friend is a friend for life, no matter how low they might sink, and that makes you a better person than I am because I'd let Adrian twist in the wind. Just promise you'll be careful. That if you feel the slightest temptation you'll drop the sponsor thing and just let his doctor's handle it."

I kissed the top of her head. "Deal. But I don't think I'll be tempted, Amber. Today I saw in Adrian what you once had to see in me, utter desperation. It's terrifying to look at, isn't it?"

"Yes."

"So I only want to help him the way you and Jenna helped me. I'm not afraid of going back to that place because I have too much to live for now. This is just about helping an old friend, okay?"

She nodded into my arms. "Okay."

Saturday was worse than Friday. Adrian broke my pinkie finger when he hurled us both to the floor in a spasm that came over him as I held him and the doctors had to put a metal splint on my finger and increase Adrian's dose of methadone. They were playing around with it, trying to hit the right dosage to match his addiction. Adrian was in a world of pain. Worse than anything I'd had to endure because his drug of choice was much worse than mine. Heroin beats coke hands down. The fact that Adrian had also been injecting his poison only made things worse. His arms were like a battlefield. He'd been forced to start on his legs, and they were just as gruesome. His once beautiful body was now nothing more than a quivering, stretch of bruised skin. I told him he looked good and went back to holding him after the doctor had taken care of my finger.

The clinic looked more like an expensive hotel than a hospital. It had thick oak paneling throughout and rooms the size of small suites. Private baths in each room. Green and white striped wallpaper in the common room where patients could get together to talk, play cards, or watch TV. Adrian did none of those things. He was in the first stages of withdrawal and spent his hours vomiting and sweating, clinging to me in fear and desperation. I held his head over the toilet, and asked the nurses for a bucket when crawling to the bathroom became too much for him. One of them brought me a standard issue white pail. The utility closet was full of them. I emptied the pail every time Adrian used it and brought it back clean, only to be soiled again. He was puking up great gobs of goo, like phlegm, only darker and somewhat bloody in appearance. A bit of food. Not much. It seemed to me he was puking up his stomach lining, and he very well could have been, because he hadn't eaten anything other than Friday's sandwich in the past five days. The vomiting continued.

It was like when you were drunk and you just kept heaving until there was nothing left and your stomach muscles hurt from the contractions. Then you got the dry heaves, and your stomach muscles hurt worse, until finally, you just passed out on the bathroom floor because it was cool and close to the toilet in case you got sick again. By morning you felt better because you'd spent the night in hell and had survived it. But Adrian wouldn't greet that morning for awhile.

His doctor came in and gave him another shot of methadone, and the spasms subsided. The vomiting stopped. I hoped they weren't trading one addiction for another. I'd heard about heroin addicts who then got addicted to the methadone meant to cure the first addiction. His doctor assured me that wouldn't happen. That they were very careful about the doses they administered and did not condone prolonged use, which was often how people got addicted to it. Spent too much time on the cure. Not enough time dealing with the ache.

Adrian was also scheduled for group therapy once the toughest part of the withdrawal had passed, and there were psychiatrists available for independent counseling if he wanted it. I was pleased with our choice of clinic. They had things under control.

"There's something different about you, Meagan," Adrian said in the fifth hour.

"I don't have a wheelchair strapped to my ass," I said.

He grinned. "That's it." Then he went to sleep for awhile.

Visiting hours ended at eight o'clock and I didn't leave a minute earlier. I'd been with Adrian all day, holding him, taking care of him, and I was exhausted. This wasn't easy work. I had a whole new level of respect for Amber. She'd done this alone. There had been Jenna but Jenna only came during the day and for Amber it was a twenty-four-hour job. No breaks like the one I was getting by leaving. No help like the help I got from the clinic staff who assured me that if I wasn't there someone else would be. This was their job, one of the nurses told me. I didn't have to feel obligated to take care of Adrian because they would. That's what I was paying them to do.

I agreed. I told Adrian I'd be back Sunday evening and kissed him goodbye. He gave me a weak smile.

"I'll be here," he said. "Where else am I going, right babe?"

I smiled back. "See ya tomorrow night."

When I returned home I was met with another crisis. This time it was Amber's. I stepped through the door and found her sitting cross-legged in the center of the couch, staring at the blank TV like it held the answer to some great mystery she was trying to solve. She didn't look at me.

"My father called," she said quietly. "My mother has breast cancer. She's scheduled for a double mastectomy on Monday. Both breasts. Gone."

I didn't know how to respond, so I didn't say anything. Amber continued to stare straight ahead.

"I needed you," she said, still without looking at me. "I needed you and you weren't here. You were with Adrian."

I felt a massive guilt crush my heart. She was always there for me and the one time she was in need, I was across town with a junkie.

"I'm sorry, honey," I said, crossing the room. "Why didn't you call me on the cell? I promised you I wouldn't turn it off again."

"You were with Adrian." It didn't look like she knew she'd already said that. It was just very important to her that I know where I was. Not with her.

I climbed over the back of the couch and sat behind her, pressing my body between hers and the cushions, and started rubbing her shoulders and neck. She relaxed slightly.

"My father said they've known for some time and that I didn't have to come to the surgery if I didn't want to." Her throat chocked. "He said it wasn't necessary. That I didn't need to be there."

She started crying and I wrapped my arms around her, feeling the sobs shake her body.

"I'll go with you," I said.

"Will you? Will you go with me?" She said it like she thought I might not, and it broke my heart.

"Yes," I said quietly.

She turned around and sobbed into my neck. Wrapped her arms around my back and soaked my shirt with her tears.

"My mother didn't even know he was calling," she sobbed. "Like it didn't matter one way or the other. Would she die without ever forgiving me for what happened to Jeff?" Then she gasped, as if saying her brother's name out loud was like speaking some forbidden word.

"It wasn't your fault, Amber," I said. "You couldn't have known your brother would get hurt and your parents have no right to blame you for that."

For thirty minutes she cried in my arms. Then she fell asleep with her head in my lap and her arm wrapped around my waist. I smoothed her hair. Watched her sleep. Darkness crept over the apartment as the sun went down outside but I didn't move. Didn't want to disturb her. For three hours I sat like that, rubbing her back, playing with her hair, while she continued to sleep and I struggled to stay awake. Not easy to do after a day of taking care of a drug addict and then returning home to find your lover in a bad way of her own. Not easy to do sitting in the dark with no TV, no radio, not even a book to read. But I owed her this. She had given me so much I owed her these hours and then some.

At eleven thirty she awoke, startled to find me still sitting there beneath her head. The apartment was pitch black and silent. She reached for the lamp. Looked at the time on the VCR.

"You've been sitting here in the dark this whole time?" she asked. "Why? Why didn't you turn on the TV or something?"

I shrugged. "You gave me a month of sleep. I think I could give you a few hours. Are you hungry?"

"Starving."

"Me too. I'll fix us something to eat."

"You don't cook," she said.

"Are you kidding me? I can whip up the best Dai Dop Voy and Kung Pao chicken this side of Chinatown."

She smirked. "We don't have a Chinatown."

"But I have an excellent dialing finger. I'll call the place on the corner. A couple of won ton soups, a few eggrolls. Be ready in fifteen minutes."

She nodded. She still looked tired. "I'm gonna take a bath while you do that, okay?"

"Okay."

Amber went off to take her bath and I ran down to the corner to get the food. The restaurant was packed with the after-bar crowd. It was only midnight but people liked to leave the clubs early so they could grab some Chinese and socialize a bit before they headed home, full and sober. I sat at a table with friends and waited for the waitress to call out my name. Summers or Reed, it didn't matter which because the order was always the same and they knew us by our faces. It would be picked up by the blond or the brunette with the highlights.

Twenty-five minutes later I strolled through the apartment door to find that Amber still had not emerged from the tub. I placed the food on the kitchen counter and walked over to the bathroom door. It was closed. We didn't close it all the way in the summer because the door tended to swell and stick due to a mixture of the heat outside and the steam from the shower or bath. Amber had forgotten. She was probably stuck inside.

I rattled the door handle. Yep, stuck. I rapped on the door. "I've got the food, Amber."

No response.

I rapped louder. "Amber?"

Again no response.

Warning bells went off in my head. Something was wrong. I banged on the door.

"Amber!" She wasn't answering me.

Panic filled me. What if she'd fallen asleep again? In the tub? I'd left her alone when I knew how prone she was to falling asleep when she was stressed. She'd been vulnerable and I'd gone out for Chinese!

I screamed her name again and pounded the door with my shoulder. It didn't budge. I backed up. Took a run at it and slammed through, splintering the door frame and falling to the floor in front of the tub. My head banged against the porcelain and a burst of pain exploded behind my eyes. I shook it away. Looked up and the darkness almost crept in front of my eyes.

She was underwater. Her face was completely submerged and her blond hair was floating behind her head. I threw myself half in the tub and grabbed a wet handful of it, pulling her out of the water by her hair and dragging her body over the edge of the tub. She didn't weigh much but neither did I and the water had made her heavier. We toppled to the floor with her landing on top of me.

She wasn't breathing. I didn't know CPR and there wasn't time to call an ambulance. She'd be dead before they could get to us.

I thought fast. My mind screamed commands at me. Do something! Anything!

I rolled her on her back. She looked dead. I freaked out and made a thousand promises to God in the course of three seconds. Things like what a good person I'd be and how I'd never leave her alone again.

Just let her live! Tell me what to do!

Red bathing suits flashed in my mind. Basil used to watch *Baywatch* and I'd hated it. He'd said the rescue methods they acted out were the real deal, that the actors were taught by real lifeguards or something on how to save a drown victim. I'd laughed at him, *then*. Now it was a matter of life and death that I remember. I was risking Amber's life on an episode of *Baywatch*! On the off chance that I might remember something, and if I did, that it would be correct.

Plug the nose, I thought. Breathe into the mouth then

pump the chest four or five times to release the water from the lungs. I didn't know if that was right but I was running out of time. I had to try something. She was dying! Maybe already dead.

I breathed into her mouth. Pumped her chest. Repeated the process. I pushed my air into her lungs and screamed at her not to die. Begged her to breathe while I pounded her chest. I didn't know what I was doing. I was just following the pictures in my head and mimicking the motions.

"Please," I cried. "You can't leave me. If you die, I'll die with you. I won't live with the guilt. I can't have more blood on my hands. Amber, please! Breathe!"

My mind flashed to Zoe and I pushed her away. Not now. I breathed into Amber's lungs. Pumped her chest with one hand crossed on top of the other. I seemed to do this forever. Couldn't stop. She might have been dead already but I wasn't going to stop. I'd give her every bit of air I had.

Suddenly, her head turned to the side and a gush of water spilled out of her mouth. Her eyes snapped open and she gasped for air. My head fell forward on her stomach.

"Oh God! Oh, thank God!"

I pulled her into my arms and leaned against the bathroom wall, sobbing. Her head rested against my breasts and her breathing stabilized and slowed to a normal pace. I crushed her to me. Wouldn't let her go for anything. We didn't talk. Then she looked up at me and gave a slow wry grin.

"Got my Kung Pao chicken?" she said hoarsely.

I laughed like a maniac. Wrapped a towel around her and brushed the wet bangs from her eyes.

"Are you okay? Do you need to go to the hospital?" I knew she didn't but it was a precautionary question. She looked as good as any drown victim could.

She shook her head. "I'm okay."

"You scared the hell out of me." The main thing was that she was alive. "You fell asleep in there, didn't you?"

Nodding, she wrapped herself up in me. "God, Meagan," she said. "What is it with us? It's one thing after another. Sometimes I think we won't live to see thirty."

I laughed. "Don't say that. You're reducing my life expectancy to about six weeks."

She laughed back. "And my own to about nine months." Then her face grew serious and she clung to me. "You didn't mean what you said about killing yourself? I heard you. You said you'd die with me. Meagan, I wouldn't want that."

"Neither would I," I said. "But at the moment all I could think was, I've killed another one through my negligence, and I couldn't live with another death on my conscience. Fortunately, you didn't die, so we both get to live."

We laughed together again.

"Okay, but don't talk like that anymore because it freaks me out." She grinned. "I don't like knowing how insane you really are."

I shook my head. "Look at you. Back from the dead five minutes and already you're questioning my sanity. Come on, let's go eat before I snap and take a shotgun to the both of us."

Amber laughed. She had learned to joke about the absurd right along with me. You had to joke about absurdity when you were plagued with it the way we were. She was right. It was one thing after another with us. Like fate was constantly challenging us to see if we would turn to each other or against each other. So far, I thought, we were winning. It was wreaking havoc on our lives, but we were winning.

I would have died if Amber had lost her life on that linoleum floor. I made light of it to her but I would have died. I meant what I'd said about the blood on my hands. I was not emotionally equipped to deal with another death that would have been my fault. I wasn't taking care of people the way I was supposed to and that's why they kept wanting to die on me. I was always in the wrong place at the wrong time. Behind the wheel of a car and under a street light I should have stopped for. In a Chinese restaurant on the corner when I should have been at home waiting for the food to be delivered to us. I always had options and I always chose the wrong one. The only time I made the right choices was when it came to business, like Divinity was saying, "You suck at the personal stuff so we'll give you this." I had a horseshoe up my ass when it came to business and a broken mirror in my pocket when it came to life. But I could put up a good face and that was half the battle right there. I could grin and bear it with the rest of them. Carry my load and pretend it wasn't heavy even when it was breaking my back. I was pretty good at that.

Amber ate her Kung Pao chicken and I watched her. Her near death had squelched my appetite and I pushed away my Dai Dop Voy, laid my chopsticks aside and watched her eat like it was her last meal. She smiled from time to time, like she knew what I was thinking, and I watched her eyes grow tired.

Beneath the splint my pinkie finger ached. It had swollen up again, but I ignored the dull throb. I knew why it hurt. I had caused it further damage when I burst through the bathroom door. My shoulder had taken the brunt of the slam but my hand had been trapped down at my side and the finger had gotten crunched between my ribs and the door. Had I kept my arm straight the hand would have stayed in the dead air by my waist and it would have been fine. But I hadn't been thinking about my hand. I had been thinking about Amber dying on the other side of the door and my adrenaline had gone haywire. Now I was coming down from the rush and my finger was throbbing. Amber was sitting across from me, alive. I didn't care about my finger.

She finished her chicken and I removed her plate. Let her have her silence. She was thinking about her mother. She was thinking how her mother could have died if the doctors hadn't caught the cancer and how she herself could have died if I hadn't come home in time to save her. Her face was like a blank computer screen that kept filling with words to project her thoughts to me. The screen would go blank and she'd refill it with new thoughts. Thoughts about how little time we had on this earth, and how we never knew when the end could come, and did she want to die someday without ever having made amends with her parents? The screen indicated that the answer was a resounding no. She wanted to forgive and be forgiven. It was as clear as the green of her eyes.

I put her to bed shortly after. Opened the window so she could feel the fresh night air blowing in from the river we didn't have a view of, and tied back the drapes so she could see the bright silver moon if she happened to wake up.

Amber loved the moon. It was the only spiritual thing about her. She was fascinated by its phases. She loved when it was waxing, when it was waning. She was thrilled when it was full, like tonight. When it disappeared entirely she looked for it. I'd catch her sometimes, gazing out the window like if she stared hard enough it might come back.

So I left the drapes open for her. So she could see the moon and know there would be another one tomorrow night, and every night after that, and that her life was as consistent as the moon and there would be many tomorrows for her as well. Plenty of time to make amends with her living ghosts. And if she did happen to wake up I would be right there beside her to look at the moon with her. It was all she ever really wanted, someone to look at the moon with her. She didn't ask for much out of life, only the simple things. It was part of what made her so special.

She didn't wake up. Not until morning and I made her breakfast. Pancakes. I didn't eat because I had awakened in the middle of the night and sat at the dark kitchen table finishing off my warmed Dai Dop Voy. Each bite had stuck in my throat. I'd almost lost her. And she had lived out that fear for an entire month while I was taking my time deciding if I even wanted to come back to her at all. She'd done it for a month and I was a wreck after one night.

She ate her pancakes and grinned around a mouthful.

"These are great," she said. "I thought you don't know how to cook."

I grinned back. "I never said I don't know how to cook I just *don't* cook. Big difference. It's a domestic thing that reminds me of taking care of Basil and I don't like it."

I moved to refill her glass of orange juice and she noticed the metal splint on my finger.

"Hey, what happened?"

I shrugged. "Adrian had a bit of a rough day yesterday. Bad tremors. Threw us both off the bed and I landed on my hand the wrong way. Broke my finger."

"This happened yesterday?" She was surprised she hadn't noticed it sooner. She prided herself on noticing things, particularly things about me.

Another shrug. I cleared her plate and tossed it in the sink.

"Why don't you do some writing today?" I said. "Get your mind off things for awhile."

She wrote almost every day but today was especially important. She needed the distraction.

"What will you do?" she asked.

"I'm going to color-code the bedroom closet. You know, group the clothes together by color and fabric."

She laughed at me. "Well, I'm not into watching your neurosis in action so maybe I will go across the hall and write for a few hours."

Color-code the closet? That was the best I could come up with? I was only trying to tell her I wouldn't leave, that I was here if she needed me, but the problem was there wasn't anything for me to do around the apartment. I could have said I would read a book, or go over some notes. Anything but color-code the closet. Then the more I thought about it, the more it didn't seem like such a bad idea. Why not color-code the closet? Maybe I'd alphabetize the canned goods in the kitchen cupboard too. They could use some kind of order.

Amber went across the hall to write and I got to work on my obsessive-compulsive projects. By the time she returned I had done the closet, the cupboard and had even used a paring knife and a spatula to rip up the black and white linoleum floor in the bathroom. I threw the bits of torn linoleum in a green garbage bag and vacuumed the dull hardwood underneath. I wasn't sure what had possessed me to do it. I'd wanted to have that floor changed for years and suspected I had only started it now because it was the place where Amber had almost died.

She was stunned when she walked in. First because I had done it all, and then because I had been able to do it with such crude tools.

"I've wanted this floor out of here forever," I said, carrying the garbage bag out of the bathroom. I inspected my work. The floor underneath wasn't bad, just scuffed. It had some residual glue stuck to it but nothing a floor guy couldn't get off with a sander.

"I was thinking new linoleum or ceramic tiles," I said, "But that floor isn't bad, is it?"

Amber shook her head. "Maybe we should stick with the hardwood. It sort of flows with the other rooms."

I agreed. "I'll call someone on Tuesday. Till then I guess we're stuck with the mess I've made."

There wasn't a mess. Just a scuffed bathroom floor that was going to drive me nuts to look at for the next few days. If Amber wasn't so stressed I probably would have rented a sander and called my father over to fix it, but she was in no frame of mind for company. I could see on her face that it was a struggle just staying awake. Her father's phone call had done a job on her but she was trying to put on a brave face.

At six-thirty I called Jenna over to stay with Amber for an hour while I went off to see Adrian, because I had promised. I also had to tell him that I wouldn't be seeing him on Monday either because of the surgery.

He was looking better already. Fairly calm for a man who had been off heroin for three days. I figured the doctors must have hit the right does with the methadone.

"So you're still with the blond narc then," he said.

I smirked. I hadn't thought of Amber as the blond narc since I stopped taking drugs.

"She's a bottle blond, right?"

I shook my head. "You'd think so because of that platinum hair but I've never seen her dye it."

"What about down below?" he asked.

I laughed. "None of your business. Why are you so interested in Amber's hair color anyway?"

He shrugged. "I'm not. Just trying to make conversation. It gets boring around here."

"You're not thinking of leaving, Adrian?"

"No. I just need something to do. Do you think next time you could bring me a Gameboy or something?"

Another laugh. "How old are you?"

"Twenty-eight."

"I'll bring you a Gameboy on Tuesday. Will you be alright until then?"

"As alright as I can be," he said. "See ya later, babe."

Adrian was the only person who ever called me babe. I liked it. From a boyfriend it would have sounded as low-class as "my old lady" but, from Adrian, it was playful. A friendly way of saying, "You're okay. You meet my criteria." Why it should matter that I meet a twenty-eight-year-old junkie's criteria was beyond me, but I had this thing about people liking me. Everyone had to or I got moody. It didn't matter if I didn't like them, they just had to like me. That's why Amber's book had once been so distressing. It made people not like me. Even people who had never known my name. They hated the book's antagonist and that was me.

I cleared my head. Old crap. No need to dwell on it now.

Amber was sleeping in Jenna's lap when I returned and I couldn't wait until this was all over with. Amber was sleeping too much and too easily. She'd spent the last two days asleep or half dead. I was impatient for tomorrow.

Chapter 15

We pulled up in front of the hospital at seven-thirty, the morning sun rising high in the sky displaying that it was going to be another hot day. I loved this sort of weather, and I almost hated to go inside, but duty called. The surgery was scheduled for eight and Amber's mother had already been wheeled into one of the private preparation rooms. We had come late because Amber didn't want to face her mother beforehand. She didn't want to see breasts, only to see them gone a few hours later. It was easier for her to deal with the aftermath. I understood. Amber didn't like to dwell on the past, and for her, her mother's breasts were already there. She would face the future instead. The scarring. The flat, marked tissue that would become a part of who her mother now was, a breast cancer survivor.

She clung to my hand as we moved through the automatic doors and rode the elevator to the second floor. We walked the long corridor and she glanced at me from time to time as if to make sure I was still there. I squeezed her hand. I wasn't going anywhere.

At the end of the hall her father stood outside the waiting room doors. He was a tall man with a crop of silver hair and a stern green-eyed stare. Amber's stare. They shared the same fierce eyes but little else. Franklin Reed looked like a self-righteous prick. The way he leaned against the door jamb with his arms crossed in front of him spoke volumes about his character. He was a lawyer, and he was always right. That's what his stance said. *Don't question me because I'm right. You've never met anyone more right in your life.* He should have been married to my mother.

Amber and I approached and he glanced down at our clasped hands. She stiffened but didn't let go. She only looked at me and I shrugged. Franklin Reed could pitch a fit if he wanted; I was not letting Amber face this alone.

We neared his side and briefly she let go of my hand to step on her tip toes and brush his cheek with an obligatory kiss.

He didn't kiss back, only bent his head so that she could respect him properly. Let her do all the work. Amber took my hand again and I thought I saw him frown but it happened too fast to really tell.

"Hi, Dad," she said, somewhat stiffly. "This is Meagan."

His eyes looked me over. He couldn't find an obvious flaw, so he turned away. "Hello, Meagan."

I extended my hand. "It's nice to meet you, Mr. Reed."

He glanced at the splint on my finger and shook my hand lightly.

"We're going to be here awhile," he said. "So you may as well call me Franklin."

I nodded. Amber squeezed my other hand. Apparently this was a good sign. If I called him Frank, he'd get upset. I knew that. I could see he was just that pretentious. It was Franklin or Mr. Reed. Period. Anyone who dared to call him Frank would get the green-eyed glare and a serious reprimanding.

Normally I would have done it just to throw him off-kilter and get the upper hand, but Amber was terrified right now and she needed me to behave. It soured my fun. Then I reminded myself this wasn't supposed to be fun, this was serious business. Surgery. A woman losing her breasts. An estranged family coming together under the fear of possible disaster. I had to be strong for Amber and I had to do it with dignity. It was going to be a struggle for me, because I thrived on putting pretentious assholes in their place.

"How's Mom?" Amber asked.

"She's doing as well as can be expected," Franklin said. "She's losing her breasts, Amber."

His tone was sarcastic and I felt Amber stiffen again. I bit my tongue so I wouldn't tell him off.

"Well, we are going to be here awhile," he said again, "so why don't we go sit down? Meagan, would you mind running down to the cafeteria and grabbing us some coffee?"

I didn't mind. I looked at Amber and she nodded that it was okay by her. Franklin went to peel a bill from his wallet and I waved it away.

"Oh, that's right," he said snottily. "Miss Big Bucks."

My turn to stiffen.

"Dad," Amber said.

He threw up his arms. "Never mind."

I left to grab the coffee. When I returned they were sitting on opposite couches across from each other and the room was cloaked in silence. No one spoke. Amber looked up at me.

"What did you buy?" she asked, indicating the bags in my hand.

I maneuvered the cups of coffee onto the table and started emptying the two bags.

"There was an old lady opening the gift shop, so I picked up a few things. A few magazines. Some snacks in case you and your Dad get hungry." I dug around the bag and pulled out a magazine and handed it to her father.

"Amber says you're into architecture. They happened to have an *Architectural Digest* down there so I grabbed it." I was being the better person, a new experience for me. It made Amber happy. Franklin didn't know what to say.

"I--thank you," he managed. He didn't know what to make of me. He'd insulted me and I'd returned with a gift.

"I'm sorry I sniped at you," he said. "I was out of line."

Amber's eyes widened. Her father never apologized, because he was never wrong. The world was a crazy, mixed-up place when Meagan Summers was in it. It made me feel good.

The hours passed slowly. Amber read a Glamour magazine and her father read his Architectural Digest. I doodled on the bottom of my boot, a nervous habit I'd taken up in high shook when the soles of all my shoes said, "Meagan loves Parker" with a heart around the words. Schoolgirl stuff. Now I was drawing a figure eight and Franklin glanced at me curiously. I put the pen down. Moved to the window and looked outside. A doctor walked in. I didn't look at him. Caught the white coat and the brown loafers and then the look of shock on Amber's face. I sighed. Of all the waiting rooms in all the hospitals in all of the world...

"Meagan?" Ken said, startled. His eyes roamed over my legs the way they had that day in his office.

My voice turned to ice. "Well, if it isn't Dr. Doom. Whose hope are you carting off today?"

Ken frowned.

"You two know each other?" Franklin asked, surprised.

"Ken is my ex-husband."

Franklin couldn't have been more shocked. He hadn't figured me for the marrying kind.

"Hi, Ken" Amber said. She was as friendly as she'd ever been. Like the three of us had never been tangled up in some bizarre love triangle that resulted in the end of my marriage and the dissolution of my friendship with Ken when I discovered he'd lied to me about the paralysis.

"Hello, Amber," Ken said. He looked at me. "I was looking for one of my patient's parents, I guess they're not in here."

"No. I guess they're not."

He tilted his head at me. "Can I speak to you out in the hall?"

I shrugged and followed him out. I squeaked my boot on the floor because I knew it would annoy him and I was just childish enough to do it. We crossed to the other side of the corridor and I leaned against the wall.

"What do you want?" I said.

He placed his hand on the wall behind my head and leaned into me.

"I want you to stop hating me. I made a mistake, okay? You'll be happy to know I've been extremely careful since. You can forgive everyone else in the world but you can't forgive me? It bothers Gwynne that I even care, you know."

I looked at him blankly. "Gwynne? What does she have to do with any of this?" Ken's eyes darted away and I gasped. "Oh my God! *You're with Gwynne?*" It was the funniest thing in the world. The woman went around picking up my discards. It made it easy to pity Ken instead of hate him. The poor guy never caught on. I shook my head like I couldn't believe a doctor could be this stupid.

"I forgive you, Ken," I said. "And I've never hated you I've just been mad at you. Now I'm just sorry for you because you never learn your lesson. The experience with me taught you nothing?"

Ken pushed off the wall and slid his pen through the top of his clipboard.

"This isn't like us, Meagan," he said. "Gwynne's not

still hung up on Amber."

"Or so she tells you. Look, it's none of my business but if you remember correctly, I didn't appear to be hung up on Amber either. I was your wife and that's what I was trying to be. I hope you and Gwynne are very happy together but I think you're setting yourself up for more hurt. Why don't you go for a straight woman, Ken? They're a lot less confused."

"Gwynne isn't confused," he growled. "You were confused. Gwynne loves me."

"I hope you're right," I said. "For your sake, I really hope you are." I turned on my heel and went back in the waiting room.

"What was that all about?" Amber asked when I sat beside her.

"Tell you later," I whispered. She couldn't appreciate the hilarity of Ken and Gwynne's involvement right now. I wanted to give her the news when she was relaxed and we could laugh about it.

The surgery went well. As well as could be expected, to paraphrase Mr. Reed. It wasn't easy getting your breasts cut off. Some women would rather let the cancer spread and kill them. I was probably one of those women. I couldn't imagine going through the rest of my life with two long scars where my breasts had once been. I couldn't imagine being deformed. It was vain, but it was me.

Amber's father had gone in to see her mother first. Then he'd ushered Amber in and I sat with him in the waiting room. The woman was just coming out of surgery. She didn't need to deal with her daughter's lover just then. I understood. She probably didn't want to meet me at all, let alone meet me after enduring something like that.

So I waited with Franklin. We didn't speak. Then after a long uncomfortable silence he looked at me quizzically and said, "You're the butterfly, aren't you?"

It never went away. He had read his daughter's book and now wanted to talk about it.

"Yes," I said. "I'm the butterfly. But I want you to know I would never hurt Amber like that again. We've reached an understanding about our past and we've let it go."

Franklin shrugged. "Amber overreacts." He tossed the

magazine on the table and I knew this conversation was going to go much further. He was going to feel me out. See how much I knew and what I thought. "Unfortunately," he said. "So do her parents. We've made a mess of this family, I'm afraid. We never knew when to let the past go and we blamed Amber for things that weren't her fault. Do you know what happened to her brother?"

I nodded. "Amber can't forgive herself for it. Maybe she could if she knew you forgave her."

Franklin gave a sad shake of his head. "It's been so many years, Meagan. I don't know why I'm even talking to you about this, but I wouldn't know where to begin with Amber. How do you erase seven years of blame in five minutes? We've given her such a hard time."

He wasn't the man I thought he was. I had misjudged him entirely. He was stern, yes, but not severe. He wanted to bury the hatchet and I got the feeling he'd been wanting it for awhile. Maybe he and his wife had discussed the possibility.

I sat beside him and patted his hand.

"You just tell her, Franklin," I said. "Just hold her and tell her you're sorry. She won't walk away. She wants her family back too. Otherwise, she'll be forced to take mine and believe me, I wouldn't wish that on an enemy."

I grinned at him and he laughed.

"I think maybe you're good for my daughter. She never would have shown up here on her own. That's why I was letting her off the hook when I talked to her about it."

"You're wrong," I said. "She would have come anyway. All your phone call did was make her cry and feel unwanted." I thought about how it had almost killed her too but didn't mention it.

"She cried?" he asked. Did he think she wouldn't have cared?

"She was very distraught." I heard footsteps in the hall and quickly patted his hand again. "Here she comes, Franklin. You have your chance, if you want it."

Amber entered the room looking tired again, and Franklin asked me if I would excuse them for a few minutes. When I came back she was smiling and I gave Franklin a happy little wave. He grinned and wiggled his fingers back. It wasn't hard for a family to come together again if they wanted to. All it took was a first step. The rest always steamrolled from there.

Franklin held onto his daughter and told me he wanted me to meet his wife. Together, the three of us went in to see Marian Reed.

I was surprised when I first caught sight of her. Aside from the brown eyes, it was like looking at Amber twenty-five years from now, and Amber was going to age well. Marian was well-preserved. With her blond hair brushed away from her face and her full rose mouth, even after surgery she was pretty. She lay on a hospital bed after just having had both breasts removed and she was as poised as if she'd been there for elective surgery, a face-lift instead of a double mastectomy. She was Amber through and through, right down to the knowing smirk.

"Seeing a resemblance?" she asked me.

I scratched my head. "It's incredible. You could be twins."

That made Marian laugh. And it was Amber's laugh that came out of her mouth. That sexy, throaty sound. It startled me. It was all too surreal. I looked at the three people before me. It was beyond reason that this family ever could have been torn apart. Now they were huddled together like none of it had ever happened. It was awesome to look at.

"Amber tells me you're a publisher," Marian said. She patted the bed, indicating that I should come closer. "Is that how the two of you met?"

I stepped up to her. "No. We met in a coffeehouse a few years ago."

"She's the butterfly," Franklin said, winking at his wife.

"*You're* the butterfly?" Marian giggled behind her blankets. "I'm sorry, but you're not what I expected."

"How so?"

"You just don't look like the punishing type. There's a kindness about your face."

"Did you just say kindness? That's the second time someone's said that to me."

Amber grinned. "Gwynne said it too."

"*Gwynne* did?"

"Yep. It was one of the many things that pissed her off."

"Amber," Marian said.

"Sorry. We have to watch our language around my parents. Anyway, I didn't tell you because I forgot."

"Who's Gwynne?" Franklin asked.

Amber shrugged. "A detour on the road to happiness."

I liked that. She knew I liked it and she gave me that grin of hers. She was doing alright. She was getting along with her family and the life was coming back to her eyes.

"I'm going to be in the hospital a couple of days," Marian said, with that same self-assured air her daughter had. "But why don't we all get together for dinner next week? The two of you will come up to the house and Franklin will cook. Won't you, dear?" She winked at her husband. Thirty-two years of marriage and these two were still in love.

Franklin sat on the edge of her bed and wrapped his arm around the back of her pillow.

"I'm an excellent cook," he said. "Roast pork and pearl onions."

Amber quickly turned her head and I swallowed back my revulsion. "Great."

She looked at her father and the two of them burst out laughing. Marian and I looked at each other; we didn't get the joke.

Amber clutched her sides and Franklin wiped the tears from his eyes.

"What?" I said.

"This one's a keeper," Franklin said to Amber, chuckling. "See the way she didn't even miss a beat. Roast pork and pearl onions! You wouldn't eat either of those things if your life depended on it."

I didn't know what to say. "Let me get this straight. This family has been back together five minutes and you've already figured out a way to tease me?" I couldn't help laughing.

"I'm sorry," Amber giggled. "My father invited us for supper when you were out in the hall."

"And you felt compelled to tell him about my strange eating habits?"

"Had to," she said. "He asked me if there was anything you didn't like. I told him."

I looked at the three grinning faces before me.

"Why do I get the feeling I'm in a world of trouble here?"

Marian laughed. "Because you are, dear. But I'll be the one to go easy on you, okay?"

I was discovering I really liked these people. When they decided to band together they just did it. Washed seven years of resentment under the bridge as if nothing had ever happened. They were an inspiring group.

"You were great today," Amber said when we got home. "I don't know what you said to my father but you charmed the hell out of him and my mother thinks you're the cutest thing she's ever seen."

"I didn't say anything," I said. "Maybe your parents just decided they don't care if you're gay."

Amber threw herself on the couch. "Oh, they've never cared about that. It was all about what happened to Jeff." I noticed she said his name without flinching. "See, Jeff was the family hero. He did everything right and he was going to follow in my father's footsteps. Become a lawyer and be my Dad's partner. When Jeff died so did the dream. That's what they couldn't deal with; that there would never be a Reed & Son law firm. Now, what did you and Ken talk about in the hall? I can't believe you called him Dr. Doom in front of my father."

I sat beside her. "I meant to apologize for that. It just popped out of my mouth." She shrugged. She didn't really care. "Okay," I continued, "Are you ready for this? Guess which happy duo have become an item."

"Who?"

"Ken and Gwynne."

"No way! When did that happen?"

I pulled off my boots and tossed them across the room.

"Don't know," I said. "But doesn't it make you the least bit curious? What if while all that time you and I were ignoring what we felt for each other they were cheating behind our backs? What if we were behaving like faithful little women and the two of them were screwing their brains out? I'm sure you noticed their odd friendship. Why would they want to be friends? At first I thought it was so they could both keep an eye on us and maybe compare notes but now I'm not so sure. Did you know Ken insisted we hire Gwynne to do the house? Flat out insisted."

Amber threw her boots beside mine.

"Gwynne insisted she was doing it," she said. "But I think your first theory was right, they wanted to watch us. I don't honestly think they were screwing around, maybe they just thought we were. Truthfully, I don't care. Do you?"

I thought about it. "No. But you know what's funny, Amber?"

She covered her ears with her hands. "Don't say it."

"Don't say what?"

"You're going to say that Gwynne always picks up your leftovers and that isn't going to make me feel very good."

I laughed. "Are you psychic?"

"No. I just know how your mind works. You find it real funny that Gwynne is always a step behind you. Like the two of you are playing some invisible chess game and it thrills you that you keep ending up as the one who gets to call *checkmate*. Gwynne was the same way. She wanted the upper hand on you and she could never get it. I told her to give it up because she didn't know how to play your game and she'd only end up losing. Not that you were playing games, but you know what I mean. You were untouchable. What did she honestly think she could do to you that you weren't already doing to yourself? You weren't trying to come after me. If anything, you were doing your best to avoid me." She smirked. "Until the day you got home from your honeymoon and made a point of exposing yourself to me in the kitchen."

Ken and I had come home early from our honeymoon and I was surprised by a morning visit from Amber. I had walked into the kitchen half-naked not knowing anyone else was in the house.

My mouth fell open. "I did not. I didn't know my shirt was open. I was too busy trying to cover up Ken's hard on. And you shouldn't have been in my kitchen anyway."

"You wanted me," she said, confidently. "I could see it on your face the second I told you your shirt was open. You started buttoning it, but you really wanted to take it off."

I laughed at her. "You're ego-maniacal, do you know that?"

"Yes." She crossed her legs under her. "I also know that if we'd been alone in the house right then we would have done it. I would have come on to you and, wedding ring or not, you wouldn't have stopped me. But that's beside the point. The point is, I think Ken is just Gwynne's way of thinking she won some small victory."

"Well she can keep him," I said. "Because I got the real prize."

Amber laughed. "If you were a man I'd say that was a sexist remark. As a woman, I don't know what the word would be. Maybe possessive. But I'm not a possession, Meagan."

"I know that. Why do you say things like that? I don't think you are a possession. I'm only saying she can keep Ken because you and I belong together. We always did. Is it okay if I say that?"

She kissed me. "Why don't we just quit with the talking altogether? I think we can work out a more physical arrangement, don't you?"

"Are you going to shut me up with sex?"

"That's the plan."

I grinned. "Good plan."

The next day I went back to work and Amber went back to writing. She was cruising though the first draft of her novel; writing at top speed and proud of the way it was coming out. She had a very structured system for writing. First she wrote by hand, filling page after page of lined paper with her girlish script. Then she'd type that chapter into her computer, save it on disk, and move on to the next chapter, following her outlines with scrupulous detail. The lined pages went into a binder and the disk sat on top of her desk, ready to be used again. In reality, she was writing two drafts at once. The first draft was the handwritten copy and the second draft was the disk -- as she sometimes rewrote the chapter as she typed.

The problem, she said, was that she couldn't type as fast as she could think. But she could write that fast, chopping up words and using her own brand of shorthand that she had started using long ago while writing essays in college.

Ted was pleased with the progress she was making.

She was working toward a deadline but if she kept up the way she was going she was never going to need that long. The deadline was a guideline and Amber was going to have her manuscript turned in long before that day arrived. I was proud of her. Ted was always gushing about her and it made me happy. Like she was my prodigy along with being my lover. Prodigy! I'd never written a thing in my life.

On Tuesday I brought Adrian his Gameboy and sat with him for an hour listening to him tell me what had gone on in his group therapy that day. He was excited about it. Glad he could unburden himself to people who wouldn't judge him.

"It's not a bad line of work, is it?" He said. "Drug counseling, I mean."

I smiled at him. The clinic staff was comprised of about a quarter of ex-users. It often worked that way. People got clean and they wanted to help others do the same. It was stamping off a debt on their karma card. A good deed done for a good deed taken. It was what good people did, and a lot of drug users were good people underneath. They'd just taken a wrong turn somewhere. Adrian was a good person. He'd just been insecure enough to fall into the clutches of a false security, and I knew how that went.

He surprised me by asking about Zeppo.

"What's he doing?" he asked. "Is he seeing anyone?"

I told him the truth. People needed the truth, especially when they were weak because it helped them get strong. Adrian took the news well. He was getting stronger already. When I was leaving he pulled me into a giant hug.

"I asked around, Meagan," he said, "and a spell in this place isn't cheap. So I want you to know I'm gonna pay you back every cent it costs you."

"Don't worry about it, Adrian," I said. "Pay me back by getting well and fixing your life."

"I'd rather give you the money," he joked.

I sighed. "Wouldn't we all?"

It had been a trying week, and it was only Tuesday. In five short days I'd managed to convince a junkie to go to rehab, break my pinkie, save Amber's life, watch a family get patched back together, and run a business all at the same time. It was exhausting, but great. I loved having a dozen things to juggle. It kept me on my toes. Even with all the chaos surrounding me I felt my life was going better than it had in a very long time. Business was thriving, I was with the person I loved, and I was learning how to be content with what I had.

The challenge still lay ahead.

Chapter 16

Summer came to an end. Fall whipped in like a seasonal fury, turning me thirty in the process. I cried intermittently for weeks. Big fat tears. Amber thought it was funny and Jenna reminded me that you were only as old as you felt. It gave me pause. I didn't feel any older than twenty and didn't look any older than twenty-five. The only thing that had changed about me was that I was now officially an adult.

Then I realized that was exactly what scared me, having to grow up. On the outside I'd been grown for a long time but on the inside I still believed in all the silly things I always had.

There was nothing wrong with that, Jenna had said. It was good that my heart refused to age, because that meant my mind and body would follow suit. She convinced me I could be as young as I wanted to be and in the end I believed her. It was better than believing it was all downhill from here.

Amber finished her novel well under deadline and Ted lined it up for publication. It was going to be another hit for Miss Reed, he laughingly told me. Amber was so excited she started making notes for a sequel. She found she enjoyed being a novelist even more than she'd enjoy being a poet. I was happy for her.

Fall brought changes for everyone. My father started grooming Josh to take over the firm when he retired and Josh rose to the challenge like a true Summers. Dad was only fifty-seven but he wanted to be a free man by the time he turned fifty-eight. I thought it was a good plan. Jenna continued to work her several jobs, because she loved every last one, and Sammy started day care.

Danny dropped out of school for two weeks then went back after I reminded her I would not give her a job. Our parents would have killed me.

Jacob still came by and his mother started college. Seamus got a new job as an engineer and started dating one of the secretaries at the plant. He was forty-six, she was thirty-one.

I knew it wouldn't last.

Ted and I continued to make our mark in the publishing world. We were doing well. *Natural Beauty* and *The Watcher* continued to turn healthy profits and the books we were publishing were hitting bestseller's lists left and right. Markham-Summers was the golden company. Hector continued its downward plummet.

Vicki Clump speedily rose to the ranks of star reporter at *The Watcher* and I kept my eye on her. I never knew when she'd become indispensable to me, but I was sure at some point she would. The girl was a pit bull, and a force unto herself. She got things done. I liked that. There would come a point when she would become very valuable indeed. So I watched.

Adrian got clean and started studying to be a drug counselor. Zeppo and Nathan broke up and Adrian asked me to put out the word that he was still interested. I passed on the news. Zeppo and Adrian got back together only to break up again three weeks later. In the fourth week they got together again. This time it stuck.

Ted and I continued to publicize our authors ourselves and eventually had to add on a PR department when it got to be too much for us. Our clients didn't want to hire their own PR people; half of them didn't even want agents or managers. They wanted Markham-Summers to handle everything because they saw how we were turning some of our very first clients into household names. We weren't just marketing their books, we were marketing *them*, and everyone wanted a piece of the action. It became a sign of victory if Ted or I decided to handle a particular author ourselves. They bragged about it when they ran into each other in the building. If one person was being handled by the PR department, it was assured the other person would have to mention that he was being handled by Meagan or Ted personally. It was like a badge of honor. Like being the chosen one.

Cicely Bower was our fastest rising star. She did TV, talk radio and dozens of magazine interviews. I pressed until her name was synonymous with the title of the book she'd written. And then I pressed harder. By fall she was famous, her book flying off shelves across the continent, and I signed her to a three-book deal with a hefty advance. I was taking her to the top and she was taking Markham-Summers along with her. She plugged the company in every interview she gave and we were flooded with manuscripts and proposals.

I had plans for Amber too. With Hector continuing his plummet I was able to buy the rights to her first three books from Hector himself for a ridiculous price. I planned on surprising her. Once her novel became a hit, which I would make sure of, I planned on having the books reprinted and released as a collection, a boxed set. Maybe for Christmas. I wasn't supposed to get involved but I was certain she'd like it. How could she not? I was going to take her even further than I'd taken Cicely Bower. Amber was going to be the lesbian Jackie Collins, I'd already planned on her commercial success. Ted might not take her that far but I would. I was going to make her a star.

It never occurred to me that she might not want to be a star. Few things occurred to me when I was focused on business. All I knew was that Markham-Summers was becoming a giant and I was going to make good use of the power that offered. What was the point of having power if you couldn't help out the people you loved? Selfish, I wasn't.

Cynthia handed me a cup of coffee and a brown manila envelope stuffed so full it had been sealed with yellow packaging tape.

"What's this?" I asked, taking the weighty thing from her hand and sipping my coffee. I groaned. Cynthia made the best coffee around.

"Ted was going through the slush pile," she said, pleased with the way I admired the cup, "and he thought this might interest you. It's addressed to you but half the manuscripts down there are." She fixed the papers on my desk by grouping them together and tapping them on the tabletop until the stack lined up. She was even more orderly than I was. "He told me to tell you it's right up your alley."

I placed the envelope on the desk. "I have an alley?"

Cynthia laughed. "It's about near-death experience or something." Gave me that sympathetic little nod because my personal life was no secret to her or Ted. They were as much family as co-workers.

Cynthia left and I opened the envelope. There was a

query letter inside. I scanned it quickly. "Hope you find this interesting". Blah, blah, blah. "Motorcycle accident". Blah, blah, blah. "A book about what I experienced in the afterlife."

It wasn't a very good query but that happened. Sometimes an author spent so much time perfecting his manuscript that he forgot the query was the first thing an editor saw. I was willing to give Mr. Garrison the benefit of the doubt. I pulled the manuscript from the envelope and began reading.

It started off slow. Several pages describing the author's life before the accident that led to his near-death experience. He had spent some time in jail for robbery. Had ridden with a gang for a few years and then met a woman who made him want to change his wild ways. I read with growing interest. The writing was bad but the story was good.

I sipped my coffee. Perhaps with a co-writer this could be turned into something publishable. I continued to read and grew more fascinated every minute. A word caught my eye at the bottom of the page. *Realm.* I nearly choked on my coffee.

By four-thirty I had read almost the entire manuscript and was in a state of shock. Nothing in the world could have prepared me for what I was reading. It was terrifying and thrilling. It was another piece of the puzzle fitting into place. Or it was someone's sick joke.

The intercom beside me gave me a quick buzz and I jumped. Amber was on the line, Cynthia said. Did I want to take her call? I told her to tell Amber I was on my way home and stuffed the manuscript back in its envelope and took it with me out the door. Amber had to see this!

I jumped in my car and sped across town. I was getting good at speeding again. I found if you battled the panic attacks often enough, eventually they went away. Within fifteen minutes I was riding the elevator in our building.

"You didn't have to rush home," Amber said when I stepped through the door. "I only wanted to know what you felt like for dinner." Amber loved to cook. Why, I didn't know, but she created these fabulous meals that were always colorful and pretty to look at. It was almost a shame to eat them.

I threw my jacket at the coat rack and it landed on the floor. Amber arched an eyebrow when I turned away from it.

"Don't worry about dinner," I said, digging into the

manila envelope and pulling out a heap of crisp white paper. "We'll order something later. Right now I wanna show you something. Cynthia handed me this manuscript today and you're not going to believe what's in it."

Amber was intrigued. I never brought manuscripts home.

"What's in it?" she asked.

I paced back and forth in front of her, flapping the pages in my hand, and not knowing where to begin. How on earth was I going to explain this? Amber watched me pace for a few moments then took my hand and led me to the couch where we always had our big conversations. She sat. I continued to pace.

"This must be huge," she said. "I haven't seen you pace like this since the day Sammy was born. Sit down, will you?"

I sat and placed the manuscript on my lap. There was no real way to begin what I was about to tell her so I started with the basics. Eased her into the tale I was about to share.

"The guy who wrote this manuscript," I began, in the calmest voice I could manage, "was in a motorcycle accident awhile back. He was unconscious for a month and this is the story of what he encountered during that time. Do you know what he calls the unconscious, Amber? *The Realm*. He calls it the Realm."

"Is that what you're all freaked out about?"

I bounced the pages on my lap. "Not even close. I'm gonna read you something, okay? And then I want you to tell me what you think."

Amber nodded and I flipped through the pages until I found the one I had dog-eared.

"Okay, listen to this: 'I met a woman in the Realm. She was a twenty-seven year old coma victim and, ultimately, she was the one who helped me decide to return to the earth plane. My girlfriend was pregnant and this woman had been in an accident of her own, which resulted in a terminated pregnancy. She thought it was very important that I go back to raise my child because she no longer had that chance.'"

I stopped reading and gauged Amber for a reaction. She was silent. Thinking. She knew what I was getting at but the pragmatic side of her nature was forming doubts, trying to punch a hole in a theory that was quite clear in just those few sentences. She folded her hands in her lap and went for the reasonable approach.

"Is it possible that it's only a coincidence?"

I didn't believe in coincidence. Things happened for a reason. I shook my head at her.

"That's what I tried telling myself," I said, "That it was just some crazy coincidence. But then I read further and what I came across erased all doubt."

She cuddled up to me. "Like what?"

"For starters this woman is named Morgan."

"Maybe a fluke," she said.

I gave her a strange look. "Would you like to hear what's on page one-o-four, Amber? I think you'll be surprised. The writing isn't great and the names are sort of silly but once I'm done you won't think it's such a fluke."

Amber pulled an afghan from the top corner of the couch and tossed it over us. I wasn't cold but it was comforting; safe. I turned so that my back was against the arm of the couch, put my feet on the cushions, and she sat between my knees, resting her back on my chest.

She turned and looked up at me. "Go on," she encouraged.

I placed the manuscript in my left hand and scanned down to the paragraph I had highlighted with a light blue marker.

"Morgan was in a dilemma," I read. "She felt she had made a mess of her life. She was married to Dr. Glen but she was in love with Amethyst, a woman she had once been involved with and who came daily to see her."

"Oh my God!" Amber gasped.

"Coincidence, Amber?"

"Glen? Amethyst? This is too weird."

"It gets weirder."

She sighed and leaned into me again. "It always does."

I grinned. "Listen to this part: 'Amethyst and Glen seemed to be fighting an unconscious war with each other. Who did Morgan belong to? In the Realm the answer was clear. Morgan belonged to Amethyst.'"

Amber wrapped my other arm around her stomach. I

leaned into her and stretched my arm so that I was reading over her shoulder.

"'Glen loved his wife,'" I went on," 'but he knew if she woke up she would leave him for Amethyst. He was angry with Morgan but he knew she never really meant to hurt him and he allowed Amethyst's visits because he believed if anyone could awaken his wife it was her.'"

"This is amazing," Amber said. "How could this guy know all this?"

"Apparently I told him. In the manuscript he goes on to say how he and Morgan often sat around chatting and how they shared everything with each other. Some of it I think I remember, Amber. He doesn't describe himself but I have this picture of a man in my head and I think it's him. He mentions Beth. Uses her real name too, I guess because she didn't come back. He mentions Jacob too. Calls him Jack. And he writes about how Jack needed a mother and Morgan had lost her child. The first time Jacob called me he said, 'You were like my mom out there', and it scared me so bad I hung up on him."

Amber nodded. "He said it again when he showed up here."

"This Garrison guy knows everything. He even mentions Gran's ring."

"He does?" She turned to face me. "Read me that part."

I turned to page one-fifteen and started at the top. "'Morgan was unsure of her destiny,'" I read. "'Every time she thought she wanted to move upward Amethyst would come and Morgan would reverse her opinion. Amethyst was as beautiful as Morgan and Morgan often said she was haunted by Amethyst's eyes." Amber smiled. "Had been mesmerized by them since the day they first met. I understood where she was coming from because Amethyst had the most gorgeous green eyes I had ever seen.'"

"I like this guy," Amber joked.

I gave her a playful nudge. "Awful writing, though. Maybe with a co-writer--- "

"Meagan."

"What?"

"Get your mind off business for two minutes and tell me about the ring. No, wait. Before you do that let me first tell you I find it incredible that you should be the topic of so many books."

I laughed. "Well, this isn't really about me, it's about this Garrison guy." I checked the cover page. "Todd."

"Whatever," Amber said. "You're in it. *I'm* even in it. You have a way of dragging people into your bizarre little world, don't you?"

"You know where the door is."

"Don't be so defensive. Get to the ring."

"Why?"

"Because I want to know something."

I cleared my throat and went back to reading. "'Morgan had given Amethyst a ring when they were together. Amethyst kept the ring after they broke up and she wore it on a chain around her neck. Morgan told me this made her happy because the ring was a symbol of an eternal bond, and although Amethyst had taken it off her finger she still wore it, meaning she had never fully abandoned the bond. The ring was a family tradition passed on to Morgan by her grandmother, whom she affectionately called, "Crazy old Gran".'"

Amber laughed. "You tell everyone your grandmother was nuts, don't you?"

"Pretty much. How else can I explain the strange things she got me to believe in? I believe in *fairies*, Amber. Not in a Tinkerbell kind of way, but still, it doesn't exactly match my rationalism, does it? Gran looked happy so I figured those fairies she claimed to be seeing were a pretty good thing. I'm looking forward to senility, I think."

Amber roared with laughter. "I'll bet you are. Tell me about the ring."

"Okay. Where was I?" I ran my finger down the page. "'The ritual of the ring was to pass it on to the person you loved. I don't know who had given it to Gran, but Gran bequeathed it to Morgan with that one stipulation attached. Ultimately, it was the ring that sent Morgan home. Amethyst placed it on Morgan's finger one day as she slept and Morgan knew what that meant. By giving Morgan back the ring Amethyst was telling Morgan that she was waiting for her to come home. Morgan left the Realm shortly after.'"

"I knew it!" Amber jumped to her feet and the blanket

fell to the floor. "Jenna didn't see how it made sense but I knew if I gave you the ring you'd come back. And it worked! Meagan, you really did come back from the dead for me!"

I grinned. "That's what I've been telling you all along. And that's also the end of Morgan's story. I'm calling this Todd Garrison in the morning. I have to know if he sent this manuscript to me because he *knew* it was me, or what."

"Obviously he knew it was you, Meagan," Amber said. "Can I be there when you meet with him?"

"If you want to be. I'll see if I can set something up for tomorrow."

"Great. Tomorrow." She was excited about this. "You know what you should do? You should call Jacob. It's kind of scary but maybe you *are* being set up for something big. You keep talking about a challenge and these coma people keep popping up in your life. Do you think it could be connected somehow?"

"I don't know," I said. "But I mean to find out."

We sat in my office waiting. It seemed to me we were always waiting for something. Amber sat in the leather chair by the wall, playing with the fairy statue she had bought me for my birthday. It was only one of many gifts she'd given me but by far my favorite. It was the thirteenth statue. I now had a coven of fairies. I kept twelve at home and the new one at the office because it was my favorite, and I spent more time at the office these days than anywhere else.

I hadn't called Jacob. I wanted to meet with Todd Garrison myself before I got Jacob involved. I was protecting him. I wanted to hear Mr. Garrison out and if what he said wasn't too frightening, only then would I get in touch with Jacob.

Amber thought it was sweet the way I looked out for the boy in what she called my own peculiar Meagan way. Sometimes she thought I was more peculiar than Jenna, because Jenna's oddities were consistent, at least. Mine were unchartered. She never knew what I might do next, but it never bothered her either. In those ways she trusted me enough that she usually just found me amusing, a mystery that spun in another direction just when she thought she'd figured me out. She was more like me than she thought, because she enjoyed the challenge.

I didn't try to be unpredictable. There was a time when I was the most predictable person around, but the accident had changed all that. I'd faced so many challenges in such a short time I couldn't help but change with them. If I didn't change I wouldn't win. The obstacles would beat me if I didn't keep coming up with new ways to beat them first. I had to stay on top of things. Look over my shoulder at every turn, lest another battle was creeping up from behind. Crazy thing was I enjoyed it. This was my life and I was getting every opportunity to live it to the fullest. I was doing what I had come back from the dead to do, live.

Cynthia rapped on the door, pulling me from my reverie. "Mr. Garrison is here," she said, poking her head inside. "Are you ready to see him?"

Amber and I rose from our chairs.

"Yes," I said. "Please send him in."

Todd Garrison entered the room like a grinning giant in a pair of jeans matched up with a shirt and tie. This was a man who didn't wear suits. The tie was as far as he went. I looked him over quickly. He was the man in my mind, only the long hair had been chopped to shoulder-length and he had grown a goatee. But the eyes. The steely grey eyes that looked colder than they were--those were the same.

He extended his massive hand. "Hello, Miss Summers."

I shook it. "Call me Meagan. Or should I say Morgan?"

He gave a sly grin. "Put the pieces together, huh?"

I laughed. "It wasn't hard. I take it you remember, Amber."

Amber stepped forward and shook his hand.

"We never did meet," Todd said, "but yes, I definitely remember Amber. The eyes. Too stunning not to be mentioned in my book."

Amber glanced away shyly. "Thank you." The only thing that could crack her confidence was a compliment from a stranger.

Todd rubbed his hands together. "So, I see things

worked out for you. Love brought you home and you decided to keep it, huh?"

"So far so good. And you? How's the baby?"

Todd nodded. "Good. Jade's pregnant again. We got married. And Zoe's going on two."

"Zoe?" I looked at Amber and felt a lump in my throat.

"We named her Zoe," Todd said. "I hope that doesn't offend you but when we were in the Realm you explained the meaning of the name. You told me it meant life and when my daughter arrived that was all I could see--life. Jade loved the name," he shrugged.

Amber was watching my face. I flashed her a quick smile to let her know I was alright. In fact, I was better than alright. I felt like in some strange way my child had lived on through her name. Zoe was alive. She wasn't *my* Zoe. But she was her namesake and that kept my Zoe real. Fate had given Todd what it had taken from me and I realized I was okay with that. I had moved on. It had taken forever but it had happened.

We sat in the chairs around my desk. Todd sat across from me and Amber pulled up a chair beside me so that we both faced him.

"Okay," I said. "I'm going to tell you what I want to do first and then we can discuss our history, if you'd like."

Todd folded his hands behind his head. "Shoot."

"I want to publish your book, Todd." His eyes lit up. "But it needs some work. So, if it's okay with you, I'd like to assign you a co-writer. The bare bones are already there. You've laid it out quite well and I can see its potential but it needs help with the grammar, the sentence structure, editing--that sort of thing. With a co-writer, I can give you a six-month deadline and we can have the book out by summer-- maybe early fall. I'm not gonna push this project just yet. Once the book is complete, we'll see how far we can take it from there. If I start pushing you, you'll only feel pressured and that won't be good for anyone."

"What about money?" Todd asked.

I chuckled. "You get right to the point, don't you?"

"Just interested."

I tapped the top of his manuscript with a pen. "We'll talk money in greater detail when the book is finished. But I'll be honest, there isn't going to be some huge advance in this for you. I have to assign you a co-writer, which will cost me money. I'm also taking a chance on you. You're a first-time author and your subject isn't exactly mainstream. It targets a select demographic, again, cutting into the money that can be made. You'll get standard royalties, for sure, and depending on what the co-writer costs me, anywhere between a $1,000 to $4,000 advance. That's as much as I can tell you right now."

Todd scratched his head. "That sounds fair."

Amber patted my shoulder. "What about me?"

"What *about* you?"

"Assign me the job. I'll be his co-writer."

I shook my head.

"Why not?" she pressed.

"Because you have a book that's being printed and packaged for shipping even as we speak. In a few weeks you're going to be too busy with publicity to focus on anything else. There will be interviews to give. A book tour."

"A book tour?" Her eyebrows shot up. "I've never had to do that before."

I sighed. This was not the time to get into this.

"You've never been a Markham-Summers client before, Amber. You can't write a novel and expect the company to promote it without any help from you. Ted would never allow it, and I suggest you talk to him about this. As for Todd's book," I said and turned to him, putting the focus back where it belonged. "I have a few writers I can set you up with. Would you prefer a man or a woman?"

Todd laughed. "If we're talking about long hours huddled away together, better go with a man. Jade can be a bit jealous."

I smiled and made a note on the top of his manuscript. *No women.*

"I think that pretty much takes care of business," I said, "We'll draw up the usual contracts and agreements when the book is complete." I settled back in my chair. We were getting to the part Amber had been waiting for.

Todd reached into his pocket for a cigarette, saw there wasn't an ashtray, and put the pack away. It was a non-smoking building but I remembered what going without a cigarette felt like and sometimes allowed clients to smoke in my office. I reached toward the bookshelf behind me, removed a glass ashtray, and slid it across the desk at him. He looked relieved as he took the cigarettes out again and lit one. He took a deep drag and grinned like I had given him gold. He looked so pleased it almost made me want a cigarette too. It had been four years but the occasional urge still crept up. I rarely felt the urge for coke anymore but sometimes wanted a cigarette. I wondered what that said about nicotine.

"So, what do you want to talk about now?" Todd asked, blowing a thick grey plume above our heads.

I watched it rise and float across the room. "I honestly don't know. Maybe you can tell me how you remember everything."

"Easy. I woke up remembering."

Amber and I exchanged a look. Jacob and I had been working for months to put the pieces together and this guy woke up remembering!

We talked about Jacob. I told Todd how Jacob had turned up in my life one day and he chuckled. "Kind of like how I just did, huh?" It was exactly like that. Only Todd had gotten the calm Meagan and poor Jacob had gotten a maniac.

We talked for over an hour, dissecting each other's memories, and fascinating Amber with our tales.

"Meagan was Victor's pain in the ass," Todd said, looking at Amber. "Every time you came around, if he wanted her for something he had to forcibly drag her away. My guide had to drag me away a few times and I'll tell you, it wasn't fun. You'd be standing in your room, looking at your guest, or whatever, and if you ignored your guide's call you'd just be yanked away. And you'd feel disoriented for a few minutes because your spirit had just been snapped in another direction and you had to compose yourself. They always apologized," he chuckled, "but Meagan drove Victor nuts. Almost never did what he wanted her to do. She was the most rebellious one of us. Did what she wanted and no one was going to tell her otherwise. Probably not even God himself if she met him."

Amber slapped the top of the desk and laughed. "So basically, you're no different dead than you are alive."

I smirked. "Guess not."

I asked Todd if he'd like to meet Jacob and he readily agreed. We made plans to get together the following week. He'd bring his wife, maybe his daughter, and we'd bring Jacob.

When he left I called Jacob and told him everything. He was thrilled to have another piece of the puzzle and said he was hanging up to go write it down in his journal before he forgot. He was so cute. Inquisitive too. One day I had been forced to explain to him what a lesbian was. He knew Amber and I were in a relationship but he didn't have a word for it. A kid at school told him not to be so stupid, that we were 'dyking out.'

Amber, as usual, thought that was the funniest thing in the world. Martha wasn't so amused. She told me I was the one who would have to explain it to Jacob since I was the one who was doing it. She wasn't anti-gay, just anti-explanation. She wouldn't have known where to begin.

I hadn't known where to begin either. How to explain a word that I, myself, didn't even believe in. I sat him down and did my best. Amber laughed all the way through it. Jenna was over with Sammy at the time and she took my feeble explanation to a higher plane. She told Jacob that words like "gay" and "straight" were only labels people used to describe different types of sexuality, but that love that existed on a higher plane surpassed such words and the only people who cared about those labels were people who didn't understand. Jacob understood.

"I don't care about those words," he'd said, "because I believe in love, like you said."

Jacob and Sammy were the future, I realized. If more kids were being raised the way they were, by the time they grew up there might not be such things as racism and homophobia.

Sammy loved Amber as much as he loved me. In his eyes, Amber was no different than Danielle or me. She was a part of his tribe. Had been since the day he was born. I was proud of the way Josh and Jenna were raising him. It was the way I would have raised my child if she hadn't been taken from me.

Amber left the office shortly after Todd. I was glad. I had another meeting coming up and I didn't want her around for it. If she knew who my appointment was with she would have refused to leave. This was a different kind of business I had to take care of. The kind she wouldn't like but the kind I was going to take care of anyway.

    I settled back in my chair and waited for my four-fifteen.

Chapter 17

It didn't take long for the shit to hit the fan. I had met with my mystery appointment, listened to her proposal, scanned the manuscript, drew up the contracts and struck a deal I had no intention of upholding. Then I waited, prepared for the kill. I struck down the only enemy I had ever had and waited some more. I knew Amber wouldn't be pleased but I didn't care. This wasn't about her. It was about taking care of business and I handled it in a way that would have made Seamus proud. He had a taste for vengeance too. I couldn't wait to tell him.

But first I had to deal with Amber.

"So I got a call today," she said over dinner three weeks later. I grinned. I knew exactly where we were headed. Cynthia had taken care of the fax that morning and I'd been wondering how the reaction was going to come about. My victim went the way I guessed she would. Straight to Amber.

I stabbed a piece of broccoli with my fork and stared at it. A fitting vegetable. My enemy had once called me broccoli. She had stood in my hospital room and wished death on me. I remembered it as clearly as if it were yesterday.

"You know what I love, Amber?" I said, thinking of the past I had only just killed that morning. I never forgot a slight. Now it was taken care of and I was finally deserving of my bitch title.

"Broccoli," I said. "I love broccoli. It's by far the prettiest vegetable, don't you think? Kind of sad the way it just lies there on your plate though. Like a pretty little tree that has no life."

Amber was watching me. I put down my fork. "I'm sorry, you were saying you got a call today?" I smiled sweetly. "Who from?"

"I think you know who from."

"Humor me."

Amber threw her napkin on the table. "I can't believe you did that, Meagan."

"Did what?" I asked innocently.

"You know very well what. Gwynne came to you with a book proposal. You bought the rights and now you're refusing to publish her book."

"Oh, that." I shrugged. The proposal Gwynne had brought me was a good one. A coffee table book about interior design, chock full of pictures of homes she had remodeled all over the country. It was a beautiful idea and I had enjoyed squashing it. "Yeah, I decided I wasn't interested after all."

Amber glared at me. She didn't like the vindictive side of my nature. It didn't come up often but when it did all hell was likely to break loose.

"You had no intention of publishing it, did you?" she accused. "You wanted your revenge for what happened that day in the hospital and you used your company to get it. That's so low, Meagan. It almost makes me ashamed of you."

I didn't like that. I shoved away my plate and glared back. "Gwynne came to *me*, Amber. Hector turned her down and she came to me. No wonder his business is dead. He wouldn't know a good book if it grew teeth and bit him in the ass."

Amber was shocked. "Then the book is *good*?"

"Oh, it's damn good. Celebrity homes--the whole nine yards. It's a shame the thing will never see the light of day."

"Meagan, you can't do this. It's unethical. Gwynne will sue you."

"Let her," I said. "She has absolutely no case. If she read her contract she would have seen that when I purchased all rights I also purchased the right to never publish it. It's a symbolic revenge. You know me and symbolism. Gwynne wanted me dead but instead her book is dead. If she had half a brain she never would have come to me in the first place."

"Sell it back to her, Meagan," Amber pleaded. "You're a better person than this."

"Unfortunately, I'm not. And I don't appreciate the way you're coming to the defense of a woman who wanted me dead. Revenge is revenge. Karma wasn't taking care of her so I did."

"You already got your revenge," Amber said, folding her arms across her chest. "You got it when you got me."

I chuckled. "Nice to see someone around here doesn't suffer from low self-esteem. I hate to burst your bubble, Amber, but this isn't about you. And before you go down the other road it isn't about Ken either. It's about a woman wishing death on me when I was almost already there and giving her back her just reward."

"Meagan, please." Amber was more stressed out about this than I would have liked. "You know the guilt you carried around about Ken for all those months before you realized you could walk? Well, that's how I feel about Gwynne. Learning how to walk again may have relieved your guilt but I don't have anything to relieve mine. Maybe if I can convince you to give her back her dream that will absolve me, okay?"

That was bullshit. I placed my hands on top of my head and leaned back in my chair. "Nice try, but no. You don't need absolution and you know it. You moved on the very day you saw Gwynne spit those awful words at a breathing corpse. Probably even before that. And you're happy Ken and Gwynne found each other because that makes what we did to them not so bad. Unless I'm wrong entirely and you feel you made a mistake when you left Gwynne for me."

"That's not true and you know it," Amber growled. "After all we've been through it pisses me off that you would even suggest it. My love for you is not in question here. I can't say I like you very much right now, but I do love you, and you damn well know it. What I'm asking is for you to be the better person here."

"I'm *not* the better person, Amber. I'm only a publisher with a taste for vengeance. That's who I am. I can be a good person in every other way but not when it comes to this. If you love me then you'll just have to accept that."

Amber rose from the table and threw our dishes in the sink. "I wish you would quit twisting the topic," she complained. "This isn't about us, it's about what you're doing to Gwynne. Now are you going to sell her back the rights or not?"

"Not."

"Then I just hope she doesn't sue you. If she can make a case for personal revenge, she just might have a chance you know. What would that do to Ted? This isn't just your company you're risking."

I gave her a silly look then laughed. "Do you think I'm stupid, Amber? This has nothing to do with the company at all.

If Gwynne sues she'll have to sue me personally because the contract stipulated that this was a private venture. It was my deal, not affiliated with Markham-Summers in any way. On paper it was a private deal between the two of us and Gwynne knows that. That's why she's calling you, because she knows there's not a damn thing she can do about it. She signed a contract selling me all rights. One that *clearly* stated I reserve the right to change my mind at any time as long as she got paid. My lawyers have already looked it over and it's 100% binding. As long as Gwynne got her money, I've upheld the only part of the deal I was required to.

As for personal revenge--prove it. You're the only other person who was in that room and heard what she said to me, so unless you're planning on going against me in court there's no proof any of it even happened. Not to mention I was in a coma at the time. Unlikely I even heard her words at all. And even if I had, so what? So she said she wished I would die. If anything that only gives *her* a motive for revenge. She won't sue, Amber. She doesn't have a chance in hell of winning."

Amber wasn't convinced. "What about Ken?" she asked. "Maybe she stole your husband and that's why you'd want revenge."

I shook my head. "Nope. That's covered too. I'd just have my lawyer subpoena Ken. The man's a stickler for the truth. He'd tell the courts I was the one who wanted the divorce because I was in love with you. Truth is, he'd get off on it so he could maintain his image as poor, long-suffering Ken. He'd tell the courts I had no motive for revenge, because he wouldn't see that I had. If pressed hard enough he'd even tell them what a good wife I was."

Amber sat at the table again, awed. "You're so frightening sometimes, do you know that? You can destroy a life and totally cover your ass in the process. Frankly, I'm glad you love me. Otherwise, I'd be waiting for a safe to fall on my head."

I placed my elbows on the table. "The thing is, I'm not destroying a life, merely crushing a dream. I'm sorry if it disturbs you but I'm not changing my mind. And you know I'd never try to hurt you. Obviously. I didn't do anything when you wrote *Butterflies*. I even let the magazine give it a good review.

Don't worry, Amber. You'll always be safe from me. It's like diplomatic immunity. And I'm not a monster." I grinned. "Well, maybe I'm a little monster."

I walked over to her and she pulled me into her lap. "Okay. I told her I'd try and I did. You're not going to change your mind and I'm certainly not going let it come between us."

"Thank you. By the way, mind if I stash some money in your name?"

"What for?"

I shrugged. "Added precaution. I've already thrown the majority of it in a few Swiss accounts." I winked at her. "Untouchable, right? But I can't make it look like I'm hiding anything either so there's a pretty good amount in accounts over here, and if you don't mind, I'd like to throw about sixty-thousand in an account with your name on it."

She laughed at me. "Do you really think all that is necessary?"

"Not really. But like you said, I cover my ass."

She shrugged. "Fine. Give me *all* your money. What do I care? But you know you're a little bit crazy, right?"

"Why? I trust you. Even if I didn't, it's only sixty grand."

"Only sixty grand! That *is* a lot of money, Meagan." She shook her head like she thought I was so silly. "You're such a nut."

"As Seamus would say, Dat I am."

The next day I returned home from work to find Gwynne sitting in my living room, legs crossed, fingers rapping an impatient beat on her thigh. Amber sat in the chair opposite her and there was a partially eaten chocolate cake on the table between them. Two plates. Only one had been used. The used one sat on the corner of the table in front of Gwynne and there was chocolate frosting smeared across it like a stain. I thought it belonged in the sink. The clean plate sat in front of Amber and it was so white and shiny it made me wonder where the cake had come from at all. She certainly wasn't interested in it.

Gwynne, I thought. She must have brought it over as some sort of edible peace offering. Too bad for her.

Amber looked nervous. She was fidgeting, rocking a little in her seat. She was also mad. I could see it in the way she looked at me. Her eyes darted to the door I had just stepped through and she watched it close behind me. Watched me remove my jacket and throw my purse on the chair by the door like she hadn't seen me do this hundreds of times before.

Neither woman spoke. They waited for me to round the couch and approach them, and I saw that Gwynne looked as great as ever. All blue-eyed and intense. I swallowed back a twinge of jealousy. Amber would never cheat on me with Gwynne. She'd never cheat on me, period.

"Hello, Gwynne," I said politely. "What brings you by?"

She got right to the point. "I want my rights back."

Amber suddenly shot to her feet like her chair had given her a shock and I arched an eyebrow at her.

"Would you like a clump of cake, Meagan?" she asked, her eyes meeting mine in an imploring way. It was the strangest thing I'd ever heard her say.

"A *clump*?"

"Yes," she said, nodding emphatically. "Gwynne had a clump. I watched her eat it."

"Huh?"

Gwynne and I both gave Amber an odd look. She wasn't making much sense but she continued to stare at me like she was willing me to catch on to something. Some sort of message in her peculiar choice of words. Gwynne gave her a disgusted look while I grappled to figure out what she was trying to tell me, because I was sure it was something.

"You can cut your own," she went on in that same nonsensical way. "Because I know you can be picky." She gave a silly little laugh. "Picky about your clump."

Picky about my clump? She had *watched* Gwynne eat hers?

It came to me in a flash and I grinned. The message was Vicki Clump. Vicki Clump who worked at *The Watcher*. Amber was trying to tell me that Gwynne had a tape recorder in her pocket and she was doing it in a way that only I would understand. It was brilliant. Gwynne wanted me to admit, on tape, that I'd screwed her over. Nice try. I couldn't help wondering why the hell people were always trying to tape me but decided I didn't care.

My grin widened. Amber saw it and dropped back into her chair. Relief on her face but anger still in her eyes. For some reason she didn't want Gwynne to know that she knew about the tape recorder and I decided I'd play it her way. Amber didn't play games, so if she was playing one now there was a damn good reason for it.

I pushed up my sleeves. "No thank you, Amber. I'm fine."

"You're sure you don't want a clump?" She was double-checking. Making sure I'd caught the meaning.

"For Christ's sake," Gwynne barked. "I'm here for a reason, Amber, so just shut up about the goddamn cake."

I sat on the arm of Amber's chair and let the anger flash in my eyes. "Don't talk to her like that, Gwynne."

A spark of hope crossed her face. "Or what?" She angled her pocket toward me and I almost laughed at how obvious the movement was. Something was definitely bulking the thin fabric of her blazer. At least Clump had had the sense to wear a thicker jacket when she'd tried the same stunt.

"Or I'll have to ask you to leave," I said, easily. "What did you think I'd do? Threaten you?" I shook my head like nothing could be crazier. "It's not in my nature to be vindictive."

Amber looked up at me and then quickly looked away. I was full of shit. I had a mean streak a mile long when I wanted. I just never used it on the people I loved. It was reserved for occasions like this.

Gwynne maneuvered herself closer. She edged forward so that she was perched on the end of her seat. "Why won't you sell me back my rights?"

Again the pocket faced me, waiting for my response. I wasn't sure but it seemed to me a tape recording couldn't be used in court. I thought I heard somewhere it was considered inadmissible evidence. I also could be wrong so I decided to play it safe. And playing it safe meant lying through my teeth.

"Didn't you get my fax, Gwynne?" I asked, sincerely. "I won't sell back the rights because I think it's a good book and I might want to use it somewhere down the road when I can get the financing together and give it the push it deserves.

Unfortunately, my money's tied up in a different project right now that's costing me more than I'd anticipated. I want to publish your book, Gwynne, but like I wrote in the fax, it just isn't possible right now. I'm afraid I really do have to put it on hold."

Amber wouldn't look at me. She hated that I could lie so well. And so easily.

"You're a fucking liar," Gwynne yelled. She sat so far on the end of the couch I thought she might fall off. She was moving in for the kill but she didn't know that I was immune to her attacks. "This is because I'm with your ex-husband. You want revenge for that!"

The pocket continued to inch toward me and I couldn't resist a jibe.

"Is there a problem with your pocket, Gwynne?" She flinched and Amber glanced up at me, wondering what the hell I thought I was doing. I smiled at her. Waved my hand like it didn't matter. "Never mind. As for your last comment, the answer is no. I do not care that you're with Ken. I divorced him because I wanted to be with Amber. You know that. I'm only sorry the two of you got hurt along the way. We never wanted to hurt anyone." That part was true. "But on the upside, you found each other, right? That's a good thing."

"We're engaged," she proclaimed snottily.

"Congratulations."

She waved a ring in my face. "We're getting *married*."

I nodded. "I understand. I'm sure it will be a gay old time."

"You're such a bitch," Gwynne growled.

Amber gave me a sideways glance and rose from the chair. Something was *really* bothering her and it wasn't my sarcasm, but she had enough class not to show it in front of Gwynne. Gwynne had never watched Amber the way I had. She didn't know the expressions I knew. The angry little mannerisms. All the things I'd made note of when I was paralyzed and had nothing better to do.

Gwynne and I stared at each other. Same old battle of wills.

"Tell me something," she said, her head indicating Amber who had turned her back on us and moved to the window. "Does she say *my* name when you're fucking her? How many times has that happened to you, Meagan?"

I gave her an amused sneer. Wasn't the least bit affected by her words.

Amber whirled around to face her. "It's never happened, Gwynne. I hate to break it to you, but you're far too lazy to be even half as good in bed as you think you are."

I burst out laughing. "Ouch. I'd hate to be on the receiving end of that one." It was so unlike Amber to insult anyone, and to do it so cruelly. I was impressed. Then she shot me a look as if to tell me I'd better stop laughing right now.

I dropped into her vacated chair and tried to compose myself, but I couldn't wipe the smirk off my face.

"Let's not get childish, Gwynne," I said. "There's no reason for it."

"*No reason?*" she shrieked. "You fucked me over!"

"I did no such thing. The plan fell through and I'm sorry about that."

I hoped she'd play the tape for Ken. He would hear the sincerity in my voice and chastise her for sinking so low as to record me.

Gwynne jumped to her feet and jabbed a finger at me. "You are one twisted bitch. I don't know what Amber sees in you."

I shrugged. "Same thing your fiancé saw in me, I suppose. I'm actually a very good person Gwynne. It's sad that you refuse to give me the benefit of the doubt."

My words angered her more. She yanked her purse from the couch and hit me with her furious eyes. "You'll pay for this, Meagan. I swear to God, you'll fucking pay!"

Well I couldn't let her get away with threatening me so I walked up to her and leaned into her ear. "Don't count on it," I whispered. "You can't beat me."

She glanced at her pocket and I grinned. There was no way her recorder picked up my words because I'd made sure my arm pressed against the fabric to muffle the sound as I spoke and my voice was so low she barely heard me herself. But she caught the warning in my eyes. This chapter was over and I had written the ending. As far as I was concerned, we were even.

Gwynne stalked from the apartment and slammed the

door behind her. Amber went in the bedroom and slammed that door. I turned the lock on the door after Gwynne and followed Amber. Whatever she was pissed about, she'd get over it. I was about to give her so much praise she'd have no choice but to get over it.

I closed the bedroom door behind me, shutting us in, and dropped down on the bed where she lay, staring at the ceiling as if I hadn't even entered. I told her she was brilliant, how much I admired the way she'd pulled it off. That she was a genius.

She kept her eyes focused on the ceiling and her arms tucked under her head like she was ignoring me.

I kept up with the praise. "How did you know?" I asked. She had to speak now.

"I saw it poking out of her pocket when she first got here. She didn't know I saw it and I knew the minute you came through the door you'd start gloating, so I came up with the clump thing. And I sounded like an idiot. But what could I do? Let her tape you confessing your crime? If I pulled you aside she'd know something was up, and I figured it was better that she got a tape full of you calmly defending yourself because if I called her on it she would have only come at you another way and I didn't know what that way would be. She couldn't get you to crack." Amber glared at me. "Not on tape anyway, so maybe she'll give up now."

She knew what the whispering had been about. She didn't have to hear it to know what I'd been doing.

"You're so cute," I said. "The way you protect me like that." I moved to kiss her but she rolled away from me, stood up, and gave me a disgusted look.

"I wouldn't have to protect you if you didn't do such things. Your antics were amusing once; now they're just sickening. I have to play stupid little games because you refuse to grow the hell up."

"Amber." I went to pull her down beside me, but she shook off my touch like it burned.

"No, Meagan. You may not care if you have to spend your life looking over your shoulder, but I do. I don't want to be a part of this sick little game you and Gwynne have been playing since the day you met."

"I never forced you to be," I said.

Her gaze zeroed in on mine. "No? If I hadn't dropped those clues, you would have told Gwynne straight out that paybacks are a bitch. *She* knew it. She brought the tape recorder because even she knew you couldn't resist a good gloat at her expense. I *had* to get involved, Meagan. Otherwise you would have hanged yourself with your arrogance."

I nodded. She was right. I would have done precisely as she'd described. I wanted Gwynne to know what I'd done to her so badly that I couldn't even resist whispering to her that she'd never beat me. Jenna would be ashamed of me if she knew. Amber was ashamed of me. Sadly, I was still proud.

"You're right," I conceded. "You totally covered my ass and I'm grateful for that. It won't happen again. I know how you hate having to be deceptive and I'm sorry you were dragged into this."

Amber would handle this situation between us a certain way. It wasn't normally my way but I thought I'd give it a try. I crawled across the bed on my knees and gave her the pleading 'forgive me' eyes and urged her down beside me. "Got any ideas on how I should thank you?"

She grinned at my attempt to be her, but something wasn't right about the grin. It didn't have that knowing edge to it. It didn't light up her eyes. It barely touched her cheeks, and there was something fierce about her expression. She was smiling at me but there was a menacing curl to her lips. Like she knew some gruesome secret she wasn't ready to share.

When we kissed I thought I was just being silly, that I'd imagined the look. Big mistake. Amber had a little game of her own in mind, and she was about to do something I would never forget.

By evening the bedroom was bathed in candlelight. The moon had risen high and full outside the window and the only light inside came from the flickering flames that danced on the tips of the wicks around us. We often burned candles in the bedroom. We were big on atmosphere.

Amber had been acting strange all evening. Every once in a while I'd catch her looking at me with that fierce expression. Staring at me, like I didn't fit the picture she had drawn for us in her mind. It wasn't about Gwynne. It was about something else she wasn't mentioning. Gwynne had just been a log on the angry fire that was burning inside her but she pretended nothing was wrong, and against my better instinct, I believed the act.

And I continued believing it. Even as I bent above her on the bed giving kisses that felt about as reciprocated as if I was kissing wood. Slowly, she warmed to me and I allowed the feelings to pass. Her mouth met mine fervently. Cotton candy. She'd returned to the carnival. She murmured my name and I smiled against her lips. I never tired of hearing her say it like that, when she was lost in me and me in her, and nothing outside us mattered.

I felt the cool metal of her ring slide across my skin as her hands moved down my back. Tickling my spine. Then the feeling again. That sense of something different. A change within her. Something growing cold in her eyes. She knew I saw it and she looked away. Leaned forward and kissed my neck. Told me she thought I was beautiful. But she was deliberating something. I could feel it in the way her lips hesitated in the air beside me, hovering slightly above my skin. Then in one awful instant it happened. Her teeth dove into the flesh of my neck at the same time her nails dug into my back and raked eight razorblade lines across it.

I shrieked and jumped away from her. "What the fuck was that? That hurt!"

"Did it hurt, Meagan?" Her eyes were frighteningly cold. She slapped me in the face, stunning me.

"*What the hell are you doing?*" I yelled. The imprint of her hand stung my cheek. My neck felt like an animal had torn into it and my back burned. Something warm slid down between my shoulder blades and I realized with horror what it was. Blood! She'd made me bleed. I turned to see, but it was too high up on my back, and I felt the small drop continue to slide downward.

Amber leaned forward to inspect the damage and smirked at a job well done. She pressed her index finger to my back, showed me the drop of blood on it, and sucked it between her lips. I was horrified. Speechless.

"It's not bad," she said.

I stared at her with my mouth open. "Have you lost your mind? You better not have scarred me."

"I'm only doing what you want," she said.

"*This is what you think I want?*" She was completely insane. Suddenly, she grabbed a handful of my hair and yanked on it so hard I was forced to follow her down on the bed.

"Let go!" I demanded. It was the vampire scene all over again. Only worse, because this was being done out of anger.

She kept a firm grip on my hair, wrapping it around her hand. "So you like it rough, huh?"

"What? What the hell are you talking about?"

She let go of my hair for a second and I rolled onto my back.

"Becca wasn't the only who liked it rough, was she?" She slapped me in the face again. I snapped and slapped her back. She just looked at me. "I wasn't informed you liked to hit back."

"Informed by whom? Amber what the hell are you talking about? *What's the matter with you?*"

She shrugged. "I'll take care of it." And she dragged me to the top of the bed by my hair.

"You're fucking hurting me!"

"That's good, Meagan."

She'd gone insane. I didn't fight back because I didn't know what was wrong with her. She was hurting me, but I didn't want to hurt her. She didn't know what she was doing, and you couldn't fault a person when they were insane like that. It was that unreachable crazy zone. Someone had obviously said something to her and she was reacting like a maniac. It was completely unlike her.

She forced my wrist against the headboard and pulled a pair of handcuffs I'd never seen before out from under her pillow so fast I didn't have time to stop her. One end snapped around my wrist and the other around the bedpost. *Now* I struggled. I whipped my arm back and forth and clanked the metal against the wood.

"Get this off me right now," I demanded.

Again she said she was only doing what I wanted. She

grabbed a red candle from the nightstand and straddling me, held it over my stomach. I was in the middle of another nightmare. Only I hadn't volunteered for this one. I was handcuffed to a bed by a woman who had gone insane and fearing what she might do to me. She started to tip the candle and I wiggled under her and fought against the cuff.

"Put that down," I said, trying to be reasonable. "Please, Amber, you don't know what you're doing. You're gonna burn me."

She glared at me. "It doesn't burn, Meagan. Remember?"

Then she must have noticed the genuine fear in my eyes because she put the candle back on the nightstand and leaned over me, staring into my face. I didn't say anything. What could I say? She'd lost her mind.

She reached under me and touched the blood on my back, showed it to me, and sucked it between her lips again.

"Stop that," I commanded. "That's really sick."

She pinned my other arm to the bed. Flashing green eyes like a child's monster.

"Oh, it's sick when I do it but not sick from the vampire, huh? The vampire you fucked for three months!"

I stared up at her. "What are you talking about? I told you everything that happened with Angus."

"You're a liar! You lie to me as easily as you did to Gwynne a few hours ago. But you're good at that, aren't you? You fucked that vampire for three months. You cheated on Ken with the bloodsucker because Ken didn't know how to get rough with you. Well, you won't cheat on me, Meagan. I'll give you exactly what you want."

I struggled against the cuff again. "That's a sweet gesture, but you're insane! I never cheated on Ken and the nightmare with Angus happened once, I told you that. But thank you for making me relive the entire fucking scene."

"It didn't happen once."

"Yes, it did."

"That's not what Seamus says."

"*Seamus?*" I could have burst into maniacal laughter. That son of a bitch! He was good. He'd warned me at the party it was coming soon. He didn't have the money for an elaborate scheme, but why spend money at all when you could creep into someone's head and get them to do your dirty work for you? Regretfully, I had to admit I could still learn a lot from my crafty uncle. "Seamus told you this? And you *believed* him?"

"Why would he lie?"

"Oh I don't know," I snapped. "Maybe because of a little transsexual named Jackie. Why would he be discussing my sexual preferences with you at all? As if he would even know them. He knew about Angus because I did tell him that. He knew that *you* knew. This is his revenge, Amber. I'm sure he didn't think you'd go *insane*, but he knew you'd confront me with it. Call him. Call him right now and I'll prove it."

Suddenly she couldn't have looked more guiltily horrified. She knew I was telling the truth the second I mentioned Jackie. I forced her to make the call anyway.

Seamus answered on the fifth ring and Amber put him on speaker. "Dis better be good," he said by way of hello. It had to be 4 a.m. in Ireland.

I dove right in. "Seamus, you tell the truth right now."

"Truth, Meggie?" He wanted to play a little first. "Do you know what time it is?" he mocked. "Four-twenty-five in da morning. It's four-twenty-five in da goddamn morning."

"Very funny," I said. "You're on the speaker and I want you to tell Amber the truth." By this point she already knew the truth, and I thought she was going to cry.

Seamus chuckled. "What's the problem, Meggie Pie?"

I rattled my cuff. "Well, for starters, I'm handcuffed to a fucking bed." She was too ashamed to unlock me.

"Dat's a shame." He chuckled again. "Wanna say hi to Sheila?" Sheila was his latest bed partner.

"Seamus, I'm not screwing around."

"Sounds like you were."

"Are you gonna tell her? Because you don't want my retaliation on this one, Seamus. Trust me."

"Okay, okay. Blondie, if you're there, I made it up. Da whole thing. About the rough stuff, the cheating--everything. I'm sorry. It was a joke."

I spotted the keys to the cuffs on the nightstand, unlocked myself, and rubbed my wrist the way they do in the movies. I started dressing. Amber watched me in guilty silence.

"Are you mad at me, Meggie?" Seamus called.

"No, Seamus." I said, pulling a shirt over my head. "This is our game and I'm not mad at you for playing it. I am, however, mad at the person who believed it."

I stalked out of the room and heard Amber say, "We'll call you back." She ran out after me.

"Meagan, I'm sorry."

I ignored her and pulled on my jacket.

"It's late," she said. "Where are you going?"

I didn't know. "Out."

She jumped in front of the door, still naked. Damn if she didn't look great. "Don't leave. I was stupid, alright? Let me take care of your back."

I pushed past her and she folded her arms across her small bare breasts. "Fine, but you're going to scar if you don't let me take care of it."

Was I that transparent? She knew exactly how to scare me into staying. Well, it wasn't going to work.

I glared at her. "I don't give a shit. I hope it does scar, that way every time you look at it, you'll be reminded of what you've done. Of how little trust you had in me to believe such stupid things."

"You're not leaving," she said, blocking the door. "We're going to work this out. Seamus told me all that stuff today, and then I saw how easily you could lie this afternoon, and I'm sorry, but it made sense."

Another glare. "What made sense, Amber? That I wanted you to slap me around? Make me bleed? Cuff me to a bed and nearly burn me? Exactly which part of that made sense to you? Or maybe it made sense that I would cheat on Ken. That I could possibly do it to you too. Don't you think if I had cheated on Ken, it would have *been with you?*"

I thought of my back and tore off my leather jacket. "Where's that aloe shit Jenna gave us?" Normally Amber would have smiled at that. She would have found my vanity funny, but not tonight.

"I'll get it," she said, darting for the bathroom.

I leaned against the couch, seething. She had believed the most asinine lies about me more readily than she'd believed the truth. She'd allowed Seamus to fill her head with such garbage that she'd even made a special trip somewhere to buy handcuffs so she could do this to me. All day she'd been planning it. When Gwynne had shown up and she'd seen how easily I'd lied to her, it had only cemented the idea in her head.

And I had the reputation as the crazy, impetuous one? I would have at least given her the benefit of the doubt before I pulled something like this.

Then I thought it was just the tiniest bit funny. '*Well, you won't cheat on me, Meagan*'. It was the most jealous, possessive thing I'd ever heard her say. That she thought I possibly *could* pissed me off, but it was kind of cute too. She was willing to turn herself into a sexual deviant just because she thought that was what I wanted. The blond narc out of control, getting off on the power trip. I told myself not to laugh.

Amber returned from the bathroom with a plastic jar of cream and a damp washcloth.

"Come back in the bedroom," she pleaded. "I'll take care of your back. I'm sorry, Meagan. It only made sense because you told me about Angus. Then Seamus started telling me all that other stuff and I don't know what happened to me. I lost it. I should have known better to begin with but you know how convincing your uncle can be. Can you forgive me?"

Eventually, yes. I could forgive Amber almost anything. She was always there for me. Even when she was mad and thinking I was the most disgusting person in the world she protected me. This thing with Seamus had been eating at her all day but still she'd protected me from Gwynne. She put her love for me ahead of her anger and disgust. She had my back. She may have scratched it to hell, but she had my back.

I met her gaze squarely. "That depends on if you've scarred me." I was being a big baby about it because I knew in my heart I'd already forgiven her.

I followed her back into the bedroom where she cleaned the marks with the cloth and tenderly rubbed on the lotion. She whispered a dozen apologies and the anger subsided.

"You won't scar," she said, twisting the cap back on the bottle and moving my hair to kiss my neck. It was tender where she had bitten me and I winced. "There's only one little line left--the one that bled--but it isn't that deep. It might scab a little, but it will go away."

I started to pull on my shirt but she stopped me. Turned to face me with those sincere green eyes.

"Don't go, Meagan. Let me love you," she said. "The way *we* make love." She took the shirt from my hands and kissed me. She knew I couldn't resist her when she looked at me like that, all sad and sexy. She was the woman in the hospital window. The one I had come back from the dead for and the first image I saw when I'd opened my eyes. She was the one who'd been at my side through everything. The one who'd never given up on me. I loved her. I had enough forgiveness in my heart only for her.

"I'm not going to scar?" I was stalling, unsure if I wanted to let go of my anger entirely.

She smiled and shook her head. "Forgive me?" She knew I did. That was why she allowed herself the amusement. Just like Seamus. The two of them thought everything was funny.

"I forgive you," I said. "Just promise you won't be so naive next time."

She touched my face. "I love you."

I laughed. "We're back to that, are we? I know you love me. You wouldn't have gone insane otherwise. And for the record, I don't like it *that* rough."

"I know what you like," she husked.

"You should, after all this time." I pushed her down on the bed and jumped on top of her. "'You won't cheat on me, Meagan!'" I mocked. She laughed.

Yep, we were back to that. Making up the only way we ever did. I wouldn't fight it. Amber was my world and I'd do anything for her. Let her do almost anything to me. As long as we were together I didn't care what we might have to face.

I found we would still have to face a lot.

Chapter 18

Jenna thought the whole thing was hilarious. I told her the story over French fries in one of those arcade/restaurant deals they have for kids while Jacob led Sammy around the place like a protective older brother. They were in the ball bin, a giant basket with a million plastic balls in it and about fifty other kids scrambling through and shrieking with joy. Jenna and I kept our eyes on them. We watched them climb out of the bin and head over to the spiral slide in the middle of the room that had a line of kids thirty-five deep.

The place was huge. It was a kid's paradise, and a parent's nightmare. Hundreds of screaming children. Parents huddled around the tables in the eating area, glad to be rid of their kids for a few hours, but desperate to block out the noise of all the giggling shrieking children. I wondered how the employees handled working here. I'd watched one waitress clean up puke, twice, and then have an icy drink spilled down the front of her shirt by a child who had taken it up on the slide, where it wasn't supposed to be, then dropped it over the side on the horrified teen waitress. The child was giggling and the teenager looked like she could kill him.

I'd shaken my head and given her an apologetic smile that she should endure so much. She'd given me a glare because she thought the smile meant the child was mine. I'd shaken my head again. No way. She laughed and walked away.

"Amber really did that?" Jenna asked, laughing. "She handcuffed you to a bed and did all those things just because Seamus told her that's what you were into?"

I glanced around us. "Well, there's a little more to it than that," I admitted, and told her about Angus.

"Well, no wonder, Meagan," she said, shocked. "If you knew about this Angus experience wouldn't you have thought the same thing?"

"Probably. But I wouldn't have gone insane."

"No, you would have gone cold and shut her out entirely." She glanced over at Jacob and Sammy, who were still in line, and popped a French fry between her lips. "These are cold. What are you doing to Gwynne?"

I blinked. "Excuse me?"

"You know what I'm talking about. For whatever reason Gwynne called me and told me all about it. This isn't good for your karma, Meagan. Give it up before it comes back to you threefold."

"I suppose you'll tell me I'm a better person than this."

"You are."

"God. Do you and Amber have a meeting before you talk to me?" I ate a French fry. "I'm sorry but the two of you don't get it. Gwynne started a fight with me the first time I saw her grab Amber in anger. I let it go. Then there were the snide comments over a dozen dinners. I let that go too. The time she confronted me in your back yard and told me I'd never get my clutches in Amber again. I was married then, so again I let it go. I kept my mouth shut so often I almost couldn't stand myself for doing so. When she wished death on me, I reached the end of my tolerance. Last week she tried to clump me."

"Clump you?"

"Yes." I told her about the tape recorder and the bizarre way Amber had warned me and again she laughed. She wasn't as ashamed of me as I thought she'd be. In fact, she wasn't ashamed at all, merely worried. Scared of how Gwynne might retaliate.

I shrugged off her fear. What could Gwynne do to me? I was as squeaky clean as my brother and his wife. Then I remembered my brother had wiped off some of their shine with his affair. Ancient history. They'd been gleaming again for some time, and I was untouchable.

"I hope you're right," Jenna said, "because if you have even one skeleton in your closet, Gwynne will find it. She's not gonna go down without a fight."

I didn't think she would. But I also didn't think there was anything she could do to me and I put the worry out of my mind. Gwynne was old news. I'd gotten my revenge and I could go back to concerning myself with whatever challenge the dreams kept telling me I would face. I was preparing myself for anything. I didn't know what fate would hit me with next so every day I imagined the worst scenario my brain could come up with and accepted it before it began. Each day I considered a new scenario, one more dreadful than the day before, and each day I accepted that this particular scenario might come true. I was building my weapons for the battle because I knew nothing that could happen could be worse than the things I was imagining. Prepare for the worst and when it turns out not to be that bad, be relieved. That was my theory. Gwynne had been a distraction but I kept to my theory.

The dreams said the challenge was getting closer and I clung to that in fear and hope. Fear that I should have to face another challenge--the biggest of my life--and hope that it would all be over soon. The waiting was driving me crazy.

I took to my goal for Amber the way I had taken to my vision for Cicely Bower. The book went out and started its slow climb. Ted wasn't pushing very hard. I made a few calls.

Todd Garrison was busily preparing his manuscript with the help of Chuck Farley, one of our best ghostwriters, and business was going forward in its usual manner. Chuck complained that Jade interrupted their work too much, so I spoke to her about it over dinner one night. We'd become friends. Amber found it odd that I, who had once been so straight-laced, now counted among my friends a transsexual, a recovering drug addict, an ex-con biker and his tattooed-to-Tuesday wife, and a small boy. The accident had changed more about me than she could have dreamed. I had gone from being corporate Meagan, the doctor's wife and near mother of a child, to publisher Meagan, the woman who was preparing for a challenge and dining with people who matched her personality in the strangest ways.

I didn't pick on Zeppo much anymore because my crowd was far weirder. Zeppo and I antagonized each other less and I grew to admire the way he looked out for Amber like the brother she had lost. I would have liked Jeff better but it wasn't for me to decide who Amber's brother should be.

We visited Amber's parents often and they treated me like one of the family. They didn't make us sleep in separate bedrooms, like I thought they would, and acted as if our relationship was the most natural thing in the word. And who was to say it wasn't? Religion? Inconsequential. The last time I was Catholic was at my eigth grade confirmation. I believed in a higher spirituality than what mere religion could offer. I had seen the Realm and not once while I was there did I get the impression that loving Amber was wrong. I wouldn't have cared if it was. If love wasn't the goal of life and death, then life and death were the things that were wrong. I would have dealt with my consequences in the after-life, but I knew there would be none.

Jade Garrison had been a tough cookie to crack. With her long black hair, pierced tongue, and tattoos galore, she was a little intimidating to look at. Frankly, she looked like she might beat you up for no reason. I got the feeling she didn't like Amber and me much to begin with but I was her husband's publisher so she played nice. By the second time we had dinner together her reserve was gone and in its place was a spunky, friendly personality. I never knew what inspired the change, only that she'd suddenly become our friend. She showed us her various tattoos and Amber joked that I had one too. Jade insisted on seeing it.

"That's not so bad," she said, when I told her the butterfly on my back was a mistake I had made when I was nineteen and my drunken friends convinced me to do it. It happened in the back room of a dirty tattoo parlor and I remember the way the florescent light overhead buzzed and flickered like it would die out at any second. The tattooist's name was Axel and he had a bald head and a dirty red elastic twisted around his scruffy brown goatee. I remembered the feel of his latex gloves. The laughter of my friends when I flinched as the needle first hit me and Axel had been forced to correct, freehand, the small mistake my flinch had caused. Axel fixed it but he wasn't very good to begin with, didn't tell me about Neosporin to prevent scabbing, and the butterfly ended up with fewer colors than I'd wanted after the area scabbed and I picked it off.

"We can fix that," Jade said, inspecting the work. "This guy Pete, he's the best tattooist around. I'll get him to do it for free."

"No way," I said. "I'm not going through that again. I wouldn't have done it the first time if I hadn't been loaded on tequila and hash."

Jade laughed. "My first was on beer and weed. Straight

hydro my boyfriend was growing in his closet." She rubbed her pregnant stomach. Don't do anything like that anymore though. Three months along and I think I'm getting fat already."

Jenna had once thought the same thing during her pregnancy. I had made it to three months and, aside from the morning sickness, I'd love being pregnant, knowing there was a baby forming inside me. It had taken awhile to get used to the idea, but once I had, I soaked up every bit of pregnancy bliss I could. I'd stared at my stomach constantly, rubbed it and sang to my unborn fetus as if she were already with me. I was doing it wrong–wrong marriage, wrong time--but I'd loved it nonetheless.

On the fourth encounter with Jade and Todd I met Zoe. She was three years old, with straight brown hair, her mother's tiny nose, her father's grey eyes, and quite oddly, my smile. Amber spotted it too and watched the way I stared at the child in fascination. I reached down to shake her little hand and she startled me by throwing herself in my arms.

Jade stiffened. "Zoe that's rude."

"She's okay," I said. But I thought Jade was thinking the same thing I was thinking, that a child with the name I had chosen for my daughter was throwing herself at me and it was too peculiar.

Zoe spent the entire evening at my side, asking me all the questions children ask. Things like: "Why is the TV over there? Do you have a cat or a dog? Can I watch cartoons?"

I was spellbound. Todd thought it was cute the way his daughter had taken to me and Amber kept giving me strange looks.

When they left, I was grinning. Amber closed the door behind them and turned to face me.

"Stop it right now," she said sternly.

"What?" I said.

She tilted her head and her eyes softened. "Honey, she's not your Zoe."

"I know that."

"She belongs to Todd and Jade."

I threw myself on the couch, still grinning. "She has my smile though, doesn't she, Amber? You saw it. I know you did."

Amber nodded. "Yes, I saw it. But that doesn't change the fact that she is not your daughter. It's a coincidence. Maybe this is your challenge—to look at this kid and not try to make her yours."

I shook my head. "I know she's not mine, that's not the challenge. But if that kid grows up to be a neurosurgeon, we'll both be eating our words, won't we?"

Amber agreed they would indeed be bitter words to swallow and we put the incident behind us. I continued to see Zoe occasionally but it wasn't like that first spark. Each time I saw her she regarded me more and more as just another silly adult. Amber and Jade both took comfort in that. I didn't consider it either way. Zoe was just another kid who had suddenly turned up in my life. I sometimes got the feeling Todd and Jade were inspecting me but I didn't react. I figured it was because they had no family other than the one they'd created with each other and they were careful who they chose as friends now. Both had lived unscrupulous lives before finding each other and I thought they were just cautious about people.

After you've crawled your way out of the gutter, you're never quite certain who you can trust. I understood their wariness, had enough of it myself, and there was nothing wrong with exercising a little caution. It was a protection mechanism and I admired them for using it.

By December Amber's book was continuing its slow climb and I set up my surprise. I called in the order to have her three previous books rebound with critic's praises on the back, and an order slip for her new novel inside. "A stunning read from the author of *When Butterflies Wear Armor* and *Gemstones & Fire,*" or something to that effect. She had never finished her fourth poetry book because she had left Hector and began working on her novel instead.

The three others were being boxed into collections. I decided on black leather boxes with shiny silver butterflies imprinted on either side. It was expensive, and maybe not worth the risk, but I was willing to chance it.

When everything was set in motion I called Amber down to the office and she bounced in like she owned the place. She pretty much did. What was mine was hers and I still gave her hell for knocking. If Cynthia told her I wasn't with a client there was no need for her to knock. Today she had taken that advice.

She plopped down on one of the chairs in front of my desk. "What's up?"

I grinned. "You are."

She shook her head. "I don't get it."

"You're going on tour, honey. One month. First stop, Edmonton, last stop, New York and *The Rosie O'Donnell Show*."

"*Rosie O'Donnell?* Why on earth would I be going on *Rosie O'Donnell*? I'm not a celebrity."

"You will be after you do the show. Half the world watches Rosie, and once she holds up your book and the public gets a look at *you* we won't be able to keep the thing on bookshelves anywhere. By the way, why isn't your picture on the jacket?"

"Because I don't want it to be." I missed the tightness in her voice.

Shaking my head, I made a note on the yellow pad in front of me. "No good. I'll schedule a photo shoot. Your picture has to be on that jacket, look at you for Christ's sake, your face alone will sell books. I've also acquired the rights to your three previous books and they're being re-printed and packaged as we speak. I'm releasing them as a collection—right in time for Christmas—so you see why the book tour is imperative. We'll need the added publicity."

Amber's eyes flashed anger, not the reaction I was expecting. "Meagan, what the hell do you think you're doing?" She jumped to her feet and paced in front of my desk. "I'm not even your client, I'm Ted's."

"Not anymore. I switched him Cicely Bower for you."

"*You did what?*"

I sighed. Picked up my pen and twisted it in my fingers, as was my habit. "Ted wasn't going to make you a star, Amber, but I will. You saw what I did for Cicely. One book and the woman gets recognized walking down the street. I'm taking you even higher."

"No you're not," she growled. "I'm not doing any goddamn Rosie O'Donnell show and you're giving me back to Ted."

I stared at her. She didn't know what she was saying. I was offering her a golden opportunity, one any of our other clients would kill for, and she was acting like I was burning her at the stake.

"I can't do that," I asserted. "Do you know how many thousands of dollars I'm investing in you? I've even pulled money out of Switzerland."

"Well, you can put it right back because I'm not doing any of it."

Anger grew within me. Clients didn't tell me how it was going to be, I told them. "You're under contract, Amber," I reminded her. She was making me pull rank.

Her eyes narrowed, monster green peering out like that day in the bedroom. She knew what I was saying. "Are you threatening me, Meagan? Are you fucking threatening me?"

I stood and matched her angry gaze with one of my own. "No, I am reminding you of your obligation to this company. Now, you're doing the fucking book tour and you're doing *The Rosie O'Donnell Show* and that's the end of it. Do you think it was easy getting you booked for that? You're not exactly famous, Amber."

She slammed her hands down on my desk. "Because I don't want to be. Look, I don't know what kind of Jackie Collins fantasy you've got going on here" (she knew me well) "but I don't want any part of it. And just who the hell do you think you are buying the rights to my other books?"

I folded my arms across my chest and glared at her. "I'm the person who owns your blond ass."

"*Owns it?*" she shrieked. "You think you *own* me? You really do think I'm your bitch! Oh, God. What's the deal here, Meagan? Are you gonna pull a Gwynne on me, is that it?"

I got up and slammed the office door then whirled around to face her. "Will you shut the hell up? Are you trying to get me sued?"

"There's no one even out there."

"I don't care. If anyone walking by heard something like that—never mind."

I went back to my desk and sat in my chair. This wasn't going the way I'd planned at all. I'd expected her to be thrilled. Pleased. Even moderately content. Not vehement. And

I'd done the worst thing of all by telling her I owned her. I didn't know why I'd said it because I certainly didn't believe it. Anger had gotten the better of me and I had to calm down.

"Switch me back to Ted, Meagan," she said, a bit more softly this time. She sensed me weakening. Something that happened for no one but her. If she had been any other client there would be no question about what was going to happen. But this was a definite dilemma. She wasn't just a client; she was also the person I loved.

I didn't answer right away.

"Meagan!" she pressed.

"Just let me think for a minute," I barked. "If you refuse to do this, I have to figure a way out so I don't lose a ton of money."

She sat in the chair and waited while I thought. I called Tim down in printing.

"How many collections of Amber's books have we run off?" I asked.

Tim put me on hold while he ran to check the print run and came back on the line. "Sixteen-hundred, Meagan."

I chewed on my pen. Okay, that wasn't so bad. I could still deal with this and not lose a small fortune. Amber was a local star so I'd just distribute the collection locally and market them as a limited edition offer.

"Stop the presses, Tim," I said, mimicking a cliché. "Don't let it get past two thousand. There's been a change of plans."

Amber looked relieved. I hung up on Tim and stared at her.

"Are you happy now? We could have made a fortune on this. Both of us."

"Is that all you care about?"

"When it comes to business, yes."

"And what about us? This little stunt of yours could have cost us our relationship."

"Yeah," I snapped, "I can really see how making us rich and turning you into a star would have destroyed us."

She sighed. "For one, you're already rich."

"And you don't want to be famous. Fine. Whatever." I threw my pen on the desk.

She frowned and relented a little herself. "I'll do the freaking tour, alright? But only two weeks of it. I'll do local TV, magazine interviews, but no Rosie O'Donnell show—and don't try Oprah and her freaking book club, either. In exchange you have to switch me back to Ted."

I crossed my legs on top of my desk. "I love how you think you're the one in charge around here."

She did the same on the other side. "Aren't I?" She folded her arms across her chest and gave a satisfied grin. "I'm not following any of your contractual obligations, Meagan. If you don't like it—sue me."

Tough Amber. She knew it was preposterous that I'd even consider such a thing. I laughed at her. Proud of the little stranglehold she had around my neck. She was strong-arming me and she knew she was the only one who could get away with it. She could rise to a challenge as well as I could when the need presented itself.

"You're a cunning little bitch," I said affectionately.

She gave a little bow. "I learned from the best."

Another laugh. "Okay. Two weeks. Nine cities in fourteen days. Local TV. Magazine interviews. I switch you back to Ted but the collection goes out and you have to do local book signings. Agreed?"

"Agreed."

I shook my head. "Now I have to find someone else to turn into a star *and* I have to lose face with *The Rosie O'Donnell Show*. See what I'd do for you?"

Amber shrugged like I wasn't doing anything much. "Book Cicely instead. I'm sure they'd rather have her anyway."

I nodded. "I'll tell Ted."

"And Meagan?"

"What?"

"Stay out of my business from now on. There's a reason we don't work together, you know. As I recall, it was your idea."

Yes, it was my idea, and I had been right about it. Amber didn't want me as her publisher. We both knew I'd push too hard but I'd gone behind her back and done it anyway. There was a lesson to be learned from that. Love and business don't mix.

So I switched her back to Ted. Cicely was glad to have me back and Amber was glad to be rid of me. The following Monday she left to start the first day of her two week tour and she took Zeppo along with her. I was glad she wouldn't be alone.

Adrian and I stayed behind, as we both worked regular jobs, and hung out together in the evenings. Marveled at how strange it still felt to be alone together without getting high. We found other ways to amuse ourselves. We went out and visited friends. Saw Holly. Took Jacob to the movies with Jenna and Sammy. Jenna commented that Jacob was preparing me for motherhood.

I gave her an odd look. How on earth did she think I'd become a mother? Last time I checked, Amber did not have a penis.

"Don't be silly," she said. "There are other ways, you know."

I shrugged. I wasn't resigning myself to a life of childlessness but I didn't quite see it happening either.

Adrian talked incessantly about how great I felt to be helping others off drugs. He was working at the rehab clinic and going to school part time to get the education required to be a drug counselor. He reminded me of a born again Christian, endless preaching. I tried not to get frustrated but he was preaching to the choir and it grew tiresome. I wanted to remain supportive but by the third day I couldn't take any more and asked him if we could about *anything* else. He laughed and told me he'd started dancing again and we talked about that.

Amber called every night from various hotels across the continent to tell me how things were going. It wasn't so bad, she said. Zeppo was keeping her entertained and they were having an alright time. I told her Zeppo better not be charging his calls to Adrian on the company bill because I knew they were talking for over an hour every night and she laughed. She said she'd already told him that.

"I know how it works, Meagan," she said. "Markham-Summers isn't being billed for his calls, just mine." I could hear the grin in her voice. She thought it was funny that I could find a way be extravagant and cheap all at the same time. I was flying them all over the continent, first class, and booking them the best hotels, but I was concerned about what the phone bills were going to cost us. For a Markham-Summers client I didn't care but Zeppo was another matter entirely. I was already paying enough for him to even be there with Amber. I wasn't paying for his damn phone calls too.

Then one night she called from a pay phone in Toronto, severely stressed.

"Our flight to Vancouver got cancelled," she crackled over the line. "They're having an unexpected snow storm up here and everyone's freaking out. We just witnessed two accidents on Yonge Street and an armed robbery. It happened right in front of us, Meagan. There were a dozen people standing around waiting to cross the street and this guy just whipped out a gun and chose one of us. Zeppo screamed like a little girl."

"Shut up," I heard Zeppo say.

"Are you guys alright?"

"We're fine but the hotel we were staying at ran out of rooms and we've been calling all over and nothing's available anywhere. There's some kind of convention in town or something."

I was thinking.

"Get us out of here, Meagan," she pleaded.

"Oh, sure," I quipped, "Now it's 'Meagan get us out of here'. What happened to 'mind your own business Meagan?'"

"Can you be right later?"

I laughed. "Okay, here's what I want you to do, Amber. Go back to the hotel you were in last night."

"We've already been there."

"Just go back, I'll take care of it. You'll have a room before you even get there. I don't know what's going on up there but I've never had a problem doing business in Toronto."

"This place is awful," she complained. "They have these homeless people called squeegee kids and we've seen at least two of them get busted by the cops for trying to clean windshields at stoplights for a dollar. People are scared of them or something. Or maybe they just don't want them near their cars."

She was telling me things that were irrelevant because she was scared. I remained calm.

"Okay," I said. "I'm going to change your schedule too. Skip Vancouver, I'll deal with them later. Did the airline say there would be flights going out tomorrow?"

"Yes."

"Okay, go straight on to Los Angeles, do the appearances there, then come home. You'll only miss a couple of bookings in total. Right now go back to the hotel and call me in an hour, or as soon as they give you a room."

I hung up with Amber and checked the schedule she'd been smart enough to leave behind because I'd forgotten to ask her what hotel I was dealing with, and made the call. The hotel had one room available but it was being held on reservation. I spoke to the manager, explained the situation, and told him I'd pay double if he conveniently lost the reservation. I felt bad for the person I was screwing over but Amber and Zeppo were not spending the night in an airport.

The next morning they left for LA and called me that night in better spirits.

"Nice weather out here," Amber said, when she called on the second evening of their stay. "You should fly out. Hell, we should move here. It's beautiful."

"Just don't get yourself caught in the middle of a drive-by," I joked. "And if you see O.J, run."

"Speaking of seeing people, guess who we saw at The Viper Room."

"You were at The Viper Room?" I asked, shocked. "How'd you get in?"

She laughed. "Guess."

"The green-eyed stare and a Versace something-or-other."

"Prada."

"I'm getting you home," I teased. "You're having too much fun while I'm sitting here listening to the Gospel according to Adrian. Who'd you see?"

"Johnny Depp."

"Oh." I wasn't impressed. "Doesn't he own the place?"

"Don't know."

"Did you talk to him?"

"No. He was talking to someone who looked like that chick from the Cranberries."

I perked up. "Really?"

She laughed again. "That grabs your attention more than Johnny himself, huh? You're like your uncle, Irish all the way. I better go though. Zeppo's bugging me to go get something to eat. We'll be home tomorrow so I'll see you then, okay?"

"Can't wait."

"Me either," she said. "Who knew I could miss you so much?"

"I did."

Last laugh. "I'll bet you did. See you tomorrow. Be naked."

I grinned. "Bye babe."

"Oh geez," she joked. "I better get home. You're starting to sound like Adrian."

We said our goodbyes and hung up. I told Adrian what she told me and he pouted about the Viper Room.

"When did *we* become the boring ones?" he asked.

I laughed. "I don't know, Adrian, but it has happened, hasn't   it?"

Chapter 19

And that was the Gods' honest truth. Adrian and I had gone from being drug addicts to respectable citizens. He took the healing route and I took the route of schedules, deadlines, PR, money management and stress. It was okay. Pressure I could deal with; boredom was what could kill me. Fortunately, since the day I learned how to walk again there hadn't been a dull moment.

Life was one surprise after another. Fights with Amber that ended as quickly as they began. Misunderstandings. Forgiveness someone had to dole out. I wondered if she found it as distressing as I sometimes did.

Everyone argued, I knew that. It was a pretty unhealthy relationship two people were in if they never fought. It meant one person was sacrificing. Whether it was their opinions, dreams, or simple everyday desires, one person was letting go of it all to please the other, and I supposed I was happy we weren't like that. I just wished the misunderstandings we did have didn't always have to be so huge.

There were times when I thought I didn't really have a substance abuse problem at all. Coke, maybe. But alcohol didn't feel like a problem. It pissed me off that everyone around me could drink but I couldn't have a pint with my uncle when I saw him or throw a drop of Bailey's in my coffee. I thought I probably could but I was too afraid to risk it. I didn't know if one thing could lead to another, alcohol to drugs, but I also didn't always feel like I had a problem. I remembered the withdrawal but I thought that was only because back then I'd felt I needed the drugs. I didn't need them now, only wondered what it would be like to experience it once in a while.

I reasoned with myself that I hadn't even been on drugs that long. Three and a half months. By junkie standards that was nothing. I had my opinions about this but I couldn't talk to Amber about them because she'd get upset if I even suggested I'd never really had a problem, so I turned to Jenna who, as usual, was able to clear the fog for me.

"You're right, Meagan," she said, "For most people three months isn't a long time, but most people don't have your excessive personality, do they? You crammed into that short time the addiction of a three-*year* junkie. It wasn't like you started with pot and eased your way into the hard stuff. You went right for the coke first time out and within a couple of weeks you were a daily user. That is addiction. It's the worst kind because it doesn't take you long to sink to the bottom. Lucky for you, it doesn't take you long to crawl back out either."

I didn't know what I'd do without Jenna. She always gave me the straight-out truth and I could talk to her about things without her being afraid I was preparing to take a fall. Jenna knew the difference between talk and action. Amber, unfortunately, did not. She thought if I said it, I'd do it. Speaking about things out loud was the first step to starting them, she thought. In most cases that was probably true but sometimes I just needed to be able to say it, to voice a doubt without it being a catastrophic event.

It was the trust issue. Amber didn't fully trust me to stay away from drugs. She said she did but a small doubt was always just below the surface and it ate at me. I knew I had caused the doubt but I also hadn't touched a drug in over two years and thought it was time she looked at that.

I ate healthily, still eighty-five percent vegetarian. I ran two miles a day on the treadmill at the gym, started kickboxing again just to burn off some of my nervous energy, and limited my caffeine intake by only drinking decaf coffees and teas. I downed spring water like I owned my own clear stream in the French Alps. I was almost thirty-one years old and I'd never been healthier in my life. I thought I deserved a break. Jenna agreed. Then she finally got me into yoga.

She was surprised the first day I showed up across the street for her class wearing flowing East-Indian style pants and a white rib-knit t-shirt. I looked like a meditator straight out of the modern Buddha book of lotus positions.

"I don't believe it," she squealed. "Six years I've been asking and you've finally come."

"This better be good, Jenna," I joked. "I better walk out of here felling like I dropped a Quaalude and washed it down with a glass of wine."

"You will," she laughed.

If I'd said that in front of Amber she would have secretly inspected the apartment for drugs. Then she'd feel guilty when she found none and want to make love when I got home. I never caught her but my gut told me she occasionally made a sweep of the apartment, just to be sure, and my gut was rarely wrong. I did business from the gut and it never failed me there.

Jenna told me I was being paranoid, that I was the one not trusting Amber, but I could see on her face she believed me and it was enough to rattle me. I wanted one-hundred-percent trust from Amber, where my own actions had reduced me to about ninety-five. Ninety-five wasn't bad. Seamus always said never trust anyone more than ninety percent because that last ten percent was your safety net. It was the thing that would give you peace of mind if you got screwed over, because you could always say, *at least I had my doubts. I wasn't completely stupid.*

I thought it was a pretty cynical attitude but I also thought he was right. Seamus was rarely wrong when it came to human nature. He knew the worst people were capable of and he was always ready for it, which also accounted for why he'd never had a meaningful relationship. He gave his trust to me instead of giving it to his girlfriends. I was the only person he believed would never let him down and it was sad because he was closing himself off to what real love felt like. I wanted him to make it work with Sheila. She was cute and kind, and just funny enough to match my uncle's crazy sense of humor. She could be good for him if he'd let her.

"Who wants to be good, Meggie?" he questioned, when I told him my theory one day on the phone.

I looked over at Amber, who was sitting in a chair by the window, reading her already-published book with an editor's eye and a red pen in her hand, and smirked. The book had been flying off shelves for months, but there she sat, editing it all over again and making notes in the margins about things she wished she had changed before it had gone to press. The book was good. Amber was a perfectionist.

"It's not a bad trip, Seamus," I said.

"What isn't?"

"Being good. It's like purifying your spirit. I'm not saying I don't still do stupid things sometimes---"

Amber looked up from her book and grinned at me.

"---but it's okay, trusting people."

"Ha," he scoffed. "Who do you trust, Meggie?"

I didn't miss a beat. "You, Amber, Jenna, occasionally Josh and Danielle, and this little boy, Jacob. He's only twelve but you know what? I'd trust that kid with my life."

"You sound like a mother, Meggie." I thought I was hearing that a lot lately.

"Or I sound like a twenty-year-old Seamus who put his trust in a little girl with pigtails."

Seamus roared with laughter. "Yeah, I trusted you. Den you mother caught you being a little con-artist with your friends in the backyard and you sang like a canary."

"Con-artist, my ass," I said. "I won every bit of that money fair and square. It's not my fault those kids were stupid enough to keep putting their collies and beagles up against my greyhound."

Amber put down her book and laughed. "You had a greyhound, Meagan? You never told me you raced greyhounds as a kid."

I nodded. "Seamus bought it for me, didn't you Old Saint Mick? But I really didn't know he was assured of winning every time until it kept happening." I switched the conversation back into gear. "Seamus, all I'm saying is give Sheila a chance. She's a nice person. Let her in."

"I'll think about it, Meggie."

When we hung up I knew he wouldn't. My poor uncle would be alone forever. He'd never get married again, never have kids--it saddened me. Then I remembered him once laughing at me when I told him this and saying, "What do you mean, Meggie? I have a kid. I have you. I been dere since the day you were born and I taught you everything I know like I would my own kid." He'd shaken his head. "You may have a mother and a father, Meggie Pie, but I'm your Da and I always will be."

He'd made me want to cry. I didn't mention that I'd never tell my "Da" the things I told him because I knew what he was saying. Da meant father to him, but also more. It meant we were bonded. I wasn't so Irish as to be calling anyone my Da and that's why the title really did belong to Seamus. He thought of himself as my younger, cooler father, and I suppose in many ways, he was. He was starting to act like Amber's father too.

"I love dat girl," he'd often tell me. He said it with such parental pride I couldn't believe I had once thought they'd been attracted to each other. Now it was ridiculous. Laughable. Seamus was a sexy middle-aged man but he was our Da.

By summer, I was also growing accustomed to having kids around me. At first it had made me impatient--the clinging, the whining, the neediness--but as time wore on I was able to deal with more than just one at a time. In the very beginning it had only been Sammy, and that was good for me. I'd been in a wheelchair and he was always my favorite person to see. He was still my favorite, only now there were other children in my life too. A twelve year old. A three year old. And Sammy who was four months shy of being four. Wasn't it just yesterday he'd been born?

I felt like there hadn't been any time in between. Like I'd just come home from London to find Jenna in labor and Amber at my side. Where had Ken gone? The marriage? The pregnancy? The accident? It felt like there had never been a Ken and never been a Gwynne. That whole year and a half seemed to slip from sight like Amber and I had never parted company.

Only we had. Because now there was Jacob and Martha and Todd and Jade and Zoe--and I never would have met any of these people if Ken hadn't happened. I might have stayed in London indefinitely, and who knew what might have happened then?

Now I was a lifetime away from all that. I was in the apartment I had almost always lived in because I loved it and I was surrounded by three giggling children who were having fun listening to my stories about fairyland. Amber was out helping Zeppo and Adrian look for a new apartment. They wanted her to go with them because Zeppo said it was always easier to find a place with a woman at your side. Landlords were less antagonistic. I was just naïve enough to think he was imagining things. Zeppo thought everyone was homophobic--even me. I couldn't help laughing at that. He could be so strange. Imagine, thinking I was homophobic. I, who was in a relationship with his best friend and hung out with his boyfriend more than I did any other man. His boyfriend was like my *brother*, and his best friend was my *wife*. He'd been there when it happened. He was clearly nuts.

When they finally returned hours later, it was with whoops of joy and a celebratory bottle of non-alcoholic wine. I took one look at the bottle and Adrian and I broke out laughing.

Zeppo walked toward the children and looked down his pointed nose at them. He whipped back his long hair and sniffed at the air like he smelled something foul. "What are you doing, Meagan, running a fucking day care center?"

Three little mouths dropped open and I whirled around to face him. "Watch your language, Zeppo. And don't start up with your ridiculous behavior. You're more of a child than they are." I pointed at the kids and Adrian and Amber laughed.

"*Me*, watch my language?" Zeppo mocked. "You have a worse mouth than a trucker."

"Not around kids I don't."

"It does look like a day care center in here," Amber said.

I shrugged. "Martha's working, Jenna and Josh went to some flea market thing, and Todd and Jade had to go for her check-up."

Amber nodded. She sat on the couch and pulled Zoe into her lap.

"What about me, Auntie Am?" Sammy said. Amber scooped him onto the other leg. She was great with kids.

"Can I go play on your computer?" Jacob asked her.

She handed him the keys to the apartment across the hall. "No internet, Jacob. Your mom doesn't want you on it alone."

Jacob shrugged. "Cool." He went across the hall while Zoe and Sammy curled up in Amber's arms.

"You gots pretty eyes," Zoe told Amber.

Amber laughed. "You *have* pretty eyes," she corrected. "But thank you. I like your eyes too."

"I have nice eyes," Sammy said.

Amber agreed. "Yep. You have the prettiest eyes I've ever seen on a boy."

"Mommy says Auntie Meg's got an eye pettish."

Amber and I looked at each other and laughed.

"It's a fetish, Sam," she said. "But it's not even that. Auntie Meg just likes people with nice eyes. Hers are pretty," she whispered, "But she doesn't think so because they're hazel."

"You know," Zeppo said, "I think we're just gonna go. You guys got this kid thing going on. Come on, Adrian."

Adrian pushed up his sleeves. "What's your problem with kids, Zep? I think they're cute." He made a little punch at Sammy and Sammy giggled.

"I like the chocolate man," he said.

Amber burst out laughing and my cheeks flushed.

"He's not made of chocolate, Sam," I said.

Adrian grinned. "But I'm just as sweet."

"Let's go," Zeppo snapped his fingers.

"Okay, okay. You're such a baby."

Zeppo scowled. "Yeah, let's just go, Toblerone."

Adrian waved at me. "Later, babe."

"Why do you call her that?" I heard Zeppo bitch as they were leaving.

I ran across the hall to check on Jacob, saw that he was just playing a computer game, and came back.

"So what time are all the parents due back?" Amber asked. Zoe had fallen asleep in her arms and she placed her on the couch and covered her with an afghan. Sammy went to play with his toys.

"Soon," I said. "Why? Does it bother you having all these kids here?"

"I don't mind. You know I love them too, I just thought we'd catch a movie later."

"Anne Heche festival?"

"Smartass."

I grinned. "That's fine. If things get around too late, we'll just go to the 9:15 show."

One by one the parents arrived to pick up their kids.

"I'm sorry we had to ask you," Jade said, throwing Zoe's toys into a knapsack. "I hope she wasn't any trouble."

I handed her a stuffed bear. "She was good. How'd the check-up go?"

Todd hooked his thumbs through his belt loops. "Good. Starting the ninth month and everything's going great."

Martha came next. She talked about work and the jerk that had pinched her ass, then left with Jacob.

We were down to one and it was 5:25.

Josh and Jenna bounced through the door, grinning at each other and giggling.

"I don't believe it," I said.

"What?" Josh asked.

"You guys just had sex."

"No," Jenna said, still grinning.

"Did so. You went to your little flea market thing, or whatever it was, and then you decided to have a quickie before coming here."

Josh laughed. "How could you possibly know that?"

I turned to Amber. "Would you like to explain?"

"You have the glow," she said easily. "My estimate is about fifteen minutes ago."

"Twenty-five," Josh said. We broke out laughing.

Jenna grabbed Sammy's truck from the floor and tossed it in the small toy box we kept for him behind one of the couches. "You guys wanna come over for supper?"

I shook my head. "Can't. I have to stay here and satisfy my pettish."

"Your what?"

Amber and I laughed. "You told your son I have an eye fetish?"

She looked at him. "What big ears. I said it to Josh. We were joking."

I laughed at her. "You never learn about that big mouth of yours, do you? It's gonna get you in trouble one day."

"With you? Hardly."

"What does that mean?"

"It means you'll never really get mad at me because you don't honestly care what I say. You know I never mean anything maliciously, so you let it go."

I thought I'd try something. "Angus," I said. Josh stiffened and I laughed. "You see," I told Jenna. "I just told you about Angus and already my brother knows."

"You told me that months ago," she defended.

"Mm-hmm, and Josh knew it that very night."

"I did," Josh said. "But don't think I *wanted* to know. I

don't know why my wife tells me these things. I certainly don't want to hear about my sister's bizarre sex life."

"Shut up."

Amber went quiet. She was embarrassed because if they knew about Angus, that meant they knew about her too. "Do you have to tell Jenna everything?" she asked when they left.

"Does Zeppo know, Amber?" She didn't say anything. I winked. "Then we're even."

On Monday it was business as usual. Schedules, deadlines, phone calls--a hundred things to do and eight hours in which to do it. I was tired of working twelve to fourteen hour shifts. Ted didn't put in those kinds of hours and I thought I would take a vacation soon. Go see Seamus or something. Unwind on the Emerald Isle.

Amber had some errands to run and she had taken the car. That left me stuck at the office until she came to get me. I wasn't going anywhere but I didn't like feeling stuck. Amber didn't think we needed two cars. My opinion differed. I sat through my fourth meeting and decided I didn't care what she thought; we were getting a second car.

Cicely Bower flounced in as my last meeting of the day. She was in the process of writing her second book and we discussed a deadline. She sat in the chair across from me and moaned. The woman was good, but she was a procrastinator. She needed a deadline more than anyone, otherwise she'd find any reason not to sit at her computer and write. She'd clean the fridge, take the dog for a walk or go shopping. She shouldn't have been telling me these things but she was. She didn't know me well enough to know her words would offend me.

I gave her a seven-month deadline and wrote nine in my book because I knew she'd be late. Cicely gave an exhausted sigh, like she'd been working in a factory all day, and left my office with a little less bounce in her step. I got on the phone.

I was talking to Tim down in printing when Amber suddenly stormed through the door, marched up to me and knocked me out of my chair.

"You fucking bitch!"

I stared up at her. What was this? Cynthia's arm

reached in and pulled my office door closed. Even she knew I was in big trouble. Amber had probably stormed past her without so much as a nod and charged at my door. She didn't lose her temper often, but when she did, you could bet it was going to be big.

I got off the floor and hung up the phone. "*What? What the hell is the matter with you?*"

She slammed an orange vial down on the top of my desk and glared at me. "Look familiar?"

Coke! I had never seen it before in my life. Not that vial of it, anyway.

"That's not mine," I said easily.

"No. Of course it isn't."

"I said it's not mine!"

She didn't like that I yelled at her. I didn't care. She was accusing me of something I wasn't doing. Her fingers angrily twisted open the lid and she dumped the contents on top of my desk. The small pile of white powder gleamed against the shiny surface.

"Go ahead, Meagan. You want your coke so fucking bad--take it!"

It didn't look bad, but it wasn't mine. I grabbed the glass ashtray off the bookshelf and used a notepad to sweep the coke into it. I didn't even want to touch it with my hand. I was afraid. I set the ashtray on the desk and desperately groped Amber's wrist.

"You have to believe me, Amber. I swear to you, it's not my coke."

She yanked herself away from me. She didn't believe me. Anger filled my head and an icy chill crept around my heart. She hadn't believed me about Angus either. When I'd first taken Adrian to rehab she thought I was stoned, and a half a dozen times in between. She made her secretive sweeps of the apartment. She'd never trusted me. I was going to burst into tears.

No I wasn't!

"I'm going to tell you this again," I said through clenched teeth. "This is not my cocaine. Why would I go around helping people into rehab if I was on coke? I don't know where you found it---"

"In your glove compartment!" she screamed. "Obviously you're so fucked up now you've even forgotten how to hide it."

I was stunned. *She'd found it in my car?* Someone had framed me. Someone had planted a vial of cocaine in my goddamn car! I racked my brain to figure out who knew I'd once been on drugs and came up empty. The only people who knew were people I loved, and surely they wouldn't frame me.

"And you can wipe that surprised look off your face," she went on. "I don't buy your phony shit for a second. That's fine, Meagan. You keep your coke because I'm moving out."

No, no, no. This isn't happening.

"It's not mine!" I yelled. A knife ground into my forehead and I staggered backwards, nearly tripping over my desk. Amber jumped but stayed where she was. I hadn't had a headache in over a year and she thought I might be faking it. I stumbled to my desk, ripped open the drawers until I found the ancient bottle of lavender oil, and rubbed it into my temples. I took several deep breaths. The knife continued to twist in my head. I thought I'd get a blood test to prove my innocence but why should I? She was supposed to believe me.

I grabbed the ashtray from the desk and shakily made my way to the private bathroom where I dumped its contents down the toilet.

Amber mocked me with fake applause. "Good show. Got another vial in your purse?"

The pressure in my head eased slightly. "I'm being set up," I said flatly.

"Of course you are. Why would a junkie like you have coke?"

My hands closed into fists and the pressure built in my head again. It was always something. "You better shut up, Amber, because you don't know what you're talking about and you're going to end up very sorry."

Tears sprang to her eyes. "I'm already sorry, Meagan. I'm sorry I ever wasted my time on you."

"Oh, that's original! I would think a writer could come up with something better than that."

She shook her head sadly. Her fingers closed around her ring and she slid it to the first knuckle, then hesitated. My eyes were wide with alarm. She knew what taking it off would mean and I was begging her in my head not to do it. *Please don't, that will destroy us.*

But out of my mouth came the warning. "Don't do that, Amber. There will be consequences."

Her eyes went deadly green. She tore the ring off her finger and whipped it at me. "Fuck your consequences!"

I felt myself sinking into a deep black hole, one from which there was no escape. We'd passed the point of no return.

"How could you do that?" I yelled. My mind burned with rage and pain. There was nothing worse she could have done than taking off that ring. It meant she was choosing to break our bond. She knew that. And she had just destroyed us.

I picked the ring up off the floor. I was not going to cry about this! The tears would have to come later, because right now I had to get away.

Amber watched with her arms folded as I stared down at the ring in my hand. I thought I felt it burning. I closed my fist around it and squeezed, pressing the broken bond directly into my palm and feeling it fill my bloodstream. The end moved up my arm, across my chest, and into my heart. My body filled with the finality I was faced with and my eyes met hers.

"I love you," I whispered. She didn't say anything. Her silence built the rage again and I tossed the ring in the wicker garbage basket by my desk, stalked passed her and flung open the office door. Cynthia jumped. She could hear the yelling coming from inside, but she'd been trying to ignore it.

"Cynthia, could you please schedule me for a blood test?" I was going away, but I would give Amber my proof first. Cynthia nodded and I turned to face Amber. "You'll see the truth then you'll pack your things and get the hell out. I won't be second-guessed my entire life."

"Gladly," she shot back. "I won't live with a junkie."

I stiffened. That was twice now she'd called me a junkie. I decided I wouldn't give her the truth after all, just get the hell away from her.

"You know what Cynthia? Never mind."

Amber scowled at me. "Scared it will turn up positive?"

"No. I just don't think I need to prove anything to you.

You wanna think I'm a junkie go right ahead. I suppose you've never thought any better of me anyway."

The outer office was empty and Cynthia did not want to be in the middle of this. She liked Amber. I was her employer and she liked me. Now she was forced to sit here and watch us break up and I could tell by the way she looked at me that she believed me. The coke wasn't mine. Cynthia knew it. Her sympathetic expression told me so.

The door to Ted's office was closed, but I knew he was in there, hiding from this the way Cynthia couldn't. Too bad. I needed to talk to him.

I picked the stapler up off of Cynthia's desk and whipped it across the room at his door. "Ted!"

"Are you crazy?" Amber yelled behind me.

"Yeah. But you've always known *that*, haven't you?"

Cynthia looked terrified. She didn't know me to be this way. I barely knew me this way. I felt completely out of control.

Ted's door swung open. He looked down at the stapler on the floor and peered up at me, handsome middle-aged face looking out through his wire-rimmed glasses. "What's the problem, Meagan?" he asked, startled by the commotion.

I stood in my doorway and he stood in his. Cynthia sat at her desk between us and Amber was behind me in my office. I switched into calculated business mode.

"Is the flat above *Natural Beauty's* offices still empty?" I asked him. I wasn't going to Ireland, I was going home. To London. To solitude.

"Yes."

"Can I use it for a week?"

"Sure, but there's no phone."

I shrugged. "Even better. I'll check on business while I'm there." Ted nodded and went back in his office. I told Cynthia to book me on the next flight out. She bit her finger, nodded, and I went back in my office and slammed the door.

"You have one week," I told Amber. "If you're not out by the time I return, *I'll* move out."

"Oh, I'll be out," she said snottily. "Don't worry about that. I'll be out by tonight."

I couldn't believe what was happening. We were actually breaking up. After everything we'd been through it had come down to these final moments and we were acting like we hated each other. The coldness crept in further. It chilled me.

"Don't bother," I snapped. "I won't be home tonight anyway. I've been set up and you refuse to believe me. *You took off the ring! You* broke our bond. I want you to *always* remember that. I would have done anything for you. In fact, I'll even leave you with a gift."

I shuffled through the top drawer of my desk. I found her papers, scribbled across them, stapled them, and threw them at her.

"The rights to your poetry," I said. "The novel stays because that was Ted's deal. I'd release you from your contract with us but I have no authority over that."

Amber was speechless. She stared down at the papers in her hands and knew I meant every word I was saying, because when business was involved I didn't screw around. I was also proving I would never "Gwynne" her.

"As for the sixty grand in your account," I snarled, "why don't you go ahead and keep that as compensation for a trying few years."

Her head snapped up. "I don't want your goddamn money."

"Consider it payment for services rendered." I was talking to her like she'd never been anything more than my whore. "I think we're done here."

Cynthia cut in on the intercom. "There's an eleven o'clock flight leaving for Heathrow, Meagan. Do you want it?"

"Yes, Cynthia."

The intercom cut out. I sat at my desk and glared at the person I thought had loved me. The person who hadn't trusted me since the day I stopped using drugs.

"Are you leaving or what?" I demanded.

She didn't move. She had started off so angry and now she didn't know what to do. I thought I'd help her decide. I picked up the fairy statue she bought me for my birthday and her eyes widened.

"Don't," she warned.

I smashed it on the floor. Hundreds of tiny ceramic pieces scattered like colorful ants. She knew I loved it and I had just destroyed it, the way she'd destroy us.

"I can't believe you just did that!" she yelled.

"Why not? Junkies are unpredictable, Amber. Get the fuck out. I don't ever want to see you again."

Tears filled her eyes again. "I'm going, but do yourself a favor, Meagan. Sign yourself into rehab before it's too late."

"Get out!"

She nodded, folded the papers in her hand, and I watched her leave, fighting the urge to run after her and beg her not to go. I had visions of myself down on my knees, pleading with her to believe me, telling her I'd do anything, just please, don't go! I did nothing.

The door closed behind her and I pressed my palms to my eyes, forcing the tears back behind them where they belonged. I choked on the sob I would not let out of my throat. It was over. For the second time in our history, it had ended on a lie, and whoever had set me up was going to pay.

Angrily, I realized it was partly my fault. I never locked my car doors. I didn't care to because it had always been safe in the garage below my building. I would start now, but now was already too late. The worst had happened. There was nothing left to fear. I had literally left the door open for disaster and I didn't know whether to laugh or scream.

The empty vial sat on my desk and I stared at it. I picked it up and squeezed it in my hand the way I had Ambers ring until the grooves in the tiny black cap left an imprint in my palm. I pulled her ring from the garbage, placed it on the desk beside the vial, and stared. I leaned forward on the desk, rested my chin on the back of my hands, and watched the ring make a dozen mocking circles as I spun it on the desk top. It danced around the desk like a pagan around a maypole. The ring of dreams. The bond of love. Broken. Everything broken. I slammed my hand on the top of it and ended its mocking ballet.

It wasn't supposed to end this way. It wasn't supposed to end at all.

I slipped the ring over the vial and tossed them both in the garbage.

Cynthia left for the day with a small knock on my door to say goodbye. Ted left for the day. I watched it grow dark outside. The phone beside me rang and I ignored it. I went downstairs to the lobby and locked the front door. Everyone had gone home. The building was empty now and it felt as cold and vacant as my heart. I went back upstairs and resumed my place behind my desk. I did nothing. The phone rang intermittently and each time I ignored it. Hours passed. It rang again and this time I snatched it up.

It was Adrian. He said he was coming to take me to rehab the way I'd once done for him.

"I am not on drugs!" I yelled, and slammed the phone in his ear.

Damn Amber! Had she gone home and called everyone? Probably. I decided I wouldn't stick around waiting for the intervention. They would come for me. Lock the doors and coax me into a rehab program I didn't need. I wondered if Amber would come too. I decided I didn't care and left the office before it could begin.

I stopped at a pharmacy and bought toothpaste, a toothbrush, shampoo--all the things I would need--then headed for the airport. I'd buy some clothes in London, I thought. I wasn't going home for anything.

By ten-forty-five I was sitting on a flight bound for Heathrow.

Chapter 20

The first thing I did when I got to London was call Jackie. I needed a friend who didn't have anything to do with anything. She picked me up at the airport and took me to the furnished, but otherwise empty, flat above the NB offices. She gave me a sympathetic shoulder to cry on and I poured out my story from beginning to end. She held me as I sobbed.

I hadn't done anything wrong, I told her. She agreed and I told her I needed to buy some clothes, that I had fled the country with nothing more than the shirt on my back.

Jackie laughed and said I sounded like a fugitive. I told her I felt like one. She took me to a few clothing stores around town where she busied herself picking out clothes for me-- everything from designer stuff to casual wear--while I stood by the cash register like a mannequin holding a gold card.

I bought everything she chose without trying anything on. Then I picked out four pairs of jeans and five t-shirts, which I planned on living in for the next seven days. We picked up some groceries and went back to the flat. I hadn't slept in thirty-six hours.

Jackie put me to bed and said she'd stick around to make me dinner but then she had a show to do.

"Guess where?" she said, doing a little sashay.

"Not---"

"Yep. The very place we met. Wanna come see Angus?"

I managed a weak smile. "No thanks. I'm really glad you're here, Jacks."

"Okay." She pulled the covers up to my chin. "Get some sleep."

Seven hours later I awoke to the smell of food. Jackie had made pasta and garlic bread. It looked great but I had no appetite.

"Eat it," she said, placing a plate in front of me. I did my best.

Jackie left after dinner with promises of returning in

the morning and I went back to bed. I felt like Amber sleeping through the pain. I woke up in the middle of the night wondering what she was doing. If she'd spent last night waking up the way she used to when she needed to see me beside her, then having that second of panic when she realized I was gone. Was she crying? Wishing she hadn't said the things she'd said? Wishing she hadn't sealed our fate by taking off the ring?

I wondered if she was okay, then chastised myself for caring. She was the one who didn't believe in *me*. And my eyes grew swollen from crying.

By the third day the offices downstairs were being swamped with phone calls from my family and Adrian, who also faxed to plead with me to please come home so he could help me with my problem. Again I didn't know whether to laugh or scream. Everyone back home thought I was on drugs. They were pleading with me, via phone messages to come home and help myself. No calls from Amber. She had given up on me. Couldn't go through the withdrawal twice. Jenna's message said Amber was sorry but she wasn't strong enough to go through it again. I had betrayed her and she was through with me. She was staying in the apartment across the hall until she figured out what to do.

She was through with *me? I* had betrayed *her?*

Two messages from Seamus. Word had even spread to Ireland like a global epidemic. *Amber's crying her heart out, Meggie. I'm worried. Come to Ireland. I'll help you.*

A message from Danielle. *Get back here, Meagan. Let me be the big sister for awhile.*

Several from my worried parents.

I called my mother and told her to tell everyone to please leave me alone. I wasn't on drugs. When I returned I would get a blood test to prove it. She kindly told me that all the blood test would prove was that I hadn't touched drugs that week. I could easily stay away from them just so I'd pass the test.

I told her to go to hell and hung up on her. I went back upstairs.

An hour later Becca came up to hand me a fax that had come from the Markham-Summers offices. We didn't look at each other.

The fax was from Cynthia and it said she had received a strange fax of her own with my name on it. It didn't make sense to her, she wrote, but maybe it would make sense to me. I was sure it would. Before I even turned to the second page I had a growing suspicion it was a gloat fax, sent by the very person who had set me up. I was right. She had waited a lifetime, but Gwynne Patterson had gotten her revenge. I read with a growing rage. Even in vengeance the woman was impatient. That was a mistake.

Dear Meagan,

Vegetables die in the winter
When the snow covers the ground and their faces
They're sniffing at the air
Breathing in dewy crystals
and they know that all will be well.
We are never lonely when we see the wind blow
and the vegetables are as pretty as any angry gemstone
when they finds the white powder too cold
Love dies sometimes
Vegetables don't grow new roots but
they find another path in the snow
I keep hope for the future and pray the vegetables
are not the last to know when the cold creeps in
and they are wrapped about the powder
Imprisoned perhaps, or merely alone
because they did not see the winter coming
A blow that comes first at the end of fall

I'm thinking of following in Amber's footsteps. What do you think?

Gwynne

It was dated the day before. I read it five times and knew it was Gwynne's way of telling me she was the one who had planted the coke. I was surprised I hadn't figured it out myself. Of course it was Gwynne. I didn't have any other enemies. She knew someone must have found the coke by now and it was time to do her victory dance.

My eyes narrowed on the page. Gwynne was going to pay for this like she'd never paid for anything in her life.

I studied the bizarre poem until certain words began to peek out at me. I underlined them with a black pen, and sure enough, a message within the message began to take form. The poem itself was a pretty good clue but Gwynne had taken it to a deeper level. She wanted me to be *sure*.

I went back downstairs and photocopied the fax. The un-coded version read:

Vegetables die in the winter
When the snow covers the ground and their faces
They're sniffing at the air
Breathing in dewy crystals
and know that all will be well
We are never lonely when we see the wind blow
and the vegetables are as pretty as any angry gemstone
when they finds the white powder too cold

Love dies sometimes
Vegetables don't grow new roots but
they find another path in the snow
I keep hope for the future and pray the vegetables
are not the last to know when the cold creeps in
and they are wrapped about the powder
Imprisoned perhaps, or merely alone
because they did not see the winter coming
A blow that comes first at the end of fall

I knew I'd cracked the code because each word she wanted me to notice looked the tiniest bit different from the rest. There was a capital letter thrown in, an "s" where it didn't belong, or a word angled slightly to the left--things that might have been hard to spot if you weren't looking for them. But Gwynne knew I'd look. She knew I was as suspicious as she was, and I'd look hard enough to catch her hidden meaning. It made me think of Amber and the Clump.

Gwynne had been having such a good time writing her little poem that she hadn't known where to stop. She couldn't have left a longer message. It was as stupid and long-winded as she was. Never knew when to shut up.

I stared down at the copy in my hand. It was the indisputable proof of my innocence. Now I'd have to see if anyone else agreed.

I added a footnote of my own to the copy--*Thanks for believing in me*--and faxed the copy to Amber. If she was staying across the hall she'd get it soon enough. Then I called Vicki Clump and told her to get me every bit of dirt she could turn up on Gwynne Patterson. Clump jumped at the chance to please me.

"I'll get started now," she said. I knew that girl would come in handy.

I felt a bit better after that. Stronger. I was back in charge and everyone would be eating their words. Jackie came by again and I showed her the un-coded fax.

"My God," she said. "Who are you, James Bond?"

I pointed at the page. "No, look at the handwriting, Jackie. She wanted me to spot it. Maybe she didn't think I'd crack the code so quickly, but maybe she didn't care. She was just having fun writing her stupid little poem."

Jackie studied the paper. "Vegetables because you were in a coma, right?"

I nodded. "That's what she called me. Broccoli, even."

"And the gemstone thing?"

"Amber."

"Makes sense."

"The best part is Amber *was* the one who found it. Gwynne's gonna pay for this, and I think my ex-husband's going to pay too."

"Why him?" Jackie asked.

"Because I told him once about the drugs. Blamed him, really. He's the only one who could have told Gwynne."

Jackie threw the fax on the coffee table and pulled her long brown hair into a ponytail. "Maybe you should sell her back the rights."

I threw up my hands. "Not you too?"

"She's dangerous, Meagan. She could have had you thrown in jail for that coke."

"I know, and she's going to pay for every damn bit of

suffering she's caused me. She ruined my relationship, Jackie. Amber and I are through because of this. She got Amber to distrust me and, well you know what Amber did."

Jackie shook her head. "I don't get this ring thing, honey."

"You don't have to. All you have to get is that Amber knew she'd destroy us by taking it off and she did it anyway."

Jackie gave me an odd look and I burst into tears.

The faxes and phone calls started up again a few hours later. The staff downstairs handled them for a while then Becca came up to tell me I better come down and deal with it because it was getting out of control.

Word of my innocence had spread like wildfire. A pile of phone messages awaited me in my old office. I sifted through the pink "guess who called" slips. My parents were sorry. My siblings were sorry. Adrian was sorry. Amber was sorry. I had been in London three days and they had done nothing but make me the source of inter-office gossip. And I was the boss!

Then there were the faxes. All Amber's. All apologizing and pleading with me to call her. They were coming every half hour. *I'm sorry, I'm sorry, I'm sorry.*

I faxed back. *Leave me alone. Move out.*

Ten minutes later Becca was at my side. "It's email now, Meagan."

"Jesus Christ."

I went back in my old office, sat at the computer and typed *You are embarrassing me. Move out,* and sent it Amber's way.

The response came back. *No. Come home. I need to talk to you.*

I was hurt and angry and I sent back one last message. *I told you that you'd regret this. I am going upstairs, Amber. These people have work to do. Stop harassing them. Stop it now. For the last time, MOVE OUT!*

I told Becca if it kept up to tell the staff to ignore it. To throw out the faxes, and there shouldn't be any more phone calls because I had called my mother and dealt with things there. I didn't know what to say about the emails, but my mother had apologized and said she'd tell everyone to stop calling. For once, she was on my side.

Then I went back upstairs and told Jackie what a madhouse Amber and my family were turning things into down there. Jackie laughed and said that was the way love went. I was still too hurt to be amused.

"You still love her, though," she said.

I shrugged. "So what? What does that change? Not a damn thing. The ring---"

Jackie groaned. "Not the ring again."

"She knew what it meant, Jackie. That's all I'm saying."

The harassment stopped an hour later but I knew it would start up again. The staff went home, glad to be released from the chaos I had brought them. Jackie and I went out for dinner then returned to watch movies and have a glass of wine. She had wine. I had a French vanilla cappuccino we picked up on the way home.

We were watching TV and I looked over at her, dying to know something I'd been wanting to know since the day I'd first met her.

"Jackie?"

She stared at the TV. "Mm-hmm?"

"Do you go out with men or women?"

Her eyebrow arched. "Are you interested, Meagan?" She teased.

"I'm just wondering, I mean, does it get lonely being a hybrid?"

"A hybrid?" she roared with laughter. "I assume you are referring to the fact that I have breasts and a penis."

I nodded.

She thought. "Sometimes it gets lonely, but then a nice guy will come along and he won't care, really. Too bad about your sexy uncle. Him, I could get into. I'm thinking of having the chop-chop operation soon though."

We went back to watching the movie. At two in the morning Jackie went to sleep in the bedroom and I stayed on the couch, staring at the high ceiling. I cried a little then passed out. At nine there was a knock on the big metal door. The offices downstairs had just opened and Becca must have been coming up to hand me another stack of faxes.

I pulled on my jeans, went to the door, and swung it

open.

"Jenna!"

"Hi, Meagan." She gave me a tired smile. She'd been on a plane all night and Jenna hated to fly.

"What are you doing here?" I didn't let her in.

"Came to talk."

"To London? You came to talk?" I leaned against the door handle and sighed. "Go home, Jenna, and when you get there tell the blond narc to stop faxing and emailing the office like a stalker."

"Tell her yourself." Jenna yanked Amber into the doorway. Green eyes on mine.

I shook my head. "Oh, no. If either of you thinks there's going to be some sort of reconciliation here you're sadly mistaken."

"You're still wearing the ring," Jenna pointed out.

"It's my *grandmother's* Jenna."

Jackie strolled out of the bedroom wearing her shirt from the night before and nothing else. "Is that Becca again?" She asked, rubbing her eyes. "They don't give up over there do they, honey?"

Jackie called everyone honey. Jenna and Amber didn't know that. Jenna's jaw dropped and Amber's eyes narrowed as Jackie came into view like a vision of morning loveliness. "Oh, hello," she said.

I sighed. "I suppose you better come in."

Jenna stepped inside, then turned back. "Amber!" Amber continued to glare at me and Jenna pulled her into the flat after her.

"Is there any of that wine left, honey?" Jackie asked.

Jenna and Amber stared at me, wondering if I was drinking again, and wondering if I was having sex with the pretty brunette. The looks pissed me off.

"It's nine in the morning," I said.

Jackie shrugged. "I'm gonna go get dressed."

"Wait." I grabbed her arm. Amber went to say something--something snide--but I pointed at her for silence, and turned to Jackie. "Tell them your name."

She looked at the two women. "Jackie. Now, if you'll excuse me for a minute."

Amber still hadn't spoken but I saw the relief wash over her face and she glanced down between Jackie's legs. I almost laughed. She wouldn't see anything. I'd done the same thing a dozen times myself and Jackie hid it well, unless she was doing a show.

I turned away from Amber and Jenna and walked into the kitchen, where I knew they'd follow.

"Here's what's going to happen," I said, taking charge in my usual way. Jenna sat on a stool at the counter and Amber stood beside her, giving me the sorry green stare that wasn't going to work this time. "I'll make the two of you breakfast and then you're out of here. You can go to a hotel or get on a flight home. It doesn't concern me either way. Jenna, you have a son at home and you don't need to be involved in this shit. And Amber," I tilted my head. Loved her. Too bad. "Nothing's changing here. You accused me, didn't believe me, and the ring is long gone."

She flashed her hand at me and I was surprised to see it back in place on her finger. She must have gone back to the office and pulled it out of the garbage. She was the only other person who had a key to my door.

I reached into the fridge and pulled out a bag of raisin bagels. There was little else in there as Jackie and I had been dining out.

"It doesn't matter, Amber," I said, undoing the twist tie at the top of the bag. "You took if off. You deliberately broke the bond when you knew its importance. I warned you but you said 'Fuck your consequences.' You didn't care about the consequences a few days ago, but you'll deal with them now."

"Don't be so childish." The first words she uttered and they were the wrong ones. "I've been apologizing since yesterday."

"Don't care." It was easy to be smug when she had flown halfway around the world to try to rectify things.

"Meagan," Jenna said. "She made a mistake."

"Yes," I agreed. "One that cost us our relationship."

Jackie appeared in the kitchen. "I'll toast the bagels. You guys go talk."

"There's nothing to talk about, Jackie. It's over."

Amber stepped around the counter. "Meagan, please. I

love you so much. Don't do this. I haven't slept since you left. I haven't eaten. I don't want us to be over."

"Then you should have believed me. I *told* you it wasn't mine. I told you I was being set up. I can't be with someone who doesn't trust me."

"But you love me." She made it sound more like a question.

"Like I told Jackie, so what? I've been without you before, I can certainly do it again. You'll find someone else, Amber. It didn't take you long the last time."

"I don't want anyone else," she said quietly.

I gave an unaffected shrug. Jenna suddenly jumped to her feet and threw her purse on the counter. "You're fucking pissing me off, Meagan."

Amber and I both stared at her, shocked.

Jenna glared. "Yeah, I can curse. I know the same stupid words you do. Now grow up and accept her apology. She found *cocaine* in your car. You're an ex-drug user. What else was she going to think? And call Seamus. He's worried sick." She sat on the stool again, exhausted from her tiny rant.

"Jenna, do me a favor and for once in your life, mind your own business."

"This is my business," she said. "I make it my business when my two best friends who belong together keep breaking up over the stupidest reasons. Don't forget, Meagan, you're the first to say you came back from the dead for this woman." Amber continued to stare at me.

"And apparently I was wrong about that." My words hurt her and she looked away.

"Really?" Jenna pressed. "Are you forgetting who she is? All she's done for you? First the coma---"

It always came back to this. The things she had done for me. Was I expected to be a saint and forgive every damn thing because Amber had once chosen to be a martyr? Was I going to have to pay for her kindness for the rest of my life? Something in me snapped.

"I know!" I screamed. I kicked the counter like a maniac and everyone back away from me. "Coma!" *Crack.* "Paralysis!" *Crack.* "Drug addiction!" *Crack.* "I was there. I know how it went!" I paced back and forth. "I can't take this anymore. I swear to God I can't take it. Every time I turn around it's the same fucking speech." I stalked past them into the living room. Amber never mentioned the things she'd done for me but everyone else did. Constantly.

She approached me. "Honey---"

"Get away from me." I marched away from her.

Jenna swiveled on her stool. She wasn't done. "Well what more do you expect from a person, Meagan?"

"Trust! I expect trust!"

"Trust is earned."

Hadn't I earned it? I turned to glare at her. Now she'd asked for it. She'd pushed too hard and she'd asked for every bit of cruelty I had within me. I stalked toward her.

"Fuck you, Jenna. You're so fucking sanctimonious. Tell me, how long did it take you to trust my brother again after he screwed his secretary?"

Jenna's head snapped in Amber's direction.

"Meagan, you promised me," Amber cried.

Jackie pretended to be busy buttering bagels.

"Yeah, well my loyalty to you disappeared the second you tore that ring off your finger." I turned back to Jenna. I wasn't done with her yet. I was going to get every bit of this out.

"Does she still work at his office, Jenna?" I sneered. "How many others, I wonder? Every time he steps out the door, do you wonder who he's going to see? If he's found someone else to fuck? Couldn't tell *me* though, huh, *best friend*?"

Jenna burst into tears.

"Meagan, stop it!" Amber yelled. "Don't take your anger out on her."

I felt bad. I said what I'd wanted to say forever, and I felt horrible. I'd never made Jenna cry and she really didn't deserve my wrath, no matter how much she was pissing me off.

I walked over to her and glared at Amber. "Now look what you've done."

"*Me?*"

I ripped a paper towel off the roll on the counter and dabbed Jenna's eyes with it. "I'm sorry. I didn't mean to hurt you."

She waved away my words. "Maybe I had that

coming."

"You didn't," Amber said. "Meagan was being a bitch."

That got her another glare. "What are you even doing here?" I barked. "I came to London to get away from you."

"Yeah, that's right. You ran away again."

"Fuck you."

Jackie placed a plateful of bagels on the counter. So far she'd kept quiet but now she said, "Go home, Meagan."

"What? Why?"

"Because it's where you belong." She pointed at Amber. "With her. Your sister-in-law is right, you're being childish. And don't get me wrong, I understand why you're upset, but I think you can find it in your heart to forgive her. Lord knows you've been crying over her for four days."

My cheeks flushed. Jackie had a big mouth. I thought up some cutting remark about her being a sideshow freak but bit my tongue. She was only trying to help.

Amber approached me again. "You cried over me, Meagan?"

I stared her down. "Exactly what kind of a glacier do you think I am? Don't you think I have feelings too?"

"I know you do, but you don't cry when you're angry. Never have." She startled me by throwing her arms around me. I didn't readily break the embrace. I didn't return it either. "Come home with me," she pleaded. "I made the worst mistake I could ever make, but I promise I will never doubt you again." Her eyes flashed suddenly. "And we're going to make Gwynne pay for this."

My own eyes widened. Amber didn't believe in vengeance. Not since the *Butterflies* fiasco. "We are?"

"Damn right we are. She could have gotten you arrested. Or me. No one fucks with us, right, Meagan?"

I took a step back. In two short days she'd acquired my sense of vengeance, and she was actually a little frightening. I didn't know what to say.

"Go home, Meagan," Jackie said again. "And, honey, drop the vengeance stuff before someone really gets hurt."

Jenna nodded. "I agree."

Chapter 21

Jackie left after breakfast and Jenna, Amber, and I spent an uncomfortable day together. We went shopping so we didn't have to be faced with any real alone time. I showed them what little of London I actually knew, because the first time I was there I'd spent most of my time working, and no one spoke about booking a flight home. We didn't know what we were doing. We were just trying to avoid the discomfort each of us felt over what had gone on.

They had been my accusers. They were the same women they'd always been but different, because they were wrong. This time I had been undeserving of their accusations. They knew it, and because they knew it, their eyes didn't meet mine easily.

A part of me was wrong too. I might not have readily admitted it but I was wrong in the way I'd turned on Jenna. I had exhausted my rage on her because she'd made me feel guilty for being angry at Amber. How could I not be angry? Hurt? She had betrayed me and then accused me of doing so to her. I didn't know what to do about it.

I gave Seamus a quick call to tell him I was alright and he asked what was going on between Amber and me. I told him I honestly didn't know. I hadn't figured that out yet.

In the evening we settled into the always too warm living room and Jenna broke the ice by discussing Josh's affair. The pain. The humiliation. She was relieved to finally be able to tell me and I felt like a piece of our friendship that had been missing since the day it happened suddenly locked back into place. She said she'd wanted to tell me for a long time but echoed Amber's age-old words that she didn't want to ruin my relationship with my brother.

By nine o'clock Jenna had fallen asleep on the couch. I covered her with a blanket and sat on the floor beside her head listening to the music coming out of the stereo and avoiding the awkward energy that suddenly filled the air between Amber and me. It hadn't been awkward since we first met, or later during the time of Ken. Now it was awkward again and it made me uncomfortable. We should have known what to say to each other, but we didn't. It had come too close to hate. We both felt it. She, when she found the coke, and I when she brought it to me. It had come to something we had never known in each other and it was frightening.

Amber fell asleep shortly after Jenna. A mixture of stress, jet lag, and the silence we'd lapsed into after Jenna had passed out. Knowing how she was stressed, I was surprised she'd stayed awake as long as she had.

I sat on the floor and watched her sleep. Could I forgive her this one? I didn't know. I thought I heard her murmur my name and leaned in to hear if she'd say it again, then I decided I didn't want to know. I put a blanket over her too and left two pillows on the chair by the couch in case they should wake up during the night and want to get more comfortable.

I looked at them. Two blond heads resting on opposite ends of the couch. One honey blond, Jenna. One platinum, Amber. I felt like a mother tucking in her twins. Only these twins would have been fraternal because one was curvy and earthy and the other was model-thin and pragmatic. One was my conscience, the other my heart.

Sighing, I turned and walked into the bedroom. I took off my jeans and t-shirt and threw on a football jersey Jackie had picked out for me because she'd said I'd look cute in it. Ken would have loved it. He liked the fresh-faced college girl look and the shirt made me look like I was dating the captain of the football team, #9. I allowed myself a small smile. If I had gone to college, that was probably exactly who I would have been dating, a fraternity boy who went to all the right parties. I wouldn't have been a cheerleader, but that wouldn't have mattered because I would have been popular in other ways. Like in high school, where I hadn't done a thing, but was friends with everyone anyway. Seamus would say I had charisma but I thought that title probably suited Amber better. Maybe I did have a kind face. Who knew?

Amber was the stunner. She walked into a room and people took notice. It was the eyes. The blond hair. The sly grin. The confident stride like she knew exactly where she was going and was determined to get there. She had a stylish beauty. She could change with the times and still look like her. Like fashion and trends were created to suit her whims. She could wear ripped jeans or an evening gown and look incredible in either one.

I was pretty, but Amber was beautiful.

She would have disagreed. She would have said I was every bit as beautiful as she was but I thought that was impossible. Not just for me but for any one. I didn't think anyone could be as lovely to look at as she was.

Another drawn-out sigh. What was I going to do about her? I couldn't stop loving her, but did love really matter in times like these? When you didn't have trust? I closed my eyes and fell asleep before I was given an answer.

When I awoke she was asleep beside me, her body curled to mine and her head nuzzled in my neck. Her hair smelled of shampoo. Fresh, like she had awakened during the night to take a shower. Her arm stretched across my neck and I smelled crushed flowers, English soap. She had indeed taken a shower then crawled into bed beside me naked.

What was she doing? She didn't trust me but she loved me. I thought perhaps she would trust me now that she had seen I could face the worst and still not turn to drugs. I had come to London alone, hurt and angry, with my emotions in worse distress than they'd seen in a long time but I hadn't cracked. I hadn't turned to a false comfort like a true addict might have. And she had seen that. She knew it would have been the easiest time for me to fall, when everyone already thought I had thanks to her, but I'd refused to go down. She would have to trust me now, wouldn't she?

My hand hesitated in the air above her head, then reached down and stroked her soft hair. She turned and grinned at me. She hadn't been sleeping at all. She knew I was awake and she'd been waiting to see how I'd react to her presence beside me. In one movement I had given her the affectionate response she wanted and I couldn't help laughing at her.

"You're such a faker," I said.

"Never with you."

"Cute, but that's not what I meant."

"Doesn't matter, it's still true. I can prove it." She

pulled my hand toward her, trying to make up her way.

I pulled it away. "Good for you."

She grinned at my shirt and propped herself up on her elbow. "I have to tell you, I find your sporty little look here quite sexy. Come on, Meagan. Make me prove it."

"I, unlike you, don't require validation." I couldn't resist the jab.

Jenna knocked on the door. "You guys up?"

I smirked at Amber. "So you're shit out of luck anyway. Yeah, Jenna, we're up."

"Can I come in?"

"Sure."

Amber nudged me and pulled the blankets up around her nakedness. Jenna bounced in the room like a burst of morning sunshine and jumped in the bed between us.

"Some Becca girl brought this up," she said, handing me a large envelope. "She said it's some pretty funky stuff and it's been pouring out of the fax machine."

She glanced at Amber and me and settled back against the pillows. "Everything alright between you two?" A curious look at Amber. A peek under the sheets.

"Jenna!" Amber slapped her hand away.

Jenna giggled. "Guess so." She lifted my end of the sheets. "You're not naked. Maybe under your linebacker boyfriend's shirt."

I ignored her. Jackie had obviously been right about the shirt.

"You said Becca brought this up?"

"Yep. I told her you were busy having sex."

"Did not." I opened the envelope.

"No, but I could have." Her head turned to Amber again. "You have cute boobs."

I smirked.

Amber laughed. "You need to go home to your husband, Jenna."

"Why? I can say you have nice boobs and not mean anything by it. Meagan has a nice ass, great legs. Danny has a cute stomach with a sexy little mole above her belly button and I won't tell you what's cute about me."

Amber gave her a strange look. "What do you do, go

around inspecting people?"

"Uh-huh."

I looked at the pages before me and gasped. "Oh my God!"

"What?" they said.

I was staring at a picture of Gwynne in bed with a man who wasn't Ken. Under that was another picture of Gwynne with the same man only now a woman was included. The pictures had yesterday's date at the bottom of them. Then there were other pages. Tax reports, bank statements and pay stubs, all leading to the fact that Gwynne was cheating on her taxes as well as cheating on her fiancé. I distributed the pages to Jenna and Amber.

"Holy shit," Amber said.

"Oh my Goddess," said Jenna. "Meagan, who sent this to you?"

I was stunned. "I told Vicki Clump to do some digging. I didn't expect her to turn up anything this fast, or this big. It's barely been two days. That girl is getting a promotion *and* a raise."

"That's it," Amber said, waving the pictures of Gwynne, who did indeed have inverted nipples. "We're nailing her to the wall with this. Gwynne is going down big time."

Jenna frowned. I took back the pages and stared down at them in my hand. I wasn't sure I wanted to be this person. I could destroy Gwynne's life with these pages and I suddenly felt very low about that. Like I'd sunk to the bottom of what I was capable of.

"What's wrong?" Amber asked, sensing my trepidation.

She saw the thought in my eyes and in a split second I made my decision and tore the pages in half.

Jenna squealed and applauded me and Amber shrieked, "No, Meagan! What are you doing? That's our proof!"

I continued to tear. I threw the scattered pages on the floor and Jenna bounced up and down on the bed like she'd never been more proud of me. Amber leaped to the floor stark naked, all modesty gone, and scrambled to pick up the tattered pieces.

"Shit! Shit! Vicki must have copies, right? Yeah, she

has to because she faxed these."

I crossed my legs under me, feeling better about myself than I had in awhile. "It doesn't matter, Amber. I'm not doing it. Some things are too low even for me."

"But Meagan, she nearly destroyed us. How do you know she wasn't planning on having you arrested for that coke?"

I thought of Gwynne's poem. Silly proof. It didn't take much to sway Amber against me or for me.

"She probably was," I said, "But you were right-- I *am* better than this. It's true, I called in the pit bull because I wanted to destroy Gwynne's life, but Christ, how low am I going to sink?" I shook my head. "I can't do it. I wouldn't like myself very much if I did."

"Good for you, Meagan," Jenna said.

"But Gwynne won't stop," Amber said. "Once she sees her little stunt with the coke didn't amount to anything she'll move on to something else."

I knew Amber was right. "Okay. I'll put Vicki's originals in the safe at the office, but I seriously hope the day will never come when I have to use them."

That pleased Amber *and* Jenna, who couldn't stop smiling at me.

Amber sat on the bed beside me and pulled the covers around her again.

"You make me nuts with the things you do, Meagan. You sign the person who got you hooked on drugs into rehab and pay for his recovery. Another person puts you in the middle of a scandal and shames your parents and you give her a job. You hand homeless people fifties like it's nothing. Gwynne comes to you with a book proposal and you totally screw her over. She retaliates in the worst way, and you tear up your proof to ruin her life. Why do you do so many conflicting things? Sometimes I feel like I'll never figure you out completely."

Jenna shrugged. "It's easy to figure her out, Amber. She has a war going on within her. She wants to be a good person but her basic nature is to strike back and go for the kill. This time the good won. Let her have that. She's *growing*."

I laughed. "Jenna, why is it you can always make me feel like a wayward child?"

"Because half the time you act like one."

I shoved her off the bed. "Go save someone else's soul. And can't you ever tell a little white lie? You're so brutally honest."

She danced around the room chanting. "Meagan's growing. Meagan's growing."

"Oh God," I groaned. We better get you home to your family before you make me change my mind about the whole thing."

Jenna skipped to the window, threw back the drapes and there was a small ding, ding, ding sound as the silver hoops at the top slid across the metal rod. The room filled with morning light. Not much, because it was raining outside, and the tiny droplets splattered against the window and dripped downward in a singular stream. It was the only thing I hated about London, it always seemed to be raining, and I had once spent many nights staring out that very window dreaming of home. Sometimes even while Ken lay asleep beside me in the giant bed that took up most of the grey room.

The entire flat was grey. Grey walls, darker grey trim around the doors and windows, it was a dreary place to inhabit for any length of time and I had lived here for seven months. Amber was surprised when she'd first seen it. I could see the surprise on her face. She knew I liked brightness. I liked rooms that filled with sunlight and were painted in soft colors. The flat was gloomy. The first time Jenna saw it she said she was glad I was coming home. When Amber saw it, after the incident with Jackie in the kitchen and when she really had a chance to look around, she said it wasn't like me to live this way and she couldn't believe I had stayed as long as I had. I told her I had liked the flat then. It was as gloomy as I was on the inside and I had served my time in it well. Voluntary imprisonment that was how I'd put it, and it sounded more like me than anything else. I hadn't run away so much as I had locked myself away, and there was indeed a difference. I had closed myself off from the world for a time, caged myself within the grey walls, threw myself into my work, and survived. That was my way.

I sat in the center of the bed, contemplating whether or not I wanted to get up and get dressed. Jenna ran back from the window, jumped on the bed, and bounced up and down like a hyperactive six year old, still chanting about my growth.

Laughing, Amber reached for the jeans I'd tossed on the floor the night before and began putting them on under the comforter she had wrapped around her.

"Hey!" I protested.

"Forget it," she said. "I'm wearing them." She pulled the t-shirt from the floor, modestly turned her back to us, and put that on too.

"Where are your clothes?" I asked.

Jenna continued to bounce happily, lost in whatever euphoria had suddenly entrapped her.

"In the living room," Amber said, sitting on the bed so that she faced me. "But I'd rather wear these right now because they feel like you."

"Aw," Jenna said. She was still jumping and the bouncing was starting to get on my nerves.

I looked up at her. She wore blue flannel shorts, a cream colored cotton shirt, and no makeup. I glanced at her legs and giggled at the blond stubble that spread across them.

"Christ, Jenna," I said, pulling on her arm so she was forced to sit and stop bouncing. "Why don't you shave those things?" She rubbed her legs and chuckled. I shook my head. "You're going to poke my brother's eye out."

"His *eye*?" She didn't get it. Maybe because she wasn't *getting* it. Amber and I laughed.

"Don't tell me Josh doesn't go down on you," I said.

"Meagan!" She slapped me with a pillow, messing my already sleep-lazy hair. I didn't care. Usually, the more tousled my hair was, the better it looked. "That's your brother you're talking about."

I shrugged. "So what? If he doesn't go down, what good is he?"

Amber laughed.

"Where do you come up with these things?" Jenna said, shaking her head. "I swear, you have two preoccupations in life, sex and money--not necessarily in that order. Your ideal fantasy is probably to have sex on a pile of money."

I whipped a pillow at her and she caught it in the air and crushed it to her chest. "First of all," I said, "I suspect, having sex on a pile of money is probably overrated." I fussed with my hair and caught Amber's loving gaze. She had a thing about me playing with my hair. She found it sexy. "Secondly, I just don't think you should spend your life having boring old missionary-position sex. What's worse than bad sex?"

"Being poor?" Amber offered helpfully.

I gave her a playful shove. "Shut up. Can't you see I'm trying to help Jenna get a decent fuck?"

Jenna placed her hands on her hips. "Who says I'm not getting a decent…sex?"

"Please," I scoffed, "my brother is such a tight ass I'll bet he's *always* on top. Do you blow him?"

"Meagan!"

Amber chuckled.

"All I'm saying is the two of you need to loosen up."

"And oral sex is that important, is it?"

I furrowed my eyebrows at her. "Yes, it's important. I know you're into the whole psycho-spiritual thing but I doubt Josh gets into mixing his spirituality with his sex. You need to get down and dirty with it once in awhile. Give him a popsicle blow job."

Amber leaned forward. "A what?"

I shook my head like I couldn't believe what was wrong with these two. "A popsicle blow job. You suck on a popsicle for awhile, until your mouth gets cold, then do it."

"I thought cold makes it shrink," Amber said.

"It never did with Basil." Amber wasn't sure she liked hearing that but she didn't say anything. I turned to Jenna. "Do you know about the prostate gland?" She frowned. "It's a sensitive spot for men," I continued, "but you have to reach it anally."

Jenna smacked her forehead. "What is the matter with you?"

"What?" I asked, innocently.

"You're telling me to shove my finger up your brother's ass."

Amber howled with laughter. Jenna was getting more comfortable with her choice of words.

I twisted a strand of hair around my finger and held it to the light. "You don't have to use your fingers. Use a vibrator with a thinner attachment." Jenna's eyes darted away guiltily. I shook my fingers through my hair again and sighed. "Jenna, don't tell me you don't even have a vibrator."

"Maybe she lets her fingers do the walking," Amber teased.

"You guys are embarrassing me."

"Why?" I said. "It's just us and we're only talking about sex." I paused to consider her circumstances. "Okay, so you don't have a vibrator. You've always been a natural girl so you find other ways, right?" She didn't answer. "Jenna, tell me you find other ways!"

She hit me with the pillow again. "I suppose *you* have vibrator?"

"Duh."

"What else?"

Amber laughed. "She's never shown you the drawer?"

"You have a *drawer* full of vibrators?" Jenna was shocked.

"Not just vibrators. Lotions, toys, Amber's last addition of the handcuffs. What else do we have, Amber?"

"Blindfolds, silk ties, feathers, those bead things." Jenna stared at us. "Oh my Goddess! You two are perverse. Just what makes you the sexpert anyway?"

I shrugged. "Two things. Basil Waite and Amber Reed."

Again Amber laughed.

"What about Ken?" Jenna asked.

"What about him?"

Amber shook her head. "We don't talk about our sexual pasts with Ken or Gwynne."

"Yeah," I agreed. "It's bad enough I have to know how many months Amber spent fisting that bitch."

"Screw you," Amber said, laughing. "You have no idea what Gwynne and I did or didn't do."

I nodded. "And let's keep it that way."

"Fisting?" Jenna asked.

I groaned. "For Christ's sake, Jenna, buy a book. Now listen to me, if you're blowing Josh and going on a prostate hunt and shoving popsicles up yourself---"

"Whoa," Amber interjected on Jenna's behalf, "you never said anything about popsicle masturbation."

"Well it's all a part of it," I said. I turned back to Jenna who was blushing. "Anyway, if you're going to be doing all those things, then damn right you're making him go down."

"I never said he doesn't," she defended.

"So what's the problem?"

"Who said there was a problem? I just don't see what all the fuss is about."

Amber and I looked at each other. Was she *serious*?

"Then he's not doing it right," I said. I thought of something funny and laughed. "Why don't you ask Amber to demonstrate?"

Their mouths fell open and it was Amber's turn to shriek my name. I thought they didn't have one sense of humor between the two of them.

"What?" I demanded, self-righteously.

"What do you mean *what*?" Amber said. "You just told your sister-in-law she should ask me for oral sex."

"Thank God you didn't say cunnilingus," I joked. "What a stupid word. Fellatio. Intercourse. I hate those clinical dictionary type words. I'm glad you called it what it is. Besides, as far as I'm concerned *everyone* should be asking you for oral sex."

She smirked and I thought, *you're not fully mine anymore anyway. I don't know what I'm going to do about you.*

She knew it. One look at my face and she knew precisely what I was thinking. We hadn't really made up; we'd just started talking about something else.

"Okay," Jenna said.

I looked at her. "Okay what?"

She whirled around on the bed and grabbed Amber's arms. "Kiss me."

I shook my head and chuckled. Amber looked at me, waiting for me to say something, and when I didn't she gave a wicked grin and leaned in toward Jenna like she was going to do it. A sudden reflex kicked into my body and I jumped between them, freezing them in place.

"Hey!"

They laughed at me.

"Oh, you talk big," Jenna said, "but when it gets right

down to it, look who's stopping the scene."

They thought they were so smart. I leaned back against the pillows, folded my arms behind my head, and grinned. "Alright, do it. Kiss."

"What about your brother?" Amber asked, looking for a reason to back out.

"He fucked another woman. I think she can kiss one."

Jenna frowned.

"What about me?" Amber asked.

I shook my head. "I don't own you. Hell, I don't even own the rights to your books anymore. What you choose to do is your own business. Now, are the two of you gonna kiss or are you a couple of chickenshits?"

"I'll do it, Meagan," Jenna warned.

I shrugged. They leaned into each other slowly then stopped.

"Well?" I pressed.

Amber took Jenna's hands in hers. "We're really going to do it, you know," she said.

I was unaffected. "So do it."

They looked at me, took in the weight of my dare, then looked at each other and inclined their heads. Slowly, they pressed toward each other and I suppressed the urge to stop them because I wanted them to lose this challenge. I wanted them to prove they couldn't do it. They looked in each other's eyes, searching for any flash of lust that would see them through this, and when they found nothing, fell away from each other, laughing. Then they made the simultaneous decision to beat me with pillows.

"You think you're so smart," Jenna said, laughing and smacking the pillow against the back of my head.

I buried my face in my hands and curled up in a ball on the bed while they hit me.

"That's what you get for threatening me," I muffled.

Amber fell on top of me and breathed in my hair. "You're such a nut."

Jenna stopped hitting and I looked up through splayed fingers, snatched her pillow from her, and turned on Amber.

"I know," I said, with a whack to her side. She raised her arms to protect herself. "You've been telling me that pretty much since the day I met you, but you know what? You're not exactly a stroll down lucidity lane either."

"We're all crazy," Jenna said, resuming her bouncing on the bed. "Meagan's insanity is just the most obvious."

I laughed and gave her a whack with the pillow. "Thanks a lot. And Jenna, do yourself a favor and get a freaking vibrator. Take charge of your sexuality."

"Yeah," Amber joked, "Cause Meagan is certainly in charge of hers."

I wasn't sure what she meant by that.

Chapter 22

Jenna flew home alone. Amber and I were going to go with her, but she told us to stay behind a few days. She'd go home and deal with the family, update them on the latest events, and she thought Amber and I should have some time away from everyone to work things out between us. We went to the airport with her and waited in the terminal until her flight was called.

"I'm proud of you, Meagan," she said again, nervously glancing at the gate. She flew so little that it was always a stressful situation for her.. "You're doing the right thing by not going after Gwynne with what you know." She hugged us in turn. "Just focus on the two of you, okay? This has been a big one but you guys can get through it. You---"

"Jenna."

"What?"

"Are you going to give me a speech or get on the plane?"

She giggled. "See you in a couple of days."

Jenna boarded the flight and Amber and I went back to the flat. She'd been in London two days and she was still apologizing. I would never apologize that much. For me, a person was either going to accept my apology or they weren't. I wouldn't beg. Amber was begging. I told her to stop. Her desperation was bothering me.

In the evening we went out for dinner with Jackie and a few of Jackie's friends, then everyone came back to the flat to party for awhile. Amber and I still hadn't talked about anything much so the distraction was good. It allowed us to be real with each other without having to get into anything serious.

One of Jackie's friends had some coke and Jackie sweetly explained that I didn't want it around us. The friend put it away. Someone else mentioned that the "vampire crew" was having a party after midnight and asked if we wanted to go check it out. I remembered, shuddered, and shook my head. Jackie laughed and loudly told everyone I had once been one of Angus's "victims". Surprised faces. I didn't look like the type.

"It was my second week in London," I said, giving Jackie a sideways glare, which she ignored.

"That explains it," said a woman with short, black hair. "Was he good?"

I looked away. "I don't know."

She giggled. "That means he was good. Did you do the group thing?"

"No. And how do you know there *was* a group thing?"

"Because the scary-looking woman with the long black hair is Mistress of the house. She'd have been the one who chose you. Angus is her lap dog."

Amber and I looked at each other. From the moment that woman had walked into the room I'd sensed a change in the energy, knew she was the boss. But I hadn't thought she'd *chosen* me. She'd pretended to not know who I was.

"Who is this woman anyway?" Amber asked.

Jackie lit a cigarette. "No one knows, honey. We call her Morticia behind her back. It's supposed to be her house, or whatever you want to call that place. She lets it look like Angus is in charge and he gets off on that."

"You know who was down there last week?" the raven-haired woman said to Jackie. "Sweet little Becca, locked away in the bondage room, as usual. What is the matter with that girl? I wonder if she shows up at work on Mondays all bruised up."

I shook my head. "Becca always looks like a librarian."

"Yeah, in a porno," someone else joked.

"Let's call her over here. Do you mind, Meagan?" They had all caught on to my name but I knew none of theirs.

I shrugged. "No phone up here and the offices are closed."

"Where's your cell, Ben?" The black haired woman asked. I took note of Ben. He handed her the phone and she called Becca.

"Becca, it's Sue." I took note of Sue. Two names down, two to go. "We're partying above your offices." She paused. "Well, don't be embarrassed. As if she cares that you're perverse. *She* did it with the vamps."

My face flushed. How did you maintain your position of authority when your employees knew your sex life?

Jackie laughed, a feminine little chuckle. "She didn't do

all of them, Sue. Just sexy little Angus."

Amber looked at me on the word sexy and Sue gave Jackie an impatient wave. "Okay," she said into the receiver. "Bye." She hung up. "You're in good company, Meagan. Becca did it with Angus *and* Morticia *and* some purple-headed Asian."

I swallowed back my revulsion. Amber must have thought we were all sick. Screwing vampires. *Sharing* them. Group sex. S&M. It turned my stomach that Becca and I had slept with the same strange man. In a roundabout way I had screwed my librarian employee. And she'd done it with the two women too. Another shudder.

"I don't like that Asian woman," I said. "She's freaking crazy."

"You know *her* too?" Ben asked.

Amber laughed. "She hissed at Meagan and nearly gave her a heart attack."

The room broke into hysterics and I shot her a look. Was nothing private?

"That Asian chick is always the cat," Sue said. "She just showed up one night…"

"The night you were there," Jackie interjected.

"…and she's been a cat ever since."

Amber was fascinated. "Let's go to this party," she said to me. "Come on, I gotta see this."

I shook my head. "*You* go. I'm never going back there again."

I went. I don't know how it happened but the next thing I knew our little party was on its way to a bigger, freakier one. We piled into two cabs. Amber, Jackie, Ben, and I in one, and Sue and the others in the one behind us. We were crunched in. Pressed against each other in the small backseat and I felt a hand stroking my hair. It better have been Amber's. We were too squeezed in to tell. I glanced at her and she smiled. It was her hand. The other sat on my thigh. I didn't move to take it. I stared out the window and watched the city pass by. Jackie told me to sit back. I was in the middle and blocking the flow of conversation. I sat back. Amber leaned into me like she was suddenly very tired and rested her head against my arm.

"That's so cute," Jackie said. "A pretty little lesbian picture."

I stiffened. "I'm not a lesbian."

Amber quickly turned away from me and looked out the window. I knew what she was thinking. She was thinking we were back to denial. She wanted to get it, but she just didn't. A part of her would always think I was deluding myself when I said such things.

"Fine," I snapped. "I'm gay. I'm the biggest dyke who ever lived."

Amber shot me a look. "Oh, you are not. But can't you at least go with bisexual?"

"Whatever."

The cab pulled up in front of the building.

"Watch Becca disappear," someone whispered as we stepped though the big wooden doors and entered the dark foyer. It was like a castle foyer, complete with a suit of armor in the corner.

We went inside and sure enough within five minutes Becca was gone.

Nothing about the place had changed. Same strange atmosphere. Same strange people. Dog chains and leather. Amber clung to my arm like she was sorry she'd wanted to come and the eerie music filled our ears. She spotted a well-known English model getting down to business in front of a pile of coke and nudged Jackie.

"Isn't that---?"

"Yes," Jackie said. "If only the general public knew about her particular predilections. What a scandal that would be."

Scandal, huh? I thought of Vicki Clump then drove away the thought. I would not ruin the life of someone I didn't even know. Maybe I should talk to Ted about getting rid of *The Watcher* altogether. Markham-Summers didn't need it anymore. With genuine shock, I realized I was going soft.

The Watcher had been good to us. It wasn't located in any celebrity-infested area, but we had our spies all over the world. It still surprised me how that worked. I supposed when you were good at your job, it didn't matter where you lived, you just took a lot of airplanes.

Being back in the vampire club made me nervous. Then I thought I wouldn't be drinking anything so my senses would be intact. Not like the last time. We grabbed a table by the platform in the corner and Amber pulled her chair very close to mine. She was freaked out by the place, the atmosphere, the S&M people, and her eyes kept darting around the room like she thought someone might attack us. I felt a small laugh tickle my ribs, as I remembered how smug she'd been when I'd first told her about this place. *I doubt anything you say could even make me blink an eye, Meagan.* Well she was blinking now.

Jackie lit the black candle on the table and Ben pulled out his coke. He took a snort off the back of his hand and offered some to us. I waved it away easily. Sue took a snort. The other two people we came with disappeared like Becca. Jackie waved away the coke too.

"No thanks, honey," she said. "I like my nose just fine."

"This table is full of prudes," Ben said.

"Get a job, Ben," Jackie said. The rest of us laughed. Amber relaxed.

Then I spotted them, or rather, they spotted me. Years had passed, but they looked exactly the same: Angus in his velvet top hat, holding his cane, and "Morticia" in her cat suit, staring at me with those cold red eyes. They could have grown dust for what little about them had changed. Angus's hair was longer now, that was the only difference. Messy dreadlocks now poked out from under the hat. He was still sexy. I nudged Amber. She looked over at them and nodded.

"He is hot," she admitted. "But I think she looks more stupid than scary."

"Not when you're half-naked and face to face with her," I said. My heart began to beat a little more quickly. Morticia terrified me and I got the feeling she knew it.

Jackie glanced over at them. "Look at the way they're looking at you, Meagan. They *remember*. Oh shit. Morticia's getting up."

I looked at her then quickly looked away. She had risen from Angus's lap, whispered something in his ear, and started coming toward us. I could feel her red eyes zeroing in like laser beams. My palms grew damp. I felt the urge to throw up and swallowed it back. Amber took a sip from the bottle of water she'd brought with her and watched Morticia approach as calmly as if she were watching this happen to someone else. Morticia reached our table, stopped in front of us, and stared at me.

"Look who's here," she said. "It's the woman who doesn't like to play." She leaned into my hair. "Change your mind, love?" She flashed her frightening fangs and I jumped. She laughed.

Amber stood up. "Keep your cat suit on, Elvira. She's with me."

Their eyes locked. Green on red. I didn't think Amber would lose. She was too calm, too focused. She placed a hand on my shoulder and continued to stare. She wasn't the slightest bit intimidated by this woman who could still frighten me whenever I saw those red eyes coming at me in my sleep.

Morticia looked Amber over appreciatively and gave an amused sneer. "You can join us too, sweetie. We'll have a little party upstairs."

Amber didn't know what to say to that. She thought her only function was to protect me. The others stared and I stood up and pushed in my chair. It was time to confront my fear. I stared into Morticia's red eyes and refused to flinch. She didn't budge either, just flashed her fangs again to intimidate me, but I tried to see what Amber saw, silliness.

"We never finished," she said to me. "Are you coming upstairs?"

"We never started," I said.

She stroked my face and I slapped away her hand. She sneered again. "Yeah, we can get rough if you want."

I saw red. What was with this "rough" shit? Her words angered me and the fear dissipated.

"You were Angus's failure," she said. "He doesn't like that. *I don't like it.* You cannot flirt with the darkness and then walk away as if it never happened. Angus tasted your blood. You are bound to him. I will taste your blood and you shall be bound to *me*. You shall be under *my* control."

Amber's eyes were wide with disbelief. They were frightening words, but I fought the impact they could have on me.

"I am not *bound* to anyone," I said.

"You give your blood too easily."

I thought I would strike her. Instead I said, "You people are sick. You're a person, Morticia, not some demon sent up from hell. Get a grip on yourself. *I've been* dead, alright, and believe me, there is no one even remotely like you there."

She flinched but didn't give up the act. "I should think not. My kind doesn't die at all."

I laughed at her. "Let me guess, you're six hundred years old, right? Seen many centuries, have you? You're seriously deluded. You need to seek professional help, because you're really fucked up." I took Amber's hand. "Let's go."

Morticia stepped in front of us, blocking our path, and again hitting me with the laser eyes. "You will not be welcomed back a third time."

"Well, now I'll have to kill myself," I mocked.

I said goodbye to Jackie, who was stunned by what she was witnessing, and Amber and I turned toward the door. Morticia came up behind us, grabbed my arm and spun me to face the large group. Amber stepped up to her but she placed a hand to Amber's chest, stopping her.

"Look at this woman's face," she said loudly, digging her nails into my arm. I yanked it away. "She is never to come in here again. Anyone who brings her in will be banished." She turned to face me. "You're out for good, love."

I shrugged. Amber and I left.

"I don't believe what just happened in there," Amber said in the cab on the way back to the flat.

"Now you know why I didn't want to go back. I was terrified she'd remember me, and the nutcase did."

Amber rubbed her eyes like she'd seen a dragon. "That woman really believes she's a vampire."

The cabby gave us a curious look in the rearview mirror and I told him to mind his own business. He dropped us off in front of the NB offices and we went upstairs. Amber was acting like everything was fine between us but I didn't feel fine. My anger had been drifting in and out all day. I thought I had forgiven her. Then I would think of her tearing off the ring and calling me a junkie and I'd be angry again. On the other hand she'd been willing to take on a vampiress who was twice her size and Amber was like me, we didn't get into physical fights with people. It wasn't in our natures to be violent and even if it were, we were small enough to get our asses kicked quite regularly. Not short –we were both about 5'7, but we were small-framed. And at least I knew some kickboxing. I didn't really need her to protect me.

I sighed. What was I even thinking? I was thirty years old. The question of whether or not I could beat someone up shouldn't even arise for me. It shouldn't arise for anyone, but particularly not a businesswoman in her thirties.

We entered the flat and the first thing I did was go to the stereo and pop in a Sarah McLachlan CD. Amber turned on the lamp by the couch and settled herself on the floor. I watched the hurt wash over her face as her mind focused on one thought.

"Why did you tell that woman you weren't bound to anyone?" She asked. Her eyes met mine and she flashed her ring at me. "You're my wife, remember?"

I looked away. I didn't answer her. The ring, it seemed, only meant something when she wanted it to.

"Meagan," she stressed. "You're my *wife*. We're bound to each other."

I sat on the floor beside her and twisted my own ring. "It's not real, Amber," I said quietly. "It's as much illusion as Morticia's belief that she's a vampire."

She got mad. "It *is* real. To *us*, it's real. It was real to you long before it even happened. You had that ring from your Gran and you believed in it. You got me to believe in it and you won't now tell me that any of this is fake. I love you."

I pulled my knees to my chest and rested my chin on top of them.

I felt the tears stinging the backs of my eyes. "You love me so much but you were leaving me. It doesn't matter that I'm not on drugs, because if I had been, you would have left me. You told Jenna you couldn't go through it with me again. That I betrayed you." The tears slipped down my cheeks and I felt a vulnerability I hadn't felt since childhood. "You would have walked out on me even though I wasn't mistreating you in any way."

She turned so that she was kneeling in front of me and locked her eyes on mine. "No, Meagan. I wouldn't have left. I was angry when I told Jenna that, but I couldn't leave you. You were the one who took off. You could have proven yourself innocent if you really wanted to but you didn't. *You* left. You said you'd never leave me again but look at where we are. I wasn't going anywhere. I thought maybe when you came home Adrian and I would have an intervention waiting."

I didn't believe her. I didn't want to be crying but I couldn't stop the tears. "When I came out of the coma you said, 'The world could tumble down around us and the sky could fall in our laps but I swear I will never give up on you.' And you were ready to give up."

Amber flinched. "I didn't say that to you when you came out of the coma, Meagan. I said it when you were *in* the coma."

It didn't matter. I'd stopped being surprised by these little flashes long ago. "Do you know how bad you hurt me? You tore off the ring and you called me a junkie."

"And then I broke into your office and took it back."

That pulled me from my self-pity and snapped me to attention quicker than anything else could have. "You broke in? Why didn't you use the key?"

She shrugged. "Couldn't find it. I shoved Cynthia's letter opener in the lock and got it to open. Don't worry though, I called a locksmith and Josh went down there to wait for him. They put a better lock on. Yours was too easy to get into. Jenna was going to slip the new keys under the apartment door on her way to work, today, I think."

"You could have just waited until I got home," I said.

"No. I had to have the ring. I wasn't coming here without it." She gave me one of her hard looks. "Now admit it's real."

Again I didn't answer.

"Admit it, Meagan."

"You'll never take if off again?" I sounded like a big baby but this was important.

"No." There was a spark of apology in her big green eyes.

I felt myself weakening. "Never? You promise?"

She stroked my face. "I promise."

I sighed. "I love you."

"Forgive me?"

"Always," I said, hugging her.

"And the ring?"

"It's as real as we are."

Satisfied, she wrapped herself around me. "Let's go home tomorrow, okay? It's too weird here."

I laughed. "What isn't weird to you?"

She didn't miss a beat. "Us."

That night I had the dream again. I was back in the Summerlands with the sweet smell of the forest around me, the lilacs in bloom. The scenery never changed, only the conversations. I wished the flowers were white daffodils and sat on my log and waited.

Victor appeared before me with his handsome, angelic face and radiant smile.

"The challenge nears, Meagan," he said, sitting down beside me.

"Are you going to be cryptic again, Victor?" He kept coming to me, but he wouldn't tell me what I was up against. I could handle a challenge, but I had to know what it was.

"That's my job," he said.

"A riddle then, right?"

Victor chuckled. "What should have been will be."

I pushed my bare feet through the dew-soaked moss in front of the log. "I don't understand."

"Soon you will," he said. "The two years in between have been to prepare you. You were not strong enough for this challenge before, so fate intervened on your behalf. The accident was no accident. And the events that followed were to strengthen you. To strengthen Amber."

"Then this is her challenge too?" I asked, surprised. This was the first I was hearing of Amber's involvement. In all the dreams and the worries they caused I assumed it was only about me, that she would be safe from it. Now I was scared.

Victor patted my hand. "You took the fall because you could. Amber became the guardian because *she* could. You were each given your duties, and though you've stumbled through them, you did not let them break you. Now it is almost time."

"Time for what?"

"Jenna knows. She won't tell you, but she knows what's coming. Remember I once told you Jenna knows things others do not?"

"Yes."

He nodded. "She knows this too. You think Jenna cannot tell a lie, but if you ask her she will deny knowing this because she is afraid of her vision. Afraid for the others involved."

I swallowed. "Others?" It grew bigger every second.

Victor stood. "It's coming, Meagan. Very soon."

"I'm scared," I said.

"You'll do fine. Both of you. The much needed growth has happened and the circle is almost complete."

Victor disappeared. I didn't bother calling him because I knew he wouldn't come back. He had said all he was going to say.

Fear gripped my heart. *It's almost here. Oh God, it's almost here.*

I woke up screaming.

Chapter 23

Amber didn't sleep on the plane. She spent the entire flight home asking me questions. I had awakened screaming, told her to grab her things, and we'd headed for the airport, lucky enough to catch two seats on a flight that was departing Heathrow in forty-five minutes.

She wanted to know if I had any idea what the challenge might be. What did Jenna have to do with it? Who were the others? What did it mean that I had taken the fall and she was the guardian?

I told her I didn't know. We dissected the dream the entire flight home and repeatedly came up blank. We skipped the meals, waved away the complimentary champagne and kept talking it through. It was coming down like lightning, I felt, all at once.

Why now? Because Amber and I had nearly ended? Because Gwynne's stunt had pushed us to the edge but we had come back? I'd been waiting two years for this challenge. I hadn't known it when I was on drugs but it was two years nonetheless. In the past months I'd been trying to figure it out. Then I'd given up. Now it was almost here.

"I took the fall because I could handle it," I said, thinking out loud. "You became the guardian because you could handle that. They've been preparing us."

"Who's they?"

"I don't know. Fate? The thing is, why could I handle the fall? I think maybe it was because I would more readily believe in things you wouldn't. I already believed in some pretty strange stuff, thanks to Jenna and my Gran, so it makes sense that I would believe in my dreams and what they were telling me. You might not. You're pragmatic. Logical. I don't know what 'guardian' means, but I'm assuming it has something to do with the way you looked out for me and kept me from slipping over the edge. That was your duty. I feel like I've been some sort of information receptor and you're the one who was supposed to put the pieces together. Then again, we haven't put anything together, have we? So maybe I'm wrong, but do you remember what Jenna once said about the magnets?"

Amber nodded. "The positive and negative polarities. How you needed them both to make the magnets fit."

"Right. She said that was us. It makes sense to me now. You and I would handle a challenge in different ways. I would go with my instinct and you would go with you brilliant mind. Perhaps we need both. Whatever this challenge is, I'm certain now we're meant to face it together."

She squeezed my hand reassuringly. "And we will."

I looked down at our hands. "I'm gonna go for blood work tomorrow, Amber. Maybe you think Gwynne's poem was a fluke or that I wrote it myself. I want you to know without a doubt that I am not on drugs."

"I don't want you to do that," she said.

"Why not?"

Another squeeze. "Because I want *you* to know I believe you without the blood work."

"Thank you. God, I'm scared right now."

"Me too."

When the plane touched down we darted through the airport and Amber reminded me we had to grab our bags. I wasn't thinking straight. I wanted to get to Jenna and force her to tell me what she knew. A quick stop at the baggage claim and we were racing for the airport parking lot, where I'd parked the Mercedes the week before.

"What time is it?" I asked, jumping behind the wheel.

"7:36."

"Good, Jenna's yoga class starts at eight. She'll be across the street at the center."

We sped across town and Amber told me to slow down, that I was going to get us killed.

"Unless the challenge is for us to die together," I said, "that's not going to happen."

We pulled up in front of the center five minutes before Jenna's class was to begin and took the stairs to the second level two at a time. Amber was running out of steam and again told me to slow down. I told her she better start kickboxing with me because she was sadly out of shape. She laughed, took a breath, and raced me to the top of the stairs. I still won.

Jenna stood at the top of the landing, greeting her students in front of a door marked, *Yoga Rm 3.*

"Hey," she said, smiling when she saw us. "You guys just get back?"

"Just got off the plane," Amber said, catching her breath.

I didn't waste time with pleasantries. "What's our challenge, Jenna?"

She gave a little jump as if I'd struck her but she recovered quickly. "What do you mean?"

I wasn't buying it. "You know what we're up against, Jenna. I know you do."

She fiddled with the drawstring on the front of her sweatpants and looked nervous. "I don't know what you're talking about. I gotta go. I have a class to teach."

She wasn't going anywhere. I poked my head in the door and addressed the dozen students. "Class is cancelled. Go home."

Amber smirked.

"Meagan, you can't just send away my students."

Jenna poked her head in the door. "Stay where you are, everyone. We're just gonna start a few minutes late tonight."

"Go home," I said again.

"Stop that," Jenna said. Amber thought it was funny.

I started pacing the carpeted hallway. Amber placed a hand on my arm and stopped me.

"As you can see, Jenna," she said. "she's freaking out. She's terrified. She had a dream last night that told her the challenge was coming and that you knew what it was but that you'd lie about it."

"I don't lie," Jenna said stiffly.

I felt the frown in my forehead. "Why did you come to London, Jenna? You were desperate to get Amber and me together again because you know this is her challenge too."

"I don't know what you're talking about," she denied.

"Don't screw with me, Jenna. You don't fly. I should have known something was up then. You've done it three times in your life. Once for your little Ethiopian excursion, once to London when Ken and I got engaged, and then again a few days ago. You're afraid of airplanes but something scared you more and it scared you so bad you wouldn't let things wait until I got home. You were determined to bring Amber to me and determined to get us back together. Now you're going to tell me what we're up against, or I swear to God I will hound you every minute of every day. And you know damn well I'll do it too."

Her eyes widened in fear. "I said I don't know anything!" She went in her classroom and slammed the door.

"She knows," I said, pacing the hallway again. "She knows what we're up against and she won't tell us."

"Okay, honey," Amber said soothingly. "Let's just go home. Let Jenna teach her class and you can try again later."

I didn't see how I had much of a choice so I relented. I went home with Amber, who then convinced me to give Jenna the night to think about it.

The next morning I woke up and called Jenna. Again she denied knowing anything. I kept calling until she burst into tears on the phone, told me to leave her alone, and hung up on me. That was twice now I'd made Jenna cry, and all in the span of a few days. Amber pleaded with me to stop. She said I was scaring Jenna more. I didn't care. Jenna knew what was going to happen to us and she wouldn't tell me. I had seen the fear on her face the night before. She didn't want to believe in whatever premonition she was having because she was afraid for the others, but who were the others?

I stopped calling for a few hours, giving her time to think. When I called back later my brother coolly informed me that Jenna had taken Sammy to visit his grandparents in Boston. I dropped the phone. She had gotten on another flight! Took her son and abandoned us!

Amber picked up the phone, spoke to Josh for a few minutes, and hung up.

"Josh said Jenna wanted him to tell us that she was sorry but she couldn't deal with this right now. She'll call us in six days. He doesn't know what's going on. He thinks we're fighting with her and he wanted to know why you're making her cry."

"Oh, God," I rocked back and forth on the couch. "She deserted us, Amber. How could she do that? How could she run out on us like that?"

Amber came up to me and tucked a strand of hair behind my ear. "Honey, Jenna isn't a part of us. We're not a threesome, she's our friend. And she's scared right now. You said it yourself, whatever it is that's coming, we were meant to face it together, and we will. We don't need Jenna. She knows that. If she thought we needed her she wouldn't have left."

"But she knows, Amber. And whatever is going to happen it's going to happen within the next six days."

Amber frowned. "Why?"

I kept rocking. "Because she said she'll call in six days. That means she's gonna call when it's over. Not only does she know what's going to happen she even knows *when.*"

I got myself together and reached for the phone. "Grab a bag. We're going to Boston."

Amber took the phone from my hand and placed it back on the table. "No, baby, we're gonna stay right here and deal with this."

My eyes narrowed. "What did you just call me?" She knew how I felt about that word and guiltily looked away. My temper eased as quickly as it flared. "Never mind. Listen, we can't just sit here waiting for disaster to strike."

"Meagan, we have to. We'll face it alone and we'll face it together. Don't fall apart on me, alright? That's not you. Right now, we need for you to be as calculating and detached as I know you can be. Call on your traits, Meagan. You know how to disconnect, so do it because we need to stay level-headed. And who knows, maybe the challenge is a good one."

That got me to laugh. I wrapped my arms around her neck. "I see you're already calling on your traits, huh, my little optimist?"

But the fact was I *could* disconnect. When I had to, I could throw up the wall and keep the storm behind it. Long ago the trait had distressed Amber, but now she was calling it out like a kid playing Red Rover, and I could see the human chain in my mind. Kids holding hands, stretched across the playground, and Amber on the other side calling, "Red rover, red rover, we call Meagan Summers and her cool reserve over". If I could break through the chain of arms, I could make it safely to the other side where sanity awaited me.

I took a breath, prepared myself, and charged at the

line. Amber smiled as she watched me win the small battle in my head and within seconds I was back from the edge.

"Better now?" she asked.

I smiled back at her. "I always did like Red Rover."

"Huh?"

"Mind games. It's how I disconnect."

Laughing, she hugged me. "You'll have to teach me that someday. Does this mean I get to be the obligatory basket case?"

"If you want."

"I don't want."

"Good. Then I guess there's nothing to do now but wait."

She dropped down on the couch and pulled me with her. "How do you want to fill the time?" A flirtatious wink.

I chuckled, "And Ken used to say *I* had a one-track mind. Obviously, he never knew you very well."

"Hey, I've been deprived. You've been mad at me. And please, don't ever again tell me you wanted sex with Ken all the time."

"I didn't really," I admitted. "Have you ever given your body because you couldn't fully give your heart?"

"Yes." She was thinking of Gwynne.

I drove away the nasty pictures my own mind created. "Then you know. As for Jenna," I started thinking of how she'd betrayed us, "this better be big enough to warrant her betrayal. I have to figure out *who* the others are."

Amber sighed. "I guess I'm not getting laid for another six days then, huh?"

I broke out laughing. "Why? I'm multi-functional."

"No doubt about that." She jumped on top of me.

Later, I called Ted and left a message on his voice mail saying I was back from London and business was fine, but that I might not be in for a few more days. I wasn't sure I wanted to go anywhere just yet. Maybe after I figured things out.

I went to take a shower and when I returned Amber was grabbing her purse from the coat rack.

"I ordered some food from Jade Gardens," she said. "I'm just gonna run down and pick it up."

I rubbed my hair with a towel and the soft curls sprang

to life. "Not without me, you're not. The last time one of us went out for Chinese, the other almost died. For the next six days you and I are joined at the hip. Give me five minutes."

Amber smiled and waited by the door while I ran into the bedroom and threw on some clothes. I ran back to the bathroom.

"Come on, Meagan," she complained. "We're just going to the corner."

I swiped a mascara wand across my lashes. "Okay, just let me dry my hair."

"The food is going to get cold. I'll just run---"

I came out of the bathroom. "Okay, I'll go with wet hair. Maybe the challenge will be not to catch a cold."

She laughed at me. "It's eighty-five degrees out there. You're not gonna catch a cold. Let's go."

We left the building and walked down to the corner, where we ran into Danielle.

"Hey," I said. "What are you doing here?"

She shrugged. "I was on my way to see you. Thought I'd bring over some Chinese and apologize."

"Apologize for what?"

"*Hello*. For letting Amber convince me you were back on drugs."

Amber leaned against the brick building. "I'm sorry, Danny. It was a misunderstanding."

"Duh. I know that now." She turned to me. "You should have seen what was going on over here, everyone was freaking out. Mom was having a complete spazz. Especially after you told her off." Her forehead puckered and she tilted her head at me. "Wet hair. You're gonna catch a cold."

Amber howled with laughter. "What kind of a paranoid house did the two of you grow up in? Were you allowed to go swimming?"

Danny gave her a strange look. "Of course. We just weren't allowed to run out and play after our baths. So, are you guys gonna be home for awhile?"

I ran my fingers through my damp hair. "Yeah, we're just picking up some food. Did you order anything yet?"

"Not yet. You guys go back. I'll order something and grab your order too."

We turned to leave.

"Hey, wait," Danny grabbed my arm. "What did you do to Jenna? Josh said she cried all day then said she had to get away from you."

"It's complicated, Danny."

"Well, Josh isn't happy."

"I don't really care. Can you do me a favor? If I give you the number to Jenna's parents' house in Boston, could you call her? I know she won't accept any calls from me. Just tell her---" I looked at Amber. "Tell her I'm sorry."

Danielle shrugged and went in the restaurant. Amber and I walked home.

"You know that really gets under my skin," she said, when we were back in the apartment. "Jenna pisses you off and *you apologize to her*. When I piss you off, you tell *me* to move out."

I was amused. "That's because I'm in love with Jenna," I teased.

"You're funny. I never should have told you that."

I stuck my hands in the front pockets of my shorts and stretched my torso. "You know this is different. I lost it on Jenna. Three times. I made her cry twice. She deserves an apology. It's harder to apologize to you because you can hurt me so much deeper. When you hurt me, I feel like a part of me gets torn away. The part of me that's you. I don't lose anything of myself to Jenna and that makes it easier to get over things."

"You can talk your way out of anything, can't you?" she said, smiling.

I cocked my head at her. "Am I out of it, Amber?"

"You know you are."

"I know. You can't stay mad at me any longer than I can stay mad at you. Why do you suppose that is?"

"Because we're soul mates?"

"Yep. Once you were my husband, now you're my wife. It seems we can't even reincarnate without each other."

"I love how you always get to be the woman," she joked.

"Yeah, and you always get the eyes."

"I wanna marry you."

"We are married."

"For real, I mean. A ceremony."

I smirked. "This isn't real?" My eyes dared her to deny it the way hers had done to me days earlier.

Glancing down at her ring, she laughed. "It's real. It's as real as we are."

"So then we are---?"

"Married," she said agreeably. "We're married."

"There you go."

Danny came back with the food and we gathered around the table in the kitchen, opening cartons and passing them to each other. General Tso's chicken, fried rice, vegetable stir-fry—there was nothing quite like Chinese when you were stressed, which was probably why we ate it so often. Danielle kept bugging me to know what happened with Jenna and I told her the full story.

"Geez," she said, when I had finished my tale, "you'd think Jenna wouldn't get so freaked out by weird stuff, I mean she *is* Jenna."

"Little Miss New Age," I agreed, laughing. Then I thought I'd have some fun with Amber and turned to her and asked "What religion are you?" I knew. I knew everything about Amber.

"I was born Catholic."

"So, hell awaits you too. I guess we'll be there together. What nationality are you?" I knew that also, I just wanted to see how she'd react.

"I'm fucking Irish too, Meagan. Don't you know anything about me?"

I smirked. That was the reaction I expected. "Here's what I know: you're not only Irish, you're also English, German and Scottish. You broke your arm when you fell off your bike when you were five. At eighteen you declined scholarships to not one, but *three*, Ivy League schools because you thought they were pretentious. How am I doing?"

She smirked back. "Pretty good. Anything else?"

I thought about the phone call I had received that morning, the one I had forgotten to tell Amber about under the day's stress. The voice on the other end had said some things about Amber I didn't like but I'd snapped out of my anger quickly and came to my senses before I could snap.

"Yes," I said, giving her a slow once-over. "I also know that five days ago you fucked Gwynne."

Danny shot Amber a hateful look and Amber's mouth fell open.

"I did not!" she screeched.

I smirked again. Danny caught it, thought I must be teasing Amber, and went back to eating.

"Gwynne called when you were in the shower this morning," I said. "She wanted to ask me how she tasted on your mouth."

Danielle gagged on her chop suey and spit it on her plate. "Jesus, Meagan. Are you trying to make me puke?"

"I didn't do it!" Amber shrieked. She shot to her feet. There was stark terror in her eyes. "I swear to you, Meagan, I would never do that. I called Gwynne and threatened her when you faxed me the poem. That's it!"

"I know," I said easily, watching the fear ebb and flow on her face. "She almost got me, but then I remembered Clump had been watching her and it would have been impossible for the two of you to get together without me knowing. I told Gwynne I didn't buy a word of it and that she better give up her little games because I knew some things about her that would make her very sorry indeed. She wanted to know what I knew but I hung up on her. She hasn't called back since."

Amber fell in her chair, relieved. "Thank God for Vicki Clump. If it wasn't for her you might have believed that and I'd have no way to disprove it. God, Meagan, I'm really sorry about the coke. Now I know how it feels to be accused of something you're not doing. How could I have ever proven to you it didn't happen?"

I shrugged. She really didn't know how it felt because her being accused hadn't lasted more than a minute and I hadn't thought the worst of her like she had of me. Of course, Gwynne didn't cough up the doctored proof for me like she had for Amber. Amber had been given a vial; I had only been given words.

"You couldn't have proved it," Danielle said. "And Meagan, don't say things like that when I have food in my mouth."

I laughed. "Pretty gross, huh? I almost puked when she

said it to me."

"The mere thought of it makes me want to puke," Amber said.

Danny threw down her fork. "Can we stop talking about puking and eat?"

Danny left after supper and I went back to thinking. I sat at the kitchen table with a notepad and a pen and wrote a long list of people I knew, trying to find a connection. These were the only *others* I had but nothing jumped out at me. I asked Amber to do the same and we compared lists. Scratched off the names of people who weren't very important to us, or who didn't seem deep enough in our circle to make sense. In the end we were left with a small group: my parents, her parents, my siblings, Sammy Jacob, Adrian, and Zeppo. These were the people we associated with most frequently.

I drew up a list of potential problems and lined them up beside the names. Jenna's family was out of the mix. She wouldn't have run to her parents if Sammy or Josh were in danger. Same thing for Amber and me. We weren't the ones who were in danger either. That narrowed things down.

Amber stared at my list.

Adrian, drugs. Danielle, pregnant. Our parents, death. Jacob, leukemia. Zeppo, AIDS.

She laughed and asked me why I came up with these particular scenarios, and how I thought any of those things, other than perhaps the deaths, would be our challenge.

"You're right." I crumpled the page in frustration. None of those things felt close to being right. I was just trying to occupy my mind. At one in the morning she finally convinced me we should go to bed.

"Maybe you should go into work tomorrow," she said, as we undressed.

"Maybe."

We fell into bed and slept.

The next morning I called Danielle to ask if she had spoken to Jenna. She said yes and that Jenna accepted my apology and promised to call soon.

"She said something strange, Meagan."

I gripped the phone. "What's that?"

"She said it comes full circle and that you might enjoy

the challenge in the end, but if she's right the bad stuff has to come first, and she can't be in town when it happens."

"Why not?" I asked.

"Don't know. She sounded confused."

"How so?"

I heard Danny shift the phone to her other ear. "She said she didn't want to see the bad stuff. When you came back the other day she started getting flashes of the bad and that's why she had to get away. You know Jenna, she just can't handle to see any suffering."

"She still won't talk to me, will she?"

"Not until it blows over."

"Shit."

Danny and I hung up. I didn't understand Jenna's refusal to tell me what she knew. Then I thought Jenna might be afraid that if she said it out loud whatever was to come would be her fault. That sounded like Jenna. She didn't want anything to be her fault. She couldn't handle to see any suffering, but she had once spent three months in Ethiopia. She made less sense to me sometimes than I did to Amber.

"Maybe she can't handle it when it's a suffering she knows she can't do anything about," Amber suggested.

"But she *can* do something about it. If she knows someone's going to get hurt she can try to prevent it."

Amber arched an eyebrow. "Jenna try to prevent fate from taking its course?"

Again she was right. Jenna didn't intervene when she thought fate was involved. She would consider it bad karma and she would believe that fate would only find another way of accomplishing its task, because when fate had a plan, nothing could truly stop it. She would only be an obstacle and that might make it angry. Such a wonderfully strange person she was, but damn, how she pissed me off.

In the afternoon Amber and I went down to the office where we both apologized to Cynthia and Ted for our behavior the week before, and gave Cynthia a huge vase of roses. She loved flowers. She placed them on the corner of her desk and I knew she would smile at them all day.

Ted said that as long as Amber was there, would she mind talking some business? Amber shrugged and followed him into his office. Cynthia handed me a stack of messages and said Todd Garrison had called that morning and wanted to know if we were available for dinner. I poked my head in Ted's door and asked Amber. Then I went in my office and closed the door. The mess was gone. The broken bits of ceramic were gone and I thought Amber must have cleaned it.

Ten minutes later Cynthia was buzzing me on the intercom.

"Meagan, Mr. Faigan is here to see you."

Mr. Faigan? Cynthia knew Ken. She'd met him several times in London and they were friendly, yet she now chose to address him like a stranger. Odd.

"Okay, Cynthia. Send him in. Is Amber still in with Ted?"

Ken strolled through the door.

"Yes, shall I call her?" Cynthia said.

I looked up at Ken. "No. If she comes out, just tell her it's okay to come in here."

"Okay." The intercom cut out.

Ken stepped up to my desk with sincere brown eyes that said he was here about Gwynne. He looked good in a blue windbreaker and loose-fitting faded blue jeans. He looked like he was going sailing. His sandy brown hair looked as soft as ever and reminded me of what it had felt like between my fingers. Ken had great hair. Floppy. Like he was part pediatrician, part surfer.

"I've come to appeal to your sense of decency," he said kindly. "I've let this go on too long."

"*My* sense of decency?" I was incredulous.

He sat in the chair opposite me. "Come on, Meagan. If you can't publish Gwynne's book right now, at least sell her back the rights."

He still believed in innocence. My ex-husband sat across from me and the look on his face told me he knew nothing about what was really going on. He didn't know that I had done it on purpose. He didn't know about the tape recorder or the coke or the phone call. He definitely didn't know about Gwynne's cheating. He believed I really wanted to publish Gwynne's book, eventually, and he believed Gwynne was hurt and somewhat victimized by my delay. He didn't know his fiancée and I felt bad for him. He was such a nice guy and he was destined to repeatedly get hurt because he always closed his eyes to the worst in people. I sighed. Poor Ken. He really was a life-long victim. But that didn't mean I had to drop my guard either.

"I'll tell you something, Ken," I said, leaning back in my leather chair. I knew the key to a successful lie was to throw in some truth so I went for it. "I wanted to publish Gwynne's book and it was a financial problem that caused the delay, but with the way she's been behaving lately—I won't. And I also won't sell her back the rights."

"She's talked to a lawyer, Meagan."

"Good for her."

His face puckered in thought and a few tiny lines appeared around his eyes. "And what do you mean by the ways she's been behaving?"

I picked the letter opener off my desk and ran its dragon head across my palm, debating my answer. I decided I didn't want to be the one to hurt him.

"It doesn't matter, Ken. All I can say is if I were you, I'd get away from that woman as fast as I could. She's not who you think she is. I'm sorry about that, because I only wanted happiness for you."

"Why? What has she done?" He asked suspiciously.

I didn't answer. Amber strolled through the door.

"Meagan, what has she done?"

Again, I didn't say anything. Amber sat on the corner of my desk and looked at me, then at Ken. "I'll tell you what that little bitch has done," she said.

I shook my head at her. "Let it go, Amber. Gwynne's not our concern right now."

Ken stood up to confront me properly. "What the hell is going on?" He was too easy to corrupt, which meant he'd been having his own doubts about his fiancée.

I stood to meet his gaze. "Don't worry about it, Ken, I'm handling it."

"Handling what?"

"Ask Gwynne, not me. And tell her if she wants to sue me, then she better prepare for the battle of her life. You once told Seamus I don't lose well. I still don't." I smiled at Amber and she smiled back. "In fact, these days I rarely lose at all. As for you, well it's none of my business, but I'd get rid of the decorator. She takes pleasure in beautifying external things because on the inside she's very ugly. Go find someone better. I told you this that day in the hospital and now I'm only surer of it. For your own sake, Ken, because I'll always care about you, I'm telling you, she is not the one."

He was dismissed. He didn't put up a fight about it and something in his expression told me he had already experienced some of Gwynne's ugliness for himself. He turned on his heel, said a curt goodbye, and left.

"So, I guess we're going to court," Amber said. I liked that she had made it a team event. We were in this together even though she'd never asked to be.

I waved away her words. "It'll never get that far."

Chapter 24

Jade and Todd Garrison lived in a middle class section of town, in a modest but friendly neighborhood. It was the low end of the middle class, an area where small brick and stucco houses lined the streets, stacked up so close that neighbors could open their windows and talk to each other without ever leaving their own kitchen tables. Some of the houses were so close they could probably even hand things to each other across the small patches of space that separated the windows. I thought I could never buy a house that sat so close to another, it would make me claustrophobic and I couldn't handle the lack of privacy. I liked living in the city, where the world disappeared behind a close apartment door, or in private neighborhoods like the one Ken and I had lived in, where trees blocked the view of your neighbors' houses and no one sat on their porches at night talking. A place where you knew your neighbor by first name only and never said more than hello as you passed him cutting his grass on your way to your car. A wave or a nod was even better. Polite but distant.

The Garrison's neighborhood was different. Even as we pulled up at seven in the evening I could see the people beginning to gather on their porches with their cigarettes and their beer while their children played ball hockey or jumped rope in the street. They watched the black Mercedes pull up to the Garrison's driveway, and come to a stop behind Todd's red Harley, and Jade's white Grand Am. They watched the two women get out carrying wine, pop, salad and a couple of plastic bags. Jade and Todd had invited us for a barbeque.

We walked down the narrow driveway and the front door swung open. Zoe skipped out in a little yellow sundress with her pretty brown hair tied in a braid at the back of her neck.

"Did you bring Sammy?" she asked excitedly. She'd had a crush on my nephew ever since the day I babysat them together.

I shifted the salad to my other hand. "Sorry, Zoe.

Sammy's visiting his grandparents."

"Oh." A little heartbroken. She got over it. "We're having a barbeque in the backyard," she announced, taking my hand. "Come on." She pulled me behind her and Amber laughed.

"Want a present, Zoe?" I asked.

She stopped in her tracks. "A present?"

"Mm-hmm. Did you lose something today?"

She kicked a stone with her sandal and it shot across the pavement. "Doggy ate my crayons."

I nodded. When I'd spoken with Jade earlier to ask what we should bring, I could hear Zoe crying in the background. Jade said we didn't have to bring anything and asked Zoe to please stop crying. I asked her what the problem was and she said Zoe had been coloring on the front porch when the neighbor's dog came over and ate her crayons. She hadn't stopped crying since and Jade was reaching the end of her patience.

I handed Zoe one of the plastic bags and she dove in.

"Crayons!" she yelled, happily. "And a coloring book!"

Amber reached into one of the bags she was carrying. "This too." She handed Zoe a tiny pair of pink plastic sunglasses with a white plastic flower affixed to the center of the frames and Zoe squealed with joy.

I didn't care for the sunglasses. Amber had picked them up while we were in the grocery store and I'd shaken my head and told her if she wanted to buy Zoe sunglasses so badly we could stop at the mall and pick her up a pair of Calvin Kleins or Ralph Laurens. She'd laughed at me and said it was ridiculous to buy designer sunglasses for a child.

"What goes through your head sometimes?" she'd said, throwing the sunglasses in our cart. "She'll love these."

"*I* don't like them."

"Do *you* have to wear them? Designer shades! They probably wouldn't even fit her face."

"Then let's get her something from The Gap, at least."

Amber was stubborn. "We're getting her these. God, if you hadn't lost your baby she probably would have come out of you wearing Nike sneakers, Osh Kosh overalls, and you would have popped a fourteen-karat gold soother in her mouth." She chuckled, not realizing her words had hurt me.

"Fuck you," I hissed, and stalked away from her.

"Shit!" She came up behind me. "You know I didn't mean anything by that. I was just teasing you."

"You think teasing about me my dead baby is funny?" I whipped a box of chamomile tea in our cart across the aisle.

"No, it's not funny. It was a stupid thing to say."

"Okay."

"*Okay?*" She was surprised I was willing to let it go so easily.

I pictured the image she'd described; the little baby decked out in brand-name attire, and I couldn't help laughing. "So, it's a little funny" I said. "But you forgot one thing."

"What's that?"

"She would have looked up at me and said 'Money.'"

Amber tilted her head. "Mummy?"

"*Money.* Any kid can say mummy."

"Right out of the womb, huh?" she teased.

"Let's just pay for your ugly-ass sunglasses and go."

"What's that word again?" Zoe asked now, her little face contorting in thought.

I shrugged.

"Mommy makes me say it and it's good." She broke out in a grin. "Thank you. I'm apost to know that myself."

We laughed.

Jade appeared on the porch, pregnant stomach coming up first. She shook her fingers through her long, black hair and frowned at us. "I told you not to bring anything."

We stepped on the porch.

"Look at you," I said, rubbing her stomach.

Jade gave a little jump. "Oh, this baby has been kicking me all day. Wanna feel?" She guided my hand to the side of her abdomen and I felt a small thump-thump coming from under her shirt.

"Feel this, Amber."

Amber stepped forward and Jade guided her hand to the same spot.

Amber smiled at the thump. "Does it hurt?"

"Nah, it just gets annoying after a while," Jade said. "Todd loves it. He starts talking to my stomach every time the baby kicks."

"When's your due date?" I asked, following her through the front door and down a dark hallway that seemed to stretch out the length of the lower level. There was a staircase on the left with a thick brown banister and a living room on the right that housed old but clean furniture. We passed the room and continued down the hall to a sunlit kitchen.

"Two weeks," Jade said, leading Amber and me into the yellow kitchen with ancient green appliances and cheesy vinyl chairs situated around an imitation wood table. It wasn't pretty, but again it was clean.

I thought Jade and Todd lived somewhat like teenagers. Or like bikers, but I didn't see much difference between the two. Old furniture, big stereo, cheap pictures on the walls like the mirrored Budweiser frames you won at a carnival. The kitchen clock was huge, shaped like a faint brown star with an off-white face and brown roman numerals. It was the ugliest clock I'd ever seen. The kitchen curtains were yellow, to match the walls, with orange and green flowers on them, and they lapped in the breeze that wafted in with the smell of barbeque.

Jade poked her head out of the window. "They're here Todd," she yelled at the backyard. "We'll be out in a few minutes."

Amber and I helped Jade carry out the food she'd prepared while Zoe scurried around our feet, telling her mother about her presents and showing off her new sunglasses. Amber smirked at me. She loved being right. I laughed.

"You didn't have to do that," Jade said as we stepped out the screen door to the back and began arranging the food on a picnic table that was covered with a red and white checkered cloth. "Is the meat almost ready, Todd?"

Todd waved his tongs at us. "Just about. We've got burgers, sausage, hot dogs, and ribs."

"Wow," Amber said. "That's a lot of food."

Jade giggled. "We forgot to ask what you like."

Todd stacked the meat on an oblong platter and brought it to the table. "I've got something for you, too," he said, grinning at me.

"You finished the book?"

"Yep. I'll give you the manuscript before you leave."

Jade looked up at him adoringly and he wrapped his thick arms around her waist. "Okay everyone, dig in."

Amber saw my hesitation about the meat and gave me the "do it" eyes. I shrugged and grabbed a burger because it seemed the least "meaty". I could cover it with condiments and tomato and lettuce and it wouldn't stick in my throat the way a steak would. Thank God there was none of that.

Jade ate like there was a small army growing in her stomach and Todd matched her. Amber had a burger and Zoe had one hot dog.

"You're eating more," Todd told her. "Try a piece of sausage."

She shook her little head. "No Daddy, it chokes me."

I coughed on my water and nearly spat it out. It was the same thing I used to say to my father. "Don't want any meat Daddy, it chokes me."

"What's the matter with you?" Todd asked, nodding at me.

"N-Nothing." I cleared my throat. "Water just went down the wrong way."

Amber gave me a strange look and I wondered if she'd caught the similarity. If she had, she wasn't going to mention it because the last thing she would want to do was encourage my strange behavior. She knew how my mind worked and she probably even knew what I was thinking as I peered at the family before us, trying to figure out how they fit the picture. They didn't. I didn't know them well enough for them to be a part of the challenge. We were friends but we didn't exactly share a history. Unless you counted coma time but that seemed to have little to do with now. We went back to eating, but not before Amber gave me what looked like a warning look.

Even if I believed they were the challenge, what did she think I would do? Start jumping up and down, screaming about how the Garrisons were a part of some grand scheme fate had planned for us? It didn't even feel right. The meat thing was just a coincidence, like the smile. Didn't Sammy have my nose? Josh's eyes, Jenna's lips, my father's teeth and Danielle's mannerisms? Sammy wasn't mine either but he shared my sense of humor and he was already showing the signs of a few auburn streaks pulling up through his brown hair. Some of that was genetics but genetics couldn't explain the similarities between Amber and Sammy. He talked like her. Made his mother buy him a pair of work boots because he thought they looked like the Doc Martens Amber always wore, and he would never let anyone tie them because he wanted the dangling bootlaces, just like Auntie Am always had. It made her laugh.

No, the Garrisons weren't a part of this, because if they were, I would have felt it right away. Jenna felt things. Sometimes I did too, and my instincts weren't saying anything much right now. Only that I wished Amber would quit giving me those peculiar looks.

Jade put Zoe to bed after dinner and promised her she could color on the porch again in the morning. Amber and I helped Jade clean and Todd started a small bonfire in the backyard. He placed candles on the now bare picnic table and called us back outside. Without the tablecloth the picnic table was a sight to behold. All through dinner I was wondering why I felt tiny grooves and indentations beneath my elbows and I now saw why, the picnic table was carved with names and dates and symbols. Todd explained that he and Jade had started letting friends carve their names into the table when they used to party a lot. The table had followed them from house to house, as they had once moved around a lot, and no one had carved into it in a very long time. He produced two jackknives from his pocket and handed them to Amber and me.

"Carve whatever you want," he said. Jade nodded encouragingly. This was special to them.

Todd cracked open a can of beer. Amber and I shrugged at each other and went to work. The conversation flowed as she carved her name and I carved mine. It seemed to take forever, prying up those little slivers of wood. When we were done Amber made me switch seats with her and she carved a little butterfly at the end of my name.

Todd stretched over the table to have a look. "Damn, now that's some handy work."

Amber laughed. "We used to do this in college. There were a few picnic tables at the back of the school." She shrugged.

I mock groaned. "You need to get over the college thing now. You're thirty years old."

"I am not."

"Excuse me. You're twenty-nine years, eleven months and ten days."

"That's better."

"You're such a child."

"Then I guess that makes you a pedophile, doesn't it?"

"Are you sick?" I turned to Todd and Jade who couldn't stop laughing. "You see what I have to deal with?"

"You?" Amber mocked. "What about me? I have to talk you down from a ledge every time you have a birthday."

"You're full of shit."

"Don't swear."

"Zoe's in bed."

"So?"

"So I can say fuck you without remorse."

"Are you saying fuck you?"

I smirked. "Yes, I believe I am."

"And there you go, being a big tease again."

"That's not sexual, that's offensive."

"I don't get offended easily. To me, the f-word is just one big tease coming out of your mouth. Especially when you're sitting here in your black hip-huggers, and your little black camisole, with your Gucci shades on top of your head, stroking your fingers through your hair when you know that turns me on." She shook her head. "The question is, what are you going to do about it?"

"I'm gonna tell you to be quiet because there are other people out here besides the two of us."

"Oh no," Jade said, smiling, "don't pull us into this. This is your own twisted little foreplay game."

I laughed. "Oh, so you want to talk about sex, do you?"

Jade pulled back her long hair and piled it on the top of her head. "Sure, what do you got?"

Amber groaned. "Believe me, Jade, you don't want to get her started. She'll say things that would make your head spin."

"I learned it from you," I said.

"Learned what from me? Sex?"

"Yeah," I said sarcastically. "I was a virgin when we met."

"You were a slut."

Jade buried her face in Todd's arm and rocked with laughter. Todd grinned.

I shoved Amber. "I was not a slut. I was a relationship junkie. When I did it, it lasted. You were the one who never had a relationship last longer than the time it took to put your clothes back on."

"That's not bad," Amber teased. "How long have you been waiting to use that one?"

Was she calling me stupid? Saying that I had to sit and think hard just to come up with something that silly? I didn't respond.

"Jade was a slut," Todd said.

Jade giggled behind her hands. "It's true, I really was. If he had long hair and tattoos galore, he was mine."

"Of course, she's more selective now," Todd joked.

I nodded. "Amber too. If it wasn't for me only God knows how many beds she'd be hopping in and out of."

"You are such a bitch," she said laughing. "And if it wasn't for me, you'd still be giving banana blow jobs and masturbating with orange popsicles."

Jade clutched her sides and Todd fell off the bench, howling with laughter.

My face flamed embarrassed. "First of all, it was cherry popsicles, and secondly, Basil made me do it."

"Oh, he *made* you do it, huh?"

"Okay, he *wanted* me to, whatever. So what? I did lots of other things too, which I will never tell you about because you have such a big mouth. Why don't you go fist Gwynne or something?"

Amber's eyes narrowed. "Who started this conversation?" She demanded.

"I don't know," Jade said, re-lighting one of the candles that had blown out. "But you certainly asked for that one. Personally, I think you got off easy."

"She always gets off easy," I sneered.

"Is that a thinly veiled attempt at sexual humor?"

Amber asked. Todd went into the house to grab another beer and his manuscript.

"Whatever."

She sighed. "Are you gonna start getting bitchy now?"

"No, but I am going to change this conversation's direction." Jade rubbed her stomach and I smiled at her. "You know, me and the fister here will come to the hospital when you have the baby, if you want. Hell, Amber could probably deliver it."

Amber was no longer amused. "Quit calling me a fister. I swear, you put something in your head---"

"And it comes right out of my mouth. Yes, I'm well aware of that."

Todd appeared at the back door, waving a thick envelope, and Jade grinned at him.

"He's been dying to give it to you," she whispered. "He's so excited." She tilted her head at me. "Did you mean that about coming to the hospital?" I nodded. "That would be great. I thought it was just going to be Todd and Zoe there. The doctor said I could let her in, because I want her to be there when her little brother or sister is born, but if you guys come too, I'll have more people there, and that will be great."

"We'll come," Amber said.

"Thanks, Fisty."

I burst out laughing and Amber scowled at me. "Now look what you've started. The next person who calls me *fister* or *fisty* is gonna get a shoe up their ass."

"A shoe or an arm?"

"Shut up, Meagan. We better grab some popsicles on the way home because you're going to need them."

Todd approached and Jade laughed. She gave him the news about our wanting to be there for the delivery and he gave a big devilish grin. Amber and I laughed all the way home. Especially because as we were leaving, Jade walked us to the car and said, "Those popsicles are cold though, aren't they? Todd likes grape." They were a fun couple.

At 4 a.m. I sat in bed with the dim lamp on beside me, reading Todd's manuscript. I thought something might come to me from reading about the Realm. The manuscript was greatly improved. Chuck had helped Todd tighten the writing, cut out the unimportant details, and lessen the observations on life and spirituality that had previously been strewn throughout the book.

Amber stirred beside me, looked up, and groaned. "For Christ's sake, Meagan. Go to sleep."

"I think I need glasses," I complained. "For the last half hour the words have been blurry and they're jumping off the page at me."

Amber sighed. "That's because you've been reading in a semi-dark room for five hours."

"I'm just trying to see if anything comes to me from reading this."

Amber sat up. "Honey, I know you're impatient, but you're not gonna find whatever answer you're looking for at four in the morning." She took the manuscript from me, placed it on the nightstand, turned off the lamp and extended her arms. "Come here."

"Why? Do you have a better plan?"

"Yes, sleep."

"You're no fun." I curled up to her, rested my head on her stomach, and kissed her belly button.

"Sleep, Meagan," she said again.

"I *know*."

Her arms wrapped around me. "And quit doing that, I'm really tired."

I frowned. "Doing what?"

"You're breathing on me."

"I'm *breathing* on you?"

"Yes, and it's making me horny. Now go to sleep."

"Okay." I rolled away from her.

"Well, don't roll away."

"Well, I don't want to *breathe* on you."

She laughed and extended her arms again. "Just come here. Go to sleep, and keep your hands to yourself."

I curled up to her again with a sigh. "You're so boring."

"At four in the morning? Yes, I am. Try me around seven."

"Screw you. *I'll* be sleeping at seven."

"So I'll wake you up in a good way."

"Amber?" I was thinking about our conversation in the grocery store.

She stroked my hair. "Mm-hmm?"

"You know I didn't mean what we were talking about earlier, right? About designer stuff and the baby? You do know I wouldn't raise my daughter --if I'd had her I mean--to be a materialistic little snob, right?"

"Yes, I know that Meagan. These are really the things you sit here and think about, aren't they? I know you. I know when you're joking and when you're being serious."

"Okay." I breathed in her hair and smiled. "I just wanted to make sure."

"Meagan?"

"What?"

"Can we please go to sleep now?"

I laughed. "Yes, we can go to sleep now." I was out before I'd finished my sentence.

Amber woke me the way she'd promised. I felt a mouth on my breast, fingers stroking me, a whisper in my ear. "Wake up, Meagan."

I ignored it and tried to go back to sleep. Her hair brushed my stomach as she moved downward, trailing a low line of kisses, bringing a soft feather with her and caressing it across my body.

"Wake up."

I groaned. "Quit molesting me and go back to sleep."

"Molesting you?" She gave a throaty chuckle and put her mouth on me again. "Wake up."

"No."

"Yes."

She did something with her tongue. I woke up.

"So what's on the agenda for today?" she asked over grapefruit and coffee. We'd risen from bed, showered, and prepared for another day of waiting.

"I was thinking we'd go check on people."

"Check on people?"

"Yeah, make the rounds. Make sure everyone's okay."

She drew a bored breath. "Couldn't we just call them?"

"Nope. I have to see their faces when I ask if they're alright."

"Okay. What are we up to, day three?"

I nodded. "Three down, three to go—maybe. I suppose it could happen sooner."

She took a sip of her coffee. "You're holding up rather well."

"You too. I just keep thinking about the dream and Victor saying we'd do fine. That eases my mind."

Amber took a last spoonful of chopped grapefruit. "You ready to go?"

I pushed in my chair. "Let's go."

So we made the rounds. Stopped by to see Adrian and Zeppo. No problems there. Swung by the office. Everything functioning as usual. Paid a visit to Danielle. Fine. Jacob and Martha. Just sitting around working on a puzzle. My parents. Saturday yard work. Amber's parents. Preparing for a dinner party.

"I guess that's everyone," Amber said on the way home.

"I guess so. Did you see the way my brother was looking at me?" He'd been at my parents' house helping Dad clean the garage.

Amber flipped through the radio stations until she found a song she liked. "Yeah, is he ever pissed at you."

I turned on the air conditioner. "He better not be screwing around while she's gone, either. Maybe I should sic the Clump on him too."

"You're doing it again," Amber said.

I steered the car onto Riverview. "Doing what?"

"Acting nosy like your mother."

"I wish you would stop saying that."

"Mind your own business and I might."

We pulled under the building. "Why are you picking a fight with me?"

"I'm not picking a fight with you."

"You are when you tell me I'm like my mother. *Seamus!*"

"What?" My yell startled her.

"We never checked on Seamus and Sheila."

"Then let's go upstairs and call them."

Seamus was fine. He and Sheila were getting ready for work. I was at my wits' end. Everyone was fine so what the hell was the problem? I finished reading Todd's manuscript. No clues there. I knew everything he'd written and there was nothing new.

Amber and I had dinner, rented a movie, and closed off another day. We fell asleep on the couch. At one in the morning, the phone rang, and a feeling of doom passed over me. This was the call. Someone was calling to say someone else had been hurt.

With my heart in my throat, I snatched up the receiver. "Hello?"

"It's over now, Meagan." Jenna said. She sounded like she'd been crying.

I clutched the phone. "How could it be over? Nothing's happened." Amber sat up beside me, and I could hear Jenna crying.

"I couldn't stop it because I didn't know how it would happen. But it *has* happened. I can feel it."

"What's happened, Jenna?"

"You'll know soon enough. I'm sorry, Meagan. I'll be home in two days."

I heard the phone move away from her ear. "Wait, Jenna. Don't hang up!" The phone went dead. "Fuck!"

Chapter 25

9:45 a.m. A call came in from a lawyer named Frederick Stone who wanted to know if I could meet with him concerning a certain situation. Would eleven o'clock be okay? Reluctantly, I agreed. I figured I may as well deal with Gwynne's bullshit now and get it over with.

By 10:47 a.m., Amber and I were sitting in the empty waiting room of a cheap-looking law office uptown. I looked at the flimsy paneling pulling away from the walls, the rip on the blue leather chair across from where we sat on the couch.

"Christ," I mocked. "You'd think Gwynne could afford to hire a better attorney than this."

Amber shrugged. "All the better for you. This guy will turn green when he hears who your representation is. Three lawyers from the Chase-Roudy group? He'll run from this like a little girl."

I laughed. Amber compared everyone's actions to those of a little girl.

An office door swung open and a tired-looking man with sloped shoulders and thick glasses came out. He was wearing a beige suit with a thick, brown-and-tan-striped tie and scuffed dress shoes that had seen better days. I grinned at Amber. Who needed the Chase-Roudy group? This was going to be a piece of cake. The man who stood before us didn't look like he could argue with his wife, let alone argue a court case.

I stood up and extended my hand. "Hello, Mr. Stone."

"Miss Summers." Limp shake. This case was mine. "And this must be Miss Reed." Amber rose and he shook her hand. "I'm glad you could come. I'm afraid we're involved in a distressing situation here."

I smiled. "You may find it distressing, Mr. Stone. I merely think your client has made a serious mistake."

He flinched. "Please come into my office," he said curtly.

Amber and I followed him into a messy room, littered with books and papers all over the floor, stacks of files on top of the desk, and more cheaply paneled walls.

"Shall we get to it, then?" he said, indicating two chairs and seating himself behind his desk.

We sat and I folded my hands on top of my black leather skirt. "Mr. Stone, I'll save you your breath," I said. "First, I should tell you that I have the best attorneys in this city. Perhaps you've heard of the Chase-Roudy group?" His eyes widened and Amber grinned. She got off on watching me control a situation from the second it began. I nodded. "I see you've heard of them. But this case isn't even going to court, Mr. Stone, and I'll tell you why. Your client has been involved in some very scandalous behavior, which I happen to have documentation of, and if she presses me, I'll use it."

"I don't know what you're talking about," he said.

I crossed my legs and met his nervous gaze. "I'm talking about pictures of her involved in orgiastic behavior, tax reports, bank statements. Your client has been cheating on her taxes and I have the proof. She's not getting her rights back— ever. Now I suggest you tell her to back off before I use this information."

Another grin from Amber. She wanted to snicker.

"I'm afraid I can't do that," Mr. Stone said.

"Why not?"

"Because my client is dead."

Amber and I looked at each other. This was no longer funny.

"Gwynne's dead?" I asked.

"Who's Gwynne?"

I looked at Amber again, confused. "The woman who's suing me to get her publication rights back," I said slowly.

Frederick Stone removed his glasses and placed them on the desk. "I don't know anything about that. My client is Jade Garrison."

A lump formed in my throat. "Jade's dead? That's impossible. We just had dinner with her two nights ago."

"I'm sorry," he said. "She and her husband were killed in a car accident yesterday afternoon."

"Oh God!" Tears sprang to my eyes. They were dead. She was pregnant and they were both dead.

Amber's eyes misted and she took my hand and

squeezed it. I stared down at it like I didn't know who it belonged to. She cleared her throat and lowered her eyes. "What about their daughter?" she asked, quietly.

I sprang to my feet. "Oh God! Zoe! What happened to Zoe?" I thought I would grab the old man and shake him.

Amber came up behind me, wrapped her arms around me and urged me back to my chair. She sat down beside me again and held my hand.

"The child is fine, Miss Summers," Frederick Stone said. "She was in day care at the time and she spent the night with one of the workers from the center."

"What will happen to her?"

"Well, that's where you come in," he said. "Normally this type of thing would be delayed until after the funerals, but as you may know, the Garrisons had no family, so the child's custody is a serious concern."

"Custody?" Another lump formed in my throat. Amber clung to my hand. We sensed where this was going.

"Miss Summers," he continued, "the Garrisons left behind a simple will, which they had drawn up two months prior to their demise. Apparently, you and Miss Reed were the only real friends they had---"

Jenna's words: It's over, Meagan.

Victor's: The circle is almost complete. What should have been, will be.

"Are you saying what I think you're saying?" Amber asked.

"Material possessions have all been left to their daughter," he said.

You weren't strong enough the first time.

"And their daughter has been left to?" I knew the answer. Two of our friends were dead and I knew what they had done.

"You, Miss Summers. With Miss Reed noted as secondary caregiver."

My head spun.

Another car accident.

It comes full circle.

A daughter.

Full circle.

The challenge.

Full circle.

I will be a mother.

Blackness crept into my head. The room grew dim and I sensed Amber kneeling before me. I saw a blurry picture of the shock on her face. She was talking, but her voice seemed to be growing very far away.

"Meagan, baby are you alright?"

"Don't call me ba---"

I fainted.

Other books by Deanna DiLorenzo:

Tell Me - Blackstone Publishing, 2013

www.ingramcontent.com/pod-product-compliance
Lightning Source LLC
Chambersburg PA
CBHW051550250626
47157CB00001B/248